HOMINID

R.D. BRADY

BOOKS BY R.D. BRADY

The Belial Series (in order)

The Belial Stone

The Belial Library

The Belial Ring

Recruit: A Belial Series Novella

The Belial Children

The Belial Origins

The Belial Search

The Belial Guard

The Belial Warrior

The Belial Plan

The Belial Witches

Stand-Alone Books

Runs Deep

Hominid

The A.L.I.V.E. Series

B.E.G.I.N.

A.L.I.V.E.

D.E.A.D.

Be sure to sign up for R.D.'s mailing list to be the first to hear when she has a new release and receive a free short story!

Hominid

Def., any of a family (Hominidae) of erect bipedal primate mammals that includes recent humans together with extinct ancestral and related forms and in some recent classifications the gorilla, chimpanzee, and orangutan
- *Webster's Dictionary*, 2015

"Well now, you'll be amazed when I tell you that I am sure the exist."

Jane Goodall, Animal Rights Activist, NPR Talk of Nation, September 27, 2002

PROLOGUE

Twenty Years Ago

Rogue River National Park, Oregon

Her heart pounding, eight-year-old Tess Brannick's eyes flew open. She sat up, pulled her dark hair out of her eyes, and strained to listen.

There was nothing. And there should have been something. She and her twin brother were in a tent on the southeastern end of Rogue River National Park. She should hear crickets, owls, animals skittering through the surrounding forest.

But there was only silence.

"What is it?" Pax asked, turning on the lantern. His bright blue eyes reflected his fear.

Even though they were twins, and separated by only four minutes, Tess had always been the big sister looking out for Pax. Tonight was no different.

She was shaking inside, but she tried to keep her voice calm. "It's nothing. Go back to sleep."

A snarl sounded from somewhere outside the tent, followed by a series of yells—her dad.

Pax latched on to her hand.

Before the trip, Tess and Pax had begged their dad to let them sleep in their own tent. He'd finally relented. Now Tess really wished he hadn't.

"Tess?" Pax asked.

A shotgun blast sounded from close by. Tess jumped. "Get out of your bag," she hissed. They both squirmed out of their sleeping bags, and Tess wrapped her arms around her brother.

When the tent flap flew open, they both screamed.

Their dad rushed in, his shotgun cradled in his arms. Gene Brannick was always calm and ready for a laugh. But now, his blue eyes were deadly serious, and no smile crossed his lips. As he crouched down in front of the twins, Tess could smell his sweat.

"I need you two to run for the ranger's station," he said. "Do you remember where it is?"

Tess was terrified, more than she'd ever been in her life, but one look at Pax's face told her she had to be the brave one. She swallowed down the fear. "Dad, what's going on?"

He shot a glance over his shoulder before answering. His hands shook, and so did his voice. "Mountain lions," he said. "You need to go."

"But Dad, they shouldn't be here," Tess said.

While other kids read comics, Tess read everything she could find on animals. She knew lions shouldn't be out this far, and that even if they were, they stayed far away from people.

"There's been a drought," her dad said. "It must have driven them farther out than before. I never should have brought you here." He stared back at her, his eyes larger than she'd ever seen them. "There's too many of them, Tess. You need to run."

Too many of them? Tess knew that shouldn't happen either. Lions were solitary creatures, unless they were young males.

Her dad placed a trembling kiss on each of their foreheads. Then he pulled them to their feet and pushed them from the tent. "Go."

A crashing sounded from the trees to their right. Her dad pulled his weapon to his shoulder. "Get to the ranger station. Now! Run! And don't look back!" he yelled.

A shadow slunk from the trees, and her father pulled the trigger.

The noise spurred Tess into action. She grabbed Pax's hand and ran. Behind her she heard footsteps. Then another shotgun blast sounded. And the footfalls went silent but a scream split the night air.

Pax stumbled. "Dad!"

Tess grabbed him by the shoulders and pulled him to his feet even as tears ran down her cheeks. "You have to get up," she cried, tears clogging her throat. "We have to run."

A crashing sounded in the trees behind them.

Tess grabbed her brother's hand. "Run, Pax! Run!"

They sprinted through the forest side by side, leaping over downed trees and small bushes.

Footfalls sounded behind them, and then more joined in. Tess's heart threatened to burst out of her chest, but she didn't dare slow, not even to look behind her.

Movement to her left drew her eyes. In the trees, a shadow was moving alongside them. As Tess glanced over, the shadow burst into a shaft of moonlight.

That's not a mountain lion, Tess thought. Whatever it was, it had dark fur and incredible height. Tess was overcome by panic. She sprinted ahead, pulling Pax behind her.

They didn't see the gully until it was too late. They stepped off into nothingness, and with screams they dropped, rolling to the ground below.

Pain shot through Tess's ankle, but she got to her feet. Pax was holding his shoulder. He threw his good arm around Tess and they hobbled across the narrow creek.

On the other side, a wall of dirt and rock blocked their way. Tess pushed Pax toward it. "Go. Climb."

"No. I'm not leaving you."

A roar behind them ended the argument. They both turned. Two lions, both skinny, their ribs showing, slunk across the creek. The lions appeared to be in no rush; this was an easy kill.

Tess's breaths came out in pants. Pax moved closer to her, his shoulder brushing hers.

"I love you, Tess," he whispered. She gripped his hand and squeezed.

The lions stalked closer. They were smaller than adults. *Probably young males.* Tess knew that male mountain lions were kicked out of their home after a year, and that they sometimes banded together. She'd felt pity when she'd first learned that. But now, she felt no pity—only fear. Because even though they were young, they would have no problem overpowering her and Pax.

A shadow cut away from the forest behind the lions and moved down to the creek. Tess jumped. *Oh God, there's another one.*

The cats whirled around. The shadow fell over them with a scream that shook Tess to her core. Before Tess could understand what was happening, one cat went flying through the air, screeching. It slammed into a tree and fell to the ground, still.

Something wet splashed on Tess's face. She reached up and wiped at it. Her fingers came away dark. Blood.

She dropped to the ground, her arms wrapped protectively around Pax.

The shadow grabbed the second lion and broke its back across its knee. Then it ripped the big cat in two.

"No, no, no, no," Pax moaned.

The shadow paused. It stood in darkness, but Tess was sure it was looking right at her. She could only make out its shape— like a man, but huge. Wider, taller. She squinted. Hairier.

Pax moaned again. The creature watched them for a moment longer, then disappeared back up the side of the gully and into the trees.

Tess and Pax stayed where they were, staring at the spot where the creature had disappeared.

"It ripped that lion apart," she whispered, not even recognizing her own voice.

Next to her, Pax only shook harder.

Tess stared into the trees, her arms still wrapped around her brother. She wasn't sure who was shaking harder, her or him.

"Tess?" Pax whispered.

But Tess couldn't answer him. Her entire focus was on the spot where she'd last seen the creature. The creature who had saved them. She pictured its height and bulk. Her eyes were drawn to the carnage it had left behind.

What kind of animal could do that?

CHAPTER ONE

Beauford, California

Today

Tess slowed the ATV to a stop at the end of the path. Tall sugar pines with heavy evergreen leaves and long cones surrounded her. In the distance, the dense forest rose and fell over hilltops. It was seven a.m., and she took in a breath, inhaling the early forest air with a smile.

She was at the northeast edge of Klamath National Forest—1.7 million acres of forest that straddled the California and Oregon border. The area was covered with a variety of trees—from Douglas firs and other pines to oak and madrone hardwoods. It was a densely packed forest—with more than five hundred trees per acre in some areas—and teeming with wildlife, from simple squirrels and chipmunks to more elusive animals such as foxes or even bobcats.

Tess's camp was a forty-minute hike from here, but this was

as far as the ATV could manage. She grabbed her pack from the back as she climbed off.

Taking a drink of water, she looked around, getting a feel for the forest. It was quiet, which she expected. Her ATV had made enough noise to chase away all but the hardiest of creatures.

She pulled her rifle from the back of the ATV. Checking that it was loaded—even though she knew she'd loaded it earlier this morning—she looped it around her shoulder, just in case in she ran into one of the hardier creatures. Bears, mountain lions, even wolverines lived in this natural safe zone. Tess respected nature enough to know that she could never be perfectly safe here.

She started to walk the trail. It was a familiar path, but there was still always something new to see. She smiled. *Best commute in the world.* She made quick time, but she didn't rush. Rushing, even on a well-known trail, was inviting injury. And besides, it's not like she had a meeting.

She knew people would probably think she was nuts to spend so much time in the woods. And to be honest, she wasn't entirely convinced she wasn't, but being out here... it did something to her. It gave her a sense of peace that the craziness of the real world couldn't.

It didn't take long for the animal sounds to return. Birds flew by overhead. Squirrels and the occasional rabbit skittered ahead of her. Every once in a while, Tess had even come across an elk in the more wide-open areas of the park. Today, an endangered spotted owl watched her from a branch twenty feet up. Above, a bald eagle sailed through the sky. *Yup—nothing better.*

For a year now, she had been making this hour-and-a-half trek into the woods, every Monday through Friday. She stayed overnight at least a few nights a month. She tried to avoid more than that. Her friends and family were worried enough about her without her living out here.

But her escape to the wild wasn't some carefree lark. It was part of a very carefully laid out plan. A tingle of excitement ran through her as she wondered what today could bring.

Up ahead, she spotted one of her field cameras. She'd placed it six feet up the tree—at five foot six, she couldn't place it much higher. She pulled it down, swapped out the memory card, and replaced the battery. She doubted she had anything special on the card, though; her subject was decidedly camera shy.

She continued on up the trail. She paused at a boulder where the path forked. To the right was her camp. She had chosen the spot for several reasons. One, it was in a very secluded portion of the park. In fact, she had never run into another human out here in the year she had been using the spot. Two, it was only a short walk from a small lake, which meant plenty of wildlife was nearby. Three, there was a clearing not too far away, so if she ever needed emergency help, there was a place for a rescue chopper to land. And four, it was a pretty spot.

But most importantly, it wasn't far from where she'd found her first footprint.

She turned left, away from the camp. The path continued over a rise and then down again. At the bottom of the hill, she stopped.

The food bag had been suspended above the trail, but now it lay on the ground, empty. She'd placed over seven pounds of food in there on Friday.

She looked around carefully, staying on the edge of the trail so as not to disturb the area. *Come on, old friend. Show me something.* She walked slowly around, seeing nothing, her hopes dimming. But then, to one side, she saw an impression. A footprint.

Kneeling next to it, Tess could make out the five long toes. The second and third toe were both bigger than the big toe, a condition known as Morton's foot. The print could easily have been mistaken for a human footprint if not for two things: the toes were disproportionately long, and the foot itself was much longer and wider than any human foot.

The animal was flatfooted, Tess noted—the print was uniform in depth—and must be very heavy, as the impression was three inches deep.

Placing her pack on the grass off the path, Tess pulled out a can of aerosol hairspray and sprayed the track. While it dried, she pulled out her white gypsum cement mix and added water. After a little stirring, it was ready. She carefully poured the plaster into the footprint.

It would take about twenty minutes to set, give or take, so while she waited she inspected the rest of the area. She found only one other print—a shallow heel mark—a short distance away. She cast that as well.

"You were careful," she murmured. She thought he had probably stayed as much off the path as possible, limiting the chance for footprints. She carefully inspected the ground around the path, but the vegetation made it too difficult to find any traces left behind. She hoped that maybe a piece of hair had gotten caught in the burrs she had glued to the tree, but no—her little traps were empty.

She headed back to the original cast. She tested it, and smiled when she met resistance. Carefully prying it from the ground, she lifted it up and gently wiped away some excess mud. She pulled out her water bottle and poured it over the underside, cleaning off the rest of the dirt. Finally, she blotted the cast with the towel she always kept in her pack.

Returning the water and towel to her pack, she took a breath, trying to calm herself and act like the scientist her degrees said she was. She needed to look at it objectively. It was possible it was just a bear footprint. She knew that when two bear footprints overlapped, they could be mistaken for her quarry.

But when she inspected the underside of the cast, she saw no sign of an overlap. Whatever had created this print was a single creature.

She looked next for the one mark she hoped she'd find.

And there it was. On the ball of the foot was an old scar that had healed over, making a jagged line.

Tess put the cast down, pulled her tape measure out of her bag, and measured the cast. She confirmed what she already knew: the widest part of the foot was eight inches, and from toe to heel, it was sixteen inches.

Tess smiled.

"Hello, bigfoot."

FROM THE BLOG 'BIGFOOT AMONG US' BY DR. TESS BRANNICK

This week's question comes from Ted Hanks in Chicago, Illinois. Ted writes:

I don't understand why people still believe there is a bigfoot. Isn't this all just a big hoax?

It's a common belief that all footprints found or sightings are the result of hoaxers. And to be fair, some are. But the pure scope of the sightings makes it difficult to swallow the idea of a hoax. Bigfoot sightings have been found not just in the United States but all across the globe: in China, Russia, Australia, Ireland, Nepal, South America, and more.

Moreover, the sightings go back hundreds of years. Native American stories have for centuries spoken of their giant brothers in the woods. And other countries have similar ancient tales. In fact, Medieval Europe even had some reports of a bigfoot being caught and held in captivity.

So is bigfoot a hoax? Well, if it is, it's one that stretches back hundreds of years and has been coordinated by unrelated cultures all across the globe.

CHAPTER TWO

Tess was heading out of town for a few days for a conference, so she had to cut her trip to the woods short. She left extra food, knowing she likely wouldn't make it back until Friday at the earliest.

When she reached the ATV, she cast one last look at the path, hating to go. She'd been seeing more and more prints in the last few weeks, and she couldn't help but feel she was close to making a breakthrough. Honestly, if she had her way, she'd spend all her time in the woods right now. The fever was hard to ignore. But she also knew there were bigfoot researchers who had spent their lifetimes searching for the elusive creature without ever catching sight of anything more than footprints.

With a sigh, she glanced at her watch. She was cutting it close. Hopping on the ATV, she pushed it as fast as she could.

Forty-five minutes later, she spied her red barn. Pulling the ATV through the open barn doors, she wiped it down, grabbed her pack, and jogged over to the cabin.

Her cabin was set on ten acres that abutted Klamath National Forest. She'd bought the property two years ago. A long porch wrapped around the front of the old cabin, and inside was a large open living room with a kitchen off to one side and a bathroom hidden off to the other. The place had two decent-sized bedrooms, one of which Tess had turned into her office, plus a loft bedroom above the living room, which could be reached by a metal staircase.

When Tess's mother learned she was buying this cabin in the woods, she had nearly had a heart attack. After losing Tess's dad, her mom had never been comfortable with them going into the woods. But she also recognized Tess was drawn to the great outdoors. They'd fought about her career choice for years. Tess knew that offering to renovate the cabin was her mom's way of saying she'd finally accepted Tess's career choice.

Tess had originally resisted, not sure she wanted anything too fancy, but she gave in eventually. And seeing as how her mother passed away only a month after the renovations were complete, Tess was very glad she did. She knew being involved had made her mother more comfortable with Tess's career choice.

Besides, her mother had been right—having a comfortable place to come home to *did* make all the difference. Tess loved being off the beaten track, but there was something to be said for modern conveniences.

When she opened the door, her ten-year-old yellow Labrador, Shelby, was waiting for her. Tess knelt down and gave the dog a good rub. "Hey, girl." Then she stepped back and let Shelby out.

Tess zipped into her office. She dropped her pack on the desk and carefully pulled out the casts she'd made. She jotted down the coordinates where she'd found them as well as the time and date, then placed them in the glass-encased bookcase across from her old wooden desk. She already had over two dozen casts in there, the majority of them with the same mark on the bottom of the foot.

Her gaze roamed over the collection, her heart rate picking up. The footprints ranged in size from fourteen to eighteen inches long and six to eight inches wide. These were proof that unknown hominids roamed the woods in Northern California.

The alarm on her phone beeped, and she grimaced. She really needed to move. With one last lingering gaze, she left her collection behind and ran for her bedroom. She had one hour to shower, pack, and get out the door.

I really don't want to go, she thought as she stripped out of her clothes and turned on the water.

But you really need the grant money, her rational side countered. She blew out a breath, acknowledging that truth. Academic curiosity might be a wonderful thing, but it didn't pay the bills. For that, you needed donors—or better yet, grants.

Tess still had money from her mom's life insurance policy, but she didn't want to touch it—not for this. Her mom had supported her, but Tess knew how much her mother had worried about her, so Tess promised herself she would use that money for something that would have made her mom smile.

And right now, she knew if she didn't get a grant at this conference, she was most likely going to have to close up shop.

She stepped into the shower, let the water run over her, and closed her eyes. *Please let me find someone as dedicated to this project as I am.*

And let them have very deep pockets.

CHAPTER THREE

Scottsdale, Arizona

Carter Hayes flipped through the papers on his desk with a scowl. *Everyone wants a handout.*

Each year, his foundation donated to a variety of philanthropic endeavors. It was good publicity, and the tax breaks were huge. But people were so greedy. *What ever happened to standing on your own two feet?*

Carter Hayes had never taken a handout in his life. He was a self-made man. After graduating Yale, he hadn't gone to work at his father's company. He'd taken his trust fund and gambled on himself. And he'd won.

He curled his lip. American Cancer Society, Children's Charities of America, the Boys and Girls Club of America. The list went on and on. And all these people wanted him to hand over his money to them.

"Sir, have you made any decisions?" Thaddeus Regan asked.

Carter eyed his assistant. Thaddeus had been with him for

over twenty years. The two had grown up together in Michigan, although they hadn't been friends; Thaddeus had been the son of the groundskeeper on his parents' estate.

Carter shoved the papers away. "I don't care. You decide."

"Very well, sir. And I may have found a researcher for your special project."

All thoughts of the charitable donations disappeared, and a tingle of excitement danced along Carter's skin. He held out his hand. "Let me see."

Thaddeus handed him a folder.

Stamped across the front were the words *Dr. Tess Brannick, PhD.* Carter flipped it open and scanned the resume quickly. She had a BS in Zoology (Anatomy & Physiology) from Michigan State University, an MS in Zoology (Anatomy & Physiology) from Kent State University, and a PhD in Anatomical Sciences (Physical Anthropology) from the State University of New York at Stony Brook. She'd also completed a postdoctoral visiting assistant professorship at Duke University Medical Center.

And she had a well-received blog called "Bigfoot Among Us." It had received over two hundred thousand hits last month.

Carter's eyebrow rose when he flipped to the next page, which detailed her blog. The topics revolved entirely around the scientific validity of bigfoot.

Carter had been obsessed with tales of bigfoot since he was a kid. He'd first seen the Patterson-Gimlin film when he was seven, and had been equal parts fascinated and terrified at the idea that a powerful eight-foot hominid was alive and at large in North America.

That year he asked his family to get him a bigfoot for his eighth birthday. His family already had a zoo on the estate, so to him, it didn't seem like such a big request. But he was given a gorilla instead. He curled his lip at the memory. The thing had never liked him. And it had been old, just sitting there, its fat belly flopping over his legs. Carter's family had finally gotten rid of it two years later.

But while Carter had lost interest in the gorilla, he'd never lost interest in bigfoot. Owning a bigfoot had grown from a childhood wish to an adult goal.

And Carter Hayes achieved his goals.

"She's well credentialed," Thaddeus said.

"So I see," Carter said.

Carter flipped through the file and stopped at a photograph. *And very attractive*, he thought. She had that girl-next-door beauty, with dark brown hair, deep blue-green eyes, and a spray of freckles across her cheeks.

"Her approach is a departure from most," Thaddeus said. "I think she may be exactly what you're looking for."

Carter flipped through the pages once more from the beginning, skimming the information again, liking what he was seeing. He paused. "What's this?" He held up a police report. He hadn't noticed it on his first flip-through.

"Her father was killed by a mountain lion on a camping trip almost twenty years ago. She and her brother were also there."

"And she still goes into the woods? Alone?"

"Yes, sir. In fact, according to unofficial reports, she and her brother were saved by a very tall unidentified animal. I believe that may be the reason behind her research."

A strong scientific background, beauty, and guts—an unusual combination. He smiled. *And the perfect one.*

"She's presenting at the annual cryptozoology conference tomorrow in San Diego," Thaddeus said.

Carter nodded, already inserting Dr. Brannick into his plans. "Make sure we have someone there to record the presentation."

"Yes, sir."

Carter flipped back to the picture. It wasn't a posed shot. She was laughing, her head tilted to the side. *Yes. She may be just what I need.*

CHAPTER FOUR

Beauford, California

Tess drove around a bend in the dirt road, revealing the white farmhouse and red barn in the treeless clearing ahead. Shelby started wagging her tail immediately. Tess rubbed Shelby's head. "I know you love it here, but you could at least act like you're going to miss me a little."

Shelby grinned back at her, her tongue hanging out of her mouth.

"Okay, fine." Tess shook her head with a laugh. She pulled to a stop in front of the wide porch steps just as the screen door opened.

Seventy-seven-year-old Madge Rollins stepped out. Her long gray hair was pulled back into a bun, her faded jeans and denim top immaculately clean. "What took you so long?"

"Sorry." Tess stepped out of the truck, and Shelby leapt out behind her. "Got back to the cabin late."

Shelby scrambled up the stairs. Madge leaned down, a grin on her face. "Hello, girl. We are going to have some fun."

Madge might have been skinny as pole, but Tess knew she was strong from her many years working the farm. Now, though, she had sold off most of the acreage, and she had people do her planting for her. Her three sons worried about her being out here alone. They wanted her to move in with them. Madge's response when they'd suggested it had been a snort, followed by: "What, so I can be a glorified babysitter? No thank you."

Her sons knew better than to try and fight her on it. Besides, Madge seemed to like her own company, and one of the boys came up every weekend to help out. Still, Tess knew Madge's sons wanted her to sell the place. And it wasn't just because of her advancing years.

Madge stood up from giving Shelby a good rub, a twinkle in her blue eyes. "So, you're off to see my boyfriend?"

Tess grinned. "Madge, you know Shawn's gay, right? And married to my brother?"

Madge cackled. "Well, he might be gay in real life, but not in my imagination."

Tess couldn't help but laugh. "I am *so* not telling Shawn or Pax that."

Madge held the screen door open. "You got time for tea?"

"I could be persuaded," Tess said, following her in. She'd checked the plane's status on the ride over—it was delayed, so she'd have a little time before her friend Sasha Bileris came by to pick her up.

Shelby headed straight for the dog bed in the corner with her toys and bones. Whenever Tess had to be out in the field for a few nights or out of town, this was Shelby's home. Tess knew Madge would like to get another dog of her own, but after what happened to her last dog, she wasn't quite ready for that.

Tess took a seat at the table, where Madge had already set out the tea and a plate of lemon cookies, and took a sip of her tea. "Any visitors last night?"

Madge crossed her arms with a sigh. "Oh, they were in a fine mood. Hooting, hollering, a few large branches came down. I'm surprised you didn't hear the racket."

A couple of miles and a large hill separated Madge's place from Tess's. The terrain tended to trap the noise on one side.

"Where about?" Tess asked.

Madge nudged her chin toward the back of the house. "Up the hill. Right about where you put those new cameras."

"Oh, crap."

Madge smiled. "I told you they don't like being spied on."

"I know. I know."

Madge was the reason Tess had bought the cabin down the road. For years, Madge had had "visitors" on her property. She'd spotted them in the distance now and then, but they kept to themselves. Every once in a while, though, Madge would come across a deer or elk that had been ripped apart. Sometimes she found footprints. And at night, especially in the spring, it wasn't unusual for her to hear them making a racket all over the place.

Tess had learned about Madge's visitors when she was a kid. She and Pax would regularly bike out to see Madge and pepper her with questions. Well, *Tess* would pepper her with questions. Tess was pretty sure Pax only made the trip for Madge's oatmeal cookies.

And Madge's nightly visitors were the reason why Madge didn't have dogs. Her last dog had been so terrified that he had reached a point where he wouldn't leave the house. Madge finally had to give him to one of her sons. It wasn't fair to the poor animal.

Luckily, Shelby was partially deaf and didn't seem bothered by the activity. But Tess knew if Shelby ever got near one, that would change. Dogs were not fond of bigfoot, and the feeling was mutual.

"Did they get close to the house?" Tess asked.

"Nah. We've established a respect of sorts. They keep to their space, I keep to mine. Never had problems before; can't sees why I'd start having some now."

"I keep seeing tracks of my friend in the woods."

Madge raised an eyebrow. "You sure it's the same one?"

Tess pictured the scar on the casts. "Yeah, same one."

"Hmm." Madge took a sip of her tea.

"What do you mean, 'hmm'? What are you thinking?"

"Seems to me he's *letting* you find those tracks. They're usually a little more careful."

Tess sat back, surprised. Madge was right. In all the cases she'd read about, no one had ever found tracks so consistently. She had just thought it was because she was so far in. But what if it wasn't?

"Why would he do that?"

Madge shrugged. "I don't know. But I'm betting he'll let you know sooner rather than later."

CHAPTER FIVE

San Diego, California

But *I'm betting he'll let you know sooner rather than later.*
Madge's words had been a constant fixture in the back of
Tess's mind for the whole plane ride to San Diego and all through
the night. Now, as she walked across the University of San
Diego's campus, she couldn't help but focus on them. Was
Madge right? Was that possible?

Tess shook her head. Bigfoot was an animal. She shouldn't
attribute higher thought processes to it. That's where people
stepped over the line from scientist to fan girl. And she planned
on staying on the side of science.

In the distance, a giant welcome banner was strung across the
brick and cement front of Meyers Hall: "The Seventh Annual
Cryptology Conference." Tess smiled at the sight. It was pretty
amazing that the university was allowing it be held here. Due to
its somewhat tainted reputation, cryptozoology was not a
specialty that had its own department. In fact, it rarely received

even a modicum of respect. Most people used the term cryptozo-ology interchangeably with pseudoscience.

But it was so much more. Cryptozoologists studied the animals that *could* be, those that were rumored to exist. And in recent years, several success stories had helped to bolster the field's reputation. The most recent find involved the Bili ape in the Democratic Republic of the Congo.

For years, the people of Congo spoke of giant chimpanzees that ate lions, fished, and howled at the moon. In fact, the animal was called "lion killer" by the native people. Of course, traditional scientists attributed the rumors to a highly imaginative indigenous group whose bedtime stories had gotten a little out of hand. Besides, the descriptions seemed to more closely match a gorilla than a chimp. It was said that it lived in nests on the ground, rather than in the trees; that it was not aggressive toward humans; that it walked on two feet for longer distances than is typical for a chimp; and that it grew to as large as six and half feet tall. All in all, it was too incredible to be real, at least for the Western world.

Still, in 1996, when word of the giant chimps got out, researchers descended on Congo. Although scat, hair, and other evidence was found, it wasn't until 2005 that the chimps were actually seen by a Westerner. Primatologist Shelly Williams was in the Congo, searching for the creatures, when a group of four of them emerged from the trees, charging at her. They were at least five feet tall, with wide flat faces, a pronounced brow, and gray fur. Yet when they noticed Williams's face, they stopped their charge and walked away.

This lack of aggression toward humans was repeated in other encounters, including those of Cleve Hicks of the University of Amsterdam, who spent eighteen months observing the creatures following the Williamses' encounter. He, too, found that they had no fear of humans, but rather seemed to recognize humans as a cousin of sorts. Which, in a sense, they were. Most primatologists classified the species as something in between a gorilla and a chimp. Some even suspected they were a missing link between humans and chimps.

But whatever they were, their discovery was a boon to the public image of cryptozoology.

A giant chimp that lived hidden in the forest for ages, Tess thought. *Just like the giant ape that lives in North America.*

The parallels were there. In Congo, there had been rumors about the existence of the Bili apes for years, but the stories were dismissed as nothing more than tall tales told by the natives—until the Bili ape was found. Similarly, Native Americans had told tales of their large brother in the woods for literally hundreds of years.

And it wasn't only Native Americans, either; one of the earliest recorded encounters with the wild, hairy men of North America was documented by Leif Ericson. In his journal, he wrote about seeing huge hairy men with dark eyes after he landed in Newfoundland around 1000 CE. The huge creatures, he said, towered over the Vikings, emitted a rank odor, and had a terrifying shriek.

Yet despite centuries of sightings—and a commonality in the descriptions of the creature, from very different native groups across the continent—bigfoot was still written off as a fairy tale.

One of the biggest barriers to widespread belief in bigfoot, Tess suspected, was bigfoot's bipedal nature. For generations, humans had felt smug in the knowledge that we were the only truly bipedal primate. Oh, sure, apes or chimps could stumble along for a few steps, but they were not two-legged creatures. Most of their travel was done on four limbs. And this faith in human exceptionalism created an unconscious bias against the idea that we might share our bipedalism with any other primate.

Recently, however, Tess had seen changes in the field that

seemed to indicate that people, and scientists in particular, might be growing more receptive to the idea of bigfoot. For one thing, a greater understanding of the diversity in the history of primates had led to more openness about the possibility of humans having a more extensive family tree.

For another, discoveries had demonstrated that bipedalism had developed independently in multiple parts of the world—and that it was *not* a strictly human trait. But perhaps most importantly, scientists coming into the field today had grown up with bigfoot. Every kid in America had heard the story by the age of eight, and that alone predisposed them to adopting a more open-minded approach.

Tess hiked her messenger bag a little higher up on her shoulder. She was pleased that science might be more open to the possibility of bigfoot, but she knew that without a grant, *she* would not be a part of furthering the field. And to get that grant, she needed to work her magic at this conference. Here she would find more people interested in the field than she could find in any other one place—which meant this was where she needed to be.

And it wouldn't hurt to give a phenomenal presentation.

So here's hoping.

Tess climbed the cement steps of Meyers Hall and pushed through the heavy doors. The large atrium was packed. Students eagerly chatted in groups. Older students, or more likely the public, wandered through as well, occasionally stopping to chat with one another. The sound of the milling crowd rose up toward the arched ceiling, which only seemed to enhance the noise below.

All told, there were easily two hundred people milling in the foyer or making their way through to the seminar rooms. And that didn't include the hundreds of others who were already seated in the dozens of presentation rooms.

Tess stepped to the side of the room, trying to calm her heartbeat. She'd had this problem often lately. Spending so much time in the quiet and with very few people tended to result in her having a small panic attack when she was assaulted with a large group of people.

Taking a calming breath, Tess watched as the lines for registration began to dwindle. After a few minutes, she composed her face and walked up to one of the registration hosts as they finished up with the last person in their line.

The young blonde co-ed smiled as Tess approached. "Name?"

"Dr. Tess Brannick."

The young woman turned to the bins lining the wall behind her. She made her way to one of them and pulled out a folder. Opening it as she walked back, she stopped, her eyes growing large. "You're the bigfoot expert!"

Tess was taken aback by the woman's enthusiasm. "Um, yes."

"I *so* want to see your session! I'm hoping someone will cover my shift so I can go. I read your blog, too. I really love it."

"Well, thanks. I appreciate that." Tess was always surprised when someone recognized her. She'd started doing the blog as a way to share what she was learning and generate some interest. But she knew that really, it was just her sitting in a room typing on her computer. She was always surprised when she learned people were actually reading it.

The young woman handed over the file. "This is all your information. Good luck with the presentation."

"Thanks. I hope I see you there." Tess took the file and stepped away.

"Well, I see you have a fan."

Tess turned to the tall, gray-haired man with the matching beard standing behind her. She grinned. "Dr. Sloane. I was hoping I'd see you."

He smiled warmly and offered his hand. "Jeff. You're done with school. We're colleagues now."

"Okay, Jeff." She knew he was right, but it was hard to shift gears from "Dr. Sloane" to "Jeff." He'd been Dr. Sloane to her for five years.

They fell in step together, heading to the main conference room. "So, I see you're presenting," Jeff said.

"Will you be attending?"

"I wouldn't miss my star student in action."

Tess studied his face. "Really?"

He sighed. "Tess, you know I wish you had chosen another area of study. You have an incredible brain, and you could do a lot. But bigfoot? It's a mocked field. No one takes it seriously. You have a promising future. I just don't want it derailed before it even begins."

"I appreciate your concern. But I need to do this. And you know as well as I that animals are being discovered every year that we've never heard of, heard of only through legend, or thought were extinct."

"But those animals are a lot smaller than an eight to ten foot ape weighing over a thousand pounds."

"The Bili ape is pretty big."

He sighed. "True. But that's just one."

"Dr. Sloane—"

He raised an eyebrow.

"I mean, Jeff. I do appreciate you looking out for me. But I promised myself that I would give this a shot. This is what I went to school for—all those degrees were so I could bring science to this search. And that's what I intend to do."

"I know. And part of me envies your ability to break new ground. I mean, if you're successful, it will not only change the field, it will change the world."

Tess felt the little trickle of fear at the back of her mind that always appeared when she thought of the ramifications of her research. She wanted to prove bigfoot existed, but she tried not to think too much about what would happen after she'd succeeded. Right now, she simply needed to keep herself focused on the work.

"But Tess," Jeff continued, "if you don't find anything or prove anything, your degrees won't help you. You may never be able to work in this field again. Your reputation will be irreparably damaged."

Tess knew he was right. It was okay to go out on a limb in science, but if you did, you had to be successful, or you risked cutting the limb out from underneath you. "I know. So let's just hope I find something."

CHAPTER SIX

Tess felt the energy of the crowd. She was almost finished with her presentation, and so far, it had gone incredibly well. Now all she had left to do she was at the question-and-answer portion, which she always enjoyed.

The room was packed. The crowd consisted mainly of college students from the university, but she also saw some of the regulars—the folks who attended almost all conferences involving bigfoot. And right now, everyone seemed to have a question or want to make a comment. Tess couldn't have asked for a better response.

She called on a student in the second row. With a crooked smile, he asked simply, "New Jersey? Seriously?"

Tess gestured to the map on the screen behind her—a map of North America with dots indicating the locations of bigfoot sightings. There had been sightings all over the US. The biggest clusters were in the Pacific Northwest and New England, but there were also plenty of sightings in the Midwest and down south in Texas and Florida.

Tess grinned. "Well, not in downtown Trenton—but in the

more remote areas of Sussex County. In fact, back in the nineteen-seventies and eighties there was a rash of sightings of a giant animal, eight feet tall with red eyes, in those more remote areas. It was called the Big Red Eye. Arms hanging by its knees, horrible stench."

"That's not possible," someone called out.

"You have to remember," Tess said, "Jersey is not all smokestacks and factories. The Appalachian Trail cuts through it. There's a substantial area for a large animal to survive, and more importantly, to go undetected."

About a dozen hands flew in the air. "Third row from the back in the red shirt," Tess said.

A man stood. He had a long beard and a t-shirt that read "Eat at Frank's." Tess prepared herself for a probably sensational question.

"Do you think the bigfoot are the same beings mentioned in the tales of Merlin and the troglodytes?"

Tess struggled not to laugh. *That's what I get for judging based on appearances.* She saw a lot of confused faces and knew she had to back up and fill them in. "I'm sure most of you have heard of Merlin—the ancient Celtic magician. What some of you may not know is that Merlin was said to have lived with a group of wild, hairy men in caves. Those men were called troglodytes.

"What's really interesting, at least to me, is that in 1735, Carl Linnaeus wrote the first codex on all the animals in the world—he called it the *Systema Naturea,* and it included nine thousand species—and in it, he said there were two types of humans: man and the troglodytes.

"Reports from more modern times say that bigfoot does indeed make use of caves and tunnels to keep away from humans. So yes, I do think it's possible that the troglodytes could very well have been another group of bigfoot."

Hands went up again, and Tess called on a woman in her thirties. "Yes?"

"So what do you think Bigfoot is?"

Tess studied the crowd while carefully weighing her answer. As a scientist, her job was to follow the data and let it determine her answer—yet she also knew that that particular answer would not go over well with the crowd.

"Right now there are two schools of thought," she said. "One holds that bigfoot is an animal, a giant ape, possibly one that has existed hidden from mankind for thousands of years. The other holds that bigfoot is actually a man, a primitive man, who for whatever reason has not developed like the rest of us."

"A man, like *Homo sapiens*?"

Tess shook her head. "No. Over twenty different types of hominids have been found in our past. We are related to them, but there *are* distinct differences. It is believed that bigfoot may be one of these cousins of *Homo sapiens*."

"But what do *you* believe?" the woman pressed.

"I believe it is most likely an ape, a giant ape."

"Apes are not ten feet tall," someone called out.

Tess smiled good-naturedly. "Well, maybe not now, but they were in the past. There was a giant ape named *Gigantopithecus* who is believed to have gone extinct one hundred thousand years ago. It was at least ten feet tall and weighed in at over one thousand pounds. Due to its size, scholars believe it made nests on the ground, like the Bili ape. At first, it, too, was considered merely a legend. That was before a molar of the giant primate was found in 1938. And soon, more jawbones and teeth were found all across Asia."

"So you really think bigfoot's a giant ape?" the woman asked.

"I *suspect* that is the truth. But hopefully, in the next year, I'll be able to prove it."

CHAPTER SEVEN

Tess keyed open her hotel room and shuffled through the door. It had been a good day, but she was exhausted. After the talk, she'd stayed to speak with members of the audience who hadn't had a chance to get their questions addressed. It had been a long but interesting two hours.

She'd been surprised that Jeff had waited. The two of them had gone for coffee. He was working on geospatial distribution of *Homo denisova* in comparison with *Homo sapiens* and Neanderthals. Tess could tell he wanted her help, and to be honest, part of her wanted to—the possible interaction of ancient humans fascinated her. But her passion was with her current line of research. Until she answered the question of what bigfoot was, she wasn't going to be able to focus on anything else.

Kicking off her heels, she dropped her bag on the desk across from the bed and pulled off her suit jacket. The worst part of these trips was always the wardrobe. The person who invented heels must have hated women.

She grabbed the remote off the top of the TV, flopped onto

the bed, and closed her eyes. *Just ten minutes. I'll relax for ten minutes, and then I'll go back down for the meet-and-greet.*

She knew that if she was to have any chance of getting funded, the meet-and-greet was where connections would be made. The presentation was just the audition; now she needed a sit down with a director.

She turned on the TV, flipping through channels without really focusing on them. Finally she shut it off and closed her eyes. *A quick nap and I'll be ready to go.*

The hotel phone rang right next to her. She groaned. *Oh, come on.*

But she slapped on her "I was not just trying to sleep" voice and answered. "Hello?"

"Dr. Brannick?"

"Yes?"

"My name is Thaddeus Regan. I am the assistant to Carter Hayes."

Tess's mouth fell open. Carter Hayes was a world-renowned businessman who had a habit of turning small ideas into million-dollar ones. "Um, yes, Mr. Regan, what can I do for you?"

"Mr. Hayes was able to view your presentation today, and he would like to speak with you."

"He was there?"

Thaddeus gave a small laugh. "No, no, of course not. But we recorded it for him. He was very impressed and would like to meet with you. Are you available now?"

Tess sat up, her eyes scanning the room for her shoes. "Sure. Where would he like to meet?"

"We've set up a video conference in the business center. Fifteen minutes?"

"Great. See you then."

Tess hung up the phone and jumped off the bed, grabbing one shoe from in front of the TV. She got on her hands and knees and retrieved the other one from under the bed. Then she pulled out her makeup case and did a quick refresher. Throwing on her jacket and grabbing her messenger bag, she pocketed the room key and made her way out the door.

Ten minutes later, she was sitting in a conference room. A monitor sat on the table in front of her with a camera aimed right at her face. Tess squirmed. She was not a fan of seeing herself on camera. It's why she wrote a blog instead of doing podcasts.

The attendant who ran the business center had left her a bottle of water. She took a sip and then tapped her pen on the legal pad she'd brought with her.

The screen in front of her beeped. Taking a breath, Tess pushed the button to connect the call.

A man in his forties with pale blue eyes and light brown hair beginning to thin at the peak appeared. He smiled, but it was not overly warm, more perfunctory. "Ah, Dr. Brannick. It's nice to meet you in person. I am Thaddeus Regan."

"Mr. Regan. It's a pleasure."

He gave her another perfunctory smile. "Please hold for Mr. Hayes."

Tess's heart gave a little leap. Carter Hayes. He'd been on the cover of *Time* magazine at least four times that she could remember, and every time they had debated whether he was a sinner or a saint. His standard mode of operation was to take over a floundering company, restructure it, and then turn it into a financially solvent corporation. But there was always a cost—pensions were lost, people were fired. His methods had gotten him likened to barbarians of old—nothing and no one was left standing when he was done.

The camera shifted as it was placed on a desk, and Mr. Hayes came into view. Tess had read that he was Scandinavian, but she would have known that anyway from one look. He had a narrow face, blond hair turning to white, and piercing blue eyes. He was a little thinner than the last picture she'd seen of him. *I wonder if he's ill or just cutting out carbs?*

"Dr. Brannick, it's a pleasure to meet you. Thank you for agreeing to meet with me on such short notice."

"The pleasure is all mine. It's an honor to meet you, Mr. Hayes."

He waved his hand. "Please. Call me Carter. I've read your recent papers and your blog."

The idea of Carter Hayes hunched over a computer reading her blog brought a smile to Tess's face. She hastily hid it with a cough.

"Tell me," Carter said. "Why do you think you've been able to continually find evidence where others have failed?"

Tess had prepared for just this question. "Usually, researchers go to a place when they hear there has been a bigfoot sighting. They stay for a few days, sometimes weeks, and then they move on to the next reported sighting. I believe that approach is misguided."

"How so?"

"Well, bigfoot know their surroundings well—they know what's supposed to be in their environment and what's not. And they tend to stay away from the things that are not supposed to be there—say, for instance, a visiting scientist. As a result, I've set up my base in an area that has had bigfoot sightings on and off for years, and I have been out there almost every day for over a year. So I'm not new to the environment—I'm now viewed as part of it. I think that's what has enabled me to get the casts I have."

"And you seem to think you're repeatedly finding prints from one bigfoot in particular."

"Yes. I noticed a consistent feature on many of the casts—a scar that tells me that they all belong to the same individual."

"Have you actually seen a bigfoot yet?"

Tess hesitated, contemplating her answer. But she knew lying would only come back to haunt her. "No. But I know one has been nearby."

"How?"

"They have a rather strong scent—if you smelled it, you would understand. It's a mix of woods, decay, and feces. It's really remarkable. I've smelled it twice, and both times I found footprints shortly thereafter."

Carter sat back in his chair. "People often refer to sasquatch or bigfoot as an animal. Is that what you believe him to be?"

Tess shook her head. "Belief has nothing to do with it. This is science."

"And what does science tell you?"

"Science tells me we need to do more research."

Carter gave a laugh, the skin at the corner of his eyes crinkling. "Good answer. So tell me, Dr. Brannick, do you think you will ever see one?"

Tess thought over all the prints she had found. She thought of the times she had felt eyes on her in the woods. But the memories of the night in the forest with her father and brother pushed to the forefront.

"It's only a matter of time," she said.

CHAPTER EIGHT

Carter closed the laptop in front of him and sat back. *Impressive.* He had queried Dr. Brannick for almost forty minutes about her research. She had a strong science background, and she was straightforward, edging to blunt. He liked that.

Plus, she was good-looking. The picture in the file hadn't done her justice. It hadn't captured her energy. Even through the monitor, he could sense her passion, her intelligence, her dedication. If anyone was going to succeed in this quest, it was Dr. Tess Brannick. And her attractiveness would be a boon when she succeeded. The media would love her.

Thaddeus quietly stood up from the couch. "Sir?"

"What is your impression?" Carter asked.

"Her pedigree is impressive. She received high marks in all her coursework, and her professors were highly impressed with her, although many expressed concern about her chosen field of study."

Carter snorted. *Academics—a bunch of smarty-pants writing articles for each other.* But Brannick was different. She was going out on her own, away from the mainstream. He respected that.

He knew that while the greatest risk was in ventures like these, so were the rewards.

"But I think it is her own personal experience that gives her the edge," Thaddeus continued. "She knows she will be successful, because she has already met bigfoot."

A childhood obsession—just like me. They were both focused on finding the beast. And together, they would succeed.

The financial windfall from the find would be astronomical. From a pure marketing standpoint, the potential profit was incalculable. And for a man known for being able to break everything down to dollars and cents, that was truly saying something. Who wouldn't pay an arm and a leg to see a bigfoot—live and in person?

But even the financial windfall paled in comparison to what else could be gained. If the hominid existed, it had a strength and build that far eclipsed that of any human. If they could harness that for the military, or figure out a way to genetically modify humans to achieve that same physique... why, that military would be unstoppable.

Of course, Carter knew he wasn't the first to have thought of the military applications of genetically modifying humans. Back during the Cold War, the USSR had attempted to merge animals and humans in an effort to increase the physical capabilities of their soldiers. It all began with a Soviet biologist named Ilya Ivanovich Ivanov, the first person to figure out how to artificially inseminate animals. The USSR contracted him to create super soldiers using a mixture of apes and humans, so he went to Congo to inseminate chimps with human sperm. But he failed. Attempts at using monkey sperm on human volunteers also failed.

Yet other attempts had demonstrated that cross-species breeding *was* possible. There was the liger, for instance: part tiger, part lion. And the zebroid: a cross between a zebra and either a horse or donkey. Grolars: a cross between a grizzly and a polar bear. And wholphins: a whale/dolphin hybrid. The list went on.

The biggest problem with the Soviet research, Carter thought, had been the use of gorillas. They simply weren't genetically compatible enough with humans. But if Carter was right, bigfoot was even more closely related to humans than apes were.

Which meant there was a stronger possibility of success.

Carter twirled his chair and grabbed the cane next to his desk. He stood and swayed. Thaddeus did not move to help him —he knew better.

The moment of weakness annoyed Carter, but it also reinforced why he needed Tess Brannick to succeed. Besides the lucrative marketing and military angles, there was a much more personal angle that Carter was counting on. Bigfoot was strength personified; perhaps the creature might provide a cure, or at least a treatment, for muscular degenerative diseases.

But even if that failed, the discovery of bigfoot would define Carter's legacy. When he passed, his name and image would live on as one of the twenty-first century's greatest discoverers. He would be forever known as the man who found bigfoot. He would not live forever, but his discovery and his name would.

"How much would help her succeed?" Carter asked.

"Five hundred thousand dollars."

Carter did a quick calculation in his mind. "Make it a million. And make sure she signs the contract and that we get twice-monthly updates."

Thaddeus back out of the room. "Very well, sir."

He turned to the wall of windows, his thigh muscles protesting even this small exercise. *Dr. Brannick, you have just become my greatest hope.*

CHAPTER NINE

After the video conference call, Tess walked back to the banquet hall in a daze. *Carter Hayes is interested in my work.* She couldn't believe it. She hit the button for the lobby as if she were sleepwalking. She crossed her fingers. *Oh, please let him fund me.*

The doors popped open, and she resolved to force the meeting with Carter Hayes from her mind. He would be a wonderful benefactor, but he was not a lock. She had to focus on other possibilities. Composing herself, she stepped out of the elevator and headed for the main ballroom.

But despite her best intentions, she couldn't stop thinking about the meeting. As a result, she spent the next hour and a half speaking with people about her work without any real idea of what she was saying. She just hoped she was making sense. The time passed in a blur, and when she finally returned to her room, it was with great relief that she slipped back into her normal clothes: jeans and boots. Her feet thanked her profusely.

But there was no time to lie down. She had another appointment—a much more enjoyable one. And sure enough, the minute she'd gotten changed, her phone chimed. She pulled it out.

We're outside.

With a huge smile, Tess hurried down to the lobby and stepped outside.

"There she is!" Pax jogged over, a giant grin on his face. He threw his arms around her.

Tess hugged him back. "It's so good to see you."

Pax pulled away, looking her over from head to toe. "You need to leave the forest more, but you still look great."

She grinned. He looked good, too—trim, tan, and his dark hair was lighter. But he also seemed a little fitter and stronger as well. "You too. It looks like married life agrees with you."

He looped his arm through hers. "That it does."

Pax's husband Shawn walked over. *And here's the reason why Pax looks so good.* Shawn was six foot six, with dark skin, dark eyes, a ridiculous amount of muscle, and a smile that lit up a room. A Navy SEAL for fifteen years, he'd given up going on active missions when he married Pax, but he still kept in phenomenal shape by putting new recruits through their paces at the Naval Special Warfare Center at the Naval Amphibious Base in Coronado.

Shawn pulled her into a hug, lifting her off the ground. "Ah, my little sister."

She laughed, whacking him on the shoulder. "Put me down."

Shawn did with a smile. "We don't like you being so far away. When are you moving here?"

"Never. But you two are always welcome to move back home."

It was their running argument. Pax and Tess were as close as brother and sister could be. And when Shawn and Pax had started to get serious, that closeness had extended to him as well. They all wished they could move closer to each other, but jobs kept them in different spaces. Pax was the marketing director for a genetic lab based in San Diego. He used to run one of the labs, but he was happier after the move to the PR position. "Fewer test tubes and more people," as he explained.

And seeing as Bigfoot didn't often hang around in downtown San Diego, moving was not really an option for any of them.

"But we are all still agreed that we're retiring together at Catalina Island, right?" Tess asked.

"We're in," Pax said. "Now let's eat."

Fifteen minutes later, they were seated at a quiet Italian restaurant. Tess grabbed a roll from the bread basket. "So, what's going on at work?"

"Oh, same old—except there was a big hubbub about a paternity test that was done at the lab involving an unnamed celebrity," Pax said. "The media has been camped out trying to get the name. I've been fielding calls all week. It's been a zoo."

"And he's loving every minute of it," Shawn said.

Pax grinned. "That I am."

Tess smiled as she watched the easy camaraderie between the two. She'd had that with her fiancée, David, too. It had been as if they could read each other's minds. The thought of David still hurt. Three years after his death, though, she was finally able to think about him without debilitating sadness. Now it was merely an ache, one that, she knew, would never completely go away. He had been young, and kind, and hers. And a drunk driver had taken him away.

Her phone rang, jarring her back to the present.

Shawn frowned. "I thought the no-phone rule was in place."

"Sorry. But I'm waiting to hear on a grant." She read the name on her screen and stood up. "Holy crap. It's them."

"Go get 'em," Pax called after her as she made for the quieter balcony.

Steeling herself, Tess answered. "Hello?"

"Dr. Brannick, Thaddeus Regan here."

"Mr. Regan. Nice to hear from you again."

"Yes, you as well. Mr. Hayes has decided to fund your research for two years. At the end of two years, depending on how the research is progressing, he will have an option to extend. Five hundred thousand dollars annually is the amount we have reached. Would that be acceptable to you?"

Tess's head spun. *Five hundred thousand dollars.* She could get new cameras, maybe hire an assistant, afford electricity and food. *Holy cow.* "Um, yes, yes. That is acceptable."

"Excellent. I've emailed you a copy of the contract. Please review it, have it notarized, and send it back to the address listed within the week. Mr. Hayes looks forward to sharing your research successes."

Thaddeus disconnected the call without waiting for a reply. But that was fine with Tess, because she wasn't sure she was going to be able to form one. She walked back to the table in a daze.

Pax took her hand as she resumed her seat. "Tess?"

She looked over at him and saw the concern on his face. Shaking herself from her shock, she said, "I've been funded for two years by Carter Hayes."

Both Shawn and Pax went quiet, then both got up and hugged her.

"I am so proud of you," Pax said.

"I knew you could do it," Shawn said.

The waiter appeared. "Is there anything else I can get for you?"

Pax grinned. "Margaritas all around. We're celebrating."

CHAPTER TEN

The next afternoon, Tess got off the plane at Susanville Municipal Airport with a groan. The sun was awfully bright. She said a silent thank-you that she hadn't driven herself to the airport.

Last night, she, Pax, and Shawn had celebrated with margaritas. Lots of margaritas. They'd left Pax's car at the restaurant and taken a cab back to his and Shawn's place. This morning, Tess had then had to rush to the hotel to grab her stuff, check out, and get to the airport.

Now her head pounded as she made her way past the gates at baggage claim. A tall brunette in khaki slacks and a sweater made her way over with a smile.

"Well, you look like hell," Abby Newman said.

Tess groaned. "Must you yell?"

Abby laughed as she hugged her. "I'm barely whispering."

"And yet..."

Abby took Tess's bag. "Let me get this. You take these." She handed Tess a bottle of water and two aspirin.

"How...?"

"Pax called. He was worried you'd be a little bad off."

Tess took the pills gratefully. She'd taken some this morning before she left, but the droning plane had not helped her pounding head.

"Sasha is meeting us at the curb. Do you have another bag?"

Tess shook her head. "Nope. Traveling light."

Abby took her arm. "Come on, lightweight. Let's go."

They headed for the automatic doors that led to the passenger pick-up area. Even from here, Tess could see Sasha's bright blue FJ Cruiser. Sasha bolted from the driver's door with a squeal as Abby and Tess stepped onto the pavement—and all the men nearby stopped to watch. At five foot two, Sasha was petite and busty, with a body that even Tess could admit was sexy as hell, long dark wavy hair, and a pouty mouth that you usually found only with a plastic surgeon's help.

Sasha wrapped Tess in a hug. "Congratulations!" Tess had called both Sasha and Abby last night with the news of the grant.

Tess hugged her back. "Thanks, but not so loud."

Sasha grinned. "Lightweight. So, I'm guessing lunch is on you?"

"You got it."

Twenty minutes later, the three of them were tucked into a booth at the back of Poor Richard's. They ordered sandwiches and drinks, and when the waitress left, Abby turned to Tess. "You ready to talk about the contract?"

In addition to being one of Tess's best friends, Abby was also a lawyer, and Tess had sent her the contract last night to look over.

Tess cleared her head and took a handful of chips. "Yeah. What do you think?"

"I think there are a lot of strings."

Tess had expected that, of course. But from Abby's expression, she could tell her friend was not happy with the number of strings.

"Okay. Tell me."

"Well, according to this, any discovery you make, Hayes gets credit for. He gets top billing. From the way this is worded, you work for him as a practically unnamed employee."

Tess had been expecting something like that, but not quite so strong. "Well, I'm not really looking for the notoriety. But how would that affect my research? How would it affect my publications?"

"You couldn't have any. Everything would have to go through Hayes and be sent out by Hayes, if he agrees."

Tess's stomach dropped "So are you saying, that even though I'm the lead researcher, Hayes will have the rights to anything I discover *and* veto power over anything I try to publish?"

Abby nodded. "And that includes all your casts, hair samples, et cetera, too."

"I can't do that. I can't hand everything over. Especially the casts." Tess shook her head, her hopes dimming. "I mean, I need the grant money, but not if he ties my hands with regard to the research. That's the whole point."

"I know. And there's another issue I'm concerned about. There's nothing in here that allows you to sever the relationship with Hayes. You would essentially be locked in for two years, and there are huge penalties if you don't come through."

Tess slumped down in her seat. "So this grant is not a dream come true after all. It's a nightmare."

Abby reached out and squeezed Tess's hand. "Let me call his people. I'll see if I can rework the contract, make it more palatable. But... if I can't do that, will you be willing to walk away?"

Tess looked away. Ever since what had happened with her

father, she had focused on this one goal: proving bigfoot exists. And she knew she was close. But with this contract, Hayes would take over. He would control every aspect of her research. She couldn't let that happen.

She sighed. "If I have to, I'll walk."

CHAPTER ELEVEN

Madge and Shelby were waiting on the porch when Sasha and Tess drove up. Madge invited them both to dinner. Sasha accepted, but Tess declined. She needed to get home and get caught up. She wanted to get everything set up, check emails, grab a shower, and have an early night so she'd be ready to face tomorrow. Plus, after Abby's review of the contract, she wasn't really in the mood for company.

When Tess pulled up to her cabin just before dusk, she smiled. Just the sight of her place lifted her spirits. Some people loved the hustle and bustle of the city, but Tess would take a little cabin in the woods any time.

She stepped out and breathed deep. Yup—this was home. She looked around, feeling the quiet. "Come on, girl."

Shelby was still in the truck. And instead of hopping out and running around like she usually did, she whined and cowered on the floor.

Tess whirled around, looking for what was wrong. But she couldn't see anything. She reached into the back of the truck and pulled out her shotgun. Whenever she traveled, she left her weapons with Madge—the shotgun, a rifle, and her Browning handgun. Teenagers had broken into empty cabins a few times, and Tess didn't want to take a chance on them finding her weapons.

"Stay there, girl," Tess said, closing the door with Shelby inside.

She walked slowly toward the cabin, straining to hear anything out of the ordinary. But she didn't see or hear anything out of place until she walked around the side of the cabin and saw some broken tree branches scattered on the ground.

She frowned. *How'd these get here? Windstorm?* No, her herb garden and flowerpots sat undisturbed on the porch. And Madge hadn't said anything about bad weather.

She walked to the back of the cabin and froze. Beside the window that looked in over the kitchen sink, a giant footprint was clearly outlined on the ground.

Tess whirled around, her heart pounding. She brought her shotgun to her shoulder. But there was nothing. The forest hummed back at her, giving no indication that a predator was nearby.

Tess began to shake. She'd never had one come this far out before. Had it somehow tracked her? But why?

Slowly she continued to make her way around the cabin. She found another print, a heel print, at the window on the other side. She moved away from the cabin, studying the ground a bit farther out. At about twenty feet from the building, just inside the tree line, she found another print.

Tess looked around, goose bumps breaking out along her skin. There was no smell that she could make out, but she had no doubt that a faint smell was what had scared Shelby. And Tess couldn't help be a little freaked out as well.

Still, whoever had visited seemed to be gone now. Tess forced the scientist part of her mind to the forefront. *Okay, get some casts and let's see who we've got.*

She headed back to the cabin, cautious of her surroundings. Nothing set off any alarm bells.

She stopped at the truck and opened the door. "All right, you big chicken, let's go."

Shelby just peered up at her from the floor on the passenger side.

Tess adopted a gentler tone. "It's okay, Shelby. I won't let anything hurt you. Come."

Shelby slowly crawled out from her spot. Tess rubbed her back. She hated how hard Shelby was shaking. And she knew that inside, she was shaking just as hard.

CHAPTER TWELVE

Tess headed down the path, her thoughts still on the footprints outside her cabin. She had slept little last night, jumping at every sound. But getting back into her routine energized her. As she rounded a mountain maple, her mind ran over everything she'd learned for the millionth time.

The feet, of course, were fascinating. They truly were amazing—more similar to primitive humans' feet than gorillas' or modern humans'. Gorillas had a divergent big toe, but there was none on the casts she'd found, or on any of the other casts found in Northwest. Instead, all the very long toes were lined up, and there was no arch.

In fact, when the foot bent to allow for bipedalism, the bend occurred almost under the ankle. That meant a full two thirds of the foot supported the being's body weight. It was both amazing and understandable. Due to bigfoot's alleged muscle mass and height, he had to weigh in excess of eight hundred pounds. The prints outside Tess's cabin confirmed that—the foot that had made them had sunk in almost three inches into the ground. Only an incredibly large animal was capable of creating such a deep print. And there was no way the ball of a foot, even a large foot, would be able to support that much weight by itself.

Tess considered what science knew about other bipeds. There weren't many. Besides humans, of course, the most famous bipedal animal was *Gigantopithecus.*

And now there's the Bili ape, too, she thought.

Of course, many animals occasionally walked on two feet for short distances, but that didn't make them true bipeds. Very few had the physiology to walk for extended periods of time.

Tess pictured the bigfoot in the Patterson-Gimlin film. *I wonder if she ever moves on all fours. Her arms are certainly long enough.* She tried to picture it, but it felt wrong. Bigfoot was too... Tess struggled to find the right word. Too *comfortable* on two feet to travel that way, she decided.

Tess was only a few minutes from her camp when something in the trees to her right caught her attention. She squinted and made her way a few feet into the brush.

A structure stood there, created out of tree branches. Each branch was easily twenty feet long, and they were layered one over the other, creating the framework for a tent.

There was no way wind could have blown these trees into this shape. Nor had these branches merely fallen from their trees. The end of the branches had no rot; they were still healthy when they were broken free. Tess tugged on one branch. It was wedged in tight. She inspected it, and saw that it had been laced through three other branches. Excitement began to build in her.

This was made intentionally.

There was no one nearby, and no noticeable footprints. Tess shrugged off her pack and pulled out her camera. She had never seen a bigfoot structure before. She'd read about them, of course. In areas where bigfoot were believed to be, it was not unusual for individuals to come across trees or branches arranged in a tepee style. But their purpose was unknown. They weren't created for shelter—they were too open to the elements.

Tess walked around, snapping shots, her certainty growing. She had always suspected that these structures were a form of communication, maybe a road sign. She placed the camera back in her pack and studied the structure again. The branch that was woven between the three other branches pointed northwest. The others made a sloppy circle.

Tess shook her head, not sure what any of that meant but convinced it meant *something*. These had been carefully arranged. There had to be a reason for it.

Tess shouldered her pack, and with one last look at the structure, she made her way back to the trail. But the structure stayed in the forefront of her mind as she continued on to her camp. *Maybe I should set a camera up near it. It might—*

Tess went still and then whirled around. She could still see the structure. She looked at the interwoven branch and then toward her camp. Her heart began to race. The branch pointed right to her camp.

She swallowed, looking around, a thin sweat breaking out on her forehead. *Is he warning others to stay away? Or warning me?*

—

FROM THE BLOG 'BIGFOOT AMONG US' BY DR. TESS BRANNICK

This week's question comes from Jane Haskell in Burlington, Vermont. Jane writes:

I've heard people say bigfoot builds stuff. Is that true?

Actually, it may be. Most people agree that bigfoot are not tool users, but tree structures have been found in areas frequented by bigfoot. In fact, there's a great website that shows the tree structures alleged to have been constructed by bigfoot in Colorado. You can find it here.

No one is really sure why they build the structures. Some argue they are announcements of life events, such as a birth or death. Others argue they are simply art. The structures are all open to the elements and therefore are not shelters. But they are solidly created. There is a plan to their construction, we just need to figure out what it is.

CHAPTER THIRTEEN

Tess spent the rest of the week going through her normal routine. But after finding the prints and the tree structure, her nights were a little rough. Bigfoot was supposed to be nocturnal, so every nighttime noise had Tess practically leaping out of bed.

But her friend made no further appearances at her cabin, and she'd found no evidence of him at the camp—although the food was gone each morning when she went to check.

She had the uneasy feeling that maybe her friend was mad that she'd left for a few days. But she chased that thought away as quickly as it appeared. *Stop giving them more credit than they deserve.*

The lack of progress had her on edge as the week closed. Which is why when Sasha called to ask her to go out on Friday, she was completely uninterested. However, Sasha refused to take no for an answer, which was how Tess ended up sitting in a booth at Poor Richard's on Friday evening, a pitcher of beer on the table between them.

"So how's the research going?" Sasha asked after she'd told

Tess about her latest commission. Sasha was an artist and was slowly making a name for herself.

Tess shrugged. "Not good. I haven't seen a sign all week."

"Oh, I forgot to tell you," Sasha said. "There was a group of bigfoot hunters in town while you were away. None of them had been in the woods before. One sprained an ankle. Two went to get help and got lost. It was crazy. Dev had to go find them."

Tess's heart gave a little leap at the mention of Dev Wilson—just as it had ever since she was a teenager.

"Well, people are fascinated with bigfoot," she said. "Do you know there's even some erotica books dedicated to bigfoot?"

Sasha's eyes went wide. "Well, that's disturbing."

Tess shrugged. "Maybe not."

"What?" Sasha's eyes grew large.

Tess looked at her for a moment before she realized how her words had been interpreted. She put up her hands, feeling a blush on her cheeks. "I mean—no. I'm not interested."

Sasha just raised an eyebrow.

"Oh, shut up," Tess grumbled. "I mean, from a scientific point of view."

"Uh-huh."

"I don't know why I try to have these conversations with you."

"Hey, *you're* the one who brought up having the hots for bigfoot."

Tess gritted her teeth. "I didn't say I had the hots for bigfoot. I said—oh, forget it."

Sasha laughed. "Okay, okay. I'll be good. Tell me why bigfoot erotica is not crazy."

Tess watched her, but she knew Sasha was done teasing. And from the way Sasha was leaning forward, Tess also knew she was sincerely interested.

"Okay, well, did you know that most *Homo sapiens* actually

have the genes of different types of hominids in their genetic code?"

Sasha's eyebrows rose. "What? How?"

"Well, apparently in the remote past, we're talking around six hundred thousand years ago, *Homo sapiens* interbred with Neanderthals. As a result, most *Homo sapiens'* genetic code has three to four percent Neanderthal genes in it."

"So we're part Neanderthal?"

"A little bit."

One of the men from the pool tables in the back let out a whoop and slapped his friend. Tess turned back to Sasha. "Of course, some people have a higher percentage."

Sasha laughed. "That's crazy. We're all a little caveman."

"And it's not just Neanderthals," Tess said. "Traces of other ancient hominids have been found in our genetic code."

"Like who?"

"Like *Homo denisova*—an ancient hominid we know very little about except for the fact that they lived at the same time as *Homo sapiens* and Neanderthals and were extremely large."

"Like, bigfoot large?"

"Yup."

"So our ancestors were a little frisky?"

"So it appears. One little cave in Denisova, Siberia, first offered proof of our mixed genetic heritage. Artifacts from the cave demonstrated that not only did different hominids live at the same time, but that they interbred. Genetic testing revealed that all three groups—*Homo sapiens*, *Homo denisova*, and Neanderthals—had interbred with one another, along with a fourth type of hominid which no one had previously known existed and which we still haven't found."

Sasha raised her beer. "Well here's to our frisky ancestors."

Tess joined the toast with a laugh.

The group of guys in the back let out a yell, and one of them shoved another one. It looked like a fight was about to break out.

A tall, muscular, copper-skinned man sitting at the bar turned his head at the disruption, then rose and headed back to intervene.

Dev. Tess's heart beat a little faster. She'd had no idea he was here.

Dev made his way to the two men, who by now were yelling at each other and shoving back and forth. Both men were about Dev's size, but whereas their bulk was due to fat, Dev's was due to muscle. Dev grabbed one guy by the shirt and pulled him away. Through Dev's t-shirt, his arms strained, and Tess couldn't help but notice just how well defined those arms were.

Tess couldn't hear what Dev was saying, but from the looks on the men's faces, it was getting through.

"Speaking of getting it on," Sasha said dryly.

Tess felt her cheeks bloom red again. She took a drink and glanced up at Sasha's knowing expression. "What?"

"You know what." Sasha nudged her chin to where Dev was escorting both men to the door. "Dev."

"There's nothing there, Sash."

"Well, tell your face that, because it's as red as my shirt."

"It's not like that."

"Come *on*. You two have been playing around each other for years. He was involved. You were involved. And right now, you're both not involved."

Tess shook her head. "I've known him since we were kids. He's Pax's best friend. It's complicated."

"No it's not. And you forget, *I've* known you since you were a kid as well. You're overanalyzing it. And he's not a kid now, as I'm pretty sure you've noticed. Oh, and by the way, he's heading over here."

"What?" Tess whirled around before she could stop herself.

Dev was still at the door. She turned back to Sasha and glared. "You suck."

Sasha grinned back at her. "And you lie. You like him, and he more than likes you. So what's stopping you?"

Tess shrugged. "Nothing. It's—it's just complicated."

Sasha hesitated. "You know I loved David."

Tess nodded.

"But it's been three years," Sasha said. "It's time to get back in the game."

"It's not that easy."

"No, it's probably not. But you've taken to this whole 'being single' thing like it's a permanent lifestyle. When David died, you locked yourself away with your dissertation, which I totally get. But then you moved back here and locked yourself away in the woods. Now I think you being on your own is less of a choice and more of a habit. And it's a habit you need to break."

Tess wanted to be mad at Sasha. She wanted to tell her to stay out of her love life, but Sasha was just echoing some of the same thoughts that had been rattling around in her own brain lately. "Maybe."

"I love you, Tess, but you need to live a little more. Unless you really are tracking bigfoot down for a little romance?"

"Um, yuck?"

Sasha laughed. "Glad to hear it." Her eyes shifted beyond Tess. "Hey, Dev."

Tess smiled. "You're not getting—"

"Hello, ladies."

Tess closed her eyes. *Damn.* She opened them to find Dev looking right at her. Standing at six foot one, he had broad shoulders, washboard abs, and hazel eyes that stood out in an almost classic Native American face with high cheekbones and a strong forehead.

After his parents—who both had ties to the Hoopa and

Klamath tribes in the area—divorced, Dev's mom had moved back with her family in Beauford, and Dev had shown up in the same seventh grade class as Pax. The two soon became fast friends, and Dev had been in and out of their house throughout high school. An attraction had bloomed between Tess and Dev, and it had remained ever since, but neither of them had ever acted on it. At first, it had been because of Pax. But then, the timing had always been off.

Sasha nudged her chin toward where the fight had broken out. "So, what was that all about?"

"One idiot accused the other of knocking the table when he took his shot. They're cooling their heels in the parking lot." He turned his full attention on Tess. "How'd the conference go?"

"Pretty good," she said, her mind going blank.

"Pretty good?" Sasha echoed. "She got a grant for the next two years with enough money to put cameras all over that forest."

Abby had been in negotiations with Hayes's people for the last week, and she said she was really close to getting it all settled. Tess was cautiously optimistic that everything would work out.

Dev grinned, showing off perfect teeth, and Tess sighed. *Why does he have to have perfect teeth too? Couldn't he have one physical flaw? A lazy eye? A crooked nose? A hairy mole on his face? Make this whole thing a little easier to ignore?*

"That's great. So I guess that means we'll be keeping you in town for another two years, huh?" Dev said.

"Looks like," Tess agreed, her gaze meeting his and her pulse leaping.

Sasha slid out of her side of the booth. "Well, I need to get going. I'm meeting a new potential client first thing in the morning."

"Oh, okay." Disappointed, Tess started to get up too.

Sasha waved her back down. "No, no. You stay. Dev, you'll see she gets home all right, won't you?"

"Be happy to," Dev said.

Sasha squeezed his bicep. "Thank you." She leaned over and kissed Tess on the cheek, whispering, "And *you* can thank me later." She stepped back. "Have fun, you two." With a wave she headed through the crowd toward the exit.

Dev slid into the booth across from Tess. He nodded at her beer. "Another?"

Live a little, a tiny Sasha yelled at Tess from inside her mind.

Tess smiled. "Sounds good."

CHAPTER FOURTEEN

Three hours later, Tess sat in the passenger seat of Dev's Jeep. They had talked non-stop since Sasha had left. It had always been like that between them. The conversation just flowed, effortlessly.

"So then he offered me the grant. And now Abby is trying to work out some of the details. She says she's close, so hopefully in the next few days it'll go through."

Dev pulled up in front of Tess's cabin and turned off the car. "That's amazing. Carter Hayes—you've actually met him."

"Well—digital him."

"That's more than most. It's really impressive. I always knew that brain of yours would take you places."

She felt a warm glow at his words. "Well, I should go." She started to open the door. Dev quickly opened his and came around, offering her his hand.

"It's okay," Tess said. "I can walk it myself."

"My mother didn't raise me that way." Dev took her hand and they walked hand in hand to the cabin.

As they walked up the steps, he said, "Pax told me you had a visitor out here while you were out of town."

That was one thing Tess had always liked about Dev—he'd never doubted bigfoot existed. Both sides of his ancestry believed, and his parents had taught him and his siblings about their brother in the woods. It's probably what had helped Pax and him bond so close together initially.

"Yeah," Tess said. "Nothing was disturbed. I just found some prints."

"You okay being out here alone?" Dev asked.

"Well, I'm not alone. I've got Shelby."

Dev laughed. "She's what, a hundred in dog years?"

"Only seventy. But still going strong. Well, besides a little arthritis in her back legs."

"Seriously, if you get any more visitors, give me a call, day or night." Dev was a deputy with the county sheriff.

Tess looked up at him, feeling like she was sixteen. "Yes, officer."

He smiled, and Tess's heart gave another little tug. "Good. And I'll make sure someone drives by here a little more often, all right?"

"I'll be fine, Dev. He doesn't want to hurt me."

"He?"

"I think it's the same guy I've seen evidence of in the woods. He's probably just hungry."

Dev pulled her to a stop, squeezing her hand. "Just be careful. I don't want anything to happen to you."

Tess couldn't seem to breathe. She leaned forward, and Dev did the same.

And then his radio squawked to life. "Dev, we've got a fight over at Poor Richard's. Are you in the area?"

Dev sighed and pulled back. He stepped away from Tess and

pulled his radio off his belt. "Yeah, I'm around. I'll be there in five minutes."

He turned back to Tess. "Well, duty calls. You good?"

Disappointed, unfulfilled. Out loud she said. "Yeah, I'm good."

He leaned down and kissed her on the cheek in a very brotherly fashion. She tried to keep the sigh from escaping her lips.

"Good night," he said.

"Night."

Dev headed down the stairs and Tess turned to unlock the door.

"Tess?"

She turned as Dev walked back up the steps. He took her face in his hands and kissed her. Tess felt like she was melting. Her heart raced, her arms wound their way around his waist, and she wanted the kiss to go on forever.

Dev pulled back and leaned his forehead into hers. "I've wanted to do that for years."

She smiled. "I'm glad you finally did."

"Have dinner with me next weekend?"

"Okay."

He kissed her again, this time briefly. "I have to go." He gave her one last look and hurried down the steps.

Tess watched him go, her heart hammering. As he pulled out of the drive, he blinked his lights at her. She waved and let herself in.

Shelby tottered over to her. Tess slumped down to sit next to her on the floor. She traced her hand over her lips, feeling Dev's lips there. Her stomach did backflips. *Oh, boy.*

CHAPTER FIFTEEN

Tess spent the rest of the weekend getting herself set up for the week ahead. She and Abby spoke on the phone half a dozen times, ironing out the details of the contract. Tess let herself daydream about what equipment she would purchase if the grant went through. At the top of her wish list was an infrared monitor. She also made sure her files were up to date and prepared a preliminary report on her methods and findings thus far to forward to Hayes.

And throughout it all, she tried to ignore any thoughts of Dev. But on Sunday she made the mistake of telling Sasha about their kiss—and Sasha immediately drove over with takeout in order to get the play by play.

Now the two of them were curled up on Tess's couch, with Shelby sleeping over by the fireplace.

"It was good, wasn't it?" Sasha asked. "Because that man *looks* like a good kisser. I mean, I can see him as one of those focused types who's completely invested in the person he's with."

Tess could feel the blush on her cheeks. "It was good."

Sasha looked at her expectantly. "And?"

"And what? What do you want me to say?"

"He put his hands where? You put your hands where?"

"He put his hands on my face."

Sasha clutched a pillow to her chest. "I love when guys do that." She sighed. "Where were your hands?"

"Um, around his waist?"

Sasha leaned back on the couch with a big grin on her face. "Aren't you glad you took my advice?"

Tess nodded. "Yes. You are officially the bestest friend ever."

"Yes, I am. And as a reward, I expect to be maid of honor and for my dress not to be hideous."

"Hey, we haven't even gone on an official date. Maybe we can hold off on picking out the china pattern."

"Nope. I have a feeling about you two. And as you know, my feelings are never wrong."

Sasha's feelings *had* been wrong a time or two, but Tess didn't say anything.

Shelby picked up her head and gave a wag. Tess looked toward the door. "That must be Abby. She's bringing over the finalized contract."

"So it's a go?"

Tess nodded with smile. Abby had managed to make sure she had the rights to all her findings, although Hayes would be prominently mentioned. And he would be allowed to announce any major discoveries first. Abby had also managed to work in an escape clause if Tess needed one. Although Tess couldn't imagine any reason why she'd want out of the grant. "Yep, it's a go."

She opened the door as Abby got out of her car and waved. And Tess felt happier than she had in a long while. She had two incredible best friends, her research was funded for the next two years, and she was on the edge of romance. She grinned. *I love my life.*

This week's question comes from Joanne Butler in Northport, New York. Joanne asks:

Is the Yeti the same as bigfoot?

Most people would argue that they are the same. In fact, across the globe, bigfoot-like creatures enjoy a number of names. There is the menk in Russia, the yowie in Australia, the yeren in China, the almas in Mongolia, and the list goes on.

However, there are some differences. For example, the almas is largely believed to be an early human ancestor, while the yeren is believed to be more similar to an ancient ape, such as Gigantop-ithecus.

And anatomical differences have been observed. For instance, the footprints found in the Pacific Northwest of the United States indicate an animal with a very human-like foot, but the Yeti prints found in Nepal indicate a divergent big toe, giving those feet a more apelike appearance. This has led some to suggest that there is not one single bigfoot around the world, but many.

CHAPTER SIXTEEN

Six Months Later

Tess and Shelby jogged down the dirt road and around the bend. Up ahead, Tess's cabin came into view. "There we go, girl."

Shelby wagged her tail and trotted ahead of Tess, heading for her water bowl on the porch. Every evening, Tess took Shelby for a long jog to make up for the fact that the dog had to be cooped up in the cabin all day. For the last few months, Dev had been accompanying them, but today he had taken on an extra shift, filling in for a sick deputy.

Tess grew warm thinking about how close they'd gotten these last six months. She couldn't imagine her life without him. And neither of them could understand why they had waited so long.

Tess headed to the barn to double-check her supplies for the morning. She'd just pulled open the barn door when her cell phone rang.

Tess glanced at the screen before answering with a smile. "Hey, Eric. How are you?"

Eric Winfree was a park ranger with Rogue River National Forest. Rogue River Park was just over the border in Oregon, north of Tess's cabin, and connected to Siskiyou National Park. Together the two parks covered over a million acres. And both parks had well-documented bigfoot sightings.

Eric had also been a good friend of Tess's father. For years after her father's death, she'd had the hardest time not imagining the incident in the woods whenever she spoke with Eric. It was Eric who had helped get Pax and her back out into the woods after they had lost their dad. And now, the sound of his deep baritone voice only brought warm thoughts.

"I'm good, sweetheart. How you doing?"

"Pretty good. Just getting everything ready so I can get out early in the morning."

Eric knew the ins and outs of all Tess's research, and he fully supported her. In fact, he kept a file in his office of all the reported sightings and forwarded them to her. And a few years back, he'd informed her that most state parks had one person in each department that unofficially did the same. The official company line might be that bigfoot didn't exist, but unofficially, park rangers knew better than most what was out in their woods. Tess had contacts in more than a dozen other state parks as a result.

"Find anything lately?" Eric asked.

"Not this last week. But I'm going to pull the memory cards tomorrow. Maybe there's something on them. How's Jeanne?"

"She's great. Wants you to come visit soon."

"I know, I will."

"We understand you're busy. Which, actually, is why I'm calling. We've had an incident."

Tess stopped what she was doing and took a seat on the ATV. "Where'd it happen?"

"Up by Handerson's Hill."

Tess was familiar with the area. "Any prints?"

"Yup. And I already photographed them for you and cast them as well."

"You're the best."

"And the couple who reported it, Bernie and Leanne Hudson, they're still in town. They're leaving tomorrow, but I told them about you, and the husband at least wanted to speak with you. I got them to agree to meet for breakfast. So if you hightail it, I can introduce you."

Tess's mind was already racing, trying to rearrange her plans for the morning. "I'll be there."

This week's question comes from Candace Wallace in Alberta,
Canada:

How can bigfoot be a *Gigantopithecus?*
I thought they only lived in Asia.

That is in fact the most common argument against bigfoot being
Gigantopithecus—Gigantopithecus *was believed to have lived*
only in Asia.

Or at least, most scientists believe that. Some speculate that
perhaps the great ape, like early humans, crossed to North America
across the Bering land bridge. The land bridge between Asia and
North America existed around one hundred and fifty thousand
years ago—during the time of Gigantopithecus. *When it existed, it*

would have been able to support a large primate. Fossil records indicated it contained a large coniferous forest and numerous deciduous broadleaf plants.

The idea isn't as crazy as it sounds. Fossils of other animals formerly believed to have lived only in Asia have been found in North America. Take for example the red panda. From 2002 through 2010, parts of two red panda skeletons were found in Tennessee's Gray Fossil Site. Apart from one found in Washington, they were the only red panda fossils to be found in all of North America. The problem was, the red panda was not supposed to live in North America. It was believed to have been limited strictly to Asia.

So how, then, did these bones end up in the US? Perhaps the red panda also crossed the bridge. But the very existence of the red panda bones in North America opens the door to the possibility that other animals also crossed the land bridge. And Gigantopithecus could have easily been one of them.

CHAPTER SEVENTEEN

T ess and Shelby pulled into the gravel parking lot of the diner just before six thirty the following morning. There were only a handful of cars there. Tess recognized Eric's old Ford Escape. After letting Shelby out to do her business, she locked her back in the truck, the windows rolled down, and a bone on the back seat.

Tess pushed through the diner door and immediately saw Eric. He stood up with a big grin. Standing at six feet tall with dark skin, a bald head, and the beginnings of a paunch, he was noticeable. Add in his personality—which seemed to bound out a few feet in front of him—and he was impossible to miss.

Eric wrapped her in a hug. "You're looking good, girl."

"You too," she said into his shoulder.

He pulled back, looking her over. "Seems to me that man of yours is treating you right." He frowned. "He is, isn't he? Because I'd be happy to have a little talk with him..."

Tess laughed. "Yes. He's great. And yes, he's treating me right."

"Good. Now, when are you two coming over for dinner?"

"I'll see what we can arrange."

"I'm holding you to that. Now come on back. Bernie Hudson's already here."

Tess followed Eric through the aluminum-topped tables. He stopped in front of a booth on the back wall. A mustached man in his early fifties, with dark brown hair beginning to gray, looked up at Tess with blue eyes rimmed in red, heavy bags underneath them. Bernie Hudson was a man sorely in need of a good night's sleep.

"Bernie, this here is Dr. Tess Brannick."

Bernie inclined his head. "Doc."

Tess slid into the booth. "Call me Tess."

"All right." Bernie stared down at his mug.

Tess could read the fear coming off him, and the embarrassment. Bernie was not a man used to being scared. Tess decided to ease into the conversation. "So, Bernie, what do you do for a living?"

Bernie looked up. "I own a roofing company. But my wife and I are avid campers. We spend every spare moment in the woods." He paused, his voice a little softer. "At least, we used to."

Tess waited, giving Bernie a chance to compose himself. "Bernie, has Eric told you what I research?"

"He said you research bigfoot."

"Yes," Tess said. "And I'm not the only one. It's a serious discipline. Since 1912, there have been over three thousand bigfoot sightings in the US alone—and of course, that's only the ones reported. A lot of the reports are never written down, or people don't even think to report it."

"Maybe because they're worried they'll sound crazy," Bernie said.

From his tone, Tess knew that was Bernie's worry as well. "Perhaps that *is* a concern. But bigfoot, or something similar to bigfoot, has been seen all over the globe. So whatever you and your wife saw and experienced, you weren't the only ones. And you won't be the last. But if you could take me through it, maybe we can help you understand a little better what happened."

Bernie continued to stare at his mug. Tess waited, knowing this wasn't an easy story for him to tell.

Finally Bernie looked up. "Like I said, my wife and I like to camp. Every year we get in the RV and take off for a month, hitting different campsites. Usually we'll park the bus and then hike in somewhere and set up for a few days before moving on to the next place. We've been doing it for fifteen years, and we've never had a problem before."

Bernie's hands began to shake. "They killed my dog."

Tess looked at Eric.

Eric spoke quietly. "We found the remains of the dog up the trail from the Hudsons' camp."

"I'm sorry," Tess said. She chose her next words carefully. "Was it like other cases we've seen?"

Eric nodded. "Yes."

Tess closed her eyes. Violence with bigfoot was really rare. They never went after humans. But for some reason they really did not like dogs.

"Why don't you start with when you first realized there was something out there?" Tess said quietly.

Bernie took a breath. "We hiked for about three hours—me, my wife Leanne, and our two dogs, Daffy and Tweety."

Tess smiled at the names.

Bernie noticed. "Don't let the names fool you. They're Shepherd mixes, over a hundred pounds easy, and tough." He again looked down at his mug. "Anyways, we set up camp, and the first night was fine, nothing out of the ordinary. But the second night, the dogs started acting weird. They got real nervous, and Daffy started growling low in his throat. I pulled them into the tent with us and grabbed my shotgun. They wouldn't settle down, though—

kept growling for about two hours. Then we heard rocks hitting the campsite. A few hit the tent. And I could hear cracking—like wood being split apart."

"How long did that go on?" Tess asked.

The tremble in Bernie's hands increased. "Until right before dawn. And then it all seemed to quiet down. I've never been so scared in my life."

He paused, his voice shaky. "After it quieted down, I decided to go out and see. Leanne told me not to go. She said we should just pack up and go. I wish I'd listened. I brought Daffy with me and a shotgun. Leanne had her rifle and Tweety. When I opened the tent I saw these rocks littering the campsite. Big rocks. I have no idea how someone could throw those. Some were easily forty pounds."

He took a trembling breath. "I didn't have to walk long to see what had made the cracking sound. Tree limbs had been yanked off trees and thrown into the woods. And they were easily six or eight inches thick. No human can do that without some sort of tool. And that's not what happened. Something ripped these things off."

"I had just decided I'd seen enough, and then the hair on the back of Daffy's neck stood straight up and she took off like a shot. I yelled for her to come back, but she didn't. Next thing I heard was her yelp... and then silence. I yelled for her again, but she didn't come back."

Tears crested in his eyes. He swiped them away. "Then I had this feeling like I was being watched. And then there was this sound—I don't even know how to describe it, and I know what animals sound like. But this was nothing I had heard before. It was a growl, a whistle, and a yell all rolled into one. I couldn't move. And I don't mean I was scared stiff—although I'm not ashamed to say I was terrified. I mean, I couldn't move. I have never in my life experienced anything like that."

He took a shuddering breath. "And then, just like that, it was gone. The feeling was gone, and I knew whatever had been there had left. I went and looked for Daffy. I found her only another twenty or thirty yards up the trail. She'd... been ripped apart." There was a hitch in his voice. "She didn't deserve that."

Eric cleared his throat. "I went to the site. I saw where the Hudsons camped and where Daffy's body was. I found two sets of footprints. One set was about ten inches long and about six inches wide. The other was seventeen inches long and about eight inches wide."

"Toes squared off? No arch? Even depth in the ground?" Tess asked.

"Yup. About two to three inches deep. Got the casts in my car," Eric said.

Tess turned back to Bernie. "Either at night or when you were on the trail, did you smell anything?"

He nodded. "Night before, there was this God-awful stink, like a mix of rotting meat, decay, and old diapers."

"What about on the trail?"

His tone was defiant. "No. But something was there."

Tess met his gaze. "I believe you."

Some of the defensiveness slipped out of Bernie's voice. "I don't know if you can give me any answers, but I just want someone to know what happened. The cops looked at me like I was crazy."

Tess knew that was probably true. Law enforcement didn't always take such reports seriously. And even if they did, what were they going to do? Put out an APB on bigfoot? The people who experienced a bigfoot encounter were often left feeling like they were on their own.

"I know," Tess said. "But I think I *can* explain why you weren't able to move."

Bernie looked at her, and Tess couldn't miss the hope on his face. At this point, she knew he'd grasp at anything that meant he wasn't crazy—anything that could inject some sort of logic into this horrible situation.

"In the animal kingdom," Tess said, "some animals have an ability to emit what are known as infrasonic vocalizations—sounds that register below a human's hearing range. Lions, elephants, even giraffes have this ability. For some, such as lions—and, I suspect, bigfoot—the infrasound is contained within their roar. But this infrasound allows a predator to stun their prey. Tell me, did you feel nauseated afterwards, disoriented?"

Bernie looked surprised. "Both."

"That's not unusual. It's the result of increased pressure on the middle ear. Your paralysis was actually a biological response to a vocal weapon. One you couldn't even hear."

Bernie stared her for a moment before speaking. "Is it crazy that that makes me feel better?"

"No. I think it's pretty normal," Tess said.

Bernie let out a breath. "I can tell you though, it will be a long time before Leanne and I go back in the woods. In fact, right now I can't imagine ever doing it again. And I grew up out there."

Eric leaned forward. "I know you feel that way now. But this is only one experience in thousands of experiences you've had. Don't let it ruin the outdoors for you."

"I know you're right. But right now..." Bernie stood up. "I think we'll be staying around people. Now if you'll excuse me, I'm going to get Leanne and get home."

Tess handed him one of her business cards. "If I can help, or if you think of anything else, please let me know."

He took the card. "Thanks, but I think I'm going to try to forget this whole thing happened."

"I understand," Tess said, looking at the exhausted and terrified man in front of her. *And I hope you can.* But she knew from personal experience that it would be a long while before Bernie Hudson felt safe again.

Watching Bernie make his way to the door, his shoulders slumped, she thought about her father's death and the tree structure pointing to her camp. Bigfoot was a powerful animal, and he was interested in Tess.

But bigfoot wasn't violent to humans. So she had nothing to fear.

A chill crawled over her. *Right?*

CHAPTER EIGHTEEN

Tess stayed and had breakfast with Eric after Bernie left. Before she hit the road, she promised she'd come for a longer visit soon and would bring Dev. She headed back to her place and made it to her camp by noon.

Her camp wasn't much. It was only about twenty yards by ten yards. She had a lean-to, a table and chair, and a giant log that she, Pax, and Shawn had pulled into use as seating by the fire pit back when she'd first begun her research. She settled into her chair, intending to work on her paper, but Bernie's story was still on her mind.

It was not an uncommon tale. People had often reported that bigfoot had chased them away from a site or thrown rocks at them. But no one had ever actually been harmed by a bigfoot.

Sightings often reported how incredibly fast they were, how long their stride was. If they *wanted* to catch someone, they could easily. And due to their musculature, no one would have a chance to fight them off. And yet, that didn't happen. Bigfoot just weren't violent creatures.

At least, not toward humans. Toward dogs... that was a

different story. There had been dozens of reports of dogs being killed by them. Even Madge had lost two dogs to the creatures.

Tess leaned her hands on the tabletop, picturing Shelby. Those incidents were the reason Tess never brought Shelby out here. The dogs that were killed were typically the more aggressive dogs—the ones who gave chase. The more timid dogs would just curl up, whimpering and terrified. Shelby definitely fell into the latter category, but still, Tess didn't want to put her through that.

Tess thought about an article she'd read about dogs' senses. It suggested that dogs might actually be able to see deeper than humans into both the ultraviolet and infrared ends of the light spectrum. This light is invisible to humans, but not so to many animals. If dogs had this ability, it would allow them to see urine trails, or to spot a hiding animal who might otherwise blend in with their background.

In addition, a dog's sense of smell is highly developed. Their nose is one thousand times more sensitive than the human nose. They have two hundred million more olfactory receptors than humans. So when a dog's eyesight and olfactory abilities were combined, it was actually no wonder that bigfoot, who seemed to be trying to hide from humans, did not like them.

Tess sat back, thinking about what Bernie Hudson had said about the strong smell. Bigfoot had been reported to have a stench, but there were many sightings where no stench was reported. Tess knew that in the ape kingdom, odor was used as a weapon. Was that what Bigfoot was doing? Trying to scare someone off, or to let them know they were near?

But dogs, with their incredibly sensitive noses, would know that bigfoot was around regardless of whether or not they emitted a stench. Which led to another possibility. Many believed Bigfoot was a master at camouflage—that he could blend into his background seamlessly. If so, people might walk right by without even knowing he was there. And as crazy as the idea was—an eight-foot hominid going completely unobserved—there was actually psychological evidence to back it up.

In 2010, researchers Christopher Chabris and Daniel Simons conducted a study at Harvard that later came to be known as the "Invisible Gorilla Test." Participants in the study were required to watch a basketball game with three-member teams wearing black or white shirts. Subjects were asked to count the number of times an individual in a white shirt passed the ball. About two thirds of the way through the video, an individual in an ape costume walked across the screen.

Yet half the subjects didn't even notice—they were too fixated on counting passes. Chabris and Simons concluded that people miss a great deal of what's happening around them, particularly if they are focused on a different task. More importantly, we are oblivious even to the fact that we are missing it.

Is that what was happening here? Tess thought. *Were people literally missing the bigfoot in front of them?*

But Tess knew that while it was possible for humans to walk right by something as large as a bigfoot and not notice it, a dog would not be so easily fooled. So did bigfoot target dogs because dogs could find them? Or were bigfoot just generally more violent than people thought?

Tess sighed and stood up. Well, she clearly wasn't going to get any work with her mind wandering like this. Perhaps she should go check out the new cameras. She'd placed them in the field two weeks ago, farther away from camp than the others, and she'd been itching to check them out.

She shouldered her pack and headed for the first location. It was a twenty-minute hike, far off the track but near a game trail, just beyond a pair of Douglas firs. She'd placed the camera in a tree, about fifteen feet up. It had taken a little climbing, but she liked the spot because the tree branches weren't very sturdy—

they'd barely held her weight—so they wouldn't support a larger predator. The only predator who could reach it would have to be either really light or tall enough to reach it without the aid of the branches.

When Tess arrived at the spot, her eyes scanned the tree where she'd placed the camera.

It was empty.

Her gaze flew to the ground. The camera lay in pieces.

CHAPTER NINETEEN

T ess knelt down and examined the bits of metal and plastic scattered on the ground. *Right. Bigfoot's not violent— except when it comes to dogs and cameras.*

She'd checked half of all the new cameras, over twenty of them, and this was the fifth camera that had been smashed. She shook her head. Madge was right—they really didn't like the things.

Blowing out a breath, she began to gather up the pieces. She had money in the grant to replace the cameras, but she was pretty sure any new ones she put up would just end up in the same condition as these. *What a waste of money.*

Tess also knew it was highly unlikely that whoever had smashed her cameras had been caught on film. Somehow, they always knew where the cameras were and managed to avoid them. *How is that possible?*

She stared at the pieces of plastic. Some people suggested that cameras emitted a low-energy signal. Could bigfoot sense them? Did they, too, see UV light? Or were they just so attuned to their surroundings that anything new was blatantly obvious?

Kind of like walking into your living room and noticing a new vase on the coffee table?

Tess looked around. "You know, you didn't have to destroy them," she said aloud.

Silence greeted her. Tess picked up more pieces. *Of course they had to destroy them*, she thought. *Otherwise I'd get a picture and the world would know they exist, and that can't happen.*

The thought brought Tess up short. Was that even possible? Were the bigfoot deliberately protecting their secrecy? That would require a pretty complicated thought process. *No, they just don't like new things in their environment.*

Tess dumped the plastic pieces into a bag and stuffed it in her pack. Her phone rang as she zipped up the pack. Tess frowned. Only a handful of people had the number to her sat phone, and they were instructed to only call if it was an emergency.

She pulled out the phone. *This can't be good.* "Hello?"

"Tess, it's Madge." Madge's voice was rushed.

Tess had never heard Madge sound anything but calm. "What's wrong?"

"It's little Mike. He's missing."

Tess pictured Madge's grandson Mike. He was five years old and mildly autistic. He was also fascinated with animals and loved to explore the woods—even if it was on his own.

"What happened?"

"He went down for a nap. We were all sitting on the porch. He must have woken up and gone out the back door. We don't even know when he left. I called the sheriff and my boys, but I knew you'd probably already be out there."

Tess shouldered her pack, the smashed cameras forgotten. She started toward Madge's place at a fast clip. "I'm about two miles away, coming in from the north. I'm guessing Mike Senior took off after him?"

"Yeah, he just left."

"Okay, good. Well, if he headed out the back, we'll catch him between us. What was Mikey wearing?"

"A red thermal shirt with jeans and brown boots." Madge paused. "I don't know what I'd do if something happened to him."

"Don't go there, Madge. We'll find him. I'll call you in an hour and a half and touch base, okay? And tell the sheriff where I'm at."

"Will do. And be careful."

"I will."

Tess disconnected the call. Placing the phone back in her pack, she started to jog, but carefully. The last thing she needed was a sprained ankle.

Mikey was a cute kid, with almost black hair and deep brown eyes. But what people always noticed about him was his smile. It lit up his whole face.

Tess frowned as she remembered the last time she'd seen Mikey. They'd been at Madge's, and he'd seen a snake. He tried to pick it up, but Madge snatched him away in time. It had been a Pacific rattler. Pure black with hexagonal markings, and incredibly poisonous. Mikey didn't seem to understand that animals could at times be dangerous.

In fact, Mikey was the personification of innocence. He lived in a fairy tale world where everyone was good, including all animals, and there were no villains. It was actually a wonderful thing. You felt better about life just being around him. But as a result, everyone in his life had to look out for him—to protect him from his overly trusting nature.

Tess picked up her pace. And out here, there were a lot of things that could harm a trusting little boy.

CHAPTER TWENTY

The land between Tess's camp and Madge's place was pretty rough, but Tess was used to hiking such unforgiving terrain. The problem, however, was that no matter how used to it she was, it was a slow process. She wasn't hiking down some well laid-out trail. She was cutting across creeks, going around downed trees, and climbing over rocks. It was taking time. Time she wasn't sure Mikey would have.

Tess paused on top of a rocky outcropping. It gave her a bit of a view of the land ahead of her. She took a swig of water, knowing she had to keep hydrated. Scanning the area, she looked for any sign that Mikey had gone this way. But she wasn't sure what she expected to see. He was small for his age, standing at only about three and a half feet, meaning he wouldn't leave much of trail, certainly not one that could be seen from far away.

Come on, Mikey, where are you? Tess looked up and saw a flash of dark fur on the ridge across from her. She went still, staring intently at the spot. But nothing moved. It had been so fast she couldn't even say for sure what kind of animal it had been.

She placed her canteen back at her hip and slowly swung her rifle back toward her. While she loved being out in the woods, she wasn't Mikey. She knew there were things out here that could kill you.

Everything was silent, and Tess's breathing seemed awfully loud. Seconds passed, but there was no further movement. *Did I imagine that?*

A bead of sweat rolled down her back. Wary, she knew she had to get moving, but as she started to walk, she was overly sensitive to movements around her.

A loud crack sounded through the woods. Tess's heart began to pound. It sounded as if a limb had been ripped from a tree.

And she could swear she felt eyes on her. She paused. Logic told her to keep going, but if there was something stalking her, it could have friends stalking Mikey—or worse, she could lead them right to him. Raising her rifle, she turned and walked in the direction of the sound.

Fifty feet away, she found the branch lying on the ground. She looked up. It had been ripped from the trunk thirteen feet up.

Tess's mouth fell open. That wasn't possible.

Oh, that's possible, a voice in her mind taunted her.

Movement to her right caused her to whirl around. Another shape disappeared behind a tree, and this time she could tell it was tall—very tall. She went still, listening, but once again the woods were silent.

On trembling legs, Tess walked forward. She reached the tree where she'd seen the shape. There was too much ground cover for any tracks. She looked up at a knot in the trunk that was at about the spot where the creature's head had been.

It was easily eight feet, maybe even nine feet from the ground.

Oh my God. Her first sighting, and she didn't have time to focus on it. She went still, listening intently, but all again was silent. She frowned.

Then she heard something. She could barely make it out. It sounded like... Her eyes went wide. Like huffs.

Stealth forgotten, Tess stormed through the trees toward the sound. *Please don't be Mikey.* She stumbled to a stop at a steep dropoff and looked down. A gully lay before her, a small stream running through it. She could barely see into it with the tree coverage. But the flash of red told her she'd found him.

Thirty yards away from him, a black bear let out a roar.

Tess pulled the rifle to her shoulder, but she didn't have a shot with all the trees. But it was a black bear, the smallest of the North American bears, easily frightened. She fired a shot into the air.

The animal leapt back, but it didn't leave. *Why didn't he—*

That's when she saw the cubs. They were tucked into the bank, caught halfway between Mikey and the momma. There was no way that mother was going to leave without her kids.

And the bear was big. It easily had to be four hundred pounds, and standing, it was probably close to seven feet. There was a good reason why bears had often been mistaken for bigfoot in eyewitness reports.

Tess looked around uneasily for the bear's mate. *Maybe that's what I saw.* Seeing nothing, she looped the rifle over her shoulder and scrambled down the steep bank into the gully. There wasn't time for a rope, but the drop was only about twenty feet, and handholds were plentiful, and she made it down with ease.

Tess walked carefully toward Mikey, keeping an eye on the bear. "Mikey," she whispered.

He turned around and smiled at her, his eyes bright. "Tess. Do you see the babies?"

Tess's heart was in her throat as she made her way slowly toward him, keeping her eyes on the mother. "Yes. I see the babies. But it's their naptime. So we have to let them sleep. Why don't you come with me?"

"But I just want to say hi." He took a step toward them.

The mother roared, and Tess knew she was about to charge. *Oh God.*

Tess dropped to one knee, lining the bear up. In seconds, she took in the bear's anatomy, following the long front leg one third of the way into the chest. The lungs would be the best takedown. Anything less and she risked just angering it.

The bear charged right toward her and Mikey.

Tess fired.

Her shot went wide, catching the bear in the leg. It let out a roar. *Damn it.*

Tess let off shot after shot, all aimed at the chest. But the bear kept coming. She got to her feet, shooting the whole time, grabbed Mikey, and yanked him behind her. She knew telling him to run was useless. She unloaded the rest of her bullets into the bear. It kept coming, and then at last it stumbled, slid along the ground, and came to a rest just a few feet away from Tess's feet.

Tess let out a trembling breath. Blood seeped into the ground around the bear. She swallowed hard, reaching behind her for Mikey. "Mikey? You okay?"

He darted around her and then went still as he stared at the bear. He turned back to Tess, his eyes swimming with unshed tears. "Why? She wouldn't have hurt us. Why'd you kill her?"

Tess pulled him to her, but he fought to get out of her arms. "Mikey, she would have killed you. I had to."

He beat his fists against her chest. "No, she wouldn't have. She was my friend."

Tess pulled him closer as his yells turned to sobs. Tess felt tears crest in her own eyes. She had hated doing it. But it was either the bear or Mikey.

Holding Mikey, she kept her eyes on the bear. "I'm sorry. I'm so sorry," she said, knowing she was apologizing to both of them.

CHAPTER TWENTY-ONE

Tess called Madge to let her know that Mikey had been found. Then she carried him away from the mother bear, pulled Mikey into her lap, and waited for the search party to reach them. The two cubs walked over to the mother as they left, nudging her with their snouts. Tess's heart ached at the sight. And every time she looked over and saw them trying to get their mother to respond, her guilt increased.

Fifteen minutes later, she could hear the yells as the search party made their way to them.

"We're here!" she yelled. Footsteps pounded toward them. Mike burst through the trees. He stopped short, looking between Mikey and Tess. "He's okay?"

"He's okay. Just a little shook up and sad," Tess said.

Mike knelt down next to them, putting his hand on Mikey's back. "Sad?"

Tess gestured down the gully to where the bear lay.

Mike went pale. "Oh my God." He yanked Mikey to him, but his eyes—suddenly terrified—stayed on Tess. "Thank you."

Tess laid a hand on Mikey's back. "He doesn't understand

why the bear was shot. You'll need to explain it to him—if you can."

Mike stood unsteadily. "I'm going to take him to Mom's."

"I'll finish up here, then I'll head there and we can talk."

"Thank you, Tess. I don't know what I would have done..." Mike blinked the tears out of his eyes.

Tess placed a hand on his arm. "He's okay. Just focus on that."

Mike gave her an abrupt nod and headed back the way he'd arrived.

Dev walked up. "Good thing you were out here."

"More than you know." She nudged her chin toward the bear.

Dev's mouth fell open. "Are you all right?"

Despite still feeling shaky, Tess nodded. "There are two cubs. Mikey wanted to see them. Can you call PAWS? See if they can come out and take care of the little ones?" The Performing Animal Welfare Society's mission was to aid and rescue abused, abandoned, or retired large animals.

"Yeah, I'll make the call in a minute." He pulled Tess into his arms. A shudder ran through her, and for just a moment, she let herself bury her head in his chest and borrow his strength.

"Are you sure you're okay?" Dev asked quietly.

Tess just nodded again, and Dev's arms tightened around her. They stayed like that for a few seconds before Tess pulled away. She looked away from the carnage and stared at the ridge above. "I'm okay."

"You did the right thing, Tess."

She watched the little cubs. "Then why doesn't it feel like it?"

Movement at the top of the ridge drew Tess's attention. Another dark shadow disappeared behind a tree. She went still.

Dev pulled out his radio. "I'll call this in."

Tess barely heard him, her eyes focused on where the shape had disappeared. "I'm going to go up top."

"Go ahead. I'll find you."

She quickly made her way out of the gully and up to the ridge. She walked along the top, her eyes scanning the ground in front of her. She was worried that what she'd seen was another bear.

Ten feet from where she'd seen the shadow, she spotted a heel print. It was easily eight inches wide. *Could be a bear.*

Carefully, she made her way forward. At the base of a Douglas fir, she saw another partial print. She turned and saw another a few feet away, this one a full print. Another five feet beyond that was its companion. Whatever had made these marks had an almost sixty-inch stride. And as she eyeballed the prints, she knew they were at least sixteen inches long.

Tess's excitement began to grow. A bear didn't make these.

She got out her gear and began taking pictures. Then she mixed the cement and poured it in the prints to make the casts. As she sat there, waiting for it to dry, she knew she'd see a healed scar on the bottom of the foot.

But why is he out here? And why let himself be seen?

Tess listened, but only the normal sounds of the forest reached her ears. A chill crawled along her skin.

And why does he seem to be so interested in me?

CHAPTER TWENTY-TWO

Carter placed the latest report from Tess on his desk. He turned his chair and stared out the window. *She's getting closer.*

Excitement began to hum through him—not an emotion he was used to. There was no challenge in business anymore. When he'd first begun, there was the thrill of the hunt and the success. But now he took little pleasure in the increasing numbers in his bank account.

He wanted something new. He wanted to forge into uncharted waters and be the first to uncover something.

But there were so few chances to be an explorer these days. Magellan, Marco Polo, Columbus, Lewis and Clark—their days were long gone. Now it was space that held the opportunity for explorers, and Carter had never had any interest in space, or in plumbing the depths of the ocean for that matter. But he'd always dreamed of being on the frontier in discovering unknown aspects of this planet: Shangri-La, lost dinosaurs, bigfoot. And now that last possibility was tantalizingly within his reach.

Bigfoot—a ten-foot primate, North America's great ape. He would be P.T. Barnum and Thomas Edison rolled into one—the great discoverer *and* the man who promoted that discovery to the world. And his name would go down in history, just as theirs had.

He knew discovering the beast was a long shot. But in the business world he'd often turned long shots into guarantees.

He turned back to the desk and tapped his call button for Thaddeus. Thaddeus opened the door a few seconds later, striding across the room.

"Sir?"

"What is the status of the equipment for Project Legacy?" Carter asked.

"It's going well, for the most part."

Carter frowned. "'For the most part'? What does that mean?"

"The engineers are having some difficulties making the cages as strong as you want them. They believe the strength you're requesting is overkill."

But they don't understand, do they? He'd contracted to have the cages built strong enough to withstand a raging elephant times two. Of course, he hadn't told them what quarry he intended to hold in those cells.

"Tell them I don't pay them to question why. Tell them to just build it."

"Yes, sir."

"In fact, move the deadline up." Carter smiled. "I think we may need them sooner than originally planned."

This week's question comes from Shirley Jones in Little Rock, Arkansas. Shirley writes:

Isn't bigfoot just a modern creation?

No, actually tales of bigfoot date back hundreds of years. In fact, a bigfoot-like creature first appeared in the Epic of Gilgamesh. The ancient Mesopotamian poem is dated at around 2100 BC. But as it recounts a Noah-like tale of a great flood, some scholars place it at closer to 10,000 years old.

According to the tale, Gilgamesh was a powerful but arrogant king who was lonely. Enkidu was a wild man who was created by the gods as a companion for him. In the tales, Enkidu was covered in hair and lived with and protected the animals of the forest.

Gilgamesh was viewed as an extremely powerful being—one third man and two thirds god. Enkidu, by contrast, was said to be one third man and two thirds beast. Yet in power, they were said to be evenly matched. And the two became inseparable friends until Enkidu's death.

There are other old tales about bigfoot, but that is the oldest one I have found.

CHAPTER TWENTY-THREE

Tess sat at her camp, struggling to figure out what was going on. It had been a week since she had found Mikey. The cubs had been brought to the rescue shelter and were reportedly doing well. Another female black bear had taken them under her wing.

And Tess had gone back to her regular activities. She did her usual chores, found a few more prints. But when she'd gone to leave more food, she'd found a pile of acorns waiting for her—as if someone was now leaving her food.

And then, last night, she had decided to sleep outside. And she could have sworn she felt someone or something tap her shoulder late at night. She'd jolted awake, but there was no one there. She'd stayed awake long after that—feeling like she waiting for something, although she didn't know what it was—before returning to an uneasy sleep.

Now she sat in her camp, leaning against a log with her sketchpad propped on her knees. She'd already drawn the cubs, Mikey, Madge, and Shelby, and she was working on a picture of her and Pax from when they were younger. But it was getting late, and she didn't plan on spending a second night out here.

"Anybody here?" she asked quietly. Of course, no one answered.

She shook her head and got to her feet with a sigh. *Okay, enough. Time to go.* She put her sketchbook into her bag.

A small rock landed two feet to her right. Tess went still.

She stared at the rock, her heart pounding. Rock throwing—a behavior associated with bigfoot. *Okay, this is what you've trained for. Focus.* But all her well-laid plans for how to deal with an encounter seemed to disappear from her brain.

She picked up the rock. A second rock flew out of the forest, landing three feet to her left this time. Tess didn't feel any threat from the rock thrower. The rocks were being lobbed gently, not aimed at her. She strained to see into the woods, but she couldn't make out anything of interest.

Well, okay. Tess took a breath and then threw the rock under-handed back into the woods. There was a silence, and then another rock landed almost at her feet. Tess smiled and let out a little laugh. Picking it up, she threw it. Thirty seconds later, a new rock landed again at her feet.

We're playing, she thought with disbelief.

They repeated the same pattern for a while: a rock would land at her feet and Tess would toss it back. But then, finally, after about five minutes, she tossed a rock and there was no response.

Tess felt disappointed. She thought about chucking another rock, but it felt as if the rules of the game had already been laid out and that would be a violation. So she waited. Leaves rustled, and Tess turned slightly to her right.

It stepped out and looked at her for only a moment before disappearing back into the woods.

Tess stumbled back, her legs feeling woozy. The creature was gone, but its appearance was permanently imprinted in her mind. It had a wide flat nose and deep-set eyes. Hair covered its upper body—due to an evergreen she could only see from its chest up. Dark hair rimmed its face, and it had what almost appeared to be a beard and mustache. But there was no hair surrounding the eyes, nose, or mouth. What skin she could see was wrinkled and dark.

And it was close to nine feet tall.

CHAPTER TWENTY-FOUR

Tess wasn't sure how long she sat there and stared at the space where the bigfoot had appeared. Ever since she was a kid, she had been focused on tracking down bigfoot and learning as much as she could about them. But to be honest, she'd never thought she'd really see one. She figured she'd use her science background to bring a higher level of analysis to the evidence they left behind: footprints, hair samples, and the like.

But now she had actually *seen* one. And her mind—her well-trained scientific mind—couldn't process it. She had known it would be tall, but she hadn't been prepared for how wide it was—at least four feet, with a large barrel chest and no noticeable neck. It was truly a monster, and yet—

It had played a game with her. It had shown itself to her. Was it the one that had been nearby when she'd found Mikey? Come to think of it, if it hadn't alerted her to its presence, she would have kept walking right past Mikey. Had it done that on purpose? Had he *led* her to Mikey?

Shadows began to fall across the camp, spurring Tess into motion. She shoved her provisions into her pack and grabbed her

flashlight, then made her way over to where she had seen the...
She hesitated. The what? Beast? That word didn't feel right.

She scanned the ground with her light, but there was no
indentation. The soil was dry, and there was a lot of ground
cover. She frowned. But it had to have been at least seven
hundred, maybe eight hundred pounds, walking on two legs. It
should have left an impression.

She looked around and listened carefully, but she saw no
movement, and only the normal sounds of the forest echoed back
to her. She considered following in the direction it had disappeared. But with darkness approaching, she knew that wasn't the
best idea. And despite its size, it moved soundlessly. And it left
little to no trail. She hated to leave, but she knew that was the
wisest course of action.

With one last look around, she stood, hiking her pack onto
her shoulders and securing it. She was done for today.

But I'll be back first thing in the morning.

CHAPTER TWENTY-FIVE

The next morning, Tess returned straight away to her camp. The first thing she noticed was the pile of rocks arranged in the middle of the space. She looked around, but she didn't see anyone. Removing her camera from her pack, she took pictures of the little pile. Then she sat back and grinned.

Tess went about her normal routine—dropping off the food stores and checking some of the cameras. She still had no pictures of the creature, and she was beginning to think that was because the surviving cameras were in the places the bigfoot weren't. Any cameras placed where she might get a shot were destroyed.

Back at her camp, she sat at her laptop, answered some emails, and wrote up some ideas for a new blog post and for a paper. She was about an hour into her paper when she got that strange feeling of being watched. The hair on the back of her neck stood straight up. Slowly, she closed the laptop, stood up, and scanned the area. She saw nothing until the rock came sailing from the woods. It hit the ground and rolled to a stop at her feet.

Tess picked up the rock and, with a practiced throw, lobbed it back into the woods. A few seconds later, another rock came sailing at her. Tess smiled.

She picked up the rock and tossed it back. A series of tosses and returns came after that, until, just like the day before, Tess threw the rock back and there was no response. Disappointment washed over her. He was leaving. She looked around, waiting, but he didn't show himself this time. No rustling of leaves, no flying rocks. No appearance of a legendary creature.

Finally, Tess took her seat again at the table with a sigh. She had no right to be disappointed. Her exchange over the last two days was more than most researchers experienced in a lifetime.

She pulled over her laptop and tried to focus on it. She scrolled back a few pages to what she had written before the rock toss. The paper detailed the theorized anatomical differences between the ape, human, and bigfoot that allowed for bipedalism —or in the ape's case, limited bipedalism.

Her eyes kept traveling back to the woods. After the fifth stolen glance, she gave herself a firm shake. *You are a scientist. Focus.*

But she couldn't help but steal one last look.

Her heart slammed to stop. And then it began to race.

He was back. And this time he was standing only fifteen feet away.

CHAPTER TWENTY-SIX

Tess's mind went blank, and at the same time, she was soaking in every single detail. He was close to nine feet tall, with a barrel chest, just as she remembered. He didn't have any breasts, which convinced her that he was male, although the definitive evidence of that was not clearly in view.

What she hadn't seen last night was that his legs were shorter than his arms, which hung halfway down his thighs. His feet were long and squat, with incredibly long toes, just like the prints she'd found.

Dark hair mixed with gray covered him except for the palms of his very large hands and around his eyes, nose, and mouth. The gray hair brought her up short. Was it a sign of age? She thought of the Yeti. Were they related? Was the Yeti always white, or was it, too, an older animal?

His eyes were a deep brown, and intelligence lurked behind them. They seemed to be inspecting her just as closely as she inspected him.

Last night, Tess had imagined what she would do if she actually had a chance to meet one, to speak with one. Slowly, she stood. "Hi."

It tilted its head, watching her. With careful moves, Tess reached into the basket she'd left on the table and pulled out two apples. She showed them to him and then, walking slowly forward, she placed them both on the end of the log that served as seating for her fire.

She backed away and gestured toward the apples. "For you."

His eyes shifted between Tess and the apples. Finally he took the apples, and then in two strides disappeared back into the woods.

Tess's legs gave out and she crumpled to the ground. She brought her hand to her mouth. *Oh my God.* Then she grinned and wrapped her hands around herself. *Oh my God.*

CHAPTER TWENTY-SEVEN

Tess sat on the ground for a good long time. Her mind couldn't stop analyzing everything she'd seen in her short encounter—or didn't see.

The bigfoot hadn't been aggressive; he had let himself be seen. He *wanted* her to know he was there. And yet, there'd been no odor. Did that mean they could control it? Turn it on and off like a switch?

Mountain gorillas were said to emit a fear odor. Was that what the bigfoot emitted? Did that mean it was more like an ape?

His face had been another surprise. She had expected it to look more gorilla-like. And while it was true that he had no noticeable neck, his face was decidedly human. The mouth was not pushed forward like an ape's. The nose was human, except flatter. And while the eyes were deep-set, they also resembled human eyes.

His torso was massive—at least four feet wide and round. He had no waist. In humans, increased exercise and fitness results in a V-shaped torso. But whereas the bigfoot had very defined musculature, his shoulders were only slightly broader than his hips.

Several theories had been advanced to explain bigfoot's large size. Among them was gigantothermy—the tendency of species to be larger in colder climates in the Northern hemisphere. This larger size allowed for increased body heat. A larger torso also allowed for a greater range of food options. The longer digestive tract would allow bigfoot to eat a coarser diet, which could explain how they could survive in an environment like the Pacific Northwest.

Tess's mind continued to draw connections between what she had just seen and what science knew. His hair had appeared thick—which meant that it would provide warmth as well as acting as a barrier to insects. Some research had suggested that bigfoot may have three levels of hair: long coarse guard hairs, an undercoat for insulation, and whiskers. And some hair samples *had* been found by other researchers. The problem had always been that there was no bigfoot standard to compare them to, so the best they could hope for was to find that it didn't match any hairs in the database. Alleged bigfoot hairs had been found to not match gorilla, human, or chimp hair, although it had been shown to have similarities to all three: no medullary structure, but with a humanlike scale pattern.

But then there were the hair samples that just seemed to further confuse the problem. In 2013, British researchers gathered samples of alleged Yeti hair for genetic testing. When they found that the samples from the Himalayas were a one hundred percent match with an ancient polar bear believed to have died out forty thousand years ago, they were shocked, but everyone thought that was the end of the story.

It wasn't. Additional testing of the sample didn't match the ancient polar bear after all. And honestly, that was a big problem in the research. Samples could be mishandled and then contaminated, making it difficult to determine which ones were legit and which weren't. But Tess was hoping that with DNA from unknown hominids being added to the databases, any sample she got might have a chance of matching.

Tess pictured the bigfoot once more. *And that was definitely no polar bear.*

Her mind continued to whirl, ticking off facts and drawing conclusions. She glanced over at her pack and realized she hadn't even thought about taking a photo. Of course, he probably wouldn't have waited around for one anyway. She pictured his long stride. No, she had played the first encounter correctly—she hoped. And maybe now he'd even stop by again.

Tess stood and wiped off her jeans with a grin. *I just met bigfoot.*

CHAPTER TWENTY-EIGHT

After Tess returned to her cabin that night, she wrote up her thoughts about her encounter. She paused at her laptop, contemplating whether or not to contact Hayes. No, not yet. She needed a little more time to think through what had happened. Hopefully she'd have more to tell for her next report.

She grabbed her keys and wallet and headed for the door. "Want to go for a ride, Shelby?" From the dog bed in the corner of the office, Shelby hopped up and padded after her.

When she reached her truck, Tess called Madge to see if she needed anything from town. Madge gave her a list, and an hour and a half later, Tess pulled into Madge's drive with a couple of bags of groceries. Madge stood from the rocking chair on the porch, a book in her hands.

Tess smiled as she got out of the truck. "Hey, Madge."

"Hey, hon. Thanks for picking those up."

Tess pulled the grocery bags from the back seat and made her way up the porch steps. "No problem. I wanted to talk to you about something anyway."

Madge held open the door as Shelby scrambled inside, followed by Tess. "Something happen?"

Tess couldn't hold back her grin. "You could say that."

"Well, dinner's about ready. Why don't you two stay and you can fill me in?"

Tess put the bags on Madge's counter and started unpacking. "That'd be great."

A short time later, Madge and Tess were settled at Madge's kitchen table with plates of meatloaf, and Tess recounted her experience in detail.

"Well don't that beat all," Madge said.

"But you've met one as well."

Madge shook her head. "Not like that. Oh, I've seen them from a distance, but any time they caught sight of me they walked away. Your friend... well, it seems like he wanted to make sure you saw him. He wanted to meet you."

Tess recalled the game of catch. "That's what I think, too. But I don't get why. I mean, these guys have been reclusive for their whole existence. Why step out now?"

Madge shrugged. "Maybe he's as curious about you as you are about him."

"Maybe."

"Or..." Madge drew out the word.

"Or what?"

"Or he wants something from you."

"Wants something? Like what?"

"I don't know. But you should be careful. These beings are intelligent, and though they may look human, they're not. I've seen what they can do to bears. You would be even easier to hurt."

A chill came over Tess as she pictured her visitor's massive arms. "I know."

Madge took Tess's hand. "I know you want to learn about them. But promise me you'll be careful."

Tess placed her hand over Madge's. "I will."

But she pictured the being in her mind. Then she pictured what it had taken for her to stop the charging bear just last week. The bigfoot was much larger than the bear, and smarter, too. If it decided to do her harm... She would never be able to defend herself.

CHAPTER TWENTY-NINE

Tess had trouble sleeping that night. Madge's concerns echoed through her mind, and she debated what to do. She thought about not going back. But how could she do that? This was what she had wanted for almost twenty years, and the truth was, she still had no hard proof. It was late by the time she fell into a fitful sleep.

She got up before the sun this morning, her concerns still there, but also a sense of hope. For some reason, the bigfoot had chosen *her* to communicate with. She owed it to him, and to herself, to find out why.

When she arrived back at her camp, nothing appeared disturbed. She checked her cameras and then her food stock, which had been depleted. She replenished it. Then she went back to her tent and sat at the table and chair, checking on her email and reviewing a paper. The morning droned on. And the sleepless night was catching up with her.

Tess closed the laptop and pushed it aside. Laying her head on her hands, she closed her eyes. *Five minutes. I'll take a quick five-minute nap and then go for a walk.*

She dozed off. In her dream, she was still in the camp, but the bigfoot returned. He stood next to her, reached out, and touched her hair. Tess stayed still, letting him. And then he disappeared.

A bird let out a screech, and Tess jolted awake.

She wiped at her eyes and at the drool that had pooled on the side of her mouth. *Lovely.*

Everything was quiet. She pushed back her chair. Her gaze absentmindedly swept the ground.

She went still.

Next to her chair were two large footprints. Her heart began to pound and her head snapped up. There was no one nearby.

She felt shaky. He'd returned. Had he touched her hair, or had that just been a dream? Even if he hadn't, he had been close enough to do so.

She wasn't sure what to think about that. Part of her felt a little creeped out. Part of her was happy that he'd returned. And part of her was confused. Why was he taking such an interest in her?

A rock landed at her feet. She paused and then smiled. She picked it up and tossed it back.

A few seconds later, he appeared in the same spot as yesterday. And she realized that the rock-throwing was almost like him ringing the doorbell to let her know he was near.

She as stunned by the sight of him as she had been the day before. A nine-foot hominid was communicating—no, actually *interacting*—with her. She slowly reached into her bag. "Are you hungry?" She pulled out the fruit she had gotten for him.

He watched her, then took a step forward.

Swallowing, Tess placed the food on the log, just like she'd done yesterday. He waited until she backed away, then he picked it up. Seconds later, he disappeared into the trees.

Tess let out a breath, feeling lightheaded.

For the next two weeks, that became their routine. Tess

would provide food. He would take it after she had backed away, then would disappear into the woods. The next day they'd do it all over again.

Then one day, it changed. Tess placed the food on the end of the log and backed away. The bigfoot picked it up and hesitated.

And then he sat down.

Tess knew her mouth had fallen open. She slammed it shut and started to talk, not even sure what she was saying, but focused on keeping her voice even. "Well, this is a nice surprise. My name's Tess."

He watched her, but said nothing, as Tess knew he probably wouldn't; from all reports, bigfoot didn't have a language. Instead, he took a bite from an apple. Tess noticed he had more gray that she'd originally thought. In fact, he was liberally sprayed with it.

"I don't suppose you can tell me your name, can you? Well, how about I call you Charlie? I don't know about you, but it actually makes me feel a little better about you being here."

She realized when she thought about him, that he reminded her of an old picture her dad had in his study of a mountain man. Tall, burly, with a big beard, covered in animal furs, she and Pax had christened him Charlie when they were kids.

Tess inched forward. He watched her from the corner of his eye as he finished up the apple. "I'm researching you guys," she said. "Trying to figure out what you are—or even just prove that you exist. Although I guess I've already done that part, at least to myself."

The idea of taking a picture crossed her mind, but she immediately discarded it. She'd thought about setting up cameras in advance, but she'd discarded that idea as well. She was making inroads here. She didn't want to do anything that might blow it.

"So, do you live around here?" she asked. "I live about a ninety-minute hike from here. Although for you, it would definitely take less time." She pictured the footprints she'd seen outside her cabin. "But I'm guessing you already know that."

She reached the edge of the log. He paused in his eating, then continued.

Tess slowly eased herself down onto the other side of the log. He went still for a second before continuing his eating. "Well, this is nice. You and me enjoying the afternoon sunshine."

Charlie polished off the rest of his food. Without a word or a glance, he stood and walked away.

Tess watched him go. And then grinned.

Wow.

This week's question comes from Shawn Tidley of Portland,
Oregon. Shawn writes:

What is the difference between bigfoot and sasquatch?

Short answer: Nothing. :)

*Long answer: There are actually more than sixty names for bigfoot
across North American tribes alone. The name "sasquatch" was
coined by Canadian journalist J. W. Burns in the 1920s. It comes
from the word Sésquac—a Halkomelem word used by the Coast
Salish Indians of Canada, meaning "wild man."*

The term "bigfoot" didn't enter the common vernacular until the

Gerry Crew incident in the 1950s. Gerry Crew was part of a construction group laying road through Humboldt County, California. He found these giant footprints around the equipment in the morning, and sometimes he found that huge pieces of machinery had been tossed. The Humboldt Times *of Eureka, California got hold of the story and photographed Crew with a cast of a sixteen-inch footprint and used the term bigfoot for the creature. And the bigfoot fascination of the modern era began!*

CHAPTER THIRTY

For the next few weeks, Tess met Charlie every day, except weekends. And each time, she learned a little more about his physiology. Unlike gorillas, he had no protruding belly—a characteristic of a herbivore—which meant he was most likely an omnivore, eating both meat and plants.

At first glance his feet appeared to be very large human feet, but a closer comparison made the differences clear. Proportionally, Charlie's feet were much wider than a human's. The average male human's foot is just under eleven inches—although some feet can be noticeably larger—but the foot tends to narrow at the arch. Bigfoot feet, by comparison, are extremely wide and have no arch. In addition, the toes are proportionally much longer than those on a human foot.

His hands were different, too. They were incredibly large, of course, but they also had webbing between the fingers. Tess was surprised to find that he had no opposable thumbs. For some reason she had expected to see them. Opposable thumbs were what allowed for fine motor movement, and most scientists agreed that it was one of the most critical factors in the development of tools.

Tess studied all these physical traits while she sat next to Charlie rambling on about nothing. Charlie didn't seem to mind. In fact, he seemed to enjoy her company. Each day he stayed a little longer.

So one day, Tess decided to try the camera. Charlie was wandering around the camp, inspecting Tess's stuff, and she was staying out of his way and letting him. *Ha, letting him. Like I could stop him.*

While he was looking at her tent, she pulled her camera out of her bag. She took a breath, then waited until he turned. She held the camera up for him to see. "Would it be okay—"

He lunged across the short distance and smacked the camera out of her hand. Then he stomped on it and let out a scream.

Tess stumbled back, tripping over her own feet in her haste. Charlie stood towering over her. Tess stared at the ground, her hands covering her head, waiting for the blow. She could hear his breath. His feet were only inches from her.

Oh, God.

Seconds passed that felt like hours.

Finally, he turned and walked away.

Tess lifted her head. He was gone. Her heart pounded and her breath came out in gasps. She shook like she was having a seizure. *Oh my God. Oh my God.*

CHAPTER THIRTY-ONE

That night Tess lay curled up on her couch, Shelby at her side. She had planned on meeting up with Sasha and Abby for a girls' night out, but after today she'd called and begged off, claiming a headache.

She wasn't sure what to do. After Charlie left, she had shook for what felt like hours. And on the walk home, she had jumped at every sound in the forest. Even now, the thought of him lunging at her sent her heart racing.

She ran her hand through Shelby's fur. "What am I going to do, girl?"

Shelby gave her a tired wag.

Dev wasn't coming over tonight, and for the first time, Tess was glad for that. She hadn't told anyone except Madge about her encounters. For some reason, she felt like telling would be a violation. Although right now, that seemed awfully stupid. Still, she didn't want to tell Dev tonight—not when she was still so upset.

Continuing to rub Shelby, Tess struggled with what her next step was going to be. Obviously, she had violated the rules of their interaction. She began to shake again when she recalled him towering over her—and that scream. She let out a stuttering breath.

Shelby raised her head, tilting it to the side. Tess reached down and hugged her. "I'm okay, girl."

But am I? She worried she'd blown all the progress they'd made. And at the same time, she wasn't sure she could bring herself to go back there again. The moment he had moved toward her, Tess had been sure her life was over. And that moment brought into crystal clarity how defenseless she was against him. If he wanted to hurt her, there was nothing she could do. She had been humanizing him, she realized that. She needed to remember that he was an animal, no matter how human he looked.

But she also knew she had no proof. She had nothing on film, no hairs, no DNA. Her interactions at this point were just a long drawn-out witness account. If she closed up shop now, she'd have nothing to show for her time. But if she didn't...

Tess sighed. If she didn't, she could find herself back in that situation again. Or worse. Was it really worth it?

She stared at the dying fire in the fireplace, but no answers magically appeared.

Ever since her father had died, she'd been obsessed with finding the thing in the woods that had helped her and her brother escape. Hadn't she done that? Wasn't her mission now over?

Her phone rang, and Tess picked it up without looking at the caller ID. "Hello?"

"Good evening, Dr. Brannick. I hope I'm not intruding."

Tess straightened her back. "Um, no, no, of course not, Mr. Hayes."

"Thaddeus tells me that your reports have been rather anemic as of late."

Tess scrambled for something to say. She hadn't mentioned anything in her reports about Charlie. In fact, her reports had barely changed. "Um, yes, but my food supplies are consistently disappearing—at least those not near the cameras."

Hayes interrupted. "Yes. Why do you think that is?"

"Well, there's some research that indicates that animals are able to pick up frequencies that we can't—perhaps cameras are emitting those frequencies. And all animals have a well-developed sense of self-preservation. I'm thinking perhaps it recognizes that something is out of place and it avoids those areas."

"Hmm. Is there a way to overcome that problem?"

"There are some newer field cameras on the market which may work. You can hide them in decoy animals, add some scents to further disguise them."

"Excellent. And I want to remind you, Dr. Brannick, what an incredible service you would be doing, not only for your career but for mankind, if you succeed in this endeavor. The things we could learn. Well, it's really impossible to imagine, isn't it? Their immune systems alone could alleviate untold human suffering. Your work may be considered on the fringe by some, but I assure you, I view it as critical for our future."

"Yes, Mr. Hayes. Thank you."

"Well, enjoy the rest of your evening, Dr. Brannick. I look forward to hearing of your progress in the weeks to come."

CHAPTER THIRTY-TWO

Scottsdale, Arizona

Carter hung up the phone and swiveled his chair to look at the view behind him. His office overlooked the lush industrial park that held offices for all the corporations he had acquired. To date there were twenty-two. Three more were scheduled for construction before the end of the year. Normally, the view gave him a sense of satisfaction. Today he was decidedly dissatisfied.

There had been nothing new in Tess's last two reports—which normally wasn't a problem. But there had been something in her voice...

He drummed his hands on the side of his chair. His gut told him that something had changed. Turning back to the desk, he hit the intercom button on his phone.

"Sir?" Thaddeus asked.

"Get me Abe."

"Right away, sir."

A few seconds later, Thaddeus's voice rang out again. "Abe is on line one, sir."

Carter hit the lit button on the phone and picked up the receiver. "Abe. How are you?"

Abe Cascione's thick Bronx accent filled the room, causing Carter to grimace. "I'm good. How are you?"

"Fine. But I think I may have a little problem that I'm going to need your help with. You received the file on Dr. Tess Brannick?"

"Yup. Was just looking it over."

"Well, I'm going to need you to do a deep background. Find out if there are any secrets hidden in her closets, any buttons that can be pushed."

"No problem. Anything in particular you're expecting to find?"

Carter paused. "I'm not sure. But she's received a hefty sum from us, and I have the feeling she's not being entirely forthcoming. I'd like some leverage if I need it."

"I have to say she looks pretty clean from what I've seen. But I'll check and see if there's anything. And even if there isn't, there *are* other ways to get the information from her."

Carter sighed. Abe always preferred the violent method of extraction. Carter wasn't morally opposed to it himself, but it could become a bit of a legal headache. And there had been a time or two when Abe had enjoyed his work a little too much.

"That's still on the table," Carter said, "but let's see what the background reveals first. We'll go from there."

"Will do." Abe disconnected the call.

Carter once again swiveled to look at the setting sun. But his thoughts were on Tess Brannick. She was a smart woman. But she had made an unwise decision.

You shouldn't keep things from me, Dr. Brannick. That is not a healthy endeavor.

CHAPTER THIRTY-THREE

By the next morning, Tess had decided she'd go back to her camp. Still, she strapped her Browning into a holster at her waist, and she brought her shotgun instead of her rifle. She wasn't sure any of that would make a difference, but she felt better having them.

Before Tess went to the camp itself, she went through the normal routine: dropping the food, checking the cameras, doing a walk around for any signs. But this morning, she was taking longer than normal. She knew she was stalling. *Suck it up, Brannick*, she told herself. *You chose to study a giant primate, not little fluffy bunnies. A little bit of fear comes with the territory.*

Squaring her shoulders, she headed for her camp. She paused on the edge of it. Nothing looked disturbed. The forest was giving off its normal sounds. Everything was as it always was. She wasn't sure if she was relieved or disappointed.

She thought about working on her paper; she'd brought a printout of it with her. When she had thought back over her interactions with Charlie, she'd realized he never showed up when she was using technology—and after the camera incident, she thought it better to be safe than sorry. So all technology was off limits—except her sat phone. That she kept with her.

But she was too restless to concentrate on the paper. So instead she pulled out her sketchpad and began to draw. The image of Charlie gradually appeared on the page in front of her. She had tried to sketch him before, but those had been more scientific drawings, trying to capture his build and musculature. Now she was just drawing his face.

She shaded in his hair and tilted her head, inspecting her work. It was actually a pretty good likeness.

When she looked up, her heart slammed to a stop. Charlie was only six feet away. She'd often been amazed by his silent approaches, but he'd never made it this close without her sensing him. She knew that humans could learn to approach others in complete silence—Apache warriors, for instance, had been known for being able to touch their victims before they even knew they were there—but the fact that Charlie, at almost nine feet and at least eight hundred pounds, was able to be just as stealthy... it was absolutely mind-blowing.

He gestured to the bag where she kept the food.

Hastily, Tess closing the sketchpad, in case Charlie didn't like his likeness being captured, and placed it on the table. She stood up, not happy at how hard her heart was hammering. "Um, sure, okay."

She went over to the bag, and Charlie took his usual seat on the log. Tess walked slowly toward him and placed the food on the ground within his reach. Then she sat on the other side of the log and tried to pretend this was just like every other time he had visited—and that she wasn't completely terrified.

Charlie ate one apple. Then he stopped and just sat quietly on his side of the log, his eyes closed. Tess thought he might have even fallen asleep. She got up and retrieved her sketchbook, then returned to the log and sat on the ground, her back against it. She began to sketch the bear and her two cubs. Charlie watched her out of the corner of his eye for a few seconds before closing them again. Tess got lost in capturing the cubs, and when she looked up again, Charlie was gone.

She let out a breath. She'd done it—faced her fear, remained objective, approached the issue clinically. Bigfoot was an incredible creature, but he was without a doubt an animal. Any thoughts beyond that, and she would be veering way off the scientific track. And she had no intention of doing that.

She stood up and dusted off her pants, then paused. A single apple sat on the log. He had left it for her. She knew that in the animal kingdom, animals provided sustenance to other animals they felt were worthy of surviving.

But another part of her wondered. *What if it's more than that?* She knew she was humanizing the action, but it still felt an awful lot like an apology.

She stood up and dusted off her pants. No. Even Shelby did things that could be construed as human—looking sorry, happy, showing emotions.

CHAPTER THIRTY-FOUR

After the apple sharing, Tess and Charlie maintained their routine. Except Charlie now always shared his food with Tess. One day, after Charlie left her camp, Tess decided to follow him into the woods. She was able to keep up with him for about fifty yards, and then he disappeared.

She scoured the area but could find no sign of him and no trail. She sighed and blew out a breath. "You're very good at this game."

Charlie stepped out from behind a tree a mere ten feet away from her. She could swear he grinned.

Then he took off again, and Tess followed. They traipsed through the woods for an hour. Every once in a while she would lose him, only for him to once again reappear much closer than she would have thought possible.

As she walked behind him, she couldn't help but notice the difference in his gait compared to a human's. Humans bobbed with each step; Charlie *glided*. His head remained completely level as he transitioned from one step to the next. And despite his long stride—his footsteps were at least five feet apart—his feet came down in a line, as if he were walking a tightrope, rather than landing to the left and right like a human's would. *Amazing,* Tess thought.

Eventually, though, Tess lost him for good. She waited, as she had before, but this time he didn't reappear, and after ten minutes, she knew he was gone. Maybe he'd grown tired of the game.

But for Tess, the experience had been incredible. Not only had she been able to observe his walk, but also his ability to soundlessly appear and disappear. She'd read the many eyewitness reports that spoke of bigfoot vanishing, but she had always written them off as overactive imaginations. Now she knew there was truth to those reports. Charlie didn't literally disappear in front of her eyes—but if she looked away, by the time she turned back he could be gone.

Tess trudged back to her camp, thankful that she had kept a mental map in her head of where she was going. Her brother Pax liked to joke that in the womb she was the one who was given a sense of direction. Pax, on the other hand, could get lost in his own neighborhood.

She reached the camp, packed up, and then stopped and looked around one more time. She squinted at the log where Charlie had sat. *Could that be...?* She moved closer and knelt down. Her heart began to race. She ran back to her pack and pulled out her specimen kit. Using the tweezers, she plucked her find from the log and then held it up.

Three long, white hairs.

Shock, followed by elation, ran through her.

I have proof.

CHAPTER THIRTY-FIVE

That night Tess sat on the couch with Dev watching a movie. But her attention wasn't on the screen or on the man beside her. It was focused on one single question: What is bigfoot?

It wasn't the first time she'd pondered the question, of course. But the strange game of hide-and-seek in the woods had demonstrated that bigfoot had a playfulness she hadn't anticipated. And then there was his walk. It was so... *refined*, for lack of a better term. It wasn't the awkward stride of an animal used to being on four feet. It was confident, self-assured.

There were always mysteries and uncertainties when dealing with ancient fossil records, Tess knew. For instance, scholars originally argued that *Gigantopithecus* went extinct due to a loss of vegetation—yet its teeth and jawbones indicated that the species was omnivorous, making that hypothesis suspect. Tess believed that the most likely cause of the species' extinction was human beings. Wherever humans appeared, they tended to have disastrous effects on indigenous populations, whether plants, animals, or other humans. And *Gigantopithecus* was believed to be a contemporary of

Homo erectus; the two may have competed for food resources. *Homo erectus*, due to their ability to use tools, would likely have been the winner in that battle, helping push *Gigantopithecus* to extinction.

We destroy so much, Tess thought. She remembered an article she'd read on animal life in Madagascar. Five thousand years ago, the African island was thriving with exotic animals. There were pygmy hippopotamuses, lemurs the size of gorillas, even elephant birds who grew ten feet tall and laid eggs approximately 180 times the size of chicken eggs today. Then, in 500 BC, humans arrived, and a short time later, all these animals were gone.

But Charlie somehow survived. Was it possible Charlie was part of a group of animals that had hidden themselves from the human world in order to protect themselves? There were documented instances of other animals doing exactly that. For example, the chimpanzees in Uganda's Kibale National Park shifted to nocturnal activity after years of human civil war and poaching. By only foraging at night, they were able to avoid human detection—giving their species a chance to survive human destruction.

Perhaps there were more hidden species than humans dreamed of; they were, after all, hiding. Like the Bili apes, which no one believed existed until just a few short decades ago.

Was Charlie a *Gigantopithecus* or some related ape? Was it possible the extinction date for *Gigantopithecus* was wrong? That it had existed longer than was currently believed? That maybe they never *truly* went extinct? The idea was not without merit, as areas with forests tended not to be great resources for creating fossils: the areas were simply too damp.

And the fossil record itself was extremely spotty. The coelacanth, a rare fish, disappeared from the fossil record 65 million years ago and was believed to be extinct—until 1938, when a live coelacanth showed up in a catch of fish in the Indian Ocean.

Their numbers had been greatly reduced—there were once ninety different species of coelacanth, and now there are only two—but the coelacanth survived. The inherent problem with a fossil record is that we can only see what *is* there, not what isn't, and proving extinction is thus a matter of drawing conclusions from the absence of observations.

Tess knew the record regarding hominids was probably no better. Researchers in Ledi-Geraru, Ethiopia had found a remnant of a jawbone that predated the oldest known human find by 400,000 years. In fact, it seemed like every year a new hominid group was being unearthed. Recently a 200,000-year-old hominid jawbone was found in Taiwan that couldn't belong to any of the three ancient humans known to have existed there: *Homo erectus*, Neanderthal, and *Homo floriensis*. It was too big, incredibly thick, and with large teeth. The only conclusion was that it must have belonged to yet another unknown group of hominids.

As time marched on and more discoveries were made, it had become painfully clear that many different types of hominids once roamed the earth, and that we know very little about most of them.

Is it possible that like the coelacanth, there are now just two: Homo sapiens *and whatever bigfoot is?* Tess sighed. *Or am I just grasping at straws? Forcing a square peg into a round hole? Trying to fit Charlie into a previously known animal category?*

"Earth to Tess," Dev called.

Tess pulled herself back to the here and now.

Dev muted the TV. "You're not paying attention to any of this, are you?"

"Sorry. Lost in thought."

"Care to tell me where you are right now?"

She sighed. "You know where."

"Ah, bigfoot. So what in particular has you preoccupied tonight?"

Tess glanced over at Dev, and her heart tripped a little. The only light in the room came from the TV screen and the kitchen island. His sharp cheekbones were more defined in the shadows. His copper skin looked even darker. When he was younger he had been cute, but now... now he was gorgeous. A girl's dream come true. *At least this girl's.*

But she shoved those thoughts aside for the moment. She snuggled into his chest. "I'm trying to determine what bigfoot actually is—an ape or a something else. And why it is they're so reclusive."

"Well, you know the Hoopa have a lot of legends about bigfoot."

Tess smiled, knowing he was about to tell her one. She loved when he did this.

"In one legend, the animals of the world got together and decided to create humans. One of the animals was bigfoot, who said humans should walk upright like they did. So humans were made to walk on two legs. Bigfoot was very happy about this, but humans took one look at bigfoot and ran away, terrified by their giant size. So bigfoot decided to hide themselves away from the humans to keep them from being afraid."

Tess couldn't help but think of the Hairy Man pictographs found in Stanislaus National Forest in Sonora. They were believed to be thousands of years old, and among other things, they depicted a bigfoot family where the bigfoot is crying. According to the legends, the bigfoot cried because the humans were scared of them.

"Is that what you think he is? An animal?" Tess asked.

Dev paused. Tess knew he wasn't stalling but giving her question some thought. He shook his head. "I can't really see that. All the stories I've heard, their ability to stay away from humans...

There's an intelligence there that is more than what an animal is capable of."

Tess nodded.

Dev kissed her on the forehead. "All right, I can see when I'm not wanted."

"No, I—"

He laughed. "Relax. I'm just going to turn in. You can join me when you're done thinking."

She squeezed his hand and watched him walk to the bedroom. She knew she was a lucky woman. Soon, though, her thoughts turned back to the problem she couldn't seem to answer.

Bigfoot had survived without human intervention for so long, and she couldn't see that they'd receive any benefit from exposure now—only harm. Once they were proven to exist, hunters would no doubt traipse through the woods trying to get at them. Tess gave the TV a disgusted look. In fact, she knew of at least two shows where the entire goal of the program seemed to be to find and kill a bigfoot. Animal or not, they didn't deserve that.

And it wasn't only the hunters who were after a bigfoot carcass. There was the commonly held belief that until a dead bigfoot was in a lab, bigfoot would always remain only a legend. Tess knew that was probably true; some would forever doubt until a bigfoot cadaver was studied. But she recoiled at the image of Charlie on some lab table somewhere.

Tess didn't question that emotion. She would do that for any animal she was close to. Shelby on a lab table was not something she wanted to envision either.

She picked up one of the two clear sealed bags from the side table. Inside, two hairs with the bulb still attached could be seen. She had the proof right here. She could send it to Hayes and have him run the analysis. She'd probably have the answer within a day.

And yet she couldn't bring herself to do it.

Originally she had wanted to rush home and send it out for testing. But by the time she'd reached her cabin, she had changed her mind. She wanted to examine it here first. She would have done it already, but Dev had been here when she arrived, and she hadn't had a chance.

And when I get the chance, then what? If she sent the sample to Hayes, he'd probably call a press conference.

But Tess needed to think this through. If she had the sample tested, her life and the bigfoots' would change forever.

And she needed to be sure that it was the right type of change.

This week's question comes from Piper Rigby in Boston, Massachusetts. Piper writes:

Hasn't the Patterson-Gimlin film been proven to be just a guy in an ape costume?

Actually, no. The 1967 Patterson-Gimlin film is the most famous footage of an alleged bigfoot ever shot, and it lasts only about thirty seconds. In the film, a female bigfoot is seen walking across a gully in Bluff Creek, California. Roger Patterson and Bob Gimlin were actually riding horses in Bluff Creek looking for bigfoot when they stumbled upon her. That short film has been analyzed and inspected dozens of times. According to different analyses, the creature in the film is somewhere between six and eight feet tall.

Of course, some have argued that the film and the creature are fake, but their arguments are based on the idea that bigfoot is not real, ergo any footage of bigfoot must be fake. Hollywood has even put in their two cents, and they agree that the detail of the "suit" was way too advanced for the 1960s. In fact, in the film, it is clear that the bigfoot has a hernia on her right thigh, causing the muscle to bulge. That much detail seems a bit much for a fake suit.

But of course, until an actual bigfoot is caught, most skeptics will never believe that the being in the Patterson-Gimlin film is anything but fake.

CHAPTER THIRTY-SIX

As Tess hiked along the trail, she noted that more leaves had begun to turn. Before she knew it, cooler weather would move in. She loved fall out here; there was simply nothing better.

She hadn't looked at the hair sample yet. She told herself it was because she hadn't had the time to dedicate to it. But really, she was worried about the ramifications of that action. And she needed to be prepared. *It's the same reason I haven't told anyone that I've actually had contact with bigfoot,* she assured herself.

Tess shook off her thoughts when she reached the camp. *As soon as I have time, I'll inspect the hair and then decide on my next step.*

She sat at her table, a printout of her latest paper in front of her. She was working on a cluster analysis to predict how many groups of bigfoot there were in the United States. It looked like there were over a dozen. Bigfoot sightings had been reported in every state except for Hawaii. In fact, it seemed like practically every state had its own name for bigfoot. There was the skunk ape down in Florida, the booger in Texas, and the momo in Missouri, along with a slew of others. *Why is it easier for skeptics to believe that thousands of people are either lying or delusional than it is to believe that bigfoot is real?*

She glanced at her watch and realized her friend was running a little late. A feeling of disappointment spread through her. *Maybe he's not coming today.*

She looked up with a frown. Cold weather would move in in another couple of months. What would happen to Charlie then? There were some who believed bigfoot hibernated, which would mean she wouldn't see Charlie for months. The idea saddened her. She looked forward to his visits. The idea of not having him around... It wasn't a good feeling.

She pictured Charlie's thick hair. But was hibernation even necessary with their coats? She knew researchers had found a gene, EPAS1, that improved people's ability to adapt to extreme cold. The gene was found in the Tibetan people who lived at high altitudes with forty percent less oxygen. Most humans would become deathly ill in that environment due to the overproduction of red blood cells causing the blood to thicken.

At first, the researchers thought they had found evidence of how modern man's genetics had adapted to the environment in which they found themselves. But what they discovered instead was that the gene was actually a gift from an earlier hominid: *Homo denisova.*

Did bigfoot have the same adaptation? Was it possible they were related to *Homo denisova* and *Gigantopithecus?* A link between the two?

Tess stood. She really needed to get her head back on her paper; she had a deadline approaching, and she wasn't sure about the coding of one of the variables for the analysis. But she couldn't come up with a better approach, and she'd found that sometimes walking helped her clear her head and get back on track.

Grabbing her pack and her rifle, Tess took off, heading north.

She was worried about missing Charlie, but there had been prior occasions when he'd arrived at the camp before her, and he had actually waited for her there. There was no reason to think he wouldn't do the same today.

Tall Douglas firs towered over her, and a few smaller incense cedars with their drooping branches crowded the trail. A flying squirrel leapt from one tree to the next farther down the path. She turned toward the lake, and fifteen minutes later had reached its bank. The day had heated up a little. She shed her sweatshirt and tied it around her waist. She smiled as she looked over the water. What was it about water that made people feel alive?

She enjoyed the peaceful scene, but she knew she should get back. If Charlie did show up, she didn't want to make him wait too long. Although it was unlikely he would show up at this point. He'd never been this late before.

But Tess doubled her pace just in case. A few minutes later, she was back at the camp. To her disappointment, it was still empty. Placing her pack on the table, she pulled out some water and took a swig.

She suddenly had the feeling of being watched. Slowly, she put down the water and picked up her rifle. She didn't see anyone, but the feeling didn't lessen—she was sure someone or something was out there. And she was just as sure that it wasn't Charlie.

Movement pulled her attention to the right, and Charlie stepped into the clearing.

Surprised, Tess lowered her gun. "Hey. I didn't think you were going to make it today."

Charlie just watched her. And Tess still felt like there were other eyes on her. "Is everything all right?" she asked.

Of course he didn't answer. Tess weighed her options. She still felt like something was watching her. Charlie *could* take care of anything that came into camp, but *would* he? Would defending Tess be a priority for him?

She placed her rifle on the table. It was time for trust. She grabbed the bag of food she'd prepared last night. She placed the food on the end of the log like she always did, then returned the bag to the table.

When she turned back, Charlie was still standing in the same spot. Tess frowned. "What's wrong? I thought you liked apples."

He watched her for a few seconds, then disappeared back into the woods. Tess stared at the spot where he had been with a frown. What had that been all about?

She still felt eyes on her, but soon the feeling began to fade. She shrugged, wondering what had been wrong with Charlie.

Just as she was planning to pack his food back up, he stepped back into the camp.

And he wasn't alone.

CHAPTER THIRTY-SEVEN

Tess took an involuntary step back. But then she forced herself to relax, or at least pretend to relax, as she took in the sight of Charlie and his guest. The second bigfoot was smaller, only about eight feet tall, and slightly more narrow.

Because in this situation smaller means almost three feet taller than me and double my width.

At a glance Tess realized the second bigfoot was a female—her hair-covered breasts gave her away. Recovering, Tess stepped forward with a smile. She spoke quietly, trying to keep her tone even and friendly, and she gestured to the food. "I see you've brought a friend. Help yourselves."

Charlie went over and picked up an apple. He tossed it to his companion, who caught it easily. Then he took a seat on the log and began eating the other one. But the female bigfoot did not take a seat and did not start eating. She stayed perfectly still, her eyes on Tess. Tess could feel the distrust—not that she could blame her.

Tess worked on keeping her expression neutral and her feelings calm. She had a feeling they picked up on behavioral signals, so Tess strove for peaceful. But there was nothing she could do about her pounding heart.

The female bigfoot sniffed the apple, then took a tentative bite. But even as she chewed, her eyes never left Tess. In another few bites she'd finished it and gestured for more.

Tess glanced at Charlie, but he didn't seem inclined to share. Tess dug into her stash and pulled out three more apples. Keeping them in front of her, she placed them on the far side of the log, away from Charlie. She backed away and gestured from the female bigfoot to the food. "Go ahead. They're for you."

The female bigfoot seemed to be considering the offer. Finally she made her way to the food. She took a seat on the opposite end of the log from Charlie and began to eat.

Never in her life had Tess wanted to take a picture more. She had not one, but two bigfoot contentedly eating while sitting on a log less than ten feet from her.

Still, Tess knew better than to even try. She knew Charlie cared about this other bigfoot, and she had no doubt that if she did anything that could be construed as threatening, well... it would not go well for her.

Tess pulled her chair away from the table—and more importantly, her rifle—and took a seat, sketchpad in hand.

The female paused and looked to Charlie, but his lack of concern seemed to reassure her. She resumed her snacking. Tess began to sketch them, part of her reeling at the incredible scene in front of her.

For a few minutes, the three of them sat there—each busy with their own activity. And Tess felt at peace. As if somehow, her sketching two snacking bigfoot was something she did every day.

She started by outlining the two of them. The female was a little slimmer than the male, but not by much. Honestly, without the breasts, Tess would have been hard pressed to tell them apart.

The female's eyes were just as deep-set, her neck just as nonexistent, her torso just as barrel-shaped. Her hair was darker without any signs of gray, leading Tess to conclude she was younger.

Tess didn't think the female was Charlie's mate, but she couldn't be sure about that. His actions to her seemed more paternal. Was she his daughter?

Tess was beginning to sketch the female's face when a screech tore through the air.

CHAPTER THIRTY-EIGHT

Tess's head jerked up and her heart began to pound. The screech sounded again. Tess's eyes flew to Charlie, who looked unconcerned. The female, though, got to her feet quickly and disappeared into the forest.

And then all was silent.

Tess's head whipped around looking for the source of the noise, but she could see nothing that would account for it. It had sounded like a growl and a whistle combined. And she knew she had never heard that sound before. Even when Charlie had screamed that time with the camera, it had sounded nothing like this.

Charlie polished off the last of his food and rubbed his hands on his hair. And then he picked up a stick and twirled it in his fingers. Nothing about his posture or demeanor suggested fear. In fact, he seemed to be in a good mood. Tess frowned over that apparent contradiction.

"So, is she part of your family?" Tess asked. She didn't know why, but she always felt the need to speak her questions out loud even though she knew he couldn't respond.

Charlie glanced over at her, then looked back to where the female had disappeared. He made a sharp bark. Tess reared back. She had never heard *that* sound before either. Another bark, higher pitched, sounded back at him.

And Tess realized what she was hearing. It was *language*. Tess's knees felt weak. *They have a language.* It might be rudimentary, but it was there. *And—oh my God—I might be able to communicate with them.*

In her wildest dreams, she had never expected this. There were some researchers who were beginning to understand that some animals may have languages—dolphins, whales. But never an animal so close to humans. It opened up a whole new aspect of their existence.

Charlie watched the woods, then turned back to his stick. The female appeared back in the clearing. A smaller figure hid behind her.

A juvenile.

The small bigfoot peeked out before ducking back behind her mother. But that one small peek was enough. Tess caught the bright eyes. She saw the face that was smoother than either of the adults' and a lighter brown color. In fact, the juvenile was almost an auburn color, not like the extremely dark brown of the other two.

The juvenile bigfoot was only about four and a half feet tall. The hair on his shoulders and head stood straight up. *Piloerection*, Tess realized with concern. Piloerection, the raising of the hair, was a common occurrence in animals when they were behaving either highly aggressively or when they were socially excited.

Let's hope this is the highly excited display. Because even though the youngest bigfoot was shorter than Tess, he was clearly much stronger. His arms were incredibly muscular, as were his legs. And like the other two, he was already wider than Tess. *Yup, definitely hoping he's just excited.*

The older female grunted at Tess. Tess stared at her for minute, then realized what she was asking for. Food.

Oh, no. She had already exhausted her fruit supply. She could go get something from the food bag she'd loaded up earlier, but she didn't want to leave, for fear they might not still be here when she got back.

But she did have her emergency stash. The stash she suspected would survive a nuclear winter. Tess went into her lean-to and pulled out her bear-resistant cooler. Keeping all her movements unhurried, she opened it and took out the box of Twinkies. She kept the stash up here not so much for real emergencies—even though she *was* convinced they'd survive a nuclear winter—but because sometimes she just needed a little sugar.

She grabbed a couple of Twinkies. All three bigfoot heads watched her intently as the wrapper crinkled.

"It's just the packaging," Tess said. She kept her voice calm as she unwrapped the Twinkies and shoved the plastic in her pocket. Then she placed both Twinkies on the log, at the opposite end from where Charlie sat.

Charlie immediately picked up a Twinkie. He sniffed it, took a tentative bite—and then downed it in one gulp. Tess laughed. Who knew Charlie would like Twinkies?

Charlie grunted at the juvenile, who stepped away from his mother, keeping his gaze on Tess. And Tess realized then that she had made a mistake—the juvenile was not a he, but a she.

Charlie held the other Twinkie out to her. She stepped over and took it cautiously. She, too, sniffed it, then licked it, then took a tentative bite. Her brow furrowed and she took a bigger bite. Her eyes grew large, and she tossed the rest in her mouth.

Tess let out a laugh, and the two adult bigfoot made a sound that Tess could swear was a laugh as well. The juvenile looked toward Tess. Tess didn't need language to know what the child wanted.

Tess grinned. "Don't worry, I've got more."

CHAPTER THIRTY-NINE

Today had been amazing. Tess had named Charlie's guests Mary and Sugar—she didn't like thinking of them in the clinical terms of "the female" or "the juvenile." She was blown away watching their interactions. Both adults had been affectionate, playful, but also disciplined with Sugar. Tess had written pages of notes, and could have written more, but her hand had started to cramp pretty badly.

Now she sat curled up on the couch with Dev next to her. She smiled as she leaned her head against Dev's shoulder. *This is pretty good, too.* And she was getting used to it. She would go out in the field all day, write up her notes, and then have dinner with Dev. Sometimes he'd already be here when she arrived, whipping something up in the kitchen. Which was wonderful, because between the two of them, he was definitely the better cook.

Shelby yipped in her sleep over by the wood stove.

"So where are you tonight?" Dev whispered in her ear.

"Actually, I'm right here."

He bent down to kiss her. Tess sighed, enjoying the moment.

When they broke apart, she leaned into him. But soon her thoughts did turn back to her visitors at the camp.

"Now you're a thousand miles away," Dev said.

"Sorry. Just a little lost in thought."

"Did you find something?"

Tess hesitated. She wanted to tell him everything—all about Charlie, Sugar, and Mary—but something held her back.

Part of the problem was that she didn't want to be disbelieved. And the truth was, it *was* a fantastic story. But she knew Dev would believe her, and not just because of their relationship. Dev was part Hoopa and part Klamath. Both tribes had a long history with bigfoot.

No, if Tess was being honest, her real reason for keeping her discovery to herself was a selfish one. Right now, the bigfoot were all hers, and she liked it that way.

"Tess?"

She looked up. In his hazel eyes she saw trust, support, and love. He was a blessing. "I found some hair a few days ago," she said.

Dev's eyebrows rose and a grin spread across his face. "Really? That's great. What did the tests say?"

"I, um... haven't gotten it tested yet."

"Why not?"

Tess shrugged. "I'm not really sure. I guess I'm worried about what the results will say."

He took her hand. "If they come back as some other animal, it's no big deal. You just keep doing what you're doing."

"And if it comes back as an unknown animal?"

"Do you think it will?"

Here was another opportunity to tell him everything—and yet she hedged. "I'm not sure. I haven't had a chance to really inspect it."

He paused. "What's going on, Tess?"

"I don't know. I guess... I'm worried about what happens if the results come back the way I think they will."

Dev frowned. "I'm still not seeing the problem."

She blew out a breath. "The thing is—what happens *after* I get the results? If it gets out that I've found proof of bigfoot, the woods will be crawling with people trying to track them down."

Dev pulled her into his arms with a chuckle. "I think you're getting a little bit ahead of yourself. And no says you have to publicize the results right away. You can announce your findings whenever you're ready."

Tess sighed. She knew he was right, but she also felt guilty about even thinking about testing the hair. "What do you think about all this?" she asked.

Tess watched Dev carefully, trying to gauge his reaction. Native Americans in the Northwest had a long tradition of regarding bigfoot with respect, almost as a family member or teacher. But they also regarded bigfoot as a flesh-and-blood being —unlike other Native American groups farther east, who viewed bigfoot as a mystical or spiritual being. And Tess knew Dev was a product of his heritage—in particular, he had a great respect for the natural world and for the beliefs of his people.

"I support you," Dev said. "I know why you're doing this. And if you prove bigfoot exists, then I'll be one of the ones fighting to make sure they're protected and left alone. The fact is, if bigfoot is still out there, I'd rather *you* find him than someone else."

He pulled back and looked into her face. "This is really bothering you, isn't it?"

"Yes. Once Hayes gets word of this, it will be completely out of my control."

"Why don't you send it to Pax? Maybe he could run it on the sly, and then you can decide what to do."

"Yeah, I'm leaning in that direction."

He kissed her on the forehead. "Well, whatever you decide, it will be the right decision."

Tess watched him go. She pictured Charlie, Mary, and Sugar. Something had changed ever since she'd watched the three of them interact.

And now she wasn't sure what the right decision was anymore.

CHAPTER FORTY

A few hours later, Dev quietly closed the front door of Tess's cabin behind him. He had an early shift and he had to stop by his own place to get a clean uniform.

As he headed to his truck, the doubts he'd had for the last few weeks crept in. Tess was keeping something from him; he could sense it. She closed up whenever he asked about her research, or she deflected his question like she had tonight. And whatever her secret was, it was putting up a wall between them.

He didn't like it. But he also didn't know how to get her to trust him. And if he was being honest, he was a little hurt by it. He had thought they were past this kind of stuff.

He pulled out of the drive and headed down the road, but his thoughts stayed with Tess. He'd been in love with her since they were kids. His mom had realized it almost as soon as he had, and had told him to just wait—it would happen. And now it had.

As far as Tess was concerned, he knew two things for sure:

One, he was going to spend his life with her.

And two, whatever she was keeping from him, it was important.

CHAPTER FORTY-ONE

The next day, Tess sat in her office, waiting for Pax to return her call. Rain was pouring from the heavens. When the precipitation had begun at five this morning, she'd hoped it was a passing shower. But the weather forecast indicated it was only going to get worse. She had really wanted to get out to the camp. Instead, she was inside, catching up on paperwork.

Which was probably for the best. She'd barely slept, thinking about Charlie and his two guests.

As she listened to the rain drum on the metal roof, she wondered what Charlie did in the rain. Did he have a shelter? Did he need one? The idea of Charlie all hunched up somewhere, soaked, tugged at her.

Before she could question that emotion, Pax's return call came through on Skype. His smiling face appeared on her screen. "Hey, sis."

Tess laughed. "Back away from the camera, you nut."

Pax laughed and took a seat at his desk.

"Is this a good time?"' Tess asked.

"Yup. Everyone's at lunch. Did you get the gift I sent you?"

Tess reached over and picked up the ten-inch plush bigfoot with a giant "Adopt me!" message on the front. "I got him. Thanks. He's a little small."

"Well, a life-size would be, what? Six feet minimum? Think of him as a pocket bigfoot."

Tess chuckled, wondering what Charlie's reaction to the little bigfoot would be. "It's just what I've always wanted."

This morning, thanks to the rain, she'd finally had uninterrupted time to dedicate to the hair sample. She had collected four strands in total: two gray, and two a dark brown. Each was between four and five inches long—and luckily the bulb was still attached at the end.

Under magnification, she had made two distinct observations. First, that the ends of the hairs were rounded, meaning they had never been cut. And second, that the hairs were clearly neither human nor gorilla.

There were some similarities between these hairs and human hair—for instance, the scale pattern was similar, and like human hairs, these did not have a continuous medullary core. But these hairs also varied in color and thickness along their shaft, which human hair did not. Tess had searched both her texts and the internet and could come to only one conclusion: no known animal had hairs like these.

The next step was a DNA test, which is why she'd been waiting anxiously for Pax's call.

"So, exactly how rusty are your lab skills?" she asked.

"Rusty? Moi? You insult me."

"Seriously."

Pax paused. "I drop into the lab every now and then to keep my skills on point. Why?"

Now it was Tess's turn to pause. "I was hoping you could run a sample for me."

A grin spread across Pax's face. "That's great! You found

something." He frowned. "But why are you asking me? Hayes must have dozens of labs you could use."

"He does, but I want to run it myself first, on the down low. Do you think *you* could run it and put the results under John Doe?"

Pax narrowed his eyes. "What's going on, Tess?"

She sighed. *Why is everyone asking me that lately?* "I just want to be prepared, depending on how this comes back. And with Hayes, it's all under his control. He could announce before I even saw the results."

"I get it. You want me to don my superspy outfit and run the analysis under the cloak of darkness." He wiggled his eyebrows at her.

Tess rolled her eyes. "I am *so* not going to address the fact that apparently you *have* a superspy outfit. And yes, with or without the outfit, if you could run the sample, I'd be thrilled. And I can pay for it."

"It might take me a while. I'll have to go in when the lab's empty."

"That's fine," Tess said quickly. "No rush."

"Okay, I'll get it done."

"You don't know how much better that makes me feel."

Pax frowned, inspecting her through the screen. "Shouldn't you be more excited about this? And what's with the 'no rush'?"

Tess knew he was right. She *should* be more excited—and more impatient to get the results. Months ago, she would have been. But something had changed. Now she wasn't just think about finding answers. She was worried about what would happen *after* she found answers. And she wasn't sure if that was a good thing or a bad one.

This week's question comes from Hilda Maldonado in Houston, Texas.

I've read a lot about the giant footprints left behind by bigfoot, and I've read about the hair and seen some of the photo evidence. But is there any other evidence?

Actually, one of the best pieces of evidence comes from Skookum Meadows, Oregon. (The word "skookum" is a Native American name for bigfoot. Dozens of locations in the Northwest have names that include the word "skookum.")

In 2000, a team of researchers from the Bigfoot Research Organization found a large imprint near a fruit trap they had left out. But it was not a footprint. It revealed an animal's buttocks, thigh, arm, and even hair. From the positioning, it appeared that the animal had lain on its side next to the mud to reach for the fruit trap. Analysis of the cast, which required over two hundred pounds of plaster, indicated that the animal was seven and a half feet tall and covered in hair.

Not only that, but bigfoot prints were found nearby, along with some hair samples—which matched no known animal.

CHAPTER FORTY-TWO

The ground was uneven, and Tess had to focus in order to not lose her footing as she chased Sugar through the trees. It had been three weeks since Charlie had introduced her to Sugar and Mary, and since then, Sugar and Mary had shown up with Charlie at least a dozen times.

Mary never stayed as long as Sugar did, but there was something very calming about her presence. Sugar, however, was anything but calm. She was full of energy. She was the most friendly of the bigfoot and the most willing to interact—even more than Charlie himself. Much like human juveniles, Sugar didn't seem as concerned as her elders were about the possible dangers of her actions.

Each time she visited, Sugar grew bolder. She'd already investigated Tess's lean-to and her packs. Tess had taken more than a few walks with her. And of course, there was the required Twinkie at every visit. Tess worried a little about getting Sugar hooked on the stuff, but the little bigfoot seemed so happy when she got to eat them.

Now Sugar and Tess were playing their own version of hide-

and-seek. Sugar always hid, and Tess always sought—and Tess rarely found her without a little help from Sugar.

But Tess had learned a lot. Sugar would sometimes emit an odor in one spot and then skip off to hide somewhere else. She could move just as soundlessly through the forest as Charlie, and she was incredibly strong. Tess might see her on the ground, then turn away and look back only to find Sugar swinging down at her from a tree limb. Sugar could also go completely still, and in an instant, she would blend into the shadows and trees. Even while looking for her, Tess would often pass right by.

As a scientist, Tess was cataloguing these physical behaviors, of course; but she was also enjoying herself. Sugar just wanted to have fun. She was a sweet child.

The thought brought Tess up short. *Child*. When had she stopped thinking of them as animals? But the truth was, she had. It was like she was finding a new tribe of humans—incredibly large, powerful, and hairy humans, but humans nonetheless.

Over the last few weeks, she'd debated how best to classify them. They had similarities to gorillas, especially in their foot shape and their torsos. But they also had distinctly human characteristics as well. What she really needed was information on that DNA sample. She'd have to call Pax again and see if he'd had any luck yet. He'd reported having trouble finding a time when the lab was empty.

She also knew Hayes was growing impatient with her, and she owed him an explanation. Yet she continued to refrain from telling him about either the hair sample or her interactions with the bigfoot.

For no particular reason, Tess felt her spirits lift; and a moment later, she felt someone watching her. This was another ability she had noticed with the bigfoot: they were like the opposite of an empath—they *projected* their feelings. And the happiness Tess was feeling right now was Sugar's.

Tess grinned and then turned quickly, pointing up at the tree behind her. "Got you!"

Sugar swung down from the tree, but she misjudged the distance, and as she landed, she bumped Tess on the shoulder—hard. Tess was knocked to the ground, the wind knocked out of her.

Sugar immediately began to pace, her nervous chatter filling the air. And then Tess felt a second presence. When she looked up, she was unsurprised to see Charlie striding through the trees. He might be okay with Tess spending time with Sugar, but never without supervision.

Charlie let out a bark, and Sugar cowered.

Tess's shoulder ached, but she wasn't seriously injured. "No, no," she said. "It was an accident. It's okay." She pushed herself to her feet and stood in front of the younger bigfoot, swallowing down her fear. "She didn't mean it. It was an accident."

Charlie stared down at her, and Tess could swear she saw a smile cross his face before he disappeared back into the trees.

Sugar put her hand gently on Tess's unharmed shoulder. Tess reached behind her and placed her hand on top of it. And with that move, she knew that all hope of scientific objectivity was lost.

And she was completely okay with that.

CHAPTER FORTY-THREE

T ess stared out the window at the rain. After coming down all day yesterday, it was finally tapering off, but she still hadn't been able to get out to the camp. She was waiting for a call from Pax regarding the sample. She was so tense. She couldn't sit still. *What is wrong with me?*

Her computer beeped behind her. She crossed the room and answered it. "Hey, Pax."

"Hey yourself."

"Any luck running the samples?"

"Oh, I'm fine. Thanks for asking."

Tess laughed. "Sorry. How are you?"

He grinned. "Wonderful, and no, I haven't been able to run the samples yet. But everyone is supposed to be out of the office at lunch tomorrow for a department meeting. I'm going to see if I can get in then."

Tess bit her lip. "I appreciate you doing this, but I don't want you to get in trouble."

"Hey, no risk, no reward, right?" Pax looked around and then slowly unbuttoned his shirt.

"Uh, what are you doing?"

"Showing you my commitment." He flashed his shirt open, and Tess let out a laugh. Underneath his uniform was a red T-shirt. Emblazoned across the front were the words "Team Sasquatch" above a cartoon picture of a waving bigfoot.

Tess laughed. "Far be it for me to dissuade a member of Team Sasquatch."

"And speaking of meetings, I need to run to one now. Call you later?"

"Okay."

Pax disappeared from Tess's screen.

Tess stayed where she was. She *wanted* to know what bigfoot was. She really did. It was why she had sent Pax the sample.

Today though, she had made a decision. She was going to cancel the grant with Hayes. She couldn't put Charlie and his family at risk.

A weight lifted off her shoulders at the decision, and she felt lighter than she had in days.

And hopefully tomorrow, she would finally be able to classify them. She smiled. Yup, tomorrow was going to be an amazing day.

CHAPTER FORTY-FOUR

As Tess walked down the path, her thoughts were on Pax and the results he might have later today. *What do I do with them?*

She was so lost in thought, she didn't immediately realize that the woods had gone deathly quiet. When she did finally notice it, she froze and scanned the area. She couldn't see anything wrong.

It's nothing, she thought. But as she continued on toward her camp, she pulled her shotgun out nonetheless. As much as she enjoyed spending time with the bigfoot, they were not the only predators out here. There were mountain lions, coyotes, bobcats, and wild pigs to worry about as well.

Arriving at the campsite, she found a few more footprints over by the log. *Damn it.* Tess grabbed a branch and quickly wiped the prints away. It was only after she'd done so that she realized with a shock that she hadn't even taken photos of them first. She sat back on her heels, bemused. *Well, I really have turned a corner.*

Shaking her head, she dropped her pack. A shadow separated from the tree ahead of her, and her head jerked up. When

Charlie stepped forward, Tess put a hand to her racing heart. "You nearly gave me a heart attack." She looked around. "Where's Sugar and Mary?"

She grabbed an apple from her pack and tossed it at him. Charlie caught it but didn't take a bite. He just stood, unmoving.

Tess narrowed her eyes and took a step closer to him. "Is everything all right?"

Suddenly, Tess felt a powerful sadness tinged with fear. For a moment it was all she could think about, and then, just as quickly as the feeling had arrived, it disappeared.

She stared at Charlie. "Those were *your* feelings."

He'd never done that before. Tess had felt Sugar's and Mary's feelings, but never Charlie's. She had begun to think that projecting emotions was an ability that only the females had.

Charlie held out his hand. Tess started. She'd held Sugar's hand, even Mary's one time, but never Charlie's. But she hesitated. Then she stepped forward and placed her hand in his. Gently, Charlie closed his fingers over it.

A sigh rolled through her giant friend. Then he stepped back, giving her hand a gentle tug.

"You want me to go with you?"

Charlie tugged again, a little less gently.

Tess put up her other hand and gestured behind her. "Okay, okay. Let me get my pack."

She pulled her hand away and quickly grabbed her bag. When she turned back, Charlie had already started walking away. She strapped on her pack and followed.

Charlie walked quickly, and Tess had a tough time keeping up. At one point, she thought she'd lost him. But Charlie almost immediately reappeared and waited, as if making sure she was still following. *This is not our normal game of hide-and-seek.*

Tess had the distinct impression Charlie was leading her somewhere specific. He led her off-trail, deep into the forest, to an area she had never been in before. She looked at the dense trees surrounding her with more than a little trepidation. "In for a penny, in for a pound," she muttered with a sigh.

As they moved through the woods, Tess did her best to orient herself, just in case Charlie decided to take off. She didn't want to be stranded. At least she had her sat phone in her bag in case of emergency, which she was very thankful for.

As time wore on, Tess could tell that Charlie was getting frustrated with Tess's slower pace. When he turned around and gave her yet another impatient look, she muttered, "Yeah, well not all of us have a five-foot gait, you know."

Finally, Charlie stopped and Tess caught up with him. She slumped against a tree trying to catch her breath. They'd been walking for at least three hours already, and Tess had a feeling they weren't done yet. She pulled out her water and took a swig.

She looked behind her, trying to memorize the trail from this perspective as well. She knew it was easy to get confused on the return leg. A path in one direction often looked very different when traversed from the other direction.

Charlie let out a howl, and Tess spilled water down the front of her shirt. Her heart pounding, she wiped her chin and looked up at him. But Charlie wasn't looking at her. In fact, the howl wasn't even meant for her; despite her pounding heart, Tess could make out a return howl in the distance—in the direction they were heading.

Charlie gave himself a nod and set off again without a word. Tess hastily tucked her water back in her pack and took off after him.

They were starting to lose the light when Tess realized the trees had thinned out. She looked up and saw a mountain peak ahead. Dread filled her. *Please tell me Charlie doesn't think I'm climbing that thing.*

Not that she couldn't—exactly. But seeing as how Charlie

seemed a little annoyed at how slow her hiking pace was, she was pretty sure he was not going to be thrilled about her climbing speed.

Charlie stopped at the tree line, and Tess stepped up next to him, trying to figure out a way to explain that it was going to take her a lot longer to climb than him. But before she could speak, she caught sight of the figure stepping out of the trees beyond him.

It was another bigfoot, at least ten feet tall.

And he did not look happy.

CHAPTER FORTY-FIVE

Tess took an involuntary step back from the new arrival. But then a calm feeling began to spread through her. She looked at the other bigfoot and felt only trust. Charlie gave her a small smile, and Tess realized that once again he was sharing his feelings.

Tess let out a breath. "Okay. Charlie trusts you, so I guess I do too."

Charlie walked up to the other bigfoot. He was two feet taller than Charlie and his appearance was more apelike. His chest was broader, his body more muscular. His head was still pointed, but it was rounder than Charlie's. His face was wider, his nose flatter, and a scar ran from just below his eye to halfway down his cheek.

I really hope that scar wasn't put there by a human.

She glanced down at the other bigfoot's feet, and she was surprised to see a divergent big toe. That was something seen in apes, and a Yeti print found in Asia had shown that characteristic as well, but Charlie didn't have a divergent big toe, and neither did Mary or Sugar.

Was it possible there were two species of bigfoot? Was this one more closely related to *Gigantopithecus*?

Charlie spoke with the other bigfoot, chattering away in the language she had heard Charlie, Mary, and Sugar use occasionally. And the more she heard them, the more complex she realized it was. It was a combination of a series of growls, whistles, and grunts in different tones.

The other bigfoot listened to Charlie quietly, only occasionally making a sound. Finally, he nodded, and Charlie gestured for Tess to walk forward.

Tess looked between the two of them. "Um, something I should know?"

The feeling of trust washed through her again. She looked into Charlie's eyes and sensed the intelligence and compassion there. And also... fear. But not of this other bigfoot. Something else was worrying Charlie.

The other bigfoot stepped up to Tess. He was almost five feet taller than her. Tess felt like Fay Wray in *King Kong*. She forced herself to stay calm—or at least not run screaming back into the woods.

"Okay, Kong," she said. "What's the plan?"

Tess could almost swear she saw him raise an eyebrow. The action looked so human, it stole away some of her fear. Very gently, Kong reached down, picked her up, and slung her onto his back.

Tess's eyes went wide and she grabbed on to his hair. "Ooookay."

Kong turned and began to scale the rock face. Tess tried to shove all the images of her plunging to her death from her mind. She only partially succeeded. One hundred feet up, she buried her face into Kong's back. She was holding on so tightly, her hands cramped. And although she hadn't been to church in a while, she began praying. *Hail Mary Full of Grace...*

Halfway up the rock face, Kong stepped onto a ledge. When he moved away from the edge, Tess realized the ledge was actually the entrance to a cave midway up the rock face. She hadn't been able to see it from the ground. Inside, Kong knelt down, and Tess slipped off his back. Her feet hit the ground, followed quickly by her butt.

Kong looked back at her and gave a snort.

Getting to her feet, Tess dusted off her pants. "Yeah, well, you try riding something about double your size and we'll see how well *you* do."

Charlie appeared at her side and looked into her eyes.

"I'm okay," Tess said, sensing her friend's worry.

Ahead, Tess could see that the cave narrowed to a tunnel, through which she could see sunlight. Kong had already disappeared through it. Charlie nudged her gently forward before stepping into the tunnel himself. Tess took a steeling breath, and with one last glance behind her, she followed him.

CHAPTER FORTY-SIX

Tess made her way along the tunnel, her nerves stretched tight. At the other end of the tunnel, all she could make out was blue sky. She really hoped it wasn't another cliff, because she was going to need a minute before embarking on another climb.

Anticipation and fear rolled over her. She had no idea where she was heading, and she knew she had gone way over the edge with this little trip. *What are you doing, Tess Brannick? No one even knows you're here.* At the same time, she knew it was an illusion that she had ever had any control here. If she had resisted… well, Charlie could have just brought her anyway.

And the truth was, she really wanted to know what Charlie wanted. She remembered Madge's words: *I'm betting he'll let you know sooner rather than later.*

So she followed Charlie through the tunnel, accompanied by equal measures of curiosity and fear. After about a hundred yards, the tunnel ended and Charlie stepped out.

Well, here goes nothing. With a deep breath, Tess stepped out behind him.

They stood on a ledge that was only a few feet above the ground. A giant valley was spread out before her, dotted with clusters of trees and with a lake on the far end.

And there were families of bigfoot everywhere.

Tess stared, her mouth hanging open. There had to be at least seventy of them. A group of juveniles, already five feet tall, played tag in one spot. A gathering of females sat nearby, keeping an eye on the juveniles while they chatted. In another area, she spotted two adult bigfoot carrying a child—a small one, perhaps only three feet tall. To his right was an adult female, carrying another small child. *They must be mates.* In fact, as she looked around, Tess could see more and more evidence of family. Men walked with women, and adults carried children or babies.

Charlie hopped off the low ledge and then gave Tess a hand to help her down after him. As she stepped down, a young bigfoot extracted herself from the juveniles and ran over to her. The bigfoot grabbed Tess in her arms and twirled her around. Tess had to swallow a yell.

Then she looked into the bigfoot's face and recognized the deep brown eyes. "Sugar?"

Sugar chattered happily back at her. She had grown at least four inches since Tess had last seen her. *Must be some sort of growth spurt.* "You've gotten so big, I barely recognized you."

Sugar crushed her in a hug, and Tess let out a yelp. Sugar immediately placed her gently on the ground, her eyes worried. Tess smiled. "It's okay. I'm not hurt."

Four of the juveniles Sugar had been playing with had followed her over. One of them chattered at Sugar, and she answered them. They moved forward slowly, the way you would if you were approaching an animal you didn't want to scare.

Talk about role reversals, Tess thought.

Four pairs of eyes studied Tess, and she looked back at them, not sure what to do. One reached out and touched the arm of her jacket. Keeping her voice calm, Tess said, "Go ahead, it's okay."

Another touched her hair. Soon they crowded around her, each touching a different part of her. Tess tried to remain calm, but when they moved in close, she lost sight of Sugar and Charlie. Her heart began to pound. They were pushing and poking at her.

"Stop it." She slapped one's hand away. One pushed her from the back, and she fell forward, catching herself on another. A hand tugged on her hair, and tears sprang to her eyes. She let out a gasp.

A howl sounded. Sugar yanked away the bigfoot who had grabbed Tess's hair. She bared her teeth and warned the others with a growl. They all quickly stepped away from Tess. Sugar then pulled Tess in to her chest. She held her with one arm and ran a hand over her hair with the other.

She's comforting me, Tess thought with shock.

Charlie chattered angrily at the juveniles, and they slunk away. Tess tried to calm her heart. What was she thinking coming here? She was so in over her head.

Charlie gestured toward the far valley wall. Tess could make out little alcoves, where more bigfoot congregated. She looked back at the tunnel. Part of her wanted to leave, to escape back to the safety of her camp. But part of her wasn't ready to go yet. And a smaller part, a part she was trying to ignore, wondered whether she was free to go at all.

Tess looked up into Charlie's eyes, and once again the sadness flowed from him. Something was wrong. And Tess was pretty sure Charlie wanted her help. Swallowing her fear, she nodded.

"Okay. Let's go."

CHAPTER FORTY-SEVEN

Tess followed Charlie across the valley. Along the way, bigfoot stopped what they were doing to stare at her. None approached or interfered, but she could feel their eyes tracking her movements across the open space. And while she wasn't sure what awaited her ahead, she looked forward to getting away from their prying eyes.

Charlie led her to a cave tucked underneath a rock overhang on the far wall of the valley. He ducked inside. Steeling herself, Tess followed.

The cave was at least thirteen feet high, but it wasn't very deep, only about twenty feet. Along the back wall sat two bigfoot next to a pile of leaves and branches. One of the bigfoot stood up, and Tess felt comforted at the sight of her. "Hi, Mary."

Mary stayed where she was, darting glances between Tess and the pile of leaves.

The other bigfoot was a male about the same size as Charlie. He backed away slowly from the pile of leaves, keeping his eyes locked on Tess and giving her a wide berth. He did not seem happy to see her. Tess kept an eye on him too, although if he tried to hurt her there was absolutely nothing she could do to defend herself.

Charlie motioned her forward toward Mary and the pile of leaves.

Trying to keep her breathing even, Tess did as he asked, her hands on her pack as if it were some sort of security blanket. As she drew closer, she noticed that there was an old blanket on top of the leaves. *That's odd.* Then she realized that hair was sticking out from under the blanket. There was someone in there.

She stepped right up to the bed of leaves, for that's clearly what it was. And now she could see that the shape under the blanket was tiny. Was this one of their babies? But why would they bring her all this way to see a baby? Why were they trusting her with this?

Charlie looked at Tess, then gestured toward the bed of leaves again. Tess knelt, aware of the eyes on her. Very gently, and with a trembling hand, she pulled back the blanket and stared in disbelief as the child turned toward her. She fell back, her hand over her mouth.

It wasn't a bigfoot child.

It was a human one.

CHAPTER FORTY-EIGHT

Tess stared at the child for precious seconds before she moved forward. She pushed the long, stringy brown hair out of the child's face. It was a girl. With shaking hands, Tess pulled the blanket all the way back. The girl wore an old dress, and her feet were bare. Tess wasn't sure, but she thought the girl was about five years old, six at most.

The girl mumbled something. Tess reached up and felt her forehead. She was burning up.

Mary kneeled down on the other side of the girl. She placed her hand gently on the child's back, and the child reached out for her. Mary scooted closer so the child could feel her near.

Tess watched the exchange in amazement. Mary cared for this child—maybe as her own child, or maybe merely as a pet, but it was obvious that she was genuinely concerned about the girl. Charlie sat down beside Mary, his eyes on the girl. Then his eyes met Tess's, and Tess felt the trust. Charlie trusted her with the health of this child. Tess turned her attention back to the girl.

"Okay. She has a fever. Why?"

She gently checked the girl, but didn't see anything that

could have caused it—until she rolled the girl on her side. Tess sucked in a breath. There, at the back of her calf, was a cut that had become badly infected. It was caked with dirt and oozing pus. *Oh, God. This is why Charlie brought me.*

Gently, Tess ran a shaky hand over the girl's hair. "It's going to be okay," she said and hoped she wasn't lying.

The girl didn't respond to her words. Tess wasn't sure if that was because she didn't hear them or because she didn't understand them.

Tess slid her bag off her shoulders, aware of the three sets of eyes watching her intently. She unzipped her bag, grabbed a towel, and tried unsuccessfully to rip it apart. "Damn it."

Charlie grabbed the towel from her and easily ripped it in two. He tried to hand it back, but Tess indicated with hand gestures that he should rip it more. He did, then gave the torn pieces to her.

Tess rifled through her pack again, grabbing her pot, her water canteen, and her lighter. She walked just outside the cave, gathered some sticks together, brought them back inside the cave, and arranged them in a neat pile beside one wall. Mary's mate watched her carefully.

Tess then picked up her lighter and brought up the flame.

With a yell, Mary's mate shoved her; Tess slammed into the wall. Her head struck with such force it left her dizzy. She crumpled to the ground and saw stars.

Mary's mate towered over her. Tess cowered, pressing her back against the wall. *Oh God.*

But before Mary's mate could strike again, Charlie darted forward, stepping between Tess and her attacker. He shoved the other bigfoot back, growling from deep in his throat. Mary's mate stepped toward him threateningly, but Charlie didn't back down. He gestured from Tess to the girl.

Finally, the mate backed away. He glared at Mary, then went

and sat next to the girl, pulling her into his lap. Tess couldn't help but notice how gentle the male was with the girl. He held her in a way that could only be described as protective.

Clearing her head, Tess got to her feet. She kept her attention on the bigfoot that had shoved her, ready to run at any aggressive moves. At the same time, she realized the futility of that plan. The bigfoot watched her just as carefully. But Charlie stood nearby, and Tess had the sense that he was warning the other bigfoot to stay back.

Turning back to the pile of sticks, Tess tried to light a fire. Her hands were trembling so hard, it took her three tries to get the lighter to work. Finally it caught. She poured the water in the pot, then placed the pot on the fire to boil.

Then she looked up at Mary's mate, who glared back at her. And Tess tried not to think about what would happen to her if the girl died.

CHAPTER FORTY-NINE

Tess spent the rest of the day cleaning out the girl's wound. She had ground up some ibuprofen and mixed it with water, and with Mary's help, had gotten the girl to drink it.

By the time darkness began to fall, Tess was exhausted. After the hike, the shock of the valley, and the stress of the little girl's illness, she was wiped. But she stayed by the girl's side all through the dark night. Occasionally she would drift off, but the girl's whimpers would awaken her, and she would replace the hot cloth on her forehead with a cool one and check her wound.

Finally, as the night turned into day, the girl's fever broke.

Tess allowed herself a small smile and tried not to cry. The girl would be all right.

Carefully Tess changed the girl's bandage, taping it in place. She looked up at Mary and Charlie, who had not left the little girl's side. Mary's mate—Frank, Tess had decided to call him— had disappeared for a few hours during the night, but he was back now, and he looked on, concerned. As did Sugar, who had come in and curled up next to the girl.

Tess nodded. "She'll be all right."

She wasn't sure if they understood her. But she was too tired to do more than that. She lay her head down on the edge of the girl's bed, closed her eyes, and slept.

CHAPTER FIFTY

T ess felt a rock jabbing into her side. She opened her eyes. *Why am I—?*

She reared back, barely able to hold in her yelp. Sugar sat three feet away, staring at her.

Her hand on her heart, Tess took a deep breath. "Morning, Sugar," she said quietly, stretching her back as she sat up. Mary was still curled up next to the little girl.

Quietly, so as not to wake the girl, Tess knelt at her side and placed her hand on her forehead. She was cool to the touch. Tess slumped next to the bed in relief. *Thank God.*

Feeling eyes on her, Tess caught Mary's sleepy gaze and smiled. Mary placed her hand on the girl's back and closed her eyes again. Sugar scampered out of the cave. Frank and Charlie were gone too.

Tess brushed the girl's hair from her face and tried to figure out what to do. Who was this girl? And how on earth did she end up here? People had spent their whole lives looking for bigfoot, and here this tiny little girl not only had found them, she *lived* with them.

Had they found her somewhere? Did she wander off from a campsite? Tess thought back to the Native American tales of bigfoot kidnapping children. Had this girl been kidnapped? Was there any way she could have *chosen* to live with them? Even if she had, she was only a child. Legally, she couldn't decide where she lived.

Tess stared at the girl and Mary's arm protectively covering her. However the girl had arrived here, Tess would not be getting those answers right now. And the best thing she could do for the girl was to let her sleep. So as quietly as she could, Tess made her way to the opening of the cave. She picked up her pack and secured it on her shoulders. She paused at the entrance, not sure how the bigfoot would react to seeing her outside without an escort.

Well, here goes nothing. Tess stepped out.

She was prepared to dart right back inside if her appearance caused any upset, but to her surprise, no one seemed to object. And they definitely noticed her. Just about everyone nearby stopped and stared. Keeping her movements unhurried, Tess walked a little to the side of the cave and took a seat with a large boulder against her back.

She just looked around, not moving, until eventually the bigfoot turned away, unconcerned. Tess let out the breath she had been holding.

She would have sat there longer, just watching. It was amazing. But there was something she had to do before she could enjoy the view.

She rose quietly and walked around the boulder, out of view. After yesterday's response to her lighter, she didn't want to risk startling anyone. She pulled her sat phone from her pack. She wasn't sure how long she was going to be out here, and she needed to leave a message before everyone freaked.

The battery light was blinking. With everything going on

lately, she'd forgotten to charge it. She glanced up at the valley walls and wondered if the call could even get through. She'd have to hope for the best.

She debated for a minute who to call before deciding on Pax. He would be the one most worried if he didn't speak with her. She quickly dialed his number. Pax answered on the second ring.

"Tess?"

"Hey, Pax."

"Tess, thank God."

"I just wanted to let you know I'd be away for a few days. But don't worry, I'm fine."

Static answered her.

Tess frowned and raised her voice. "Pax? I said I'll be away a few days, but I'm okay."

More static sounded. And then the phone died.

Tess stared at it. *Damn.* Well, Pax had heard her voice—she hoped. He knew she wasn't in danger. It would have to do.

Tess put the phone back in her pack, walked around the boulder, and took a seat closer to the cave entrance. With her back against the valley wall, she watched with amazement the scene in front of her.

She had noticed the family groups yesterday, but now she had a chance to really study them. She saw juveniles playing together, but there were always a few adults nearby, and the few times the juveniles got out of hand, they were quickly reprimanded by the adults. Tess even caught sight of a few babies, some of them possible newborns. Plus she saw at least two bigfoot that were obviously pregnant.

This must be a breeding ground. The bigfoot probably gather here to help protect and provide for the children. And when they're old enough, they probably even bring them here to find a mate. Some researchers had hypothesized the possibility that bigfoot had family units, but most discounted it. They said bigfoot was a loner. While it was true that bigfoot shied away from humans, apparently they enjoyed being in each other's company.

Over at the lake, Tess spotted a few bigfoot swimming—and they were incredible swimmers. That was perhaps what surprised her the most. Gorillas hated the water and stayed away from it. They didn't even drink much water, preferring to get their water from plants. But the bigfoot dove and swam liked they'd been born for it. Tess pictured Charlie's webbed fingers. *Maybe they were.*

She tore her gaze from the swimmers as some juveniles raced by playing some sort of tag. Tess couldn't take it all in. It was incredible.

And it made sense. In all the sightings of bigfoot, very few ever reported seeing a juvenile. But the juveniles had to be *somewhere.* So maybe they did separate during the years, then came back together solely for breeding purposes. Or maybe they stayed together year round and only the older ones were allowed to go off alone—probably to forage for food.

And Charlie's existence here also suggested they did not write off older members of their groups. Everyone had a purpose. Everyone had a part to play.

Tess watched everything unfolding in front of her with new eyes. This was a cohesive group—a tribe. If not for their size and all that hair, they could be any group of humans.

She caught sight of Kong standing across the valley with a group of like-sized individuals. *Well, almost human.*

Kong and his companions held themselves apart from the rest of the bigfoot. Almost like a guard—a general and his lieutenants. Like Kong, the others of his group were more muscular and taller. The more Tess compared them to the smaller bigfoot, the more convinced she became that they were two different species. As she watched Kong, Tess couldn't help but wonder about his divergent big toe and think about all the subtle differences in the reports of bigfoot around the world.

At the same time, her mind whirled at what she was looking at and what it all meant. She had not discovered a single unknown group—she'd discovered *two*. Two that intermingled, two that lived together and in all likelihood bred together. *Amazing*.

Sugar disappeared into the cave and reappeared soon after. Tess felt the worry coming from her, so she rose and made her way back into the cave.

The little girl was moaning softly in her sleep. Tess mixed some more ibuprofen with water and brought it over to the girl. Mary pulled the girl into her lap and held her while Tess held the cup to the girl's lips.

"That's a good girl," Tess said as the girl began to take small sips. Slowly, the girl downed it all. Then Mary leaned back against the wall, the girl snuggled in her lap. Tess watched the two of them, etching the memory into her mind. It was the picture of maternal love.

Tess turned to return the cup to her bag and nearly bumped into Charlie and Frank. Frank's eyes latched on to the girl and then Mary, who was cooing softly to the girl. Frank didn't even glance at Tess as he went to join his mate. Mary handed the girl over to him, and with a gentleness belied by his size, Frank held the girl snugly in his arms.

Charlie grunted at Tess before turning and walking out of the cave. Tess paused and then followed him, sensing that was perhaps what he wanted. Sure enough, he was waiting for her outside, and as soon as she stepped out, he started to walk across the valley. Tess struggled to keep up, and Charlie slowed.

They passed an apple tree, and Charlie reached up and snagged a couple. Tess grinned. Apparently he hadn't really needed her apple supply after all.

Tess realized they were heading for the entrance. Her heart plummeted. She wasn't ready to go home yet. But Charlie turned before reaching the tunnel, leading Tess to a path that cut up along the side of the wall of rock. It ended at a wide ledge overlooking the valley. Charlie sat down.

Tess could see everything from here. She looked at Charlie and realized no one would be able to see him up here. He blended in too well with the surrounding rocks. She sat down next to him. He handed her an apple. Tess realized they had reached a pivotal point in their relationship. Charlie was now feeding her.

Tess took a bite as the sun began to dip toward the horizon. Neither of them spoke, which for Charlie wasn't unusual. But for the first time, Tess didn't feel the need to either.

She just smiled and enjoyed the sunset.

CHAPTER FIFTY-ONE

The paperwork on Pax's desk had shrunk significantly in the last two hours, and he thought he'd done a pretty good job of burying himself in it and pretending he wasn't completely terrified that something had happened to Tess.

He picked up the printout showing the results of her sample. He'd left her a message as soon as he'd gotten it, and she still hadn't called him back. At first he'd told himself she was just in the field; then he'd called her late last night and he'd told himself she had decided to stay overnight. But in his heart, he knew something was wrong. Shawn had tried to reassure him, but Pax had seen the worry behind Shawn's words. He was just as concerned.

For now, Pax was letting himself be convinced that Tess's sat phone was out of range—even though they'd bought it precisely because it wasn't supposed to be *able* to go out of range.

His phone rang and he glanced down. *Finally.*

"Hey, Pax," Tess said.

"Tess. Thank God."

Static answered him.

Pax frowned. "Tess? Tess? Are you there?"

More static, plus small bits of words. "—out—day—but—"

Then the phone went dead. Pax stared at it. He quickly dialed her back, but the call went straight to voicemail.

With trembling hands he dialed Dev. "Pick up. Please pick up."

"Hello?"

Pax's words rushed out. "Dev, have you spoken with Tess?"

"Uh, no, not since yesterday. Why? What's wrong?"

"I just got a call from her, but it was all static. I haven't heard from her since yesterday. Something's wrong."

"Pax, calm down, you don't know—"

"Dev, please, just go by her cabin and make sure everything's all right, okay?"

There was a pause. "I'll head there right now."

Pax grasped the phone. "Good, great, thanks." He disconnected the call and immediately called Shawn. It went to voicemail. *Why is no one picking up their phones?* He left a message explaining what was going on. Then he paced his office waiting for Dev to call back, praying he was overreacting.

CHAPTER FIFTY-TWO

Dev had just pulled into his parking spot at the police station when Pax called. He had been expecting Tess to call. He had the early shift, which is why he hadn't stayed at Tess's last night. He'd tried to call her last night but she hadn't answered. Now Pax couldn't reach her either.

He pulled out of the parking lot and headed for Tess's, telling himself everything was fine. But he still pressed down on the accelerator a little heavier than usual. Twenty minutes later, he pulled up at her front porch. Even from the car, he could hear Shelby's howl.

Fear prickled his skin as he sprinted up the porch stairs and opened the door. Shelby barreled out of the door and down the stairs, relieving herself as soon as she stepped off the last step.

Dev's fear grew. He stepped into the cabin. "Tess?"

No answer. He made a quick search of the cabin, but Tess wasn't there. Her answering machine light blinked at him. He hit play and heard Pax's message, as well as one from Sasha. Both were from yesterday. His pulse picked up. She hadn't checked her machine last night. And she always checked her machine.

He didn't want to worry Pax, but right now *he* was starting to worry. He called Tess's cell and her sat phone—no answer. He called Sasha, Abby, Madge, and Eric. None of them had heard from her, and all Dev had accomplished was worrying them as well. He assured each of them he'd call as soon as he found her.

He stood in her living room, looking around, trying to come up with any other possibility. Then he pulled out his phone, telling himself that he would be reasonable and calm with Pax. But he couldn't help but notice the shake in his hand as he dialed.

CHAPTER FIFTY-THREE

Pax looked again at the results on Tess's sample. They were not what he'd been expecting. But he had the sneaking suspicion Tess wouldn't be nearly as surprised. Her behavior around this whole thing was weird—not rushing to get the results, keeping the information from Hayes. *What's going on with you, Tess?*

He placed the results back in the manila folder and slumped into his chair. He turned so he faced the giant wall clock behind him. It would take Dev at least twenty minutes to get to Tess's cabin from his place. Time seemed to crawl by. By the time twenty minutes had passed, he could barely keep himself in his chair.

"Hey."

Pax whirled around. Shawn stood in the doorway, holding a bag of takeout and two coffees.

Pax was so happy to see him he wanted to cry. Shawn placed the bag and drinks on the desk. Pax got up and hugged him. "I left my phone in the car when I picked up the coffee," Shawn said. "I only got your message just now. I was already on the way over."

Pax stepped back. "How'd you manage that? Don't you have grunts to beat into submission?"

Shawn smiled, and Pax's heart gave a little leap, like it always did. "I just told them to keep running until I get back."

Pax nodded and then his head jerked up. "You're kidding, right?"

"Sort of. But I did send them on a ten-mile run. I thought you might want a little company. I guess you haven't heard from Dev yet?"

"No, I thought—" Pax's phone rang, and he pounced on it. "Dev?"

Dev's voice was even, measured. "Now, Pax, I need you to stay calm."

Pax slumped into his seat on shaky legs as he put the call on speaker. Shawn came and stood behind him, his hand on his shoulder. "What happened?" Shawn asked.

"Tess isn't here. It doesn't look like she's been here since yesterday. Shelby obviously hadn't been out in a while."

"Shelby's there?" Pax felt lightheaded. He knew that whenever Tess was planning on staying out, she dropped Shelby at Madge's. There was no way she'd leave Shelby alone overnight.

"I'm going to head out for her camp and see what's going on," Dev said. "And I'll put out a BOLO on her and make sure the rangers are aware. But she's probably at her camp, maybe twisted an ankle or something."

Pax stood up, plans running through his head. "I'll be there first thing in the morning."

"*We'll* be there," Shawn said.

Pax nodded. "We'll be there."

"We don't know yet—"

Pax cut him off. "We'll be there in the morning. Best-case

scenario, I'll make her pay our airfare for worrying me to death. Worst-case scenario..." Pax choked, his hand flying to his mouth.

Shawn reached over and took the phone out of his hand. "Thanks, Dev. We'll see you in the morning." He disconnected the call.

Pax slumped back in his seat, listening to Shawn arrange flights for the two of them. But all he could picture was Tess. She'd never leave Shelby unattended.

A few minutes later, Shawn knelt down in front of him. "We'll find her, okay?"

Pax nodded, but it wasn't because he agreed. It was because he really, really hoped Shawn was right.

CHAPTER FIFTY-FOUR

Dev filled up Shelby's food and water bowls, then locked her back inside Tess's cabin. He made his way quickly to Tess's barn and gassed up her other ATV. He turned the key and said a little prayer of thanks when it flared to life.

He followed the path Tess normally took, noting that it was relatively dry. Its elevation had caused most of the water to run off. He saw tracks from the other ATV, but he suspected they were at least a day old.

Forty minutes later, he spied Tess's ATV parked at the end of the trail, and his stomach dropped. He quickly pulled up next to it. Not allowing any of his fears to overcome him, he took off at a fast clip for her camp. Another thirty-five minutes and he was there. He stepped into the silent camp. Nothing. He checked the lean-to. Nothing. Her bear-resistant cooler was empty except for two boxes of Twinkies.

There was no sign that Tess had been here, at least not today.

Dev studied the ground around the camp. He wasn't an expert tracker, but he could hold his own, and he caught sight of

Tess's footprints heading north. He followed them, trying to calm his now-racing heart.

Ten minutes later he came to an abrupt halt. He stared at the print on the ground in front of him, his heart all but stopping. The print was easily sixteen inches long and eight inches wide.

Oh God, Tess, what have you gotten yourself into?

CHAPTER FIFTY-FIVE

Tess spent the next morning watching over the little girl. Finally, around noon, the girl opened her eyes.

Tess looked down at her and spoke quietly. "Hi."

The girl reared back, but Charlie was there, making soothing noises. The girl clutched his hand.

Tess kept her voice gentle. "My name's Tess. Your friends brought me here to help you. You were hurt."

The girl shook her head.

"You weren't hurt?" Tess asked.

"Not friends," she said, her words halting, like she hadn't spoken in a while. She licked her lips. "Family."

Surprise filtered through Tess. For some reason, she had assumed the girl couldn't speak. But seeing as she spoke perfect English, it was clear that she hadn't been out here her whole life. So when *did* she get here? And how?

As Tess looked at the pale little girl, she knew now wasn't the time to have that discussion. "I can tell they care about you very much," Tess said.

The girl closed her eyes again, her hand still clasped in Charlie's. Charlie looked down at her. The affection in his gaze was undeniable. After a while, the girl's breathing turned even. She'd fallen back to sleep.

A short time later, Mary came in and replaced Charlie, and Sugar arrived as well, curling up next to the girl. Frank stayed outside, standing at the entrance of the cave with a few other bigfoot, but he poked his head in every few minutes. Sometimes he stared at Tess, but he always checked on the little girl.

Tess watched all this in amazement. The girl hadn't been lying. They were her family. They doted on her. They were concerned for her. They had even risked exposure to bring Tess to heal her.

Tess drew her knees up to her chest and rested her chin on them. Now what? The girl would heal and grow stronger. But she couldn't live with them forever. The bigfoot were designed for the outdoor life. Their hair kept them insulated from both bugs and cold. Humans had no such insulation. And the girl's dress was slowly turning to rags. Tess supposed she could get the girl clothes, but that would only be a stopgap.

The thought brought Tess up short. She realized the other huge difference between humans and this other group of hominids: the bigfoot had no possessions. They used what they needed from nature, but they kept nothing. Even the bed in the cave was solely for the little girl. No other family member had such a bed.

That partly accounted for why the bigfoot were so difficult to find. They brought nothing with them and left nothing behind, no evidence of their passage.

Tess's eyes drifted to the girl. *Unless they have a little human girl with them.*

Tess looked at each member of the girl's family. She knew they could protect the girl from many of the dangers she would face, but not all of them. The cut was evidence of that.

And the girl must have a human family, too. Were they looking for her? Was there some mother walking into this little girl's room each day, her heart breaking a little more at the sight of the unused toys and bed? Did she have a sibling who was missing a sister?

Who was the girl? Where had she come from? How long had she been with this group? The questions rolled on and on. But the biggest one blinked like a neon sign above the rest: What was Tess going to do about her?

If she left the girl here, the girl could be in danger. Did Tess have the right to deny a family a reunion with their missing child? But to get the girl home, Tess would have to almost certainly reveal the bigfoot.

And they wouldn't want to let the girl go, either. That much was obvious. So then what? Tess wouldn't be able to convince them. And they could most definitely stop her.

Tess ran her hand through her hair. *What the hell am I going to do?*

CHAPTER FIFTY-SIX

Queens, New York

Abe Cascione disconnected the call and pulled open the file on Tess Brannick. Over the last few days, Carter had placed a few unreturned calls to Dr. Brannick, and now the good doctor had failed to hand in her last report. Carter wanted Abe down there to see what was going on.

Abe smiled. *And hopefully to offer a little encouragement the way only I can.*

He rifled through the file before stopping at the pictures of Tess. The first was an academic shot from her doctoral program. Even in the conservative pose and dull gray suit, her attractiveness was apparent. The second shot was more casual. She was standing with one arm around her brother and the other around her brother-in law. Two other females flanked the trio: her friends Sasha Bileris and Abby Newman.

After Hayes had contacted Abe about her, Abe had conducted his own research. It was amazing how much information was available online. People really needed to be more careful. Tess carefully controlled her public image, but her friends and family were far less circumspect. The picture was from her friend Sasha's Facebook page. Abe took in Tess's bright smile, her long legs. *An All-American beauty.*

He picked up the phone and dialed. His call was answered on the second ring.

"Hello?"

"Mrs. Cameron, I need a flight to—" He flipped back to the first page and grimaced. "Beauford, California. It's a small town somewhere near Oregon. Get me as close as you can."

"Do you want me to arrange for a car and hotel as well?"

"Yes to the car, no to the hotel. I'll figure that out when I get there."

"Very well. I'll have it ready first thing in the morning. Is there anything else?"

"No. That's it for now. I'll need you in the office at six in case I need anything else. And you'll need to keep your phone with you at all times while I'm away."

"I'll be there. And I already live with my phone."

"Good." He disconnected the call.

Beauford was a tiny little town in Northern California located along the Bigfoot Scenic Byway. Abe scoffed. *Bigfoot Scenic Byway.* He'd looked up the name just to make sure it wasn't fake—it wasn't. It was an 89-mile road that cut through the Klamath National Forest. An eighteen-foot statue of bigfoot was supposed to tower over the beginning of it. That area of northern California was reputed to have the largest number of bigfoot sightings in the country.

Bunch of idiots believing in fairy tales. But even he had to admit, the idea of seeing one, and better yet killing one, was awfully appealing. He'd read the doctor's professional description: "research into an unknown bipedal hominid residing in North America." Academic speak for bigfoot.

But why the hell would Carter be interested in the professor?

He pictured the enigmatic CEO. Carter was Abe's main employer, although Abe took the odd job here and there. Just quick kills—in and out. Carter's jobs were usually more involved.

Abe picked up the picture. *A watch-and-see mission. Maybe I'll see if Mrs. Cameron can find me a few quick jobs while I wait.*

CHAPTER FIFTY-SEVEN

Over the next few days, the girl got stronger and stronger. And Tess learned her name: Missy. Tess couldn't recall any missing children by that name, but that meant next to nothing. It wasn't as if Tess kept a mental registry of every missing child. Besides, Bigfoot were theorized to travel long distances, perhaps hundred of miles; the girl could have come from any of the areas around the national forests.

And that was a lot of area. Klamath Park connected to three other national forests: Six Rivers Park, Siskiyou National Forest, and Rogue River National Forest. Together they comprised nearly five million acres over two states.

On Tess's fourth day with the bigfoot, Charlie brought Missy along with him and Tess for their nightly routine of apples and sunset. The girl lay curled in Charlie's lap, munching on an apple and glancing at Tess occasionally through the corner of her eyes.

Clearly the girl wasn't comfortable with her yet. Tess leaned back and took a bite of apple. When she was done chewing, she said, "Do you know how I met Charlie?"

The girl frowned. "Charlie?"

Tess nudged her chin toward the bigfoot. "That's what I call him. And then there's Mary, Frank, and Sugar."

Missy smiled shyly. "I call him Teddy."

"Like a teddy bear?"

Missy nodded.

"Well, Teddy and I met at my camp. And the first thing we did was play catch."

Missy's eyebrows rose. "What?"

Tess explained about meeting Charlie for the first time and then how she'd come to meet Mary and Sugar.

Missy smiled when Tess mentioned playing hide-and-seek with Sugar. "Sister's good at hiding," Missy said.

"She's *really* good," Tess said. The three of them sat contentedly for a few moments before Tess spoke again. "So how did *you* meet them?"

Missy bit her lip and looked away. Tess glanced up at Charlie, who was watching the exchange quietly, but Tess felt trust coming from him. He wanted her to bond with the little girl. And he wanted Missy to know that as well.

"I used to play in the woods," Missy said quietly.

"That must have been nice," Tess said.

Missy hesitated, darting a glance at Tess. "I saw Mary one day, and then I started leaving her some food. We became friends."

Tess knew she had to tread lightly here. "And how did you come to live here?"

Missy looked at Tess, and tears sprang into her eyes. "I don't want to talk about it," she said with a shaky voice.

"It's okay, honey. You don't have to. I'm just glad you found such good—such a great family."

Missy turned and buried her head in Charlie's chest. As she

did, the hair fell away from her neck, exposing a red circular mark.

Tess stared at the spot, feeling shaky. Because Tess had seen that kind of mark before, but only in pictures. And it could only have been made by one thing: a cigarette.

CHAPTER FIFTY-EIGHT

Abe Cascione lay on his stomach in his tent a few hundred yards from Tess Brannick's cabin. He'd been camped out here for days now, and he'd seen no sign of the good doctor. But her cabin had been busy with people coming and going. Something was definitely up.

Pax Brannick stepped out of the cabin next to his husband, Shawn. The two of them headed to the barn, trailed by the dog. Abe shook his head. *Two men married—times have definitely changed.* A minute later, the ATV pulled out with Shawn aboard, heading into the woods. Pax appeared with the dog, and the two of them headed down the road.

Abe waited until they were out of view, and then he crawled out of his tent. *Finally.*

He walked to the front door and tried the knob—unlocked. He never understood people. *Why on earth would anyone ever leave a door unlocked?* He eased the door open and slipped inside. He made his way straight to the office, not sure how long the brother would be away. Sometimes he took the dog for a long walk, sometimes extremely short ones.

A map of the park was taped up on the back wall. Some areas were crossed off, others circled. Abe grunted. *They're searching for her. So she* is *lost.* He shook his head. *What did she expect, running around in the woods all this time?*

He took a picture of the map and then rummaged through the desk. He found a list of names, all of them crossed off. He recognized some of them from his background check. They were calling all of Brannick's associates.

He took some photos of the other papers on the desk, then walked over to the bookcase with the glass doors. At least three dozen large casts lay there. *Damn, those are big.* Almost all the footprints were over a foot long, and even the smaller ones were incredibly wide. *Maybe she* will *find a bigfoot.*

In the bottom right, he noticed a little bag. *What have we here?* He opened the door and reached in. The clear baggy held two pieces of hair. The bag itself was labeled with coordinates, time, and date. Abe smiled as he slipped the bag into his pocket. *I think you may just have to come with me.*

He closed up the case, gave the room one last scan, then headed out. It had been at least eight minutes, and he didn't want to chance getting caught. Carter wanted this quiet. Translation: boring.

He let himself out and returned to his tent. Just as he ducked inside, he spied Pax and the dog returning. He watched the cabin for a few minutes after they entered, but all was quiet. They had no idea he'd been there.

He pulled out his phone and dialed.

Thaddeus answered. "Mr. Hayes expected your call hours ago."

"Then he shouldn't have told me to do this quietly. Quiet takes time."

"Fine. What have you found out?"

"They have a few search parties out looking for her, so she's definitely missing."

"Are they getting close to finding her?"

Abe rolled his eyes. "I have no idea, as I don't know where she is. But from what I can tell, they're doing a grid search, covering specific areas before moving on to the next. They really don't seem to have any idea where she is."

"That's disappointing. Did you find anything else?"

Abe held up the bag with the hair. "Nothing worth reporting."

CHAPTER FIFTY-NINE

Over the next few days Tess managed to coax more details out of Missy. She learned she was an only child and that her mother had died a few years back. She and her father had lived in a cabin on the edge of the woods, although Missy didn't know where it was located. She had been to kindergarten for a little while, which meant she was at least five years old, as Tess had suspected.

Missy didn't seem to know how long she had been with the bigfoot, but given how well she was accepted, Tess was sure it had been a while. Tess herself had seen how the rest of the bigfoot doted on her. Missy really had been accepted as one of them.

Tess didn't want to press the girl for information, and Missy was very reluctant to speak about her life before the bigfoot. But Missy loved to talk about her life *with* them. She told Tess all about Frank carrying her on their long treks. She told her about the games she played with Sister and the other juveniles. And Tess realized—even if Missy didn't—that Missy had missed talking with another human. There were times when she seemed to ramble on nonstop as if she'd been storing up her words the whole time she was with the bigfoot and now she needed to get them all out at once.

Tess didn't mind. It was nice to have someone to talk to—someone who could talk back. And Tess was really starting to care for the little girl. She could see why the bigfoot enjoyed having the girl with them. Missy was almost perpetually happy.

But while Tess was enjoying her stay, the lower level of hygiene was really beginning to get to her. By the seventh day, Tess knew she needed a bath. She stunk. And while the bigfoot might not mind, she certainly did.

After a breakfast of a few apples, Tess decided she couldn't take it anymore. She grabbed her pack and headed for the lake. She stopped where Missy was playing some sort of rock game with Sugar, observed by Mary. "I'm going to the lake," Tess said. "Do you want to come?"

Missy turned to Sugar and let out a series of grunts. Tess was dumbfounded. *She speaks their language.* In all Tess's time here, this was the first time Missy had done so. The possibilities of that one discovery nearly overwhelmed her. With Missy's help, she would actually be able to communicate with them.

Missy stood, as did Sugar and Mary. "We'll come."

Tess didn't respond at first. She was still dealing with the shock of learning Missy could speak the bigfoot language.

Missy tugged on her arm. "Tess?"

Tess pulled herself back to the present. Mary and Sugar had already started down toward the lake. Tess forced a smile to her lips. "Sorry. Okay, let's go." She and Missy jogged to catch up with the other two.

The foursome made their way down to the lake. As they drew nearer, Sugar scampered ahead with Missy on her back. They were just like any other siblings.

At the edge of the water, Tess hesitated, wondering about the water's temperature. But the bigfoot had no such qualms, and neither did Missy. They all dove right in.

Taking off her boots, Tess dove in after them. The first brush with the water chilled her. *Wow, that's cold.* She stretched out and swam halfway across the lake. As she treaded water in the middle, she began to warm up. She watched the others. Missy was swimming after Sugar—it looked like a game of tag, although there was no way a young human girl could keep up with a bigfoot.

Then Sugar dropped under the water. Tess waited for her to reappear. She didn't.

Tess frowned. Her heart began to beat faster. *She should be back up by now.* Mary floated on her back, unconcerned, and Missy swam around happily, but Tess felt her anxiety building.

Then a hand grabbed her leg, and she screamed. Sugar burst out of the water behind her.

Sugar let off a barking laugh, and Mary and Missy joined in. Tess held her hand to her chest, afraid her heart would pound its way out of it. Then she splashed water at Sugar. "That was mean." Sugar dove under again, avoiding the spray, and reappeared out of range.

Tess shook her head and chuckled.

As she treaded water, she got an up close and personal view of the bigfoot's swimming abilities. They really were incredible swimmers. They splashed water at one another, and raced across the lake at impressive speed. And Mary could hold her breath underwater just as long as Sugar had, if not longer.

What was most surprising, though, was what a good swimmer Missy was. Tess considered herself a pretty decent swimmer, but she was a distant fourth when compared with the other three.

Still, at one point Missy swallowed some water and started to struggle. Before Tess could even move, Mary and Sugar were at her side. Mary quickly flipped onto her back and Sugar lifted

Missy up so that she could lie on Mary's stomach. *Her very own bigfoot pool float,* Tess thought.

An hour later, Tess pulled herself to shore, knowing that if she stayed in a second longer, someone would have to rescue her. She lay back on the grass, thankful that the sun was warm. After a time, the other three joined her and lay next to her. Tess smiled. *Just four friends just enjoying a warm afternoon.*

Mary was the first to get up, followed by Sugar. Tess groaned as she sat up. She had actually been really comfortable on the ground. She looked over at Missy, who gave her a shy smile.

Missy's hair was matted. Her dress was torn. She was a miserable mess, but there was such a look of contentment on her face. "You had fun, didn't you?" Tess asked.

Missy nodded.

But Tess's gaze traveled to the dress she wore. It really was a disaster. She grabbed her pack and pulled it over. "You know, I may have something in here for you."

"Really?" Missy asked.

Tess rummaged through and found her old blue t-shirt in the bottom. "Here we go." She shook it out and held it up to Missy. It came past her knees, but it would work. "What do you think?"

Missy's eyes grew large, and a smile broke across her face.

Tess dropped the t-shirt. "Okay, turn around and I'll help you put this on." Missy did, and Tess pulled the old ratty dress off of her.

And she barely managed to hold in her gasp. Her hands shook as she looked at Missy's back. There was a mass of old scars, most of them cigarette burns. She put a trembling hand to her mouth.

"Tess?" Missy asked.

"Sorry, sorry," Tess said, forcing herself to sound normal. "Here you go." She pulled the t-shirt over Missy's head and helped the girl get her arms through the sleeves.

Missy turned back around. She ran her hand over the material and grinned. Then she threw herself at Tess. "Thank you."

Tess wrapped her arms around the little girl, trying to block out the image of her back and just focus on the girl's present joy. "You are very welcome."

"I'm going to show Sister." Missy wiggled out of Tess's arms and took off at a run.

Tess watched her go, her heart heavy. Wherever Missy had come from, it had been a cruel existence. And now she had found peace. How could Tess take her away from that?

But at the same time, Tess knew that as Missy got older, there was more and more of a chance that she would get hurt. And if she stayed out here too long before returning, she'd never be able to fit back in with human society.

Tess ran her hands through her hair. She had no idea what the right thing to do was in this situation. But she knew that whatever decision she made, Missy would be the one to deal with the consequences.

CHAPTER SIXTY

Grand Rapids, Michigan

Tyler Haven stared at his reflection in the mirror. Light hazel eyes and chiseled cheekbones stared back at him from under thick light brown hair sculpted to look carefree. Tyler leaned forward and squinted at a red spot appearing on his cheek. *I'll have to use a stronger cleaner tonight.*

He pressed a small amount of powder over the spot, blending it in to his skin to make sure no one could tell he was using makeup. He had a reputation as a tough outdoorsman. It wouldn't do if anyone learned about his pre-show makeup ritual.

He sat back and inspected every inch of his face. Then he stepped back farther and inspected his outfit. His dark wash jeans were just tight enough to accentuate his physique without looking like he was trying to. His tight t-shirt showed off his well-developed chest but it was washed enough to have more of a care-less attitude. *Perfect.*

He stepped out of his trailer.

Tyler's assistant, Meg Tilly, who'd been leaning against the side of the trailer, jumped to attention and rushed over to him. "Mr. Haven, they're ready for you."

Tyler brushed past her. "We're set up out back?"

Meg struggled to keep up with Tyler's long-legged stride. She pushed her glasses up her nose, clutching her reports and clipboard to her chest. "Um, yes. Just like you wanted."

Tyler nodded. The light would look good on him. And the trees surrounding them would give the story a little extra credibility. "What about the guest? What's his name again?"

"Um, Billy Bob Franklin."

Tyler struggled not to roll his eyes. Billy Bob? He was willing to bet the guy was about four hundred pounds and owned one shirt. He really needed to get off this show. His talents were being completely wasted. "Right, right. Did you explain to him what we need?"

Meg nodded her head, and her glasses slid down to the end of her nose again. "Yes. He, um, knows."

They rounded the corner of the cabin. The small crew was already set up. Two chairs had been placed on the dock; the lake would serve as a backdrop. Tyler paused, glancing up. He'd need to move his chair to the right a little more to make sure the sun hit him just right. Which would leave the sun directly in the eyes of his guest, but hey, fans weren't tuning in to see Billy Bob Franklin every week.

Billy Bob stood with his one of the cameramen. What was his name? Frank? Fred? Anyway, Tyler was glad to find that Billy Bob was not as hillbilly as he'd thought. A little overweight, but his shirt was a button-down and his dark hair was recently cut. *I can work with that.*

Pulling on the Tyler Haven charm, he walked forward with a smile. "Mr. Franklin, thank you so much for agreeing to do this. You're really helping out a lot of people."

Billy Bob's jaw fell and he shook Tyler's hand robotically.

Then he seemed to gather himself together. "Mr. Haven, I'm a huge fan. In fact, your show is the reason I was out here. Call me Billy Bob—everybody does."

"Well, we all appreciate you taking up the cause. Why don't we go ahead and get started?" Tyler led Billy Bob over to the chairs and directed him to the one facing the sun. Shifting his own chair, Tyler took a seat and felt the sun hit him from behind. Perfect. Across from him, Billy Bob blinked a little in the sunlight.

"Ready?"

Billy Bob ran his hand along his thigh. "Uh, sure."

Tyler turned to the camera. The cameraman counted down with his fingers from three and then pointed at Tyler, who smiled.

"Welcome to *Bigfoot Must Die*. Each week we bring you horrifying tales of the monster that lives among us, preying on innocent souls in the woods. Today, we have a special guest. A true hero who faced a bigfoot and did what needed to be done. But before I get ahead of myself, let's let the man tell you himself. Billy Bob?"

Billy Bob looked like a deer in headlights. "Um, yeah?"

Great. Tyler cut in. "Is it true you saw two bigfoot when you were out in the Rogue River State Game Area?"

"Uh, yes sir."

"And that's in Michigan, the Northwest corner of Kent County, correct?"

"Uh, yes sir. It is. They were standing in the forest as clear as you are to me."

"How far away were they?"

"No more than twenty feet."

Tyler let out a whistle. "That is awfully close. How tall would you say they were?"

"Well, one was easily eight, maybe nine feet tall. The other was a lot shorter, maybe four or five feet."

Tyler leaned forward. "And you were in fear for your life, weren't you?"

"Well, not really. I mean, they weren't paying me any attention."

Tyler glared at Meg, who took a step back. *Prepared, my ass.*

"But if they wanted to hurt you, they could have without a thought, isn't that right?"

Billy Bob nodded his head repeatedly. "Oh, yes sir. I mean, even the little one—its arms were huge. If they had decided to take me out, there'd have been nothing I could do."

Tyler nodded. They were back on track. "So tell us, what happened next?"

"Well, the big one, he walked off. So I watched the little one through my scope. And I must have made a sound, because it turned toward me. It looked at me with these big brown eyes. I swear, it looked almost human."

"And then?"

"Well, it turned to leave. So I shot it in the neck. That thing doesn't belong here. It's not normal. It's the only thing I could do."

Tyler leaned forward. "Because you were in fear for your life."

"Yes, sir, I sure was. Especially after the big one came tearing back. It was screaming. I've never heard a noise like that. I took off running for my truck and drove off."

Tyler shook his head. "I can't blame you. I don't think anyone can. But you returned to the spot later, didn't you?"

"Yup, about two hours later I came back with two friends. But the one I shot was gone. And I know I killed it. I got it right in the neck."

"What do you think happened?"

"I think that other one took it away. I should have taken him out."

"No, protecting yourself was the right thing to do. And I'm glad you shared your story with us today."

Billy Bob sat a little straighter. "Well I think it's important people know what's going on. And I'm glad I can help people understand the danger that's out there."

"And you have." Tyler turned to camera. "If you ever come across one of these beasts in the woods, remember these words: the only safe bigfoot is a dead bigfoot."

CHAPTER SIXTY-ONE

Tess had been with the bigfoot for ten days, and each day she'd learned more about them.

For one thing, every night a handful of them went out and hunted—both males and females, although females with young children stayed behind—and brought back whatever they found to share with the group. For the first few days, these hunting parties had not been inclined to share with Tess, but eventually that had changed as well. They offered her part of their spoils. Not that Tess always wanted it—raw meat was not exactly her favorite—but she ate at least a few bites so as not to insult anyone. Then she stuck with the fruit.

She also observed that they ate leaves, which might tend to make them more like gorillas. But ancient humans also ate leaves. Just like these bigfoot, humans were omnivores—eating basically anything that would help sustain them.

Tess couldn't help but think about the research on the EPAS1 gene when she curled up for the night. Although Missy always snuggled near someone for warmth, and Tess always needed her blanket, the bigfoot never seemed to get cold.

The bigfoot used the caves, but they didn't really need them. The ones with infants tended to stay in caves, but the rest stayed outside—even in the rain. Tess was pretty sure Charlie and his family only used one for Missy's benefit. Was that because they, too, had the EPAS1 gene, like the Nepalese who could live at high altitudes? Was that why bigfoot didn't need shelters? Were they actually genetically programmed to not be as bothered by the cold?

Were they actually *Homo denisova*? Or were they possibly a new species, perhaps hinted at by the jawbone discovery in Taiwan in 2014? Not for the first time, Tess wished her sat phone was working. She really wanted to know what Pax had found out from that hair sample.

Another behavior she noticed was that while the females did the bulk of the child rearing, the children were kept in line by the whole group. Any misbehavior was swiftly handled by whatever adult was nearby. One day, Tess saw a young male pinch an apple from another juvenile, and before the thief had gotten more than a few steps, one of the adult males let out a roar. The juvenile stopped dead and dropped to the ground.

Tess had practically dropped to the ground as well—the scream was that terrifying. The adult bigfoot stormed over to the offending child, and Tess braced herself for the violence. But it never came. The adult stood over the juvenile for a few moments. Then juvenile stood up and returned the stolen fruit. And that was that. The juvenile went back to playing with his friends. It was remarkable.

But despite the shared responsibilities for hunting and keeping the children in line, the bigfoot did have a hierarchy of sorts. Charlie was clearly the leader—the whole group deferred to him—which was probably why he was the one who had brought Tess in. If anyone else had brought a human to this place, the guest would likely not have fared as well. And Kong obviously ran security. He and his lieutenants could often be seen around the periphery of the valley, watching the group. Some of them were always on the other end of the tunnel, and Tess assumed they were keeping a close eye on the land around them.

The guards were primarily male, and entirely of that larger type of bigfoot, but Tess had seen a few females that resembled Kong as well. And although the two types of bigfoot mingled with each other, they did show some tendency to self-segregate.

More than anything Tess wanted to grab some hair samples of the two types of bigfoot and run some tests.

Not for a journal article or conference presentation. No, she wanted to know for herself. She'd spent her life searching for answers to the questions she'd had since that horrible night in the woods, when her father died. Now she had those answers, and they'd only led her to new questions.

And new worries. Tess glanced over at Sugar, who was standing in the middle of her group of friends with Missy hoisted up on her shoulders. Missy had a giant smile on her face, and every once in a while one of the other bigfoot would reach up and pat her leg or back.

Tess thought back to the one phone conversation she'd had with Pax after arriving here. She wasn't sure how much of it he'd understood, but even if she'd put his concerns to rest then, she'd now been gone a long time. Her friends and family would be getting worried. Shelby, too. She missed them, and it was time to get back.

At the same time, she really hated to leave. She watched a female walk past, carrying a small bigfoot only about two feet tall. The infant let out a cry, and the mother quickly cuddled him closer. *How can I leave this?* But she knew she had to.

One more day, she told herself. *Just one more day and then I go.*

CHAPTER SIXTY-TWO

The next morning, Tess woke with a start. A wail echoed through the valley. She looked around, but there was no one in the cave. Even Missy was gone.

Tess hurried outside and found all the bigfoot gathered in the middle of the valley. More cries joined the original, one by one, until the valley rang with sounds of despair.

Tess's heart pounded as she made her way toward the group. *What happened?*

She moved as close as she dared and climbed onto a rock to get a better look. In the center of the pack stood Frank, holding a silver-haired bigfoot in his arms.

Tess's knees went weak; the air left her lungs. Her mind struggled to accept what she was seeing. *No.* "Charlie," she choked out.

Frank let out a scream and fell to his knees. Mary and Sugar rushed to his side. Missy pushed through the group and joined them.

Tess put her hand to her mouth. They were the picture of a family in grief. She watched Frank—his anguish was powerful, overwhelming. Tess had always thought that Mary was Charlie's daughter. But now she saw the truth: Mary was Charlie's daughter-in-law. It was Frank who was Charlie's own child.

Kong appeared at the other end of the valley then. He was holding an entire tree, with the roots still intact. The bigfoot parted to allow him through. He strode between them and stopped ten feet from Frank. A group of male bigfoot approached and wordlessly began to tear up the earth. Giant chunks of ground were thrown to the side. Kong stood waiting, his face impassive.

When the hole was completed, the diggers stepped back, and with a shudder, Frank got to his feet. Tess bit back a sob when he stumbled under Charlie's weight, but he shrugged off another male's attempt to help him. He walked over to the hole and gently placed Charlie inside. Then he knelt there, one hand on Charlie's chest, before stepping back. Mary took one of his hands. Sugar took the other. And Missy wrapped her arms around one of his legs.

Kong gently placed the tree on top of Charlie. He held it there as the diggers refilled the hole with the displaced dirt. Each clod of dirt hid Charlie more and more from her view. She wrapped her arms around her stomach. *This can't be happening.*

In only a few minutes, the tree stood firmly on its own, and Charlie was gone. The men and Kong backed away.

Then, one by one, the members of the tribe walked up to the mound and bowed their heads. Some placed a hand on the trunk of the tree. They walked away in groups of two or three, until at last only Mary, Frank, Sugar, and Missy were left. Then they too walked up to the tree and lay their hands on it, their heads bowed.

Missy placed her hand on the mound of dirt. Even from her vantage point, Tess could see the little girl's shoulders shaking. Missy stepped back and turned to Frank, who leaned down and picked her up. Together the four of them walked back to their cave.

Tess wiped the tears from her cheeks. Her scientific mind recognized that this was why no one had ever found the remains of a bigfoot. But she barely acknowledged that thought. All she could think about was the kind man who had watched the sunset with her every evening, the man who had shared apples with her. The man who had introduced her to this magical place.

Man, she thought, wiping another tear from her cheek. When she began all of this, she thought she had been tracking an animal. Getting to know Charlie, Sugar, and Mary, that had changed. They had become *people*.

Tess made her way down the rocks on wobbly legs. Her mind was assaulted by memories of Charlie. The most powerful of these was the look of affection he had in his eyes whenever he looked at Missy.

Tess's chest felt heavy and her eyes stung with tears.

Checking to make sure no one was going to stop her, she made her way slowly to Charlie's grave. When she reached the tree, she placed her hand on the trunk just as the other members of the tribe had done. "Goodbye, Charlie," she said. "Thank you for being my friend."

The other bigfoot had seen her approach the grave. She knew that. Yet none had intervened. They had accepted her. She glanced down at the upturned earth. *He* had accepted her.

This time she let the tears flow down her cheeks. *I'll keep them safe, Charlie. Whatever I have to do, I'll keep them safe.*

CHAPTER SIXTY-THREE

For the next two days, Tess watched the tribe mourn. Frank was the hardest to watch. He sat in one spot, staring into the distance. He wouldn't allow anyone to come near him except Missy. Missy would lie cuddled in his lap, or would lean against his back and brush his hair down.

Tess longed for her camera to take a picture. At the same time, the moment was so heartbreaking, she wouldn't have felt right violating it. *Some scientist I've turned into.*

And Tess knew she needed to get back to her world. She wanted to stay, but she knew if she didn't touch base soon, a full-fledged search party would be out looking for her, if it wasn't already—and she shuddered to think what would happen if they came here. She had promised Charlie she would keep the bigfoot safe, and to do that, she needed to leave them. Perhaps she could go home, touch base, and then return.

Tess sat up, her back aching from the hard ground. She stretched to work out the kinks and then stood. *It'll be good to sleep in a real bed.*

But even the prospect of her soft mattress didn't dislodge the sadness at having to leave. It wasn't just that they were an undiscovered group of hominids. The scientific angle of this visit had long since vanished. It was the peace here, the contentment she experienced. *This is what life should be.*

She grabbed her pack, which now seemed almost foreign to her, and stepped out from the alcove. A group of juveniles were playing some form of tag—their favorite game, it seemed—with Sugar and Missy in the middle. Sugar spied Tess and loped over. She chattered happily about something. Tess smiled and nodded, which seemed to be all Sugar wanted before she headed back to her friends.

Tess felt a longing to go with her. And a sadness at watching her go. But she shoved it aside. She would contact everybody back home, assure them she was fine, and then head back here again. This wasn't goodbye.

A group of women sat along the edge of the grass, keeping a watchful eye on the juveniles. Tess scanned their faces but didn't see Mary among them. With mild surprise, Tess realized it was easy for her to tell them apart now.

Across the valley, Kong stood with a group of his men. He was staring at Tess with hard eyes. Tess gave him a nod, and he nodded back before turning to his companions.

Then a group of bigfoot emerged from the tunnel across the way. Mary was among them. Tess was glad to have found her even though she dreaded the conversation to come. And it wasn't just the fact of the goodbye that caused her worry, but the realization that she might not even be able to explain to Mary what she needed.

A small kernel of fear took hold. Would they let her go? She considered getting Missy to try and translate for her, but she thought she should try on her own first.

Banishing her doubts, she crossed the valley to Mary. Mary saw her coming and broke off from her group. Tess gestured to an outcrop of rocks. "Sit?" It would be easier to communicate if she wasn't staring up at Mary, trying to see her face.

Mary took a seat, and Tess sat a little above her so they were almost at eye level.

Tess gestured to the tunnel, then pointed to herself, and then back at the tunnel. "I have to go," she said.

Mary stared at her intently, her face unchanged.

"Home. I have to go home."

Tess felt sadness wash over her. She took Mary's hand. "Me too. But it's time."

Mary held Tess's gaze for a long moment before she stood, Tess's hand still clasped in hers. She pulled Tess forward and let out a yell, followed by a series of grunts and hoots. Across the valley, the bigfoot stopped what they were doing and looked over. Most of them then returned to their activities, but some walked toward Mary and Tess. Were they coming to say goodbye?

Then Tess saw a few of the juveniles go over to Missy and pat her on the head. Sugar picked Missy up and hugged her.

"No, no!" Missy yelled, banging on Sugar's chest. But Sugar held on. Frank walked over and took Missy from Sugar. He cradled her in his arms and headed toward Mary and Tess.

Tess frowned, trying to figure out what was going on. And then it hit her.

She stared up at Mary, a new grief bubbling up in her at the sadness she was about to cause. "You want me to take her."

CHAPTER SIXTY-FOUR

Missy lay curled in Frank's arms. As Tess stared up at Frank, she saw the double heartbreak on his face—the loss of his father and now the loss of his adopted daughter.

Tess had worried about Missy's wellbeing here. Apparently the bigfoot had shared those worries. And as much as they cared for Missy—and Tess knew they did, very much—they must have realized that a human girl was not cut out for this life. She needed to go back to her people. So they had made the decision that Tess had been too timid to make. They were putting Missy's wellbeing above their own.

A few of the bigfoot walked up and laid a hand on Missy's back. Missy stayed in Frank's arms, her arms wrapped around his neck in a death grip. Tess understood what the girl was going through. Missy had found her safe place, a place where she was loved and cared for. And now she was being sent away.

Finally, the other members of the tribe drifted off, and only Missy's immediate family—Sugar, Mary, and Frank—remained with Tess. Sugar leaned up and placed a kiss on Missy's cheek.

Then she leaned her head into Missy's and stayed there for a moment before turning and sprinting away.

Tess looked away, tears springing to her eyes. Mary stepped up beside Frank and whispered into Missy's ear. Missy switched her grip from Frank to Mary.

Tess took a step away, giving them some privacy. A shadow fell over her, and she looked up to see that Kong was standing beside her. She shook her head, marveling at how someone so big could move so silently.

He nudged her shoulder, and she turned back toward the little family. Frank had walked away now, his shoulders lower than she had ever seen. It was just Mary left. She clutched Missy to her, tears running down her cheeks.

Tess walked up to her. "I'll take care of her. I promise."

Tess was fully aware of the responsibility she was taking on— but she also had perfect clarity at that moment. She knew exactly why she was here. Charlie had watched her, had made sure she was someone he could trust Missy with. This whole last year had been an audition. An audition leading to this exact moment.

Tess put a hand on Missy's back, just like she'd seen so many others do. "Missy, honey, it's time to go now."

Missy only tightened her grip on Mary.

"I know it's hard, honey, but we do need to go. It's a long walk."

Missy wouldn't even look at her.

Kong took Missy from Mary's arms. Missy let out a wail, but Kong didn't react. He just held her and walked toward the tunnel.

Mary watched her go, and Tess felt her pain. Tess took Mary's hand and gave it a squeeze. "I will take care of her," she promised.

Mary stared into Tess's eyes. Love flowed over Tess then. The feeling was so strong that tears rolled down Tess's cheeks.

"I know," she said.

Tess turned, wiping her cheeks. She headed for the tunnel, shouldering her pack, but really shouldering so much more.

CHAPTER SIXTY-FIVE

K ong carried a crying Missy down the cliff face while one of Kong's lieutenants carried Tess. At the bottom, Tess climbed off the bigfoot, and without a sound or gesture, the large hominid climbed back up.

Tess then turned to Kong. Missy had gone quiet in his arms, but she could see the small girl's shoulders quaking. Tess pointed at Missy. "I'll take her."

Kong ignored her and started to walk through the trees. Tess stared for a minute before scrambling after him.

They walked together in silence for almost two hours. And to be honest, Tess was grateful for the silence. She needed the time to process what had just happened. Every few minutes she would glance at Missy and wonder what exactly she had gotten herself into.

Too soon, Tess began to recognize landmarks. Kong was taking them back to her cabin. *Huh. I didn't realize he knew where I lived.* She paused. *I'm not sure how I feel about that.*

After another hour, Kong stopped suddenly, and Tess nearly

walked into him. Kong didn't appear fearful, but his head was tilted to the side, listening. There must be a human up ahead.

Tess looked at Kong, her eyes going wide. "Give her to me. You have to go. Quickly."

Kong handed her Missy. Tess adjusted the girl in her arms. Somewhere along the way, Missy had fallen asleep, making her dead weight.

A snap of a branch from behind Tess caused her to turn. She scanned the forest. No one was in sight yet, but she knew they were close. She turned back to tell Kong to go—but he had already disappeared.

Tess waded through a small brook and rounded a corner when a voice to her right stopped her.

"Tess?"

She turned, and smiled at the tall, muscular man staring at her with an incredulous look on his face. "Hi, Shawn."

CHAPTER SIXTY-SIX

Dev trekked through the woods scanning the ground for any sign that someone had been through here recently. Tess had been gone for two weeks, and no one had heard a word from her for almost that whole time. She never went out of touch for this long. Pax was manning the radios back at Tess's cabin and keeping all the searchers organized so they didn't run over each other. Shawn was out searching like he had been everyday since they had arrived.

But so far, there had been no sign of her.

Dev pulled out his canteen and took a swallow of water. He knew how easy it was to get turned around out here. And if Tess had gotten hurt...

Dev pictured the hikers he'd found last fall. One had broken his leg. The other had stayed to help. But the coyotes had found them before the searchers did.

A tremble worked its way into Dev's limbs.

Tess is smarter than that. She knows how to handle herself in the woods. She's holed up somewhere, waiting for us to find her.

Dev shoved his water back in his pack. And he intended to do just that.

"Dev," Shawn's voice called over Dev's radio.

He yanked it from his belt. "Dev here."

"I've got her," came Shawn's reply.

Dev stopped, feeling the breath leave his lungs. "Is she all right?"

"She's fine. And she's brought a friend."

Dev felt his eyes go wide. He pictured the giant print he'd found near Tess's camp. "A bigfoot?"

Shawn laughed. "No. This one's feet are pretty small."

"Where are you?"

"I'm east of the cabin, just past the old brook. We'll be at the cabin in another fifteen minutes."

"I'm heading to you now."

Dev shoved the radio in his pack and started east. Before he knew it he was flat out running. He sprinted through the trees.

Five minutes later, he heard Shawn's voice and Tess's answer. He rounded an oak and saw her walking down the path next to Shawn.

Dev took a second to calm his racing heart. He looked Tess over from head to toe. She was a little dirty. Her clothes had seen better days, but she also had no noticeable injuries.

She was beautiful.

She caught sight of him and smiled. It was as if the sun had appeared after a month of rain.

He ran up to her, pulled her into his arms, and twirled her around. She laughed and wrapped her arms around him.

He placed her on the ground and went to kiss her. She ducked her head away. "I am so gross right now."

He held her face in his hands. "I *so* don't care." He caught her in a kiss and felt the planet tilt back into its proper orbit.

Tess leaned in to him. "I missed you too."

"Well, don't worry about the two of us over here," Shawn drawled.

Dev kissed Tess one more time and stepped back, looking at Shawn for the first time. His gaze fell on the little girl and his eyes grew large. "Who have we here?"

"Her name's Missy," Tess said, placing her hand gently on the girl's back.

Dev stared at the cigarette burn on the girl's forearm. A tingling of recognition dawned in the back of his mind. Carefully, he pulled the girl's hair back from her face.

Shock tore through him and he let the hair drop back over the girl's face. "It can't be."

"You know her?" Tess asked.

"Not exactly. But I was part of a countywide search for her. It ended when her father was arrested."

"What was the charge?" Shawn asked.

Dev's gaze went back to the little girl. "Murder."

CHAPTER SIXTY-SEVEN

Tess stared at Dev in disbelief. "Whose murder?"

Dev nudged his chin toward Missy. He spoke quietly. "Hers."

Shawn opened his mouth to ask something more, but they were interrupted by a shout. Pax was running toward them, Abby and Sasha on his heels. The three of them swamped Tess, hugging her as if the world were ending.

"I'm okay, guys," Tess said.

Pax wiped at the tears in the corner of his eyes. "You never do that again, do you hear me? Do you have any idea how worried I've been? We've all been?"

"What he said," Sasha said. She pulled Tess in for another hug.

"I know, I know. I'm sorry. I really am," Tess said.

Abby hung back and watched Tess. "Are you really okay?"

Guilt crashed over Tess. She had never thought that Shawn and Pax would be here and that everyone else would be so worried. "I am. But we need to get her back to the cabin."

They all looked over at Missy with surprise. "Who is she?" Pax asked.

Tess opened her mouth, then shut it. "Let's head back to the cabin and then we can all sit down and talk—*after* I've had a really long shower."

Tess could tell by the looks on everyone's faces that they wanted to argue, but thankfully they all kept their tongues. "You need me to take her?" Dev asked Shawn.

"No, it's okay. I've got her. She doesn't weigh anything," Shawn said.

They headed back to the cabin. Tess had never seen anything so beautiful. Shelby caught sight of her and let out a howl from the front porch, then hobbled down the stairs. Tess broke into a run and met her halfway, dropping to the ground. Shelby whined and barked, letting Tess know exactly how unhappy she was at her for being away so long.

"I know, I know. I'm sorry. I won't do it again, okay?" Tess said before standing.

Missy began to stir, and Tess quickly made her way over to her. She put her hand on Missy's back as the girl's eyelids fluttered open.

Missy's head swung from side to side as she took everyone in.

"It's okay, Missy. These are my friends," Tess said.

"Let's all back away and give Missy a little time to adjust, okay?" Pax said.

Everyone headed to the front porch, leaving Tess alone with Shawn and Missy.

Missy's breaths came out in little pants.

"It's okay," Tess said calmly. "They won't hurt you. They're my family. They're all my family."

Missy's gaze latched on to Tess's and wouldn't let go.

Tess took her hand. "I promise." She gestured to Shawn. "This is my brother-in law, Shawn."

Missy looked up at him.

"Hey there, beautiful," Shawn said softly. And Tess had the distinct impression that Shawn's size put Missy at ease.

Tess indicated the cabin. "That's my home. Would you like to see it?"

Missy looked at the cabin, then at Shelby, then back at Tess, a question in her eyes.

"Shelby's my friend. Would you like to meet her first?"

Shelby was staring up at Missy, her tail wagging. Finally Missy nodded.

Shawn knelt down slowly. Shelby walked up, her tail still wagging, her head held low. Missy reached out tentatively. Her hand came to rest on Shelby's back. Shelby wagged harder and licked Missy's face. Missy smiled. And Tess let out a breath.

Okay. It's going to be okay. But then she remembered Missy's scars and caught Shawn's concerned look.

Well, at least for the moment it is.

CHAPTER SIXTY-EIGHT

An hour later, Tess had gotten in a quick shower and had managed to get everybody out except for Dev and Shawn. Tess was worried that too many people would make Missy nervous.

She had originally intended for only her and Dev to stay, but when Shawn started to leave, Missy's fear had been apparent. Something about him made her feel safe. So Shawn had agreed to stay too.

The only way Tess had managed to get Sasha and Abby to leave was to send them on a shopping trip to pick up some things for Missy. Pax was making a food run. Although Tess appreciated everyone's concern, to be honest, *she* needed less of a crowd as well.

Tess threw on her most comfortable sweats and did a quick blow-dry of her hair before pulling it back in a ponytail. As she looked at herself in the mirror, she could hear Shawn and Dev talking low in the other room. She thought about everything that had happened over the last two weeks. *What am I going to tell them?*

She had puzzled over that ever since she'd realized Missy would be coming with her. Her original plan had been to tell everyone that she had been on the trail of a family of bigfoot for the last two weeks but had lost them. But now that she had Missy with her, that story wouldn't hold water. How was she supposed to explain finding a little girl? *A girl Dev knows something about.*

Well, she'd put it off as long as she could. She stepped out of the bedroom. The first thing she saw was Missy asleep on the couch. Tess had given her a bath and tried to wash her hair as best she could. But it was so matted she knew she would either need professional help to untangle it or a good pair of scissors. That could wait until tomorrow.

Right now, Missy looked like any other kid. She lay curled up in one of Tess's t-shirts. Shelby lay next to her, and Missy's arm was flung over the dog's back.

Dev and Shawn were talking quietly at the kitchen island, a coffee mug in front of each of them. Tess nodded at the mugs. "Any chance there's more of that?"

Shawn stood up and kissed her on the forehead. "Absolutely, sweetheart." He headed for the counter to pour her a cup.

"You all right?" Dev asked, curling his hand around hers.

Tess enjoyed the feel of his hand in hers and gave his hand a squeeze. "Yeah. I'm fine."

He raised an eyebrow.

"Really. I'm sorry I worried everybody."

Shawn put the mug in front of her. "You ready to tell us how you came across Missy?"

Tess hesitated. She turned to Dev. "You said you knew her. Who is she?"

Dev glanced over at the couch and then dropped his voice a little lower. Shawn and Tess leaned in. "She's Melissa Hargrove. She went missing from east of Crescent City over a year ago."

His words stirred the embers of a memory. "I remember that case. Her dad was some sort of criminal, right?"

Dev grimaced. "In and out since he was a teenager for a string of low-level offenses."

"Wait," Shawn said. "Crescent City? That's over a hundred miles from here. You're telling me that little girl walked that distance?"

Tess focused on her mug, thinking how easy that distance would be for a bigfoot to cover, even with a little girl perched on their shoulder. "Are you sure it's her?"

Dev nodded. "Trust me, that little girl's face haunted my dreams and the dreams of a lot of other people for a long time. We searched for weeks, but we never saw any signs of her. She was just gone."

Shawn frowned. "How does a little girl end up in the woods alone? Where were her parents?"

"Her mom died of an overdose almost four years ago. Her dad moved them to a place on the edge of the national park. And he was a piece of work."

Tess pictured the old scars on Missy's body. "Was there a record of abuse?"

"Not when she disappeared—just a lot of suspicion," Dev said. "She'd just started kindergarten. The law had to get involved just to get her to school. Her father got warnings half a dozen times about attendance. And some of the teachers were concerned about the girl's mental state."

"Her mental state?" Tess asked.

"She was withdrawn, didn't interact with other kids. As one put it, she was scared."

Tess's heart broke as she thought about Missy's tortured childhood. And then she'd somehow found peace with a new family, only to have that pulled away from her as well.

But another thought pulled Tess up short. "She won't have to go back to him, will she?"

"I don't know. It's a little complicated," Dev said.

"But he's in prison for her murder, right?" Shawn asked.

"No. Without a body, they couldn't make that stick. But he *was* found guilty of a slew of child abuse charges. They had pictures of old scars, so they were able to make a case."

"That poor kid," Shawn mumbled.

"Before her disappearance, Missy had been meeting with the school psychologist. She drew some pictures that raised a lot of red flags. In fact, they were about to bring a case of child abuse against her father when Missy went missing. It was widely believed he killed her and then hid the body—hence the murder charge."

Tess gasped. "That's horrible."

"What will happen now?" Shawn asked.

"I don't know. But I'm going to have to notify people that she's back." Dev looked at Tess. "You know that, right?"

"Yeah," Tess said.

"So, now it's your turn to talk. How did you come across her?" Dev asked.

Tess looked away. "It was two days ago. I heard a noise I didn't recognize. When I investigated, I found Missy. Her foot had gotten stuck under a rock. She cried out."

"Did you see anyone else around her? Did she say anything?" Dev asked.

Tess shook her head. "No. It was just the two of us. It took two days to hike back out because I needed to slow down for her. And then you guys found us."

Shawn caught her gaze and then looked away. He gave an abrupt nod. "Good thing you found her."

"Yeah," Tess said.

Dev watched her before standing. "Well, I'm going to go call in and let them know she's been found. Do you want me to call Dr. Avery and see if she can come out and look her over?"

Tess shook her head. "No, not until tomorrow. Let's let her adjust a little bit first."

Dev turned to Shawn. "You staying here tonight?"

"Yeah. Pax and I will," Shawn said.

"Okay, good. I'll head back then. I think there's going to be a lot to do." He turned to Tess. "Walk me out?"

Tess nodded, and together they stepped out onto the porch. Tess closed the door behind them.

Dev pulled her into his arms. "I am so glad you're back. I can stay tonight, if you want."

She shook her head. "I'd like you to, but I need to focus on Missy. Make sure she's okay."

"I figured that. But I'll be back after I touch base with Sheriff Cowley."

"Okay." Tess hesitated. "How much of big deal to you think this is going to be?"

"It's going to be a circus," Dev said.

Tess closed her eyes, knowing he was probably right. "Look, I don't want her exposed to that. She's been out there a long time. Too many people will overwhelm her."

"I'll try to keep it to a minimum, but she's going to have to talk to some people."

Tess let out a breath. "I know, I know."

Dev kissed her on the lips. "I'm so glad you're back."

Tess let herself enjoy his warmth. She had missed him. Being in his arms reminded her just how important he'd become in her life.

Dev pulled back and looked down at her. "You know, I went by your camp when you went missing. I followed your trail. And I noticed there was another trail going in the same direction as yours."

Tess's heart pounded and her mind raced.

Dev continued. "You know, when Missy went missing, her father swore up and down that he didn't do anything to her. He said bigfoot took her."

Oh, no.

Dev took Tess's face in his hands. "You don't have to lie to me. And you don't have to tell me today. I know you're exhausted. But I hope you know you can trust me."

Tess felt like crying. "I know. It's never been about trust."

He kissed her on the forehead. "Good. Now get some sleep. We'll talk later."

She watched him walk away, wishing she could tell him to stay. But she needed to talk to Missy. She needed to get their stories straight before the circus began.

CHAPTER SIXTY-NINE

Tess watched as Dev's Jeep disappeared. He knew she wasn't telling the truth. And she hated herself for keeping secrets from him. She was going to come clean, she really was—she just needed a plan first.

She leaned against one of the porch railings. But why hadn't she just come out and told him everything already? Why hadn't she told all of them? She'd known about the bigfoot for weeks. And now with Missy...

She sighed. What was the right thing to do here? She knew she'd need to tell people what had happened, but she had to be very careful who knew, or the tribe would be in danger.

She felt so tired. Maybe after she slept a little she'd be better able to face the decisions ahead of her. Right now, she just wasn't capable of any rational decision-making.

She let herself back into the cabin. When she closed the door, Missy's eyes popped open. Tess hurried over to her. "Hey. It's okay. It's just me." She sat next to Missy on the couch, and the girl climbed into her lap. Tess rubbed her back. "It's okay. You're safe."

Shawn sat on the other end of the couch.

"Do you remember Shawn?" Tess asked the girl.

"He carried me," Missy said.

"That's right, I did," Shawn said gently. "Are you hungry?"

Missy nodded, her eyes big.

"How about I go make you something?"

"That would be great," Tess said.

Shawn smiled. "Be right back." He headed to the kitchen.

Tess watched him for a moment before she turned her attention back to Missy. "Missy?"

Missy looked up at her.

Tess kept her voice as gentle as possible. "Tomorrow, some people are going to ask you questions about where you've been."

Missy ducked her head into Tess's chest.

"I know. I'll see if I can get them to limit how many people speak with you, but you *will* have to speak with some of them." Tess paused, trying to figure out what she needed to say. The only way to protect the bigfoot was to not mention them at all. But how did she tell Missy that without putting too much pressure on her?

"For now, can you just say that you were by yourself in the woods? That you weren't with anyone? I don't think people will understand about your family. And we need to keep them safe."

Missy's bottom lip trembled.

Shoot. Tess hugged her. "It'll be okay. We just won't tell anyone about them, and that way they'll be safe, okay?"

Missy's shoulders shook. "I kept getting hurt. I couldn't keep up with them. So they gave me away." Tears trailed down the girl's cheeks.

"No, no. It's not like that." Tess turned Missy so she was looking right in her eyes. "They did this to protect you. They know the forest isn't a place where you can survive without help. And they risked everything to protect you. They found me. They risked being discovered so that they could get you somewhere you could be safe."

"But they don't want me."

"Oh, honey, they do. Charlie…" Tess stumbled over the word, a stab of grief robbing her voice for a moment. "He made sure I would be able to take care of you. And Mary, she made sure as well. Even Kong was making sure I would be able to take care of you. They love you. They did this *because* they love you."

Tess hugged her tightly. "I saw how difficult it was for them to let you go. They wanted you more than anything. But they put your safety above their own. They love you."

"Are you sure?" Missy asked, her voice both hopeful and scared.

"There is nothing in this world I am more sure of. They love you with all their hearts. And when you love someone, you put what they need ahead of what you want. They could have kept you, but they knew that one day you could get really hurt and they wouldn't be able to save you. And they couldn't take that chance. They care too much about you."

Missy sniffed. "I miss them."

Tess put her chin on the top of Tess's head. "I know, honey. I do too."

"Will I ever see them again?"

"I hope so, sweetheart. I really hope so."

CHAPTER SEVENTY

A few hours later, Tess eased herself away from the bed, where she had settled Missy. It was just past seven. They had slept away the afternoon. Missy was sound asleep with her arm wrapped around Shelby. Shelby lifted her head as Tess rose, but Tess held up her hand. "Stay," she said softly.

Before falling asleep, Missy had cried her little heart out for her family. And Tess had cried right along with her at all the cruelties this one little girl had already faced. And she was terrified of what the future might hold for her.

Tess left the door slightly ajar, so she could hear if Missy woke. Although she hoped the girl would sleep right through until morning.

"She asleep?" Shawn asked from his spot on the couch.

Tess sank down onto the other end of the couch, curling her legs under her. "Yeah."

"Did you get any sleep?"

"A little." She spied Pax in her office, on the phone. "Who's he speaking with?"

"Work. He's arranging to take a little more time off."

Guilt ate at Tess. "I'm sorry for—"

Shawn cut her off. "Don't you say you're sorry. Because what you are is important to us, and we're here for you."

Tess leaned her head on his shoulder. "Thank you for everything. I don't know what I'd do without you two. And you've helped Missy feel safe. I can't thank you enough for that."

The front door opened, and Dev stepped in. Tess started to get up, but he waved her back down.

He leaned down and kissed her on the cheek before taking a seat across from her. "I spoke with Crowley. He's not happy about it, but he agreed to hold off speaking with Missy until tomorrow."

"Thank you," Tess said.

"And I have some more good news—I looked into Missy's custody situation, and her father's parental rights were revoked when she went missing. Even if he wanted to, he couldn't get custody now. So he won't be standing in your way if you want to file for custody." Dev paused. "You... do want to file for custody, right?"

Tess wasn't sure about much right now, but she knew keeping Missy with her was part of the plan. "Yes. I need to know she's taken care of, safe."

"She's been through a lot, hasn't she?" Shawn asked.

Tess nodded, feeling her weariness pull at her.

"Tess?" Dev asked.

"Hmm?"

"We'll help you however we can, but we need to be prepared. Is there any chance someone took her and that they'll come after her?"

Tess shook her head. "No. No one will be coming for her."

"But she wasn't alone out there, was she?" Shawn asked quietly.

Tess debated what to say. She knew she needed to keep the

tribe's secret, but she also knew she was probably going to need some help in order to do that.

She looked at Dev. She knew he would believe her. And he would protect Missy just as strongly as she would.

Her gaze shifted to Shawn. Her brother had chosen well: Shawn was reliable, confident, and just basically a good man. But he was also pragmatic. He respected what she did, but he had healthy doubts about what was out there, if anything. Like a lot of people, he accepted that footprints could be found, but he never really believed in a full-fledged bigfoot.

Well. He was just going to have to get past that.

Pax got off the phone and joined them. He plopped down on the one remaining chair. "Okay, Tess. I've arranged for anyone that needs to speak with you to go through either me or Abby first. And Abby is looking into the legal status of fostering Missy."

"I don't know what I'd do without all of you."

"And you'll never have to," Pax replied.

Tess met Dev's gaze. He sat watching her, waiting for her to decide whether or not to explain what was going on. She let out a breath. "There's something I need to tell you guys."

CHAPTER SEVENTY-ONE

Tess recounted her whole experience with the bigfoot, beginning with finding Charlie's tracks and finishing with Kong disappearing into the woods when he realized Shawn was near. When she was done, Dev, Pax, and Shawn just were staring at her, their eyes wide.

Dev spoke first. "Why didn't you tell me any of this? I mean, back when you first met one of them."

Tess shrugged. "I don't know. It just... It almost felt like I was going to jinx everything if I told anyone what happened."

"What do you want us to do?" Shawn asked.

"Help me keep them safe. They're not animals. They're—people. And if anyone finds out about them, they *will* hunt them down. You know that."

"Maybe not," Pax said. "Not all people are—"

Tess shook her head. "No. You don't understand. In academic circles, the common belief is that no one will believe in bigfoot until someone provides a dead bigfoot—one that can be dissected on a lab table. Someone *will* track them down, kill them, and then reap the rewards of that discovery."

She pictured all the shows she'd seen, hunters giddy at the prospect of taking down a beast like bigfoot.

"You're sure they're not violent?" Shawn asked.

Tess pictured the juveniles playing in the valley, Mary and her family mourning Charlie's death, and the incredible gentleness they had shown to Missy. "No," she said softly, "they're not violent. In all the bigfoot encounters on record, no one's ever been killed. The worst that's happened is that a human has hurt themselves running away."

"And if they're as big as you say they are, they'd certainly be able to catch anyone they wanted, and hurt anyone they intended to. So clearly they don't intend to," Pax said.

He was on her side, just like always. "I think we make them nervous," she said. "They know what we're capable of. They go out of their way to stay away from us. I've heard people say that we need to find them so we can protect them. But they seem to be doing a fine job of that on their own."

"There was really one with you right before I found you?" Shawn asked.

Tess smiled at the incredulous look on Shawn's face. "I call him Kong. He's about ten feet tall and close to a thousand pounds. He carried Missy and only handed her to me when he realized you were nearby."

Shawn shook his head. "It seems impossible."

"I know. But they took care of Missy all this time. And..." She paused. "And I think the reason they came to me in the first place was so that I would bring Missy back. They realized she wouldn't survive with them."

Pax sat back. "Seriously?"

"Yeah. They loved her. And it killed them to let her go. But they did it so she would be safe. And now I need to make sure she *is* safe—and that they are as well."

Pax gave a laugh that held no mirth. "Well, at least you

haven't set yourself up for too difficult a task. But what are you going to do about Hayes?"

Tess started. She had completely forgotten about her grant responsibilities. She shook her head. "Before I went to their valley, I had decided to break the contract. I'll pay back all the money I've received. I can't let them get any evidence that bigfoot exist."

"Do you have the money to do that?" Dev asked.

"I haven't actually spent all that much. I should be able to cover it with the money from Mom's estate."

"You haven't mentioned anything in your updates to him?" Shawn asked.

Tess shook her head. "No, nothing. I had some hair samples that I was planning on sending out to them, but I held off. Now I'm glad I did."

Pax frowned. "A hair sample? Like the one you sent me?"

"Yeah. Did you run it, by the way?" Tess asked.

Pax nodded. "I thought I was going to surprise you with the results, but now they seem a little anticlimactic."

"What did they say?" Dev asked.

"The DNA in the hair sample wasn't a match for either human or ape DNA. But it did match a hominid."

"*Homo denisova,*" Tess said.

Pax leaned back with a sigh. "See? Anticlimactic."

"So they're not apes?" Shawn asked.

Tess thought about Kong. "No. Although I think there are actually two groups of hominids. One of them might actually be *Gigantopithecus,* or at least a close cousin. But no, they're not apes."

"So what are they?" Shawn asked.

"They're humans."

"They can't be humans," Pax said.

"I don't mean to say they're identical to us, of course," Tess explained. "The term 'human' is really broad. Some people define it as *Homo sapiens*. Others define it as any living being that's not an animal. In fact, hominid is a synonym for human. That means in one sense, all hominids are humans."

"So they're more like us than they are like animals?"

Tess shrugged. "So it seems. In fact, most people think denisovans are closer to us than Neanderthals are. Each year, we seem to find more evidence of new hominids that have existed on this planet—more than twenty at last count. And now we know that many of them even coexisted."

Shawn's eyebrows shot up. "Coexisted?"

"For the longest time," Tess said, "academics thought each group was isolated, with no overlap. But fossils keep popping up demonstrating that we've shared this planet, at multiple points in our history, with other humans."

"This is all a little out there," Shawn said.

This time it was Tess who shook her head. "No, it's really not. It's just that we humans have always considered ourselves unique, the top of animal kingdom. The idea that we aren't, even if it's backed by science, is tough to accept. But it doesn't make it any less true."

"How's that possible? I mean, twenty hominids," Shawn said. "We all must have at one point had the same ancestor. So how did we evolve differently?"

"Probably DUF1220," Pax said.

Everyone stopped and stared.

"What?" Pax said. "I'm in PR now, but I do have multiple degrees in the biological sciences. And I keep up with the field, thank you very much."

Shawn cocked an eyebrow. "So what's the deal with DU-whatever-it-is?"

"It's a protein, and researchers believe it may be responsible for increases in human brain capacity. It's what in essence allowed us to evolve. In fact, it's even suggested to be a cause of autism," Dev said.

"I hadn't heard about a link to autism," Tess said. "How so?"

"In autistic individuals, the brain develops extremely rapidly during the first few years of life. Autistic individuals with a higher number of copies of DUF1220 have more severe symptoms of the disorder—repetitive behaviors, communications difficulties, and social deficits. In short, having more copies of DUF1220 results in an increase in brain development. It's a whole new direction for autism research."

"So you're suggesting that maybe different hominids have different numbers of these particular genes, resulting in different hominids?" Shawn asked.

Pax shrugged. "It's just an idea."

"Well, we do know that around six million years ago humans started producing an increased amount of DUF1220, which is what separated us from chimps," Tess said. "Remember, humans and chimps share 99.8 percent of our DNA. So maybe Pax is right—maybe we started developing different levels of DUF1220, creating different hominids."

"And your bigfoot is one of these hominids?" Shawn asked.

"According to the lab results, that seems to be the case," Tess said.

"But if bigfoot *is* a *Homo denisova*, basically a cousin of *Homo sapiens*, why don't they still interact with us?" Pax asked. "You said they did in the past."

Tess looked at Dev, and she knew he was thinking the same thing she was. He turned to Shawn and Pax. "There's this old tale among the Hoopa about the creation of man by the animals, including bigfoot." He recounted the same legend he'd told Tess —the one about animals creating humans, the humans being afraid of the bigfoot, and the bigfoot hiding themselves away so as not to frighten the humans further.

When he was done, Tess said, "I think the story may be true —at least in part. *Homo sapiens* probably really were terrified of bigfoot—or *Homo denisova*. At first, anyway. But then we developed tools, and they didn't. They don't have an opposable thumb, so they don't have the level of dexterity necessary to make use of tools. As a result, we began to outpace them technologically—and I'm guessing we weren't exactly kind about that."

"We probably started killing them off at a fast clip," Shawn said.

"That's my theory," Tess said. "They shifted their behaviors. They became nocturnal. They shunned people. And that's how they've managed to survive."

"It sounds impossible," Pax said.

"It *does* sound impossible," Tess agreed. "Except for the small fact that they exist. And now that we know they exist, we need to make sure that no else does."

"Okay. So how?" Dev asked.

"Well, first, no one can know where Missy has really been this whole time. She was alone in the forest for this last year, okay?"

The men nodded back at her.

Tess turned to Pax. "And I need those results destroyed. No one can know what we found."

"That won't be a problem," Pax said.

Tess let out a breath, feeling relieved. "Good. I have another hair sample in my collection case, which I'll also toss, and then—"

"What hair sample?" Shawn interrupted.

"Part of the sample from Charlie. I only sent Pax some of it. The rest is in my office in my bookcase."

Pax exchanged a look with Shawn. "You mean with your casts?"

Tess narrowed her eyes. "Yes. Why?"

Pax spoke slowly. "I've been using your office since we

arrived. I must have looked at those casts dozens of times. I don't remember seeing a hair sample."

Tess stood up, concerned. "It's there. You must have overlooked it." She hurried into the office. Dev, Shawn, and Pax followed her.

Tess made her way to the case, and her eyes went immediately to the right-hand side of the bottom shelf—the place where she'd placed the hair sample.

That spot was now empty.

Tess unlocked the cabinet and started searching every shelf methodically, pushing casts aside. Dev helped. Tess's panic increased as she continued to look and continued to find nothing. "Where is it?"

When she reached the last shelf, she turned around, stunned. "It was here. I swear it was here."

Pax moved to the desk. "You're sure there's not somewhere else you might have placed it? In your desk maybe?"

Tess shook her head. "No. I put it in the case. But where is it now?"

Dev shook his head. "You're asking the wrong question."

Tess looked up at him, confused.

Dev's voice was grim. "You should be asking who took it."

CHAPTER SEVENTY-TWO

Tess woke up before the sun had broken the horizon. She had been so exhausted last night after speaking with the guys, she had thought she'd sleep forever. And for a while she did sleep deeply, but then Missy had cried out just after midnight, and Tess had pulled her into her arms, and rocked her. It had taken a while, but Missy eventually had drifted back to sleep. Then Tess lay next to her, holding her hand. Before long she also headed back to dreamland.

Tess watched the little girl sleep now, wondering how she had gotten here. Tess had never planned on having a child on her own. Certainly not one who was six and was going to need quite a lot of help to adjust.

But the truth was, the girl had worked her way into Tess's heart. There was no way Tess could trust her wellbeing to someone else. And Tess knew she needed to keep Missy safe, along with her secret family. She owed all of them that much. But the task ahead of her was terrifying.

She slept on and off for a little while longer, but gave up as the sun crept over the horizon. She had too many questions and concerns rolling around her mind. Foremost among them: Who had taken the hair sample? She knew it had to be Hayes, somehow. Which led to the next question: What would he do when he got the results?

Quietly, she rolled off the bed. Missy was curled up with her hand wrapped in Shelby's fur. Tess smiled and then stepped outside the room, closing the door behind her.

"Coffee?" Shawn whispered from the kitchen.

She looked up in surprise and made her way over to him. "I thought I was the only early bird."

"Nope. But Pax is still out. He hasn't slept much for the last week."

Tess cringed. "I'm so sorry."

Shawn waved her words away. "Hey, you were doing what you needed to do. And it's good for him. Gives him a little taste of what's to come."

"Why? Is he planning on increasing the stress and worry in his life?"

"I was thinking more of the lack of sleep which we're hoping might be heading our way soon."

Tess was momentarily confused, and then a smile spread across her face. "You guys are adopting?"

Shawn smiled. "We heard back from the agency. They might have a baby for us in about two months."

Tess hugged him. "That's great. I'm so happy for you two. And I guess that means I'm going to be an aunt."

"Yup." Shawn raised an eyebrow. "And maybe a mother as well?"

Tess glanced back at the bedroom door. "I don't know. It's such a big step. I mean, you guys have been talking about this for two years. Two weeks ago, I wasn't even thinking about it. Heck, two *days* ago I wasn't. It's a lot to take on."

"But you can do it," Pax said as he climbed down the ladder from the loft. He hugged Tess.

She returned the hug. "Sorry. Did we wake you?"

"I heard your voices, but honestly? After these last two weeks, I am *more* than happy to be woken up by you. Our little friend still asleep?"

"Yeah."

Pax leaned into Shawn, who put an arm around him. "Did you tell her?"

"I told her about the adoption agency. I thought I'd leave the other part to you," Shawn said.

Tess looked between the two of them. "What other part?"

Pax grinned. "Well, we thought that if the adoption went through, our little rug rat was going to need some family around. So we were thinking it would be good if we moved back here."

Tess went still. "Are you serious?"

Shawn and Pax grinned.

Tess threw her arms around both of them. "That would be incredible. But what about the Navy? And Pax's work at the genetics lab?"

Pax shrugged. "I can do a lot of stuff remotely, and Shawn has been asked to develop a training program for the state police."

"And I can do that from anywhere," Shawn said. "I'll have to travel anyway. We both will, now and then, but it will be worth it."

Tess stepped back, wiping at a tear in her eye.

"Hey, what's that about?" Pax asked.

"Nothing, it's just—I've missed you guys. And the idea of you being around, well... it's kind of exactly what I need to hear today."

"Well, we're really only moving for the free babysitting," Pax said.

Shawn shook his head. "His attempt at humor. I keep telling him he's not funny."

"I'm hysterical," Pax said.

Tess laughed. "Yes you are."

Pax's face turned serious, and he took Tess's hand. "And we're here for you too. I know taking Missy on is going to be a lot. But you don't have to do it alone."

Tess felt a lump in her throat. "Thanks, guys."

The door to the bedroom creaked open, and Missy's big eyes stared out at them. Tess smiled. "There's our girl now. Are you hungry?"

Missy watched them before giving a timid nod.

"How about some of my famous chocolate chip pancakes?" Tess asked.

Missy's eyes got wider.

"Never had them before?"

Missy shook her head.

"Well, you are in for a treat. Come on—you can help me make them." Tess held out her hand to Missy. And held her breath. The only way this was going to work was if Missy started to trust her.

It seemed like the seconds passed by incredibly slowly. But then Missy opened the door all the way, walked over to Tess, and took her hand.

Tess let out the breath she was holding and tried to force back the tears that wanted to leak from her eyes. "Okay, let's get to work."

CHAPTER SEVENTY-THREE

Scottsdale, Arizona

Thaddeus strode into the office. "Yes sir?"

"Any word from Brannick?" Carter asked.

"Nothing yet, sir. Would you like me to call Abe?"

Carter waved Thaddeus away. "No, I'll handle it myself."

Thaddeus departed, and Carter picked up the phone and punched in the number. He drummed his fingers on the desk.

Abe's voice finally came over the line. "Yeah?"

Carter didn't waste time with hello. "Has Brannick been found?"

"Actually, the search for her was just called off. I swung by the sheriff's office and learned she's back."

"Good. Now where the hell was she?" He paused. "Is she hurt?"

"From all reports she's fine."

"So where the hell has she been?"

"I'm not sure—"

"Find out. Now."

"Will do." Abe disconnected the call. Carter started at the receiver, anger rolling through him. The man had no respect. Carter would have dropped him years ago, but for some jobs, you needed someone like Abe—someone who wasn't so worried about legal versus illegal. Unfortunately, those type of people tended to come with some rough edges.

Carter pulled over Brannick's last report. There was nothing in here. She had been making progress, and then it was as if everything had stopped. *Or she was covering something up.* Had she found them and wanted to keep the credit for herself?

Well, if so, that wasn't going to go very well for her. Carter Hayes had a legion of lawyers who would make her life hell if she tried to go around the contract and lay claim to *his* discovery.

You are becoming a disappointment, Dr. Brannick.

CHAPTER SEVENTY-FOUR

Tess toweled off Missy's shorter hair—which was much shorter now. Tess had decided that scissors were the only option; even the world's greatest hair stylist would not have been able to unravel those knots. So she'd cut off a good ten inches, with Pax hovering at her elbow giving advice. Now Missy's hair hung in ringlets that just reached her shoulders.

Tess grinned as she wrapped the towel around Missy. *Not bad.* "Okay. Let's go find you something to wear."

She gathered up the bags that Sasha and Abby had picked up yesterday. Walking over to the bed, she spread everything out—and struggled not to groan. It was as if something pink and sparkly had exploded all over her bed. Apparently, her two friends had been reliving their little girl dreams of being a princess.

Wary, Tess turned to Missy, hoping she liked something. And that it wasn't too much for a girl who'd basically been in rags for the last year.

Missy's eyes were wide, and she reached out a hand to touch a pink and purple tulle skirt.

"Um, is there anything you like?" Tess asked.

Missy looked up at Tess, then back at the bed. "These are for me?"

"If you want them. My friends got them for you."

Slowly Missy pulled the skirt over and hugged it to her chest.

Tess knelt down. "That's a good choice. Let's see." She pushed through the pile, finding a white shirt with a picture of a ballerina in a similar skirt. "Do you want to wear this with it?"

"Yes," Missy said quietly.

Tess quickly picked out some underwear, socks, and sneakers —all with yet more sparkles on them. She helped Missy dress. When they were done, Missy stood looking down at the skirt, not saying a word. Tess couldn't tell if she liked it or if she was completely freaking out.

She turned Missy by the shoulders and led her over to the standing mirror in the corner. "Well, what do you think?"

Missy stared at herself in the mirror. She reached out a hand, like she was surprised that the reflection was really her.

"Do you like it?" Tess asked.

Missy stared at herself for another long moment, then a smile spread across her face. She shook her hips, watching the skirt swirl around her. She let out a laugh and then twirled in a circle.

Tess laughed with her, watching the joy spread across Missy's face. And then Missy turned and flung her arms around Tess, nearly knocking her over. "Thank you."

Patting Missy on the back, Tess swallowed the lump in her throat. "You are very welcome."

CHAPTER SEVENTY-FIVE

Tess spent the next hour showing Missy around the cabin. The girl loved the stuffed bigfoot that Tess kept in her office and now had it clasped in her arms. But Tess could tell she was getting a little overwhelmed, so Tess brought her to the coffee table and pulled out a jigsaw puzzle Abby and Sasha had added to the bag of clothes. They sat down and worked on it together for the next fifteen minutes, until Tess heard Dev's car in the drive.

"Can you sit with her?" Tess asked Pax.

"I would love to." Pax plopped down on the other side of Missy. "Did I ever tell you how awesome I am at puzzles?"

Tess smiled as she stepped out onto the porch. But her smile didn't last when she saw Sheriff Hank Cowley stepping up to the cabin with Dev.

Missy would have to speak with people—Tess knew that. But she had hoped to give Missy a couple of days before she had to be questioned. Dev had tried to put the sheriff off, but Hank had insisted on seeing her this morning.

Dev gave Tess a reassuring smile. She gave him a small one in return before turning to the sheriff. "Hank."

Hank took off his hat as he made his way up the stairs toward her. He ran a hand over his comb-over, flattening the few long white hairs he had left. "You've caused some people quite a bit of bother, little missy."

Tess ignored the "little missy." He called everyone under the age of fifty either little missy or junior. "So I hear."

"And I also hear you brought Melissa Hargrove back with you."

"Yes. I found her a few days ago."

"Well, how about we go see her?" Hank said.

Tess stepped in front of the door, blocking Hank's way. He raised an impressively bushy eyebrow at her.

Tess gestured to the Adirondack chairs to the right. "I was thinking we could speak out here first. She's been through a lot, and I'd like to keep her interactions to a minimum."

Hank eyed her for a minute before sighing. "All right." He took a seat in one of the chairs. Tess took the other, and Dev leaned against the railing across from them.

"So, where exactly did you find her?" Hank asked.

"Out by Willow's Bluff. She was down by the creek."

Hank narrowed his eyes. "That's tough country out there. She was alone?"

"I didn't see anyone with her, or any evidence of anyone with her."

"And what were you doing that far out?"

Tess shrugged. "I was scouting out to see if there were any spots that I might be able to stake out with my cameras."

"That's state park land. You wouldn't be able to just put up cameras," Hank said.

"I know. But with my grant, I could petition the parks and see if they'd grant me access."

"The grants through Carter Hayes," Dev cut in. "He tends to get doors opened."

"So he does," Hank mumbled. "Now, how come you stayed away so long? From what I hear, you tend not to disappear that long."

"No, usually I don't. But the weather was good, and I didn't have anywhere to be or research to do. So I thought I'd just scope everything out so I could form a plan and get the cameras out as quickly as possible."

"And you didn't think to let anyone know you'd be away for so long?"

Tess cast her eyes down, hoping she looked ashamed of herself. "I should have, I know. But my sat phone was dead, and I just really wanted to get finished. And seeing as I found Missy, I'm glad I did."

Hank grunted. "Suppose so. Have you asked her if she was with anybody? If anybody hurt her?"

"Yes. But she's a little fragile, and to be honest, I don't think she's spoken much for the last year. So it's taking her a little time to get used to speaking again."

Hank rubbed a hand over his head. "Well, her reappearance has us in a bit of a pickle. That father of hers was put away for her disappearance."

"Will he get out?"

Hank shook his head. "No, at least not right away. The child abuse charges were pretty steep. In fact, he may even be up for more charges now that Missy's back."

Tess cringed at the thought of Missy having to face a court-room full of people. "She's not up for testifying."

"Well, maybe not today, but in the future," Hank said.

Tess felt lightheaded at the thought.

"Dev here says you want to take the girl in," Hank said.

"Yes—I feel responsible for her. And she feels safe around me, Pax, and Shawn," Tess said.

Hank got to his feet. "Well, I guess we'll see what the court thinks about that. But now I think it's time for me to speak with her."

Tess opened her mouth, but Hank put up a hand. "Tess, I know you're worried about the girl. But I have ten grandchildren. I promise I'll treat her like I'd want someone to treat them in this situation. All right?"

Tess nodded reluctantly. "Okay."

FROM THE BLOG 'BIGFOOT AMONG US' BY DR. TESS BRANNICK

This will be my last blog. For various reasons, I've decided to take down my website. Thank you for all your support and interest. So here's one last question. This week's question comes from Fiona Hamilton from Phoenix, Arizona. Fiona writes:

I want to believe bigfoot exists. But I just cant get past the fact that no one has caught one. Why do you think that is?

Well, that's the million-dollar question, isn't it? One of the things you have to remember is that bigfoot seems to stay in areas that are completely isolated from humans. Take for example where I am— Northern California. Here, there are four state parks: two in California and two in Oregon. They're all connected and cover five million acres.

To put that in perspective, New York City covers an area of twenty-one thousand acres. These four state parks cover an area twenty-five thousand times larger—an area that is densely packed with trees and no humans. If we're talking about an intelligent being, which we are, who knows the land much better than we do, it's really not that surprising that when we go stomping into the woods, we don't catch sight of them, much less actually physically catch one.

But I think the best explanation may come from David Rains Wallace in his book, The Klamath Knot: Exploration of Myths and Evolution:

"What if another hominid species had emotionally outgrown Homo sapiens, *had not evolved the greed, cruelty, vanity and other 'childishness' that seems to arise with our neotenic nature? What if that animal had come to understand the world well enough that it did not need to construct civilization, a cultural sieve through which to strain perception? Such a creature would understand the forest in a way we cannot."*

And maybe, we should just leave them on their own to live that life.

CHAPTER SEVENTY-SIX

Two days later, Missy sat on the couch next to Pax with her eyes glued to his phone. Hank had been by again, but he had gleaned no additional information. Each of his questions made Tess's heart beat faster, but Missy had said nothing about her other family.

Tess leaned over the back of the couch to get a better look at the screen in Missy's hands. "Uh, what are you doing?"

Pax looked up with a grin. "Showing her how to use the phone."

Missy swiped at the screen and brought up a kids' game.

"She's a natural," Pax said.

Tess shook her head. "I wouldn't have thought that was a priority."

"Hey, in this technologically advanced society, learning technology is as important as learning your ABCs. Speaking of which, I've downloaded an app to help her with that as well."

Tess sighed, but she knew it was probably a good thing. Missy *was* going to have to get used to technology again. So far, Missy's assimilation had gone well. Of course, it had all happened in

Tess's cabin and the woods around it. Tess hadn't taken Missy into town, and the only person who had come by the cabin besides Tess's immediate friends, family, and the sheriff was the pediatrician. The doc had visited yesterday and she said Missy was in good health, although she was going to need some shots.

The pediatrician also agreed to keep quiet about Missy, but Tess knew it was only a matter of time before the world knew that Melissa Hargrove had been found. Tess worried what would happen when news got out.

Abby had managed to get Tess immediate temporary custody, and she had a court date scheduled for a week away, at which time Tess would have to demonstrate her plan for Missy. Which meant school, friends, counseling. Tess felt overwhelmed by everything she needed to do. But it was good to have the deadline, as she needed to get things into place sooner rather than later anyway. She'd set up a meeting with the school principal today, followed by a meeting with the school psychologist.

And if she didn't get moving, she'd be late. She picked up her bag and glanced at Shawn. "You're okay with her?"

Shawn smiled. "We've got this. And you'll only be gone for a little bit."

Tess nodded but made no move to leave. She wasn't really worried about whether Shawn and Pax could handle it. She was worried about whether *she* could handle it. She hated leaving Missy. She stepped over to the couch and sat next to Missy.

Missy glanced up at her with bright eyes. "I won."

The screen in Missy's hand showed fireworks exploding, with the words "Well Done!" splashed across them.

Tess wrapped her arm around Missy. "That's great."

Missy turned back to the phone, and Tess pulled it gently from her hands. "I need to speak with you for a second."

Missy looked up at her expectantly.

"I have to go out for a little while."

An expression of fear crossed Missy's face. "You're leaving?"

"Only for a short time. I need to speak with some teachers at a school, and then I'll be right back."

Missy's eyes looked troubled. Tess would have given anything to know what she was thinking. When Missy spoke, her voice was small. "But you will come back?"

"Oh, honey, I will always come back. We're family. Families stick together."

Missy shook her head. "Not always."

Tess had no answer for that, because it was true. "Maybe. But *we* will. It's you and me kid, okay?"

"Okay," Missy said softly, but Tess got the distinct feeling she didn't believe her.

Tess turned to Shelby. "Come here, girl."

Shelby got tiredly to her feet, her tail wagging. She stopped at Tess's side and put her chin on Tess's lap.

"Do you know Shelby and I have been together for ten years?" Tess said.

Missy's eyebrows shot up.

"And Pax and I have been together since before we were born."

Pax sat down on Missy's other side. "Yup, it's true."

"*Our* family stays together," Tess continued. "And now *you* are part of it. And that's not going to change, okay?"

Missy threw her arms around Tess. "Okay."

Tess hugged her back, promising herself she would do whatever was necessary to make Missy feel safe and to give her the home she deserved.

She was heading to the door when her phone rang. She glanced at the screen before answering. "Hey, Dev. I'm just—"

His words were rushed. "You need to turn on channel nine. It's about Missy. I'm heading to you now." He disconnected the call. Tess stared at her phone.

"What's going on?" Shawn asked.

"That was Dev. He said there's something on the TV we need to see."

Pax gestured to Missy. "Why don't you guys go watch it in your bedroom? Missy and I will stay here."

Shawn and Tess hustled into the bedroom. Tess grabbed the remote and quickly tuned the TV to channel 9. A well-dressed male anchor sat behind a desk. In the corner of the screen was a cartoon figure of bigfoot, and the words "Missing Girl Found" were emblazoned across the bottom.

The anchor smiled. "Stay tuned for our interview with the father of Melissa Hargrove, the girl who just has been found after having gone missing for over a year. And you won't believe who he says took his daughter."

Tess sat heavily on the bed. *Oh no.*

CHAPTER SEVENTY-SEVEN

Tyler flung himself onto the couch in his trailer, his hand over his face. *Bigfoot Must Die* was a huge hit for the cable network, but he was getting so sick of the constant travel, not to mention his idiot guests. This latest one, Cletus Hargrove, was perhaps his worst. The man obviously hadn't bathed in a while, and his shirt—which Tyler was pretty sure was his best—had holes at the armpits and barely covered his giant stomach. Tyler curled his lip just thinking about the man. What he wouldn't give for a well-dressed, well-spoken person to spot a bigfoot. Now *that* would be something different.

A quick knock sounded on his trailer door before it flung open. Tyler didn't open his eyes. Only his producer, Seth Hruby, would dare to do that.

The two had grown up together, then had gone to Hollywood together to make their fortune—Seth behind the camera and Tyler in front. Tyler had the good looks and charisma; Seth had been born with a hooked nose, premature balding, and a round figure that no amount of diet or exercise had been able to change. But he was smart and always seemed to know what would draw in viewers. As much as Tyler hated to admit it, Seth was a big reason why the show was such a hit.

Seth shoved Tyler's feet off the couch.

"Hey," Tyler said.

"Shove over. You have to see this."

With a grumble, Tyler sat up. "No, I don't think I do. I think what I have to do is find a bar where my feet don't stick to the floor and find someone soft to bury myself in for a few hours."

"Later," Seth said. "First you need to see this."

With a heavy sigh to make sure Seth knew just how put out he was, Tyler waved him on. "Fine. Go ahead."

Seth put his iPad down on the table and pulled up a video clip. Tyler blew out a breath, picturing the beer he could be drinking. Seth was good, but too focused. The man just didn't know how to cut loose.

A video appeared on screen, paused, showing a man in a prison uniform. "Dale Hargrove was sentenced to twenty years following the disappearance of his daughter Missy, age five," Seth said. "But Missy has just reappeared, and some reporter was lucky enough to get in and speak with the prisoner. And Dale has some interesting ideas about where his daughter has been for the last year."

Seth hit play.

A haggard man in his fifties, Dale Hargrove had a beard and mustache and looked a little on the emaciated side. But when he spoke, his face was full of life and more than a little anger. "I told the police when she went missing, it was them sasquatch that took her. Missy—she kept drawing these pictures of them and she said they were her friends. And then she goes missing. And now she's back."

"Why do you think she came back if she was with them?"

"They probably got tired of her. She's a lot of work. But make no mistake, the only persons that harmed that girl were the bigfoot."

"But what about the child abuse charges against you? Are you saying you're innocent?"

"Damn right I'm innocent. It was them—*they* hurt her. People better look out. If they took my child, they might take yours too."

Seth paused the video again and looked over at Tyler with a big smile on his face. "I think we just found our way to the big leagues."

CHAPTER SEVENTY-EIGHT

The TV interview with Dale Hargrove had been the starting gun for a full-on race to see which reporter could get the first interview with Missy. The cabin had been besieged, as had Tess's phones and email. Some reporters had made it all the way to the front door, but either Dev or Shawn had been there to run them off. For a week, Tess and Missy holed up in the cabin, feeling like prisoners. And any time Shawn or Pax ventured out, they were hounded, as was Dev.

They'd had their court case yesterday, and the judge had extended Tess's temporary custody. If all went well, it would be converted to permanent custody in six months. Tess was thrilled, and surprised at how quickly Missy had become such an important fixture in her life. It was hard to remember a time before she had Missy with her.

The judge had been kind enough to set the court date very early in the day, so they had managed to avoid all the press—at least on the way there. They hadn't been as lucky afterward. Outside the courthouse, Tess's truck had been swamped. Missy was terrified, and Tess knew she needed to get the girl away from everything, if only for a little while. She decided right then and there that she was taking the girl to her campsite.

The next day, it wasn't even dawn yet when she, Shawn, and Missy ducked out the back of the cabin. Shawn rode one ATV and Tess rode the other with Missy sitting in front of her—with Tess's extra helmet on, of course. Missy smiled almost the whole ride. Tess hugged her and checked on her every few hundred yards, afraid the sound of the machine might spook her. But Missy seemed to love the ride.

At the end of the driving trail and the start of the walking trail, Tess parked in her usual spot, feeling nostalgic. For a year, coming here had been her regular daily routine. And now it felt as if she hadn't been out here in forever. A lump formed in her throat as she realized Charlie wouldn't be visiting her today—or any other day.

Shawn pulled up next to her. "I see why you like it out here. It's beautiful."

Tess climbed off the ATV and helped Missy down. "It sure is. It's really come to life since I was last here." It was true—the leaves were now changing color.

Tess grabbed her pack off the back of the bike and Shawn grabbed his. "It's usually a forty-minute walk from here," Tess said. "But it might take longer with Missy."

Missy grabbed Tess's arm. "Let's go. Let's go."

"Or maybe not." Tess knelt down to look the girl in the eyes. She had debated time and again whether to bring Missy out here. Part of her worried that Missy would try to go back with the bigfoot if they showed up, and part of her worried that her heart would break if they *didn't* show up. "Remember, whatever happens, your home is with us. But your bigfoot family loves you and always will."

Missy's bright eyes turned serious. "I know."

Tess studied the girl, looking for some sign that she really did understand. But until they saw the bigfoot again, she wouldn't know for sure.

Tess stood up and held her hand out to Missy. "Okay, my little friend, let's go."

CHAPTER SEVENTY-NINE

Abe stretched out in the hotel chair. The media was swarming all over the cabin, and Abe could see that not much of interest was going to happen. So, he decided he was owed a nice steak dinner and soft bed.

The phone rang as he was finishing up his omelet on the balcony of his room. He wiped his mouth and answered. "Hello, Thaddeus."

"What's going on? Mr. Hayes is not happy he's learning the girl's identity along with the rest of the world. And now there are all these rumors about bigfoot. Other people are getting involved."

Abe popped a grape in his mouth. "Nothing I could do about that. Once she found the girl, that was out of my control."

"Mr. Hayes wants to know about this girl and where she was found. More importantly, he wants to know if there's any chance she was actually with a bigfoot."

Abe rolled his eyes. These shirts never understood what it took to get that kind of information. What did they think? The woman wrote down an entire accounting of where they'd been and with who and that Abe just needed to steal it?

"We need to find a way to find out what actually happened," Thaddeus continued. "Do you have any way of doing that?"

Abe pushed his plate to the side. "I may, but it'll cost extra."

"You have been paid. The amount for the job was agreed on before you even began."

Abe could picture Thaddeus's face getting redder by the second. "True, but the job is evolving. The risk to me is evolving, and what you want is changing."

Abe could sense Thaddeus seething on the other end of the line. Abe smiled. *Sometimes I just love this job.* "What if I could find proof that she had indeed found bigfoot?" he said.

Thaddeus spoke slowly. "Proof? What kind of proof?"

"A hair sample."

Thaddeus paused. "If the hair sample bore fruit, Mr. Hayes would be very appreciative."

"Well, why don't you put a dollar amount on his appreciation and we'll talk."

"You're sure you can get a hair sample?"

"I saw one in her display case. I can get to it." Abe pulled the little packet from his pocket. He hadn't let it out of his possession since he'd taken it from the cabin. He'd had a feeling it was going to be worth a nice chunk of change, and apparently he was right.

"But how will you get to it with the media and everyone else camped outside?"

Abe smiled. He'd let them stew for a few days and then overnight it to them. "Well, that's why it'll be extra. And why you'll pay me for the extra work and risk required."

CHAPTER EIGHTY

Tess sat in her chair in the camp. Shawn was sitting in the lean-to reading a book, and Missy was leaning against the log, coloring in a coloring book. It had been a peaceful day. In fact, since Tess had returned from the bigfoot's valley, this had been the most peace she had experienced. There was no ringing telephone, nobody driving by just to get a peek.

She closed her eyes. *I should have done this sooner.*

So far there had been no sign of their bigfoot friends, but Tess had seen footprints that told her they'd been here recently. Her smiled faded a little as she watched Missy. Missy hadn't said anything, but Tess knew she was disappointed that they hadn't shown up. Tess wasn't sure what to do about that.

She sat on the ground next to Missy, throwing an arm around her and hugging her in to her side. Missy's coloring had really improved. "That's beautiful," she said.

"Thanks," Missy said shyly.

A shadow passed over them, and Tess looked up. Mary was standing there, a mere ten feet away. She met Tess's gaze and then gazed at Missy. Tess could read the love in that look.

With a catch in the back of her throat, Tess nudged Missy. "Someone's here to see you."

Missy looked up—and went still. And then she was a flurry of movement, sprinting across the space and throwing herself at Mary. Mary caught her, hugged her, and twirled her around.

Then Mary froze. Her eyes narrowed, the hair on the back of her neck stood up, and she emitted a growl from deep in her throat.

Tess whirled around in alarm. She'd forgotten about Shawn. He sat inside the lean-to, staring at Mary, his mouth hanging open.

Tess got to her feet and put her hands up toward Mary. "It's okay. He's a friend."

Missy chattered something in Mary's ear. The hair on the back of Mary's neck lowered.

"Shawn, why don't you come out here?" Tess said. "And move slowly."

"You sure it's safe?" he asked.

"Um... no? But I think it's probably the right move."

"You are *not* filling me with confidence, Tess."

"Sorry."

Shawn slowly crawled out of the lean-to and stood, keeping his empty hands in front of him. Missy clambered down from Mary's arms and ran to him, throwing her arms around him. Shawn ran a hand gently over the little girl's hair, but he kept his eyes on the large bigfoot.

Tess felt the air crackle with tension, but then, like a popped bubble, it was gone. Missy hurried back to Mary and wrapped her arms around the bigfoot's leg.

Shawn stood next to Tess. "I know you already told me about this, but seeing it with my own eyes, that's something altogether different."

Sugar appeared from the trees behind Mary. She, too, kept

her eyes on Shawn as she hurried over to pull Missy into a hug. And then, surprise of surprises, Frank appeared. Missy went still, and with a cry, she ran for the eight-foot-tall bigfoot. He lifted her quickly but gently, hugging her to him.

Shawn gasped, and his voice was filled with awe. "Oh my God."

Tears in her eyes, Tess slipped her hand into Shawn's. "Now you understand why we need to keep them safe."

Shawn spoke softly. "Yes, I do."

CHAPTER EIGHTY-ONE

High Desert State Prison

Susanville, California

The sound of inmates could be heard from the cafeteria down the hall. Tyler straightened his shoulders, keeping a scowl on his face while trying to ignore the fear racing through him. Next to him, Seth looked completely unconcerned as they followed the corrections officer down the hall. And for a moment, Tyler felt jealous, because he was pretty sure Seth's confidence wasn't faked.

At the end of the hall, the officer ran his card through the scanner next to a locked door. A loud buzz filled the air, and the door slid open. Tyler and Seth stepped through, accompanied by prison guard Nate Holmsfeld.

Nate, a skinny, nervous man with acne scars, shifted his feet. "Now, I could really get in trouble for letting you guys speak with him outside of visiting hours."

Tyler nodded at Seth, who reached out to shake Nate's hand, passing him a hundred-dollar bill in the process. "We appreciate you making the exception," Seth said.

Nate slid the money into his shirt pocket. "I *do* love your show." He smiled, showing off teeth in desperate need of a dentist's cleaning. He led Seth and Nate to a small visiting room where inmates spoke with their lawyers.

Tyler straightened his shoulders, liking the respect he was being shown. Nate opened the door and ushered them in. "I'll be back with Dale in a little bit. You guys will have to wait here."

Tyler flashed him the Haven smile. "No problem."

Nate straightened up. "Great. Thank you." He disappeared through the door, locking it behind him.

Seth pulled out a chair and took a seat. But Tyler was too keyed up to sit. He paced. The room was gray like the rest of the prison. The walls were solid cinderblock. An old scarred metal table sat in the middle of the room, a chain lopped across the middle. Tyler nudged his chin toward the chain. "What do you think that's for?"

"To attach handcuffs."

"Yeah, that's what I figured," Tyler said, as if he'd also realized that. He imagined himself in a movie, role-playing the street-hardened cop who came to the prison to interrogate a witness. He could see his name in neon lights.

And if he could just get *this* witness to cooperate, Hollywood really would take notice.

As if on cue, the lock rattled. Tyler placed himself on the side of the room away from the door, with Seth in between. Seth took notice of the move and gave Tyler an exasperated look. But Tyler knew it was the right move. After all, he was the face of the show. He couldn't get hurt, now could he?

Nate stepped through the doorway with Dale Hargrove in tow. The man was smaller than he appeared on TV, only about five foot five. And the orange prison uniform dwarfed him. In fact, he'd had to roll up the bottoms of his pants to keep them from dragging on the ground.

Tyler pushed off from the wall, his hand extended. "Mr. Hargrove, it's a pleasure to meet you. I'm Tyler Haven."

Dale looked at his own cuffed hand and then shook Tyler's hand awkwardly. "Nice to meet you. We get your show in here. I'm a big fan."

"Of course. Oh, and this is my producer, Seth Hruby."

Seth nodded at Dale from the table but didn't get up.

Nate escorted Dale over to the table and helped him sit. "You want him cuffed to the table?"

"Of course not." Tyler grinned at Dale. "We're all friends here."

Dale smiled back.

"I've got rounds. You guys okay for about thirty minutes?" Nate asked.

Tyler's heart rate picked up. He'd thought the guard was going to stay.

Nate nudged his chin toward the table. "There's a panic button there if anything goes wrong. It'll go right to the main guard station. But, try not to push it, okay? Or I'll get in a lot of trouble."

Tyler puffed up his chest. "I'm sure we won't need it."

Nate looked between the three of them before letting himself out the room and once again locking it behind him.

Silence fell in the room. Dale broke it. "So, I guess you guys want to hear about Missy?"

Tyler crossed his arms over his chest. "It's an interesting story."

Dale leaned back in his chair. "What's in it for me?"

Tyler smiled. "We can include an interview with you on the show."

Dale shook his head. "I've already been on TV. I want out of here."

Tyler stared at him. Was he crazy? There was no way—

"That might be possible," Seth said, "but we'll need to hear what you've got first. If it's worthwhile, we'll see what we can do to help you. You know what they say, you scratch my back..."

Dale shifted his gaze between the two of them, then nodded at Seth. Tyler bristled at the insult. So, Dale thought Seth was the power here. Well that just—

Dale started to speak again before Tyler could do anything to correct his misconception. "It started when we moved out to the cabin, after my wife died."

Tyler stowed his annoyance and tried to look sympathetic. He'd practiced the look in the mirror plenty of times, and he was pretty sure he pulled it off. "I'm sorry about that."

Dale shrugged. "She wasn't much to look at, but she took care of the house, so I guess that was something. Anyway, after she died we moved to the cabin. Rent was cheaper."

"How long ago was this?" Seth asked.

"Maybe three years? Anyway, Missy liked to play in the woods. She'd be gone for hours at a time."

"How old was she then?" Seth asked.

"Around four, I think. I asked her about it, and she said she played with some friends. I thought she was crazy. Her mom was, you know. But then I started finding these footprints around the place. I mean, these were giant-sized and not human, I don't care what anybody says. And Missy, she starts drawing these pictures of her and these giant bigfoot. So I knew she'd seen them."

"Did you ever see them?" Tyler asked.

"Once. I'd been away for a few days and drove up to the cabin. Caught one in the headlights, peering in the windows of the cabin."

"Was Missy in the car with you?" Seth asked.

Dale looked surprised. "Nah, she was home."

Tyler didn't like how Seth was taking over his interview. "What makes you think she was with them this last year?" he asked.

"Before she disappeared, they started coming around more often, yelling, banging trees."

"Any idea why?" Seth asked.

Dale shifted his gaze away. "Nah. But anytime Missy cried, they'd show up. And that girl was a crier. And as soon as she was gone, they were gone too."

"Why would they take her?" Seth asked.

Dale shrugged. "Who knows? Now, when do you think you can get me out?"

"We'll see what we can do," Tyler replied. He crossed his arms over his chest. "Tell us a little more about where your cabin was located."

Tyler and Seth peppered Dale with questions until Nate returned. Dale got up from his chair as Nate stepped over to him. "So, when will you guys be able to get me out?" Dale asked.

"We'll be in touch," Seth said.

Nate eyed Seth and Tyler. "Hang tight for a few minutes while I drop him off. Then I'll escort you guys back out."

"Will do," Tyler said.

The door closed behind Nate and Dale, and immediately the smile dropped from Tyler's face. He turned to Seth. "So what do you think?"

"I think that guy is a piece of garbage the world would be better off without."

Tyler stared at him. "What are you talking about?"

Seth's mouth fell open. "You're kidding, right?"

Tyler raised his hands. "What?"

Seth's mouth slammed shut and he shook his head. "He let his four-year-old daughter wander around the woods alone for hours. He left her for days at a time. And have you read the report on him? The girl had cigarette burns on her body."

Tyler shrugged. "So? That's got nothing to do with us."

Seth's mouth became a tight line. "I keep forgetting how little you care about anything not directly related to you."

Tyler glared. "What's that supposed to mean?"

Seth let out a breath. "Nothing. Let's just focus on the story."

"I *was*. Now, if Dale is right, this is the story of a lifetime."

"True."

"So we need to just get verification."

Seth narrowed his eyes. "What did you have in mind?"

Tyler smiled. "I think it's time Missy had her close-up."

CHAPTER EIGHTY-TWO

They had stayed at the camp as long as Tess had dared. She didn't want to head back to the cabin in the dark, but she also hated taking Missy away from her family again. The bigfoot had stayed with them right until the end. In fact, for the first time, it was Tess who left first.

When Tess had at last told Missy it was time to go, Missy had looked at her with big, sad eyes before turning to hug her other family. Tess felt the sadness at their goodbyes. Mary had even hugged Tess, much to Tess's shock.

The walk back to the ATVs was a subdued one. Missy looked asleep on her feet, so after a while, Shawn picked her up and carried her. She fell asleep a few minutes later.

Tess put a hand on Missy's back. "She didn't sleep much last night. She was too excited at the thought of seeing them."

"I still can't believe they're real. But I could see how much they love this little girl."

"They entrusted me to take care of her. I can't let them down."

"You won't," Shawn said.

Hours later, back at the cabin, Tess was curled up on the couch, not really thinking about anything. In fact, she was intentionally trying to keep her mind blank. There were just too many weighty topics for her to focus on.

A sound came from the bedroom. Tess tilted her head, straining to hear. It was Missy; her cries were muffled, but Tess could just make them out. She hurried into the room and knelt down next to the bed. "Missy, honey? Are you all right?"

Missy shook her head, burrowing deeper under the blankets. Tess rested her hand on the trembling girl's head. "Honey, what's wrong?"

Missy shook her head again. Tess looked around as if somehow there was an answer in the dark bedroom. She turned on the small light next to the bed and took a seat beside Missy, nudging her over. "Make some room, kiddo. Do you think you could tell me why you're crying?"

Missy sniffled. "I miss them."

Tess sighed. "I know, honey. And I know they miss you too."

"I don't understand why can't I live with them."

Tess let out a breath. "The bigfoot are amazing people. But their life is suited for people like them. It would be too hard for you. And they're worried that one of these days you would get really hurt, and they would be unable to save you."

Missy nodded, but didn't stop sniffling. "I know." Tess held her close, rocking a little.

Missy looked up after a few minutes. "Could they come live with us?"

Tess smiled at the image of Frank and Mary sitting on her couch and Sugar raiding her fridge. But then the smile dimmed. "I wish they could. But not everybody understands what kind of people they are. Some people would try to hurt them or put them in a cage. It wouldn't be fair to them. They live in nature. They're part of nature."

"I wish I could live like that too."

"You know, I think humans would be better people if we lived a little more like them as well. The bigfoot take nothing from nature but what they need. They have no possessions. I'm not a very materialistic person, yet compared to them..." She sighed. "Not everyone will see it that way. And in order to protect the bigfoot, we need to make sure that nobody knows they exist."

"But they do exist."

"They do. And they love you, just like you love them. And it doesn't matter if you can see them or not see them, they will always love you."

Missy's voice was small. "What if they forget about me?"

"Oh, honey, I saw how much you mean to them. They will never, ever forget you."

Fresh tears appeared in Missy's eyes. "It's not fair."

Tess pushed back Missy's hair. "No. It really isn't. And sometimes, that's how life is—unfair."

"It shouldn't be that way."

"No, it shouldn't."

Missy lowered her head. Sobs shook her shoulders. Tess rubbed them, and she felt like her own heart was breaking. She hugged Missy to her.

"Go ahead and cry. I'll be right here."

CHAPTER EIGHTY-THREE

S eth put the car in park just past the cabin. Tyler looked around him with distaste. They were in the middle of nowhere. They'd arrived in town this morning and had learned where Tess Brannick lived as well as a few things about her just by asking around town. But they had wanted to wait until Tess's brother and brother-in-law were gone before approaching the cabin. Apparently the brother-in law was huge; no need to deal with *that* if they could avoid it.

They'd also learned that Brannick was dating a deputy from in town. But Tyler wasn't concerned about that. He knew that as soon as he smiled at the poor girl, she'd be putty in his hands.

Seth nudged his chin toward the cabin. "You sure you don't want me to come with you?"

Tyler took off his seatbelt. "No. I think this little meeting requires the personal touch."

Seth snorted. "Okay. Good luck."

"Luck is for amateurs." Tyler flipped down the visor and inspected his reflection. He pushed his hair a little to the side and smiled. *Perfection.*

He opened the door and stepped out. Dusting off his jeans, he headed for the cabin. An old Labrador lay sleeping on the front porch.

Tyler kept an eye on the dog as he walked up the stairs. For some reason, dogs never seemed to like him. And to be honest, he didn't really care for the walking flea magnets either. He didn't trust anything that didn't fall for his charms.

He knocked on the door, and the dog lifted her head. She rose slowly to her feet and let out a low growl.

"Take it easy," Tyler said.

The door opened, and Tyler gave a grunt of surprise. He'd been expecting some old gnarled hippie chick. But this woman... well, she was gorgeous in that girl-next-door kind of way. He smiled. *This is going to be easier than I thought.*

Tyler went to lean against the doorway, but the Labrador's snarl stopped him. He glanced warily over at the dog. "Uh, can you call off your dog?"

"No. Who are you?"

Tyler turned back to her, his full-watt smile in place. "Dr. Brannick, I'm Tyler Haven."

"And?"

Shock flooded him. Was it possible she didn't know who he was? "From *Bigfoot Must Die?*"

"Oh, I know who you are," the woman said. "What I don't know is why you're standing on my porch."

"Well, I heard about the young girl you found, and I think it's important for the world to hear her story."

Tess laughed. "No, it's not." She started to close the door.

Tyler put his foot in the door. "I really think we should talk."

Tess reached beside the door and pulled up a shotgun. "And I really think you need to leave before I get annoyed, or my dog gets *more* annoyed."

Tyler took a step back, his hands up. "I think we maybe got off on the wrong foot."

"I don't think there's any way on this earth that you and I could possibly have gotten off on the *right* foot. Now you have thirty seconds to get off my property before I start filling you with holes."

Tyler pulled up another full-watt smile. "Now, Tess—"

"Twenty-five seconds."

Tyler narrowed his eyes. "No need to be such a bitch."

Her eyes hardened. "Ah, so now I'm meeting the *real* Tyler Haven. Get off my porch."

He backed down the stairs and crossed the dirt drive. Tess stepped out onto the porch, keeping her gun trained on him, her dog at her side.

Tyler didn't turn his back on her until he reached the car. He ripped the door open and flung himself into the passenger seat.

Seth was trying to hide a grin but completely failing. "So... how'd it go?"

Tyler gritted his teeth. "Shut up and drive."

CHAPTER EIGHTY-FOUR

Tess watched Tyler Haven drive away. When he was gone, she let out a breath and began to shake. *Damn it.*

"Tess?" Missy called quietly.

Tess whirled around. Missy stood to the side of the door, peering out, her eyes large.

Tess knelt in front of the girl. "It's okay, honey. Nothing to worry about." She pulled Missy into the house, and Shelby trotted in as well. Tess shut the door and returned the shotgun to its usual place.

"Who was he?" Missy asked.

Tess knelt down again so she was eye to eye with her. "Just a man who wanted to ask you some questions about where you've been."

Missy's eyes went large. "Do I have to talk to him?"

Tess shook her head. "No. He's not a cop, not a social worker. He's just nosy."

"I don't want to talk to him."

Tess pulled the girl into her arms. "And you won't have to. I promise."

Missy's next words were muffled into Tess's shoulder. Tess pulled back. "What was that, honey?"

"Will he come back?"

Tess pictured Tyler's face—not the fake one he put on for the cameras, but the real one. "No. I think he's gone," she said, lying with every word.

CHAPTER EIGHTY-FIVE

Darkness had started to fall by the time Pax and Shawn returned from town. Tess had called them after Tyler had left to see what they could find out about him and his show.

"Anything?" Tess asked when they arrived.

Pax slumped onto the couch. "Tyler and his producer have been talking to everybody in town about the bigfoot hereabouts, as well as you and Missy."

Tess shook her head. "Damn it."

Shawn grabbed himself a water from the fridge, then joined them. "Well, Tyler seems to be rubbing people the wrong way, but his producer is said to be less obnoxious. A few people say they told him about their sightings."

Tess groaned. "Oh, that's so not good. So what do you think happens next?"

"Well, it's a given they're going to do a show here," Shawn said. "I don't see any way of stopping that."

"Don't they need permits?" Tess asked.

Pax frowned. "Yes, but the mayor is on their side. And all she can see is tourist dollars."

Shawn placed his hand on Tess's shoulder. "Abby said the order of protection should go through tonight. The show won't be able to come within five hundred feet of you, Missy, or this place."

Tess looked to the open bedroom door, where Missy lay curled in bed with Shelby. "Somehow, that doesn't make me feel better."

"It shouldn't," Pax said. "I called some of my friends who are in the industry. Tyler's a piece of work. He probably thinks this is his ticket. He's not going to go away quietly."

Tess sighed. She hated that they had to deal with this idiot when they had so many more important issues to deal with. "Yeah, I have the feeling we haven't seen the last of Tyler Haven."

"Did Abby send Carter the notice about the contract?" Shawn asked.

"Yeah, and she assures me it's airtight. I've arranged to pay the money back, so I am officially done with Carter Hayes. At least that's one headache gone."

Pax wrapped his arms around Tess, and she leaned her head in to his shoulder. "Well, bright side," he said, "we won't have to worry about Carter Hayes anymore."

Tess pictured the enigmatic businessman. His interest in bigfoot bordered on obsessed. But he would respect her decision, wouldn't he?

"I hope you're right," she said softly.

CHAPTER EIGHTY-SIX

Carter listened impatiently to the CEO droning on about the merits of his corporation. *Oh, please.* The man didn't see the potential in his own company. He kept going with the same old approach his father had gone with. Which in this day and age meant the company would be all but dead in a few short years.

But Carter saw what this oaf could not. He saw that with a few tweaks, this company could lead the way not in circuit chips, but solar. That's where the future lay.

His phone beeped. Results back.

"Mr. Gerund, we'll have to pick this up at another time." He disconnected the videophone without waiting for a response. Gerund needed to think Carter was barely interested in him. It would help seal the deal at a much lower rate and with much less bother.

Carter hit the intercom button. "Thaddeus."

Thaddeus opened the door a few short seconds later and

made his way quickly to the desk, a few sheets of paper in his hands. "Here you go, sir."

Abe had finally managed to snag the sample and had overnighted it. Carter had had it analyzed immediately.

Carter grabbed the results from Thaddeus, and his eyes greedily scanned it. The top half of the page explained the methodology, which Carter ignored. His attention flew to the chart at the bottom of the page. First, the samples the DNA profile had been compared to were listed: brown bear, black bear, human, along with a dozen others. The column on the right indicated that all had been discounted.

Except there was a *similarity* to humans. If he was reading this correctly, that meant this sample came from a creature in the human family, just not a *Homo sapiens*.

Carter flipped to the second page. This page held the more detailed analysis—and it reported exactly what he had been hoping for. The sample matched the family tree of *Homo denisova*. The hair wasn't from an ape. It wasn't from a human. It was from something else.

She found them.

Carter looked down at his legs. "She's done it."

"Sir?" Thaddeus asked.

"We're going to need to move fast. Arrange a videoconference with Brannick immediately."

"Um, sir, she's canceled the grant."

Carter's head whipped up and his eyes narrowed. "What?"

"Well, as I told you, after she went missing for those two weeks, she returned with a little girl. A girl who had herself been missing for over a year."

"So what?"

"Well, according to Dr. Brannick, she's going to halt her research in order to spend time with the girl."

Women and their stupid maternal instincts. Carter's voice was hard. "She can't cancel the grant. We have a contract."

"Actually, sir, she can. Her lawyer worked wording into the contract that allows her to bow out at any point. She has seven business days to return any funds she's used."

"So we have no leverage over her?"

"No, sir. I'm sorry."

Carter glared. "That is not acceptable."

"I know, sir. But Abe is still in the area. I can have him speak with her."

Carter mulled that over. He liked Dr. Brannick. He even respected her. But she had reneged on her word, and that he couldn't allow.

"Do it. And make sure he convinces her to fulfill her contract —*however* he needs to."

CHAPTER EIGHTY-SEVEN

Tess pushed Pax toward the door. "Seriously, go out, have some fun."

"No. We're fine," Pax insisted.

"I love you both, but you need a little time alone. Just go have a nice dinner. Forget about all this craziness for a little while."

Shawn arched an eyebrow. "I could go for a little dinner."

"Good. Now out, both of you. And you're not allowed back here for at least another hour and a half."

"Are you sure?" Pax asked.

Tess smiled. "I appreciate you guys and everything you've done for me. Now go take a little time for yourselves. The media's calmed down a little bit, and Dev said he'll call if Tyler or any of his crew leave town. Missy and I are just going to relax, okay?"

"Okay," Pax said. "But if you need us—"

"We won't," Tess said, opening the door.

Shawn picked up Missy. "Come here, my favorite little girl." He gave her a big hug. Pax reached up and kissed her on the cheek, and then Shawn handed her over to Tess.

"Bye, guys," Missy said.

They headed out onto the porch. Pax turned. "You're sure you don't want—"

"Go," Tess said. "Now."

He laughed. "Okay, okay. I'm going."

Tess smiled as Pax climbed into the car with Shawn. She and Missy stood at the porch railing and waved goodbye. But when the car had disappeared from view, the smile dropped from Tess's face. She scanned the forest around them. She felt like someone was watching them.

Missy tugged on her shirt. "Can we make cupcakes?"

Tess focused her attention on the little girl. "That sounds great. Go wash your hands first."

"Yes!" Missy exclaimed, and she ran into the house.

Tess smiled, but the hair on the back of her neck began to rise. She scanned the trees again. But there was no one there. *You're jumping at shadows.*

Still, as she headed into the cabin, she made sure to lock the door securely behind her.

CHAPTER EIGHTY-EIGHT

Tess and Missy had assembled all the ingredients for the cupcakes on the counter when they heard a knock on the door. Shelby raised her head with a growl.

"Tess?" Missy asked, fear behind her eyes.

"It's probably just your uncles." Tess pulled her phone out of her pocket and pulled up one of Missy's games. "Here. Why don't you go play this in our room while I see what they want, okay?"

Missy took the phone and headed to the bedroom. Tess kept the smile on her face until Missy closed the door; then she dropped it. Damn reporters. She stomped over to the front door. Without opening it, she said, "Who is it?"

"Dr. Brannick? My name is Abe Cascione. I work for Carter Hayes."

Tess sighed and leaned her head against the door. *Crap. I think I would have preferred if it was a reporter.*

"Could I have just five minutes of your time?"

Tess debated what to do. Ever since she'd canceled the grant contract, she'd been expecting something like this. Carter Hayes was not known for giving up easily. She'd already ignored over a dozen calls from him.

She blew out a breath as she unlocked the door. *Five minutes, and I never have to deal with this again.*

But the minute she got a good luck at Abe, Tess rethought her decision to open the door. With a bald head, a boxer's nose, and clothes about two decades out of style, Abe Cascione was not what she would have expected one of Carter Hayes's employees to look like.

Shelby stood just behind Tess, growling softly. *Shelby doesn't like the look of him either.*

Tess stood in the doorway, blocking his entrance. "I've told Mr. Hayes that the contract is done. I've paid him back the money. There's nothing to talk about."

Abe smiled, but the sight only chilled Tess. "Well, you see, Mr. Hayes tested one of those hair samples you collected, and he knows there *is* something to talk about."

Tess's surprise was followed by outrage. "You're the one who stole the sample."

"I have no idea what you're talking about."

Tess started to close the door. "I think this conversation is over."

Abe grabbed the door and shoved it back hard, sending Tess stumbling backward, slamming into one of the club chairs.

Shelby lunged at Abe and grabbed on to his leg. Abe slammed his fist into Shelby's back. Shelby let out a yelp, and Abe kicked her hard in the side, sending her sliding across the floor. Missy appeared in the bedroom doorway with a gasp.

"No! Hide!" Tess yelled as Abe grabbed Tess by her hair.

Abe leaned down and put his mouth right next to her ear. "You know, I'm pretty sure this conversation's just beginning."

CHAPTER EIGHTY-NINE

Pax watched the trees rush by on the side of the road. Shawn reached over and took his hand. "You okay?"

Pax squeezed his husband's hand. "I'm good. Just thinking."

"About what?"

"Tess, Missy, our soon-to-be little one. Everything's changing."

"Are you okay with that?"

"Yeah. I just want to make sure we're there for them. All of them."

"We will be."

Pax's phone buzzed. He picked it up and peered at the screen. "Speaking of which." He answered the call and put it on speaker. "Hey, you must be psychic. We were just talking about you two."

Silence greeted him.

Pax frowned. "Tess?"

Missy's small voice came over the phone. "He's hurting her."

Pax's stomach dropped, and he felt his heart all but stop. "Shawn."

Shawn had already thrown the car into a U-turn and was tearing back toward Tess's cabin. "Talk to her," Shawn ordered, his eyes on the road.

"Where are you, Missy?"

The girl's breaths came out in pants. "In the closet. Tess told me to hide."

"You did the right thing."

"But he's hurting her."

Pax wished he could hug her through the phone. She sounded so scared, so alone. "We're coming, sweetheart. We're coming."

CHAPTER NINETY

Tess lay on the floor of the cabin, her ribs aching. She spit out a wad of blood. "So this is how Hayes gets people to do what he wants?"

Abe reached down and yanked her up by the hair. "He's a determined man. He understands that different problems require different solutions."

"And what? I'm a problem?"

Abe laughed. "Not for long." He flung her toward the couch. Tess's knee banged into the coffee table and she let out a grunt. The crayons Missy had been using this morning went flying, along with the glue.

Her eyes traveled to where Shelby lay. The dog hadn't moved since this brute had hurt her. Her blood began to boil. As she pushed herself up against the couch, her hand slipped between the cushions and brushed something metal. *Scissors.* She grasped them and slid them up her sleeve.

Turning, she glared at Abe. "What do you want?"

"I want to know exactly where you found that hair."

"Why?"

Abe shrugged. "I have no idea. But that's what the boss wants."

"And if I don't tell you?"

Abe smiled and cracked his knuckles. "Oh, you will. The only question is how much pain you want to experience before you do." He nodded toward the bedroom. "And how much *she* experiences."

Tess clenched her fists. "You will *not* touch her."

"Well, that's up to you now, isn't it?"

He reached for her. Tess slipped the scissors out of her sleeve and into her hand. When he grabbed her hair and pulled her up. Tess shoved the scissors into his chest in an upward motion, right under his ribs.

He let out a yell and backhanded her. Her cheek exploded with pain, and she crashed back onto the couch.

Abe stared down at the scissors sticking out of his chest before he lunged for Tess. "You bitch!"

She scrambled off the couch, but slipped and landed with a thud on the floor. Crawling away on her hands and knees, she stumbled to her feet and ran to the kitchen.

Abe yanked the scissors out of his stomach, then marched toward her menacingly. "You know, I *was* being nice. But now I'm pissed."

Tess backed up against the stove. Behind her, she wrapped a hand around the handle of the frying pan she'd used to make eggs that morning. As Abe charged at her, she swung for all she was worth. The pan slammed into his shoulder and he stumbled sideways with a grunt. She brought the pan back up, backhand, and caught him under the chin.

The front door flew open and Shawn sprinted across the room. He grabbed Abe by the back of his shirt and his neck, yanked him off his feet, and body slammed him, face first, into the ground. The floor shook with the force. Shawn grabbed the back of Abe's head and slammed his face into the ground again for good measure.

Pax appeared in the door, his eyes wide. He started for Tess, but she waved him off, pushing away from the stove. "Missy. Get Missy. Bedroom."

Pax changed direction and disappeared into the bedroom.

"Shawn?" Tess asked. Tess had never seen Shawn angry before; he was always so easygoing. She had sometimes wondered how he was as a SEAL. And now she knew. He was a warrior through and through.

"He's out," Shawn said. "You okay?"

Tess grimaced. "I'll live." Her ribs ached, but she forgot all about them when she remembered Shelby. She ran over and knelt at the dog's side. "Hey, girl."

Shelby didn't get up, but she was awake and breathing. She gave a whimper and a feeble wag of her tail.

Tess lowered her head to Shelby's. "You'll be okay. We'll get you fixed up like new."

She raised her head as Pax reappeared, Missy wrapped protectively in his arms. He knelt down beside Tess.

"You okay, Missy?" Tess asked.

A tear rolled down the girl's cheek as she nodded. Tess wiped it away. *She's shed too many tears for one so young.*

"She called us," Pax said. "Told us you were in trouble."

Tess rubbed Missy's back. "You did the right thing. I'm so proud of you." Then she glared at Abe. Shawn still had the man pinned to the floor, his arms behind his back, and Tess could feel Shawn's anger.

She was angry too. Furious. She wanted to kill Abe for scaring Missy, and that desire scared the hell out of her.

She turned away from him. *Bastard.*

But she knew *he* wasn't the real villain here. Abe was just a puppet—one whose strings had been cut.

It was the puppet master she still had to worry about.

CHAPTER NINETY-ONE

Tess walked behind Shawn as he carried Shelby outside to Madge's truck. She wanted more than anything to go with Shelby to the vet, but she couldn't leave Missy alone, and she didn't think the cold, sterile waiting room of Happy Tails—the one and only vet in the area—was what Missy needed right now.

Madge opened the passenger door of her F150, and Shawn gently placed Shelby on the seat while Madge put her arms around Tess. "Don't worry, sweetie. I'll take good care of her. And I'll call as soon as I know anything."

Tess only nodded, not trusting herself to speak. Shelby had been her constant companion for ten years. She couldn't imagine her life without her.

Madge's face went cold when she spotted Abe in the back of Dev's cruiser. "You make sure Dev doesn't let that piece of garbage make it to the jail alive."

Tears in her throat, Tess gave a little laugh, knowing Madge meant every word. "Not sure he can do that, but I like the idea."

Madge gave her another squeeze before heading for the

driver's door. "Take care of that little girl, and I'll take care of this one."

Tess walked to the open passenger door where Shawn stood rubbing Shelby's head. He looked at Tess. "She's tough. She'll be all right." He clapped Tess's shoulder and headed back inside the cabin.

Tess leaned down to kiss Shelby's head. "You have to be all right, you hear me? You and I have to take care of our little girl, okay?"

Shelby gave her a tired wag.

With a shuddering breath, Tess stepped back and closed the door. Madge revved the engine and pulled away. Tess watched them go, wrapping her arms around herself.

Once again, the image of Abe kicking Shelby appeared unbidden in her mind. Tears burned the backs of her eyes. People called bigfoot monsters—but she'd seen no evidence of that. It was humans who were the real monsters. Monsters who killed or hurt one another for their own gain.

And it was Carter Hayes who had sent that monster after her. Which meant he was a monster too—one with deep pockets and a long reach.

Tess wrapped her arms around herself, feeling cold but knowing it wasn't from the air surrounding her. This cold went much deeper. She looked back at her little house. The day she'd bought it, she had been filled with optimism at what the future held. And now...

Now I need to figure out a way to protect everyone I care about from being destroyed by Carter Hayes.

CHAPTER NINETY-TWO

Tess sat on the bed with Missy, rubbing her back, Dev at her side. Tess's ribs ached, and Dev wanted her to go to the hospital, but she knew they weren't broken—although it wasn't for lack of trying on Abe's part.

Yet even bruised ribs proved to be pretty painful. Every time she moved or even breathed too deeply, pain shot through her side. Shawn had wrapped her chest tightly, but she still gasped when she moved too quickly.

After Tess had seen Shelby off, Missy had run to Tess and had refused to let her go. She'd stayed in Tess's lap the entire time Dev and Hank had questioned her. In fact, she hadn't fallen asleep until just a short while ago.

"She doesn't deserve this," Dev said quietly.

"No, she doesn't." Tess hated that she couldn't give Missy a peaceful home. The poor girl had started with the world's worst father and then found peace in the most unlikely of places, only to have it yanked away again. And now she had Carter Hayes adding more violence to a young life that had already seen too much of it.

She curled her fists, wanting to hit something. *How could anyone be so cruel?*

"Are you coming?" Dev asked.

They were going to talk about their next steps, but they'd agreed to wait until Missy was settled.

"I'll be out in a minute."

Dev kissed her on her cheek. "Take your time."

Thirty minutes later, Tess was still sitting beside Missy. She couldn't seem to make herself leave. A shadow fell across the bed as Pax made his way into the room. He sat gently on the bed next to Tess. "You two okay in here?"

Tess nodded.

"Sasha and Abby are here for the talk."

Tess nodded again but made no move to leave.

Pax put a hand on her shoulder. "You don't have to lie to me. You've never been very good at it."

She clasped his hand but kept her gaze on Missy. "They're so determined to get to the bigfoot, they're willing to hurt a little girl to do it. How do I fight that?"

"We'll figure out a way."

"She's already been through so much. I—" Tears choked off her words.

Pax pulled her into his arms. Tess let the tears flow. She knew if she didn't, they'd eventually overwhelm her. After a few minutes, she pulled back and wiped at her eyes. "Thanks."

"That's what twin brothers are for."

"I suppose we need to go talk to the gang. Figure out our next steps."

Pax gestured to Missy. "I'll stay with her. You guys can fill me in later."

"You sure?"

Pax placed his hand gently on Missy's back. "Yeah. I'd rather she not be alone, and to be honest, I'm too angry to think straight right now. So I won't be much help."

Tess took a long look at her brother. She could see that he was angry. His jaw was taut, and his eyes had a hard edge to them. Pax was rarely angry. Even growing up, he was always the even-tempered one.

Tess took his hand. "Just being here, you're helping. Thank you for putting your life on hold."

Pax shook his head. "We haven't put our life on hold. We just put our jobs on hold."

Tess kissed his cheek. "Well, whatever you want to call it, thank you."

"You're welcome. Now go, before you make both of us cry again."

Tess leaned down to kiss Missy on the forehead. She sucked in a breath as pain pierced her chest, then winced as a sharp inhale caused her yet another piercing pain.

"You okay?" Pax asked, concerned.

Tess stood. "No. But I will be as soon as we take down Carter Hayes."

CHAPTER NINETY-THREE

As soon as Tess stepped out of the bedroom, Sasha flew across the room and engulfed her in a hug.

At Tess's first gasp of pain, though, Sasha jumped back. "Sorry, sorry."

Tess let out a breath as the pain passed. "It's okay. I'll risk a little pain for a hug any day."

Sasha shook her head, her lips forming a tight line. "I can't believe that asshole did this. To you, Missy, and Shelby." Her hand flew to her mouth and tears sprang to her eyes.

Abby came over and threw an arm around Sasha. "It'll be all right. We'll figure out a way to keep them safe."

Tess settled onto the couch next to Dev. He took her hand. "You need anything?"

She squeezed his hand. "This is all I need right now."

Abby and Shawn took the two club chairs, and Sasha sat on the couch next to Dev. Abby looked around the group. "Okay. We know Carter Hayes is behind this. The question is why, and how do we keep him at bay?"

Tess exchanged a glance with Dev; he met her look with a

nod. He would keep her secret if she wanted him to, as would Pax and Shawn, but she knew that to form a real solution, they were going to need more than that.

She took a breath. "I found a sample of bigfoot hair a few weeks ago. While I was away, someone broke in and took it. I'm guessing it was Abe, the man who attacked me and Shelby. And I believe he gave it to Carter Hayes."

Sasha frowned. "So why does that matter? I mean, you provide him samples as part of your grant, right?"

Tess hesitated.

Abby answered for her. "She terminated her contract with Hayes."

Sasha's eyes went wide. "What? Why would you do that? That was your dream grant."

Tess sighed. "It was. But then things changed."

"What changed? Missy?" Sasha asked.

"No. It started changing before that. I just didn't realize it." She took a breath and looked around the group. "It began with a friend I call Charlie."

CHAPTER NINETY-FOUR

The storyboards were lined up along the wall in Tyler's camper. He pointed to the one in the bottom right, which depicted Tess's cabin. "We need to get those shots early in the morning, before anybody's up. And maybe late at night, when the shadows fall across it. That'll give it a nice ominous feel."

"I can use a lens that will darken the shot, increase the appearance of shadows," Tyler's cameraman said. Tyler had no idea what the man's name was, despite the fact that he had been with Tyler for three years.

Tyler slapped him on the shoulder. "Great."

The door to the cabin opened and Seth stepped in. Tyler turned back to the cameraman. "Make sure everything's ready to go first thing in the morning."

"Will do." The cameraman gathered his stuff and slid out past Seth. "Seth."

Seth nodded at him. "Oscar."

Oscar. Of course. And of course Seth knew the man's name. Seth knew everybody's name.

Seth walked over to the storyboards, and Tyler took a sip of his coffee with a smile. This was the first time he'd created the storyboards himself. Usually Seth did it. But Tyler hadn't wanted to trust this story to him. After all, this was going to be *the* story.

Tyler gave Seth some time to look everything over. Finally, he couldn't wait any longer. "Well?"

Seth turned around. "What's this?" He gestured to Tess's cabin.

"We're going to get some shots of the cabin. And I was thinking we could spend some time out there and hopefully get a few shots of the kid."

Seth's mouth fell open. "You want to stalk a kid?"

Tyler waved him away. "She's news whether she likes it or not, which makes her fair game."

"She's *six*, Tyler. And she's probably traumatized. And you want to—what? Leap out at her from the trees?"

Tyler sat back surprised, envisioning that. "Actually, that's not a bad idea. We could—"

"What is *wrong* with you?" Seth yelled.

Tyler stopped and stared at Seth. "What's wrong with *me*? What the hell is wrong with *you*? This is the show that's going to send us into the stratosphere, and all you've done is drag your feet."

"Do you even know what happened to them today? The woman and that little girl? They were both attacked in Brannick's cabin."

"So?"

Seth ran his hand over his face. "Look, you want to go out into the woods and shoot some footage—fine. You want to interview some people in town or even that useless father of hers—fine. But the kid's been through enough. She doesn't need us traipsing around and traumatizing her some more."

"Been through enough? Seriously? That *kid* is our ticket to national exposure. And if she's already been traumatized, us asking her some questions won't make it any worse."

Seth stared at Tyler. Seconds dragged by.

"What?" Tyler demanded.

"You know, we've been friends since we were kids. And I know you're amazingly self-involved. But I never imagined you'd put your personal goals ahead of a kid's welfare. This is wrong."

Tyler felt the blood rush to his cheeks. "No, what's wrong is that my *producer* is trying to ruin what could be the best show of my career! What's *wrong* is that instead of leading this charge, you're standing in the way."

Seth pointed at the storyboards. "You really don't see that *this* crosses a line, do you?"

"There *is* no line. Not when it comes to a story."

Seth shook his head. "I can't do this. I *won't* do this."

"You're refusing to help? This is your job."

Seth turned and headed for the door. "Not anymore."

CHAPTER NINETY-FIVE

S asha wiped at her eyes. "So they gave her to you to keep her safe?"

"Yes. They loved her—still do. But they knew she couldn't survive out there. I get the feeling that wasn't her first illness."

"That's just amazing. I mean, they really exist. And they're... Well, what are they?" Abby asked.

"They're something unique. They're a primitive type of human," Tess said. "Actually, 'primitive' is not the right word. They're a *different* type of human. I mean, if you saw them together, you'd understand better. But they respect nature. They understand it. They have no possessions—none at all. I think that's why no one's found them before. They can just pick up and move without having to take a thing with them."

"Would it really be so bad if they were found?" Sasha said. "I mean, I'd love to see something like that."

Tess shook her head. "See them how? Put them in a zoo? Give them a little cell where people can peer at them? Or worse, have some hunter take one or more down, drag the bodies back, and show them to the world? It would be a media circus. And their way of life would be completely destroyed."

"It would be like the European settlers rousting the Native Americans," Dev said quietly.

"Or any other conquering group," Shawn said. "And besides, they seem to be getting along just fine without us."

"Any chance we could make that argument to Carter Hayes?" Sasha asked.

Tess shook her head. "We could, but I'm certain it wouldn't change his mind. The financial incentive for finding bigfoot is mind-boggling. I mean, here's a close human relative who is incredibly strong and fast. And Hayes has contracts with the military. He would have to be looking to exploit that. See if there was a way to adapt their strength and speed for our use."

"Not to mention the marketing angle," Shawn said.

Abby nodded. "The merchandizing rights alone would be through the roof. He'd make millions."

"So how do we stop him?" Sasha asked quietly.

No one answered her. Tess suddenly felt overcome with guilt. "I never should have signed that stupid contract. I could have just done my research as I always have, and no one would have known anything. But I never thought I would actually *find* them. I mean, not like this. I thought if I was lucky I'd find some better prints or hair, maybe get a clear picture of one of them. But a group? A society? Actually interacting with them? *Living* with them for two weeks? Nothing like that ever even crossed my mind."

Dev squeezed her hand. "You can't beat yourself up for that. I mean, people have been looking for bigfoot for centuries. And no one's found them."

"Actually, that's not entirely true," Tess said. "There were reports that in the Middle Ages in Europe, a few bigfoot were captured at different times. But because there was so little communication between groups, it didn't destroy their way of life. That's all changed now. With our instant global communication, the entire world will know about bigfoot mere seconds after their existence is announced. And people from all over will pour into these woods, and into every other area that is hypothesized to house bigfoot. We'll destroy everything."

Everyone went quiet—all of them thinking about what could essentially be genocide if they didn't stop Hayes.

"Okay," Abby said. "Let's start with our legal options. Bigfoot is not a legally recognized creature. In fact, there's only one county in the United States where it's been declared illegal to kill a bigfoot."

"So, if someone kills one, it's no big deal?" Sasha asked, her eyes wide.

"Unfortunately, yes," Abby said.

"Any way to change that?" Tess asked.

"Well, it kind of depends on their legal categorization. If we can get them declared human, then the usual penalties would apply."

"Unless someone declares self-defense," Shawn said.

"Well, yeah," Abby said. "And I suppose if they're as big as you say they are, it wouldn't take much to convince a judge that someone felt their life was in jeopardy."

"And if we have them declared an animal?" Dev asked.

"Then I'm guessing they'd be protected by the endangered species law. But even then, it'll take over a year to get them put on the list, at a minimum. And if someone kills one, they can still say that they thought they were in mortal danger."

"So the law's not going to be much help," Tess said.

"It might," Abby said, "depending on where the bigfoot are. If they're in an area where hunting isn't allowed, like private property or a state park, we could prevent people from hunting them."

Tess's hopes dimmed even further. "They're not. At least, they weren't the last time I saw them."

"And even if they were, do you really think that would stop Hayes from going after them?" Shawn said. "He'll just pay someone to take the prison time. And there are plenty of people who'd be willing to take that job on for the right price."

"Okay, so what do we do?" Tess asked.

"We need to hit him where it hurts," Shawn said.

"And where's that?" Sasha asked.

"His wallet."

"Okay," Tess said. "And how do we do that?"

Only silence greeted her.

Tess closed her eyes. *This is impossible.*

CHAPTER NINETY-SIX

Three days later, they were no closer to an answer. And real life—and the responsibilities that came with it—were beginning to intrude. Tess stared at the bills in front of her. Now that she had turned down the grant, she had to figure out a way to make some money. She'd already spoken with Eric, and he'd told her that the state park service was hiring. But even with his help pushing her application through, it was going to take some time.

Missy came running up to Tess. "Can I go outside?"

Tess forced her negative thoughts away, placing her hands on Missy's hips. "What's that, honey?"

"I finished my letters and numbers. Can I go out?"

Dev stood up from the couch where he'd been helping Missy. "Yup. I checked them over, and she did everything perfect."

Tess tried to ignore the image she had in her mind of Abe lurking out in the trees. *He's still locked up,* she told herself. "Okay. But stay near the cabin."

"I will," Missy said.

She ran for the door. Tess watched her go with mixed feelings. The therapist had said it was important for Missy to regain some independence, and small things, like playing outside by herself, were critical in that. But Tess was still uncomfortable with the idea.

At least Dev had gotten a few people from his tribe to set up a small camp a ways down the road; they were keeping the reporters away. Only people with actual business were permitted to come by now.

Dev sat down across from Tess. "Everything okay?"

Tess bit her lip as all her worries came flooding back. She shook her head and gestured to the papers in front of her. "I'm feeling a little overwhelmed."

"Why don't you let me help?"

Tess shook her head before he even finished getting the question out. She tried to pull her hand away. "No. I'm not taking any money from you."

"Hey, stop. Look at me."

Dev waited. Finally Tess met his gaze.

"This is not charity," he said. "I love you. I love Missy. Don't force me to stand by while you shoulder something alone you don't need to."

Tess's heart began to beat a little faster. "You love me?"

"I thought that was kind of obvious."

"Maybe... but a girl likes to hear the words."

Dev tugged her over to him and onto his lap. "I love you, Tess Brannick. You are the most amazing woman I have ever met, and I am going to love you until the day I die."

"I love you too, Dev."

Their lips met, and Tess felt her worries slip away. She wasn't alone in this.

Shelby began to growl, and Tess lifted her head. "What's the matter, girl?"

Shelby was staring at the door, the hair on the back of her neck standing up.

And then from somewhere outside, Missy screamed.

CHAPTER NINETY-SEVEN

Tess bolted out of the cabin with Dev right behind her. A man and woman, with *Bigfoot Must Die* emblazoned across the back of their sweatshirts, had Missy backed up against a tree. The man held a TV camera.

"Come on, Missy," the woman said. "We just want to know who you were with when you were gone."

Missy shook her head, her eyes impossibly large.

Tess was overcome by rage and a need to protect. "Get away from her!" she yelled as she sprinted across the yard.

The couple ignored her. Tess shoved the man and his camera, sending him sprawling.

The woman leaped back, and Tess advanced on her, her hands fisted at her side. "Get out of here."

The woman spluttered, "We have—"

Dev grabbed the woman from behind. "You are under arrest for trespassing and harassment."

The man stumbled to his feet, his lip bleeding. "You need to arrest *her* for assault!"

Dev narrowed his eyes. "You'll be lucky if *I* don't hit you. Tess, hold her."

Tess gripped the woman while Dev cuffed the man's hands behind his back. Then he took the woman from Tess. "I've got this. You get Missy."

Tess nodded, trying to calm down. She was so angry she was shaking. Taking a breath, she turned. When she saw Shelby painfully trying to climb down the stairs, her blood boiled even more.

Missy was still backed up against the tree, her eyes locked on Dev and his two captives. Tess knelt down in front of her. "Missy? Honey?"

Missy's big eyes turned to Tess. Tears swam in them. Tess pulled Missy into her arms. "It's okay, honey. I've got you."

Missy's shoulders shook, and each sob was like a stab to Tess's chest. She wrapped Missy in her arms and turned for the cabin. At the stairs, she looked over her shoulder and glared at the two who were now locked in the back of Dev's car. Someone needed to teach Tyler Haven a lesson. And if the world was even slightly fair, he would learn that lesson soon.

CHAPTER NINETY-EIGHT

Abe strode out of the Beauford courthouse without even a glance at the high-priced lawyer walking beside him. *Asshole probably wants a thank-you.* He grunted. *Right—for doing his job.*

His phone rang, and he knew without even looking who was on the other end. He punched the answer button as he walked away from the lawyer. "Yeah?"

"What the hell happened?" Carter yelled. Abe paused in mid-step. He'd never heard Carter angry before.

"That brother-in law of hers came back. Guy's built like a mountain. Oh, and I'm fine. Thanks for asking."

"I don't care how *you* are. I pay you for *results*, and these are not the results I was expecting."

Abe clenched his jaw. His knuckles turned white from gripping the phone. He didn't need this overfed suit telling him what he should be doing. But at the same time, Carter *was* his meal ticket.

"Is there any chance Brannick will tell us what we need to know?" Carter asked.

"Doubtful. Unless you want me to go after the little girl. She'd probably do anything to keep that one safe."

Carter blew out a breath. "No. I never should have agreed to this approach anyway. She's one of those do-gooder types; she won't be cowed. And now I'm guessing she won't let anyone near that little girl."

Abe knew he was probably right. Although he wouldn't mind a rematch with the big guy. Of course, he planned on bringing a gun for that fight—just to even the playing field.

"Is there another play?" Carter asked.

Abe paused. Inside the jail, one of the guys from that stupid reality show had been in the cell next to him, crying almost non-stop. That was not a man set up for hard time.

"You don't really care about her, though, right?" Abe said. "You just want to know where the bigfoot have been?"

"Yes."

Abe smiled as an idea popped into his mind. "Well, I may have just the thing."

CHAPTER NINETY-NINE

The trees around them blocked out what little light was left in the sky. It would be dark soon. Tyler turned to Oscar. "You have the shot ready?"

"Yup. As soon as the rest of the light disappears, we're ready to go."

Tyler looked around, uneasy. He might host a show that was based on incidents in the wild, but personally, he was much more comfortable in the lap of civilization. The truth was, he'd never even been camping. Whenever the show called for shots of him in a tent, he'd pop in and do the shots and then go right back to his trailer.

"You, uh, you're sure you know how to get back, right?" Tyler asked.

Oscar grinned. "Got the GPS. We're good."

Tyler had to admit, the cameraman's confidence helped calm his nerves. The man seemed to know his way around the woods. Tyler had decided to do this shoot with just him and Oscar. Partly because he thought it would make for better TV if it looked more

Blair Witch Project than Hollywood, and partly because the network had been making noise about budgets. And that meant either cutting down on some of the crew or losing the trailer.

The trailer was not negotiable.

Besides, his other two crewmembers were still in jail. He couldn't believe that bitch had had them arrested. Didn't she understand what freedom of the press was? What exactly was her problem? They were just trying to get some footage of the kid. It's not like they were going to hurt anyone.

He paused. Maybe they could show how Tess Brannick was actually putting the kid in danger. *Out here, middle of nowhere... It could work.*

Tyler pulled out his cell phone, but he couldn't get a signal. *Damn it.*

The brush near him rustled and Tyler jumped. A squirrel darted out. Tyler didn't like it out here. It was too quiet. Eerie.

And for the shot they wanted, they had to wait until it was pitch black. Tyler felt more than a little creeped out. He would normally try anything to avoid being out in the woods at these times.

Finally, about twenty minutes later, it was dark enough for what they needed. Tyler took three breaths, getting his game face on, then said, "Okay Oscar, let's roll."

The light on top of Oscar's camera bloomed to life, bathing Tyler in its glow. The brightness eased some of Tyler's fears and reminded him why he was doing this: people needed to know. *And I need to move on to bigger things.*

"We are standing on the very spot where Tess Brannick said she found little Melissa Hargrove. Missy had been missing a year before she was found. No one knows where she was during that time, and Missy isn't talking. But her father is—and *he's* convinced she was taken by a bigfoot."

Tyler waited while Oscar panned the area. "Okay, that's enough. Back on me."

The light came back to him. "This area of the Pacific Northwest is rife with sightings of bigfoot. In fact, the famous Patterson-Gimlin film was shot only a few short miles from here, in Bluff Creek."

The sound of wood striking wood echoed through the area. Tyler went still. "Did you hear that?" he whispered.

Oscar nodded.

Tyler swallowed, trying to keep his voice even. "Um, observers have often reported hearing bigfoot striking trees with large pieces of wood. That may be what we just heard."

The sound came again. Tyler scanned the area but he couldn't tell from where it originated. It was almost like it was everywhere at once.

He turned back to the camera. "This audio evidence lends more support to Dale Hargrove's claim that bigfoot took his daughter. As does the secrecy that now surrounds her. Her current legal guardian is refusing to allow the girl to be interviewed by the press. And that has to make a person wonder why? Why not just let the girl tell her story?"

Tyler smiled at his words. *Man, that was good.*

"Because maybe, just maybe... Tess Brannick is holding out so that she can break the story herself. Is that really in the best interest of this poor child?"

The sound of wood on wood came again, and then once more.

Tyler's head jerked up. "I think the bigfoot are getting angry. We're in their territory, and they're letting us know they don't want us here. For our own safety, we're going to head out. But we will be back at first light to investigate and look for proof of our nocturnal visitors."

Oscar took the camera off his shoulder, keeping the light on to lead the way. "That was good."

"Yeah. It was. Now let's get out of here."

Oscar dropped to one knee. "Let me just run this back and make sure we have everything we need."

"Fine, fine. Just do it quickly."

Tyler felt the hairs on the back of his neck rise. He could feel eyes on him. And he didn't like it. He stepped away from the circle of light and peered into the trees. Was there someone there?

A grunt sounded behind him—Oscar. Tyler spun around just in time to see the cameraman slump to the ground, taking the camera down with him. The camera's light shined directly into Tyler's eyes, blinding him.

Then a tree branch snapped off to Tyler's side. He started to turn, but a branch caught him in the chin and chest hard enough to lift him off of his feet. He slammed to the ground and knew his jaw was broken.

Pain tore through him, but his need for survival overrode it. He started to crawl away.

Then a blow slammed into his back, knocking him onto his belly in the dirt. And he went numb. Which was good, because the blows continued to rain down on him. And soon he welcomed the black that enveloped him.

CHAPTER ONE HUNDRED

Dawn was just breaking when Abe tossed the duffel in the back of his truck. He stretched out his back. *A rewarding night.*

He drove for an hour to the site he'd picked out earlier and then carried his bag over to the fire pit he'd set up. Pulling some lighter fluid out of the bag, he doused the wood, struck a match, and set it aflame. The wood caught quickly. He pulled out his cell phone as he began tossing everything from the bag into the fire.

Thaddeus answered quickly. "Yes?"

"Good morning, Thaddeus. How are you?"

Abe could practically feel the glare through the phone. "Is it done?"

"Is what done?" Abe pulled out the sixteen-inch carved wooden foot molds he'd had made. They strapped to the bottoms of his boots—and he had to admit, they had done a pretty good job. He tossed them in the fire as well.

"Is—Have you—The situation Mr. Hayes wanted addressed, has it been addressed?"

"You mean is that tool from the reality show dead? Yeah."

Thaddeus's spluttering came through loud and clear. "You can't talk that way!"

"Relax. No one will be overhearing this conversation. And I don't really see how you guys can order violent acts and then get all squeamish when I talk about them."

"Fine. But it was arranged as planned? No one will know you did it?"

"Of course not. But more importantly, it won't even look like a human did it. You've got your situation. Now I expect to be compensated for my part."

"Of course. I'm wiring the remainder of the fee to your account as we speak."

"Great. Well, that's my part of this little situation concluded."

"Very well. I'll let Mr. Hayes know."

"Tell him I'll be out of touch for a few days."

"You've got another job?"

"No, just taking a little vacation. Think I'll get in a spot of hunting."

CHAPTER ONE HUNDRED ONE

Dev hiked through the woods, his distaste for the task ahead of him growing with each step. According to the ex-producer of *Bigfoot Must Die,* two members of the crew had gone out in the woods two nights ago to do a shoot, and they hadn't returned.

From the quick chat Dev had had with the two crewmembers he'd arrested at Tess's cabin, he knew the group was not as woods-savvy as they tried to appear. It was likely they had simply gotten lost. And he wasn't exactly thrilled about being part of the search party that had to go out looking for them. *Like I don't have better things to do. Serves them right for trying to capitalize on Missy's situation.*

And in fact, Dev had *plenty* of better things to do. And at the top of that list were Tess and Missy. Tess was stressing herself into exhaustion trying to come up with a way to thwart Hayes, and the last thing she needed was this reality show headache adding to her already sizeable worries.

Generally, Dev wasn't responsible for searching for every idiot that got lost in the park, but missing celebrity idiots were apparently a special case. Fortunately, he had a good idea where to start looking. He'd gotten into Haven's RV and seen the storyboard—he knew they intended to go to the spot where Tess and Missy had first been found.

He curled his fists remembering the rest of the storyboard, including the notes about getting shots of Missy and Tess.

A shadow passed overhead, and Dev looked up to see a large black bird with fingerlike tips on its wing—a turkey vulture. It joined another three turkey vultures flying in wobbly circles farther ahead.

Dev's stomach dropped. *Oh, shit.* Turkey vultures were carrion birds—they fed on fresh carcasses. He picked up his pace.

He heard the snarl before he reached the spot. When he arrived, four coyotes were already feasting on what was left of the bodies. Dev aimed his shotgun in the air and pulled the trigger twice. The coyotes backed away, but didn't run. He hoped he didn't have to kill them. One made a move for the bodies again.

Damn it. Dev aimed and pulled the trigger. The buckshot caught the animal in the rib cage. It let out a yelp and fell to the ground, its back legs running but not going anywhere.

The other coyotes scattered. Dev approached the wounded coyote. It would not survive. "I'm sorry," he said. He put the poor beast out of its misery.

Then he turned from that carnage to the human carnage. He blanched at the condition of the bodies. Chunks of skin and muscle were gone. One person's arm had been tugged off and dragged several feet away. The other body was missing a hand and leg. And the faces... It was hard to tell *what* they were, never mind *who* they were.

No, proper IDs would require much more than a visual. All he could tell was that one guy was white and the other was most likely Latino—or really tan. But he knew all he needed to know from the television camera that lay not far from one of the bodies. The words *Bigfoot Must Die* were stamped on its side.

Dev pulled out his radio, hoping he could get a signal from here. He knew he should feel some sympathy, but the image of Missy's terrified face wouldn't let him. *Dead out-of-towners. This is going to be a nightmare.*

D ev paused outside Tess's cabin door. He really didn't want to bring her this news. But she needed to know.

Taking a breath, he opened the door and stepped inside.

When Tess caught sight of him, her whole face lit up. Dev would never tire of seeing that expression on her face, and he really hoped she never tired of providing it. She got up and hugged him. "Hey. I tried you earlier but couldn't reach you."

"Yeah. It's been a little crazy."

"Everything all right?"

"We need to talk. Something's happened." He looked around. "Where is everybody?"

She led him over to the couch. "Pax and Shawn went for a walk with Shelby and Missy. What's going on?"

Dev sat down next to her. "Tyler Haven and one of his crew were killed two nights ago."

Tess's hand flew to her mouth. "Oh, that's awful! What happened?"

Dev recounted coming across the bodies in the woods. Tess paled, and Dev knew she was recalling her father's death.

Her voice was a little shaky when she spoke. "You know I didn't like the guy, but no one should go out like that."

Dev pulled the pictures out of his pocket and handed them to her. "These were found near the bodies."

Tess's eyes grew wide. "Bigfoot prints? That's not possible."

"Tess, these prints, found right near two dead bodies... It's getting people pretty worked up."

"But bigfoot aren't violent."

"Are you sure?"

"I'm sure." There was no doubt in her voice.

"Then how did these prints come to be there?"

Tess took the photos to the kitchen island and turned the lights on above it. She pulled her magnifying glass from the utensil drawer. "Did you cast these?"

Dev came over and stood beside her. "Yeah, but I had to leave the casts back at the station."

She squinted at the pictures and frowned.

"What is it?" Dev asked.

"How far apart are these?" Tess pointed to two footprints in one photo.

"About three, maybe four feet."

"That's too small a stride." She flipped through the other photos, and her frown increased. "And look at this."

Dev leaned forward. It was a close-up of one the footprints. "What about it?"

"The toes—they're wrong. They're not long enough. The foot's too narrow as well. And look." She placed three photos down, right next to each other.

"What? They all look the same to me."

"They do, and that's the problem. There should be a little difference between them. All feet bend, dip, and shift a little. These don't." She glanced up at him. "How damp was the ground?"

"Not too bad, but we got that rain the night before these guys disappeared."

"How deep were the imprints?"

"Maybe a half inch?"

Tess shook her head. "They're forgeries."

"What?"

"These prints are, what—sixteen inches long? And the ground was damp? A bigfoot should have sunk into the ground at least two or three inches. That's one of the ways to spot hoaxers—they can't get the prints deep enough. Humans can't simulate the weight distribution."

Dev grabbed the photos and flipped through them.

"Hold on." Tess ran into her office and returned a few seconds later carrying her own photos and a cast. "Compare them to these."

Dev noticed right away that the cast Tess held was thicker than the one he'd made earlier. The foot was much wider, and she was right—the toes were longer too. "I don't know that this will make much of a difference. You say they're not bigfoot prints, but you can't explain why you're sure of that."

"There are other experts. You could call them in—"

"I don't think we have time for that. The mayor is in a frenzy. These deaths, following the return of Missy... Beauford just became bigfoot central."

Tess closed her eyes. "Oh, no."

"The mayor scheduled a press conference for tomorrow morning. I think you should be there."

"What do you think she's going to say?"

"I don't know, but I know it's not going to be good."

C arter sat at his lunch table, a white linen napkin draped across his legs, a twenty-four-hour business channel playing in the background. He glanced up from the financial report he was reading to glare at the TV screen. It had been two days. *Two damn days, and nothing.*

Everything was set up, at least everything that could be set up without raising suspicions. They just needed to get the word.

Thaddeus walked in from the front office and picked up the remote. "I think you'll want to see this." He switched to a news channel.

An African-American anchor faced the camera, her perfectly made-up face serious. "A grisly discovery in Northern California has rocked the reality TV world. TV personality Tyler Haven was found dead in Klamath National Forest along with his cameraman, Oscar Frankel. A cause of death has not been released, although one source at the medical examiner's office stated that the bodies had to be identified through dental records.

"Haven was the host of the popular reality show *Bigfoot Must Die*, which chronicled humans' experiences with bigfoot in the wild. Fans of the show have bombarded the show's website and the governor of California's office with demands that the truth of the attacks be released. Many are stating their belief that a bigfoot, a legendary half-man/half-ape creature, is responsible for the killings. Governor Edwards's office has not released a statement yet but is expected to later this afternoon. We now go live to the town of Beauford, California, where—"

Carter hit the mute button on the console on his desk. On screen, a reporter interviewed a man who held two fishing poles over his rather large shoulder. Carter barely registered the image, though; his mind was churning. Finally he turned to Thaddeus. "Make the call."

Thaddeus picked up the phone on Carter's desk and dialed a number from memory. "Carter Hayes for Governor Edwards."

Only a few seconds later, Thaddeus spoke again. "Good morning, Governor. Please hold for Mr. Hayes." He handed the phone over to Carter.

Carter took it, forcing a jovial tone to his voice. "Harrison, it's been too long."

Tess and Pax entered the town hall meeting room just before ten a.m. and took positions along the back wall. Tess had worried that people might pay them too much attention, but as she looked at the chaos in front of her, she realized that was not going to be an issue. Everyone was too busy yelling and talking to their neighbors to notice Pax and Tess.

There were a lot of faces here that Tess didn't recognize. Missy's father's story had drawn a lot of attention, and bigfoot enthusiasts had been descending on Beauford ever since, traipsing through the woods and hoping for a sighting.

And then there was all the media that had descended on the town. There were so many TV vans parked along the road from Tess's house, hoping to get a glimpse of Missy or even of Tess, that Sasha had had to sneak Tess and Pax underneath a blanket in her back seat. Tess couldn't believe this was all happening. It was surreal.

Pax reached over and took Tess's hand. She squeezed it, glad he was with her.

The door off to the side of the podium at the front of the

room opened. Dev walked out, followed by Hank and a fifty-five-year-old heavyset blond woman—Mayor Catherine Sonner.

Catherine had been the mayor for the last seven years, and everyone agreed she'd done a good job. Although everyone also agreed there wasn't much to do besides make sure the winter and summer festivals ran smoothly.

Catherine stepped up to the podium, and Hank stood to the right and slightly behind her. Dev stood on her other side. His jaw was taut, his body tense. He was not happy. Tess's anxiety rose.

The mayor waved for quiet, but a few people still murmured in the audience. She frowned and placed two fingers in her mouth. With the aid of the microphone in front of her, she let out an eardrum-shattering whistle. Silence reigned, with more than a few people placing their hands over their ears and wincing.

Catherine gave them a grim smile. In addition to being mayor, she ran the biggest lumberyard in the county. She was used to dealing with tough men. If half the stories Tess had heard about her were right, a group of cranky townsfolk and excited out-of-towners was nothing to this woman.

"Thank you," Catherine said, the evidence of a two pack a day habit clear in her throaty voice. "By now, you have all heard about the deaths of Tyler Haven and Oscar Frankel out in the state park."

A murmur passed through the audience; Catherine glared, and it silenced. "The medical examiner has concluded the autopsies, but the bodies were in such bad shape due to the coyotes that he can't conclusively say what killed them. Although he did say the likelihood of them both dropping dead of natural causes at the same time was unlikely."

Some people tittered at Catherine's attempt at a joke.

"As a result, we have had to use other means to ascertain what happened," Catherine said.

Tess's gaze flew to Dev. He curled his fist and stared straight ahead. Whatever Catherine had determined, Dev did not agree with it. Hank, however, seemed to have no such reservations. A smile ghosted across his face before he covered it with a small cough.

The mayor continued. "The crew was filming a scene for *Bigfoot Must Die*, a reality show based on the search for bigfoot. Well, I think it's safe to say, they found him."

Tess's jaw dropped. *What the hell?*

"On the taped segment, the crew heard a bigfoot in the area. They were preparing to leave due to fears for their safety. And that's when the tape ended. In addition, we found some extremely large footprints in the area. I think it is safe to assume that the two unfortunate members of this show did indeed find the object of their search, and that they paid the ultimate price for it."

Tess couldn't even think beyond the stupidity of that statement.

The mayor paused and eyed the room before continuing. "The town of Beauford has issued a twenty-thousand-dollar reward for the person who can find and kill the monster responsible for this attack."

The crowd began to murmur excitedly. Catherine didn't seem to mind this time.

"What about hunting permits?" someone yelled.

"For the immediate future, hunting permits will not be required. This reward is open to anyone—be they a resident of Beauford or not. That is all. No questions."

Tess could not believe what she had just heard. The mayor had just put a death warrant out on the bigfoot.

She turned to Pax, whose eyes were huge. "What are you going to do?" he asked.

Tess shook her head, feeling numb. "I have no idea."

CHAPTER ONE HUNDRED FIVE

Dev was furious as he followed the mayor and sheriff out of the meeting room and back to the mayor's office. As soon as the door closed he turned to the mayor. "What the hell was that?"

Catherine narrowed her eyes. "Watch your tone, Deputy."

"With all due respect, there is nothing in the ME's report or on the tape that proves a bigfoot killed those two men."

Catherine took a seat behind her desk. "You're missing the big picture, son."

Dev imagined vaulting over the desk and strangling her. "And what might that be?"

She smiled. "Tourist dollars. Bigfoot is a huge money-maker. People are fascinated by him. And if we have proof of a bigfoot in the area, it will bring tons of people to our little town."

"Do you have any idea how reckless you're being?" Dev said.

Catherine frowned. "I don't see that at all."

Dev gripped his hands behind his back to keep them from reaching for her neck. "Every year when hunting season starts, we have a massive increase in gunshot wounds. Why? Because people get drunk and then fire at their friends, thinking they're a deer. Now you're going to have every yahoo within driving distance, and probably beyond, heading here with a gun and a case of beer." Dev was yelling by the end of his rant, and had to rein in his anger.

"Now son, I think you're exaggerating," Hank said. "Most hunters are decent, responsible individuals."

"Yeah, and the key word there is 'most.' Because the few that aren't will be out there too. Not to mention people who've never hunted before. And then there's the bigfoot investigators. They'll show up here, banging trees, making calls, and someone will take a shot at them thinking they're the real deal."

"Well, it's your job to keep the peace then," Catherine said.

"My jurisdiction does not extend into the woods. We can't patrol the woods. You *do* get that, right?" Dev said.

Catherine's eyes narrowed. "I warned you once about your tone, Deputy. If I have to do it again, there will be repercussions."

Dev curled his fists, his anger only growing hotter. These two were going to get a whole lot of people hurt, if not killed. He turned to Hank. "I have some vacation time coming. I'd like to take it beginning now."

Hank looked between Dev and Catherine. And Dev knew what he was thinking. He was lucky to have Dev, and bigger enforcement agencies would be happy to get him. If he didn't keep Dev happy, he was likely to lose him. What's more, he knew that everything had Dev said was true. And Hank was going to need a good deputy when everything went to hell.

Hank stared at a spot on his tie. "Well, maybe just a few days. But then I'll need you back on duty."

"Fine." Dev turned on his heel and headed for the door. He yanked it open, and it took a herculean effort to not slam it behind him. He stormed down the hallway past small groups of people talking excitedly. Others were quickly heading for the doors.

Dev stepped out into the fresh air. An angry car horn drew his attention to the right. An old F-150 slammed to a stop as a black Tahoe cut it off. Both drivers launched themselves from their cars, screaming at each other over their hoods. And both were out-of-towners.

Dev shook his head. He knew this was only the beginning. It was going to get worse from here.

Tess and Pax rushed back to Tess's cabin after the meeting. When Tess opened the door, Shawn and Missy looked up from the puzzle they were doing on the coffee table. Missy ran over and hugged Tess.

Tess ran her hand over Missy's hair. "There's my favorite girl. You and Shawn have made a huge dent in that puzzle."

Missy grinned and retook her seat.

Shawn smiled. "She's good at these. I thought I'd have to help her, but *she's* helping *me*."

Pax moved over and sat next to Missy. "Can I help?"

"Sure." Missy pushed some of the puzzle pieces toward her.

"Uh, Shawn, could I talk to you for a minute?" Tess asked.

Shawn frowned before a quick glance at Missy had him covering it and getting to his feet. "Sure."

They stepped out onto the porch, and Shawn closed the door behind them. Shawn crossed his arms over his chest. "What happened?"

Tess quickly filled him in on the meeting. Shawn's face grew grimmer and grimmer as she spoke.

Tess looked out into the trees. "I know they'll probably be safe. But I feel like we need to warn them."

Shawn nodded. "I agree. But do you know where they are?"

"I'm guessing at the valley. And if they're not, well, that would be great, because that would mean they've moved on."

"I'll go with you."

Tess smiled at him. "I was hoping you'd say that. But that still leaves the bigger problem: how do I make them understand they're in trouble?"

Shawn considered. "Yeah, that is a problem."

Tess looked through the window at Missy. She looked like any other six-year-old—but she wasn't. "Missy could get them to understand," Tess said quietly.

Shawn held up his hands. "Whoa. We can't take her out there. It's too dangerous."

"I know. But I also don't have any idea how else to make them understand. She's the only one who stands a chance of doing that."

Shawn looked inside at Missy as well. He blew out a breath. "There's no good option here. If she doesn't come with us and we can't convince them, and then they get killed, she'll be inconsolable."

"But if we take her, we place her in danger. And it's our job to keep her safe."

"What do we do?" Shawn asked.

Tess felt completely out of her depth. "I really don't know."

D ev was emptying a few things out of his desk, and he frowned when a man in a dark suit walked past the double glass doors of the sheriff's office. They normally didn't get people dressed like that around here. He slid his drawer closed and stepped around his desk to get a better view. The man disappeared into Catherine's office.

Dev stepped back and caught the eye of the other deputy in the room.

"What's going on?" Becky Martin asked. Becky had been with the department for twenty years and knew all the ins and outs of the town.

Dev shook his head. "I don't know. Some suit just went into Catherine's office."

Becky came over and leaned on the desk across from Dev's. "I can't believe you're leaving me with all this going on."

"Sorry. But I think I'm going to be needed more elsewhere."

"I agree. You need to watch out for Tess and Missy. Lord knows, people will probably be fighting each other trying to get in to speak with them."

Dev groaned, picturing exactly that. "I know. But I *am* sorry to be leaving you with this mess."

Becky grimaced. "Hey, it's not your fault. It's her royal highness." She tilted her head toward Hank's office. "And Sir Sits-a-lot."

Her radio squawked and she pulled it off her belt. "Go for Martin."

"Becky, we've got a report of a fight over at Poor Richard's."

Becky rolled her eyes. "Great. I'll be right there."

She gave Dev a hug. "Take care of them and I'll see you in a few days. And give me a call if I can help."

"Will do."

Just as Becky was heading out the door, Catherine came storming through it, and Becky had to step quickly aside. Becky looked from Catherine to Dev. Dev knew she wanted more than anything to stay and find out what was going on. But she blew out a resigned breath and headed down the hallway.

Catherine stormed right past Dev to Hank's office. She slammed the door behind her, but it didn't catch. Dev sidled up next to the door to listen.

"I can't believe this!" Catherine yelled. "Finally something good happens in this town, and now this!"

"What are you talking about?" Hank asked.

"I just got a visit from one of the governor's people. He told me the governor has said we cannot offer a reward for hunting down bigfoot. In fact, he's just declared that anyone going out and searching for bigfoot should be arrested."

Dev smiled. *Finally, cooler heads.*

"Why would he do that?" Hank asked.

"He says he doesn't want California looking like a bunch of idiots who believe in bigfoot, so he won't let any public funds be used for a reward. And *I'm* certainly not forking over twenty grand. Instead he's sending in a private military group. Some private donor offered their services."

Dev's mouth fell open. This just kept getting worse and worse.

"When are they arriving?" Hank asked.

"Sometime tomorrow," Catherine said.

"How many of them?"

"I don't know, but it sounds like a few dozen. And they've apparently got a half dozen or so helicopters as well. They're going to turn the park into a war zone."

Dev had heard enough. He gathered his bag from his desk and hightailed it out of the office. He all but sprinted for his truck. He needed to warn Tess.

And she needed to warn her friends.

D inner was finishing up, and Tess still wasn't sure what to do. The tribe had survived for centuries without her help. They could survive this, right? Wasn't she just being self-centered to think they needed her to look out for them? Besides, they were incredibly attuned to the sounds of the forest. They would know the hunters were coming.

By the time the dishes were cleaned and put away, she had just about convinced herself they would be all right.

Then Dev showed up.

As soon as he walked into the cabin, Tess knew things were even worse than she feared.

Pax took one look at Dev's face and said, "Hey Missy, have you ever seen *The Little Mermaid*?"

Missy shook her head.

"Well, that needs to be rectified right now. Tess, is it okay if we use the TV in your bedroom?"

"Sure, no problem."

Shawn, Dev, and Tess waited while Pax disappeared into the bedroom with Missy and closed the door behind them.

Then Tess whirled on Dev. "What happened?"

"There's a private military force coming out to search for them."

Tess's jaw dropped.

"What? How the hell did *that* happen?" Shawn asked.

Dev shrugged, but his eyes were hard. "The governor has some affluent friend who convinced him it was more politically advisable to allow him to conduct the search than to use public funds."

"Hayes," Tess said quietly.

"That's my guess, too," Dev said.

Tess sank onto the couch. "It makes the most sense. He was *not* happy when I returned the grant money. He's really interested in bigfoot. And then there's the hair sample that went missing and the guy he sent after me. Obviously he's not opposed to violence. It has to be him."

Shawn took a seat across from her and Dev sat beside her.

"So what do you want to do?" Shawn asked.

"Missy will be destroyed if something happens to them," Tess said. "But how can I risk her out there? And without her, how can we convince them of the trouble coming their way?"

"I'll go with you," Dev said.

"Me too," Shawn added. "And if they care about her as much as you say, they'll help make sure nothing happens to her."

Tess stared at the framed picture she'd put on the mantelpiece. Missy had drawn it a few days ago. It showed Missy with Tess, Shawn, Pax, and Dev. But if you looked closely, you could also see the shadowed figures in the background. Missy was beginning to accept that this was her world now, but her other family was never far from her thoughts.

And Tess knew that if they didn't help the bigfoot now, Missy would forever hold it against her—and herself. "If we do this, keeping Missy safe comes above everything, right?"

"Yes," both men answered.

Tess turned to Dev. "When is the force arriving?"

"Sometime tomorrow."

Tess blew out a breath. "Well, I guess than means we're leaving at first light."

Daylight hadn't yet broken the horizon when Tess woke up the next morning. She stared at the ceiling for an hour, listening to Missy's quiet breathing next to her. She hoped she was doing the right thing. They'd stayed up late last night getting everything together. And they had a plan. But a lot of things had to come together for that plan to work right.

She slipped from the bed. Coffee, some eggs, and she'd be ready to face the day—she hoped.

Tess pulled the blankets up to Missy's chin and smiled as Missy snuggled deeper under them. One thing Missy had loved since she'd returned was the bed. The softness of it delighted her. And the pocket bigfoot that Pax had sent her lay snuggled in her arms.

Tess walked out of the room and closed the door softly behind her. Dev and Shawn were already awake, sitting at the kitchen island, mugs in front of them. Dev gave Tess a hug. "How you doing?"

Tess wrapped her arms around his waist and leaned into him.

"Good. I'm ready to get this show on the road. Everything go okay last night?"

Dev nodded. "Yeah, they'll be there."

Tess sighed, feeling a little relief. "Good."

"Have some coffee," Dev said. "We've got another hour before daylight, and then we'll get going."

Shawn placed a full mug in front of her. She took a sip, reveling in the warmth, then looked up at Shawn. "You sure Pax is up for this?"

Last night, Tess had been shocked when Pax said he was going too. Pax was not known for roughing it.

"One of them saved his life too when you guys were little," Shawn explained. "He's paying a debt. Besides, he wants to be there for you and Missy."

"But is he up for it?"

Shawn faked affront. "Hey. He's married to a Navy SEAL. He knows how to take care of himself."

"Well, when you put it that way."

But her fear for Pax lay at the back of her mind, right next to her fear for Missy, Shawn, Dev, herself, and the tribe. *Please let us all come home.*

She took another sip of coffee and appreciated that no one commented on how much her hands were shaking.

CHAPTER ONE HUNDRED TEN

An hour later, dawn burst out bright and beautiful. Tess stepped onto the porch with Shelby by her side. The air was a little crisp, but she knew that would burn off by mid-morning, leaving behind a beautiful day.

Madge's old red pickup pulled into the yard with her ATV in the back. Tess had called her yesterday to see if they could borrow it.

Madge stepped out and Tess walked down to greet her. "Thanks for coming."

Madge pulled a shotgun from her truck, slung it over her shoulder, then grabbed a rifle too before closing the door.

Tess's eyebrows went up. "Um, you expecting trouble?"

"Nope. But it never hurts to be prepared." She handed the rifle to Tess. "I've never had a better gun than this one. It was my granddaddy's, but I clean it and shoot it regularly to keep it in shape. I want you to take it with you today."

Tess looked away. "Madge, it's—"

Madge took Tess's arm in a strong grip. "I know you're not going out for a little hike." She nodded toward the house. "And I know where that little girl's been this last year. Don't worry—I don't plan on telling anyone. But I also know that our mutual friends are in trouble, and your little last-minute hike has something to do with that."

Tess wanted to look away from Madge's probing gaze, but she couldn't. So she nodded instead.

Madge released her arm. "Well, Granddaddy's rifle may just come in useful. Because from what I hear, there's gonna be a lot of folks running around with their own guns."

Tess took the rifle. "Thanks, Madge."

"If I were younger, I'd insist on being out there with you. But seeing as I can't, I'll keep an eye on Shelby."

"If we're not back by tomorrow, call Abby. She knows what to do."

Madge tightened her mouth but nodded.

Tess turned toward the steps, paused, then turned back. "If I don't make it back, can you take care of Shelby?"

Madge opened her mouth to protest.

Tess took Madge's arm this time, but more gently. "Please."

Madge gave her an abrupt nod and pulled her into a rough hug. "Just make sure you come back. You're supposed to bury me, not the other way round."

Madge pulled away and disappeared into the cabin. Tess watched her with a heavy heart, hoping that nobody was going to have to bury anybody anytime soon.

CHAPTER ONE HUNDRED ELEVEN

The three ATVs roared down the path. Tess had Missy snuggled in front of her, and although she knew the stakes were high, she let herself enjoy the ride. It had been too long since she'd been out here, and it felt good to be back. And judging by Missy's smile, the girl felt the same way.

She had told Missy that they were going to see her family—and that her family was in danger. Missy had taken it surprisingly well. Tess supposed that perhaps she shouldn't have been surprised to find that Missy so easily accepted that the world was full of evil people.

Tess led the way and stopped her ATV at the usual spot. Her legs felt a little numb from the continuous vibration of the bike, and she shook them out when she dismounted. Then she turned and helped Missy dismount.

The boys gathered near. "About a forty-minute walk from here to your camp, right?" Dev asked.

"Yeah," Tess said. "And then it's about another three hours from there to the valley."

"You don't sound so sure about that," Pax said.

"Well, I was following Kong last time and didn't look at my watch."

"Kong?" Pax asked.

"He's one of the big ones," Tess said.

"I thought his name was Frank," Shawn said.

"The one *you* met was Frank," Tess explained. "Kong's the one who brought me back. He's much bigger."

Shawn paled a little.

"Come on, guys," Missy called.

"You heard the boss," Pax said. "Let's go." He hurried after Missy, who smiled and ran ahead. Shawn started after them.

Dev took Tess's hand. "We'll be okay. We'll get there in time."

"Promise?"

Dev didn't answer her; he just kissed her softly on the lips. Tess wished he *had* answered her, though, even if it had been a lie. Because right now, she needed to believe the lie.

CHAPTER ONE HUNDRED TWELVE

Abe sat at the table outside the coffee shop across from city hall. He took a bite from his egg sandwich as he waited for the show to begin.

Five minutes later, a black jeep pulled up and a gray-haired man in green fatigues stepped out. Abe shook his head. *Private army assholes*. The man strode up the steps of city hall and disappeared through the double doors. Abe took one last sip of coffee before throwing a twenty on the table and crossing the street. Two younger men in fatigues stood waiting next to the Jeep.

Abe schooled his features and headed for them with a giant smile on his face. "Hey, you the guys going to track down bigfoot?"

Neither of the men responded.

"Man, what a sight that's going to be. I know a lot of people around these parts who'd love to be going with you." He paused. "But not me. No sirree, I'll leave that to you young hero-types."

One of the men smirked.

"Yup, you guys are genuine American heroes. Say, could I shake your hand?"

One of the guys shrugged and extended his hand. Abe gripped it and placed his other hand on the man's shoulder. "Be careful out there, and good luck."

Abe nodded at the other man still keeping his smile big. Then he headed down the street and around the corner. He dropped his smile as soon as he was out of view.

He made his way to his rented SUV and opened the back. After scanning the street to make sure no one was around, he pulled over his duffel, pulled out the receiver, and flipped it on. The light glowed green, and the screen displayed GPS coordinates. Yup, the tracer he'd placed was working fine.

It wasn't long before the light started to move. Abe patted the big gun case next to the duffel. *Time to go bag me a bigfoot.*

CHAPTER ONE HUNDRED THIRTEEN

They made good time to Tess's camp. Tess looked around— it was already beginning to look abandoned. She glanced at the log where she and Charlie had first sat, and immediately a vision of Frank holding Charlie's body appeared in her mind.

Tess took a deep breath. She promised to take care of them. She needed to do that.

Pax pointed to the sky. "What's that?"

Tess looked up. A black speck to their east was heading in their direction.

"A chopper," Dev answered, reaching for his binoculars. He watched it for a few seconds, then lowered them. "It's not a county one. Maybe news?"

"Maybe," Tess said, knowing occasionally they flew over the area when there was a news story. And a private military force tracking through a national forest was definitely a news story.

Shawn pulled out his own binoculars and focused on the target. He went still and then lowered them. "That's an older military chopper."

"Well, I guess they've arrived," Dev said. "How many people can that chopper hold?"

"Maybe four or five, plus the pilot. Not enough for an invasion force. But that's not the problem."

"What's the problem?" Pax asked.

"It's not unusual for those choppers to be fit with heat signature cameras. They're looking for your friends from the air."

Tess looked again at the chopper. If it stayed on course, it would come awfully close to the valley. "We need to move faster."

Shawn shifted his pack to his front and then lifted Missy onto his back. "Come on, little girl, time for a piggyback ride."

Miss squealed and wrapped her arms around Shawn's neck. There was a giant grin in her face. Tess only saw it for a split second, though, because she was already hurrying off into the trees.

They moved at a fast pace, and they only took one short break for water and a snack during the first hour. And during that time they saw three more choppers. They didn't run into any of the military on the ground, but with the air getting as crowded as it was, she knew it was only a matter of time.

Ahead, Tess spotted a tall mountain maple that had grown around a large boulder. She remembered that tree, although she wasn't sure which way to go from here.

Up ahead another chopper reappeared, heading back the way it had come. They had kept track of this one because unlike the others, its flight path would take them very close to the valley. Tess looked over at Shawn. "Do you think they found them?"

"Maybe. Or they could just need to refuel."

Tess looked in the direction the chopper had appeared from. Maybe the bigfoot had heard it and had been able to hide before it could get a reading.

"Which way?" Dev asked.

"I'm not sure," Tess said.

"It's that way." Missy pointed off to the right a bit.

"You're sure?" Shawn asked

"Mm-hmm."

Tess shrugged. "Sounds good to me."

It was another hour before they stopped again. Tess took a swallow of water. Her legs were beginning to feel numb, but she knew they needed to press on.

Then, without warning, she felt absolutely terrified. Her head whipped from side to side.

"They're here," Missy whispered.

Tess looked at the guys. "Do you feel that?"

They all nodded. Dev pulled his shotgun from his pack.

"No," Tess said. "No weapons. They're warning us away. Let me have Missy."

Shawn squatted down, and Missy scrambled off his back. She ran over and took Tess's hand. "Do you know where they are?" Tess asked.

Missy pointed. "That way."

"You guys stay here. We'll be back," Tess said over her shoulder.

Dev stepped forward. "No chance."

Tess put up her hand. "Trust me."

Dev held her gaze. "You have five minutes, and then we're coming after you." Shawn and Pax nodded their agreement.

"Okay."

Tess went in the direction Missy had pointed. As soon as they were out of view of the boys, she said, "Can you tell them we need to speak with them?"

"I think they already know that," she said softly.

Tess looked over her shoulder and jumped. The bigfoot standing behind her was ten feet tall, with a scar along his cheek. *Kong.* "Can you tell him the tribe is in trouble? That bad men are coming after them?"

Missy stepped forward, but Kong ignored her, his gaze fixed

on Tess. Tess could feel his anger. *Damn it, why did it have to be Kong?*

Finally he looked down at Missy, and for a split second, Tess saw his expression soften. Missy began to speak with him. When she was done, he looked back at Tess.

"You need to go," Tess said. "They're coming." She knew her words wouldn't be understood, but she hoped her tone conveyed the importance.

He grunted and said something to Missy.

"He wants us to come with him," Missy said.

Tess thought of where the boys waited and shook her head. "We can't split up. It's not safe."

Missy relayed what she'd said, and Kong disappeared into the trees.

Tess looked around. "Um, what did he say?"

"Nothing. He just left."

Tess sighed. "Well, great. Come on, let's get back to the guys before they storm in after us."

The three men had their weapons in their hands when Tess and Missy returned.

"What did I say about weapons?" Tess growled.

Shawn gave her a pointed look. "Tess, this forest is crawling with the usual dangerous animals as well as a paramilitary force. We're not dropping our guns."

"Okay. Good point," Tess said.

Pax hugged Missy. "Did you find them?"

Tess nodded. "We ran into Kong. Missy told him what was going on and he wanted us to come with him. But then I said you guys couldn't be left behind, and he just disappeared without a word."

"So what do we do now?" Pax asked.

"Well, we've warned them, which is what we had wanted to do. So... I guess we just head back," Tess said.

Pax looked around the group. "Does anyone else feel like this was all a big build-up with little payoff?"

Tess wrapped her arm in his and teased. "Well, sorry I couldn't make it more exciting for you, but—"

"Tess," Dev said, a warning in his voice.

Tess followed Dev's gaze and saw Kong stepping out of the woods. "Everyone put down your weapons, now," Tess ordered.

From the corner of her eye she saw them follow her orders. And she also saw three of Kong's lieutenants stepping out of the woods as well.

They were surrounded.

Tess examined the four bigfoot that surrounded them. They were all dark brown and stood between ten and eleven feet. None of them looked happy or even peaceful. They were the second type of bigfoot, the more aggressive ones like Kong. *Oh boy.*

"Nobody make any sudden moves," Tess said quietly.

Missy held onto Pax's hand, and Tess could see him shaking.

Kong looked over the entire group before finally letting his gaze rest on Shawn. Tess wasn't surprised. Shawn was by the far the biggest and strongest of their group, so according to Kong, that would probably make him the alpha. Kong stalked toward him.

"Shawn, don't move," Tess said. "Look at the ground."

Shawn kept his eyes fixed on the ground, and Kong walked right up to him, stopping a mere foot away, a growl low in his throat. Shawn didn't move.

Kong stood there for a full minute, almost daring Shawn to do something. But Shawn remained perfectly still. Finally Kong backed up, and Tess let out a breath. Next to her, Pax nearly lost it. "Oh my God," he whispered.

Tess held on to his arm. "It's okay. He was just testing to make sure Shawn wasn't going to try to fight him for alpha status."

"Okay?" Pax hissed. "He nearly ate my husband."

"They don't eat humans—I think."

Pax glared at her.

"I'm fine," Shawn said. "He kind of reminds me of one of my old drill instructors."

He was joking, but Tess could see how shook up he was.

"Should I be insulted or happy he didn't think *I* was the alpha?" Dev asked.

"Happy, definitely happy," Shawn muttered.

Kong grunted, and Tess's head snapped back to him. "Missy? Do you know what he wants?"

"He wants us to go with him." She raised her eyebrows. "All of us."

Together they hiked behind Kong for a few minutes, but Tess could tell he was getting frustrated by their slow pace. Finally he stopped and grunted something to his friends.

"Missy?" Tess asked.

"He's going to give us a ride."

Pax's eyes went large. "What does that mean?"

Kong walked over to Tess and Missy, then turned around and knelt down. Tess understood. She picked up Missy and helped her onto Kong's back. Then she climbed up herself. Kong stood.

Tess looked over her shoulder, unable to hide her grin at the men's expressions. "Your turn."

Each of the other bigfoot knelt down in the same manner. The men exchanged glances. Finally Shawn stepped forward and climbed on. Pax and Dev followed, one on each of the other two bigfoot.

Pax grinned. "This is actually kind of cool. I really wish I had a camera right now. Hey, you think they'd let me take a selfie with them when we get there?"

Tess opened her mouth to answer, but just then Kong took off at a run, and it was all she could do to just hold on. She could understand now why their pace had been frustrating Kong—right now they were practically flying through the trees.

In mere minutes they had reached the base of the cliff that led to the valley. Without even stopping to catch his breath, Kong headed up. Behind her, Tess heard Pax give a little yell as Kong's companions started to climb, too.

When they reached the ledge with the tunnel, Kong knelt to allow Tess and Missy to clamber down. Kong immediately ran down the tunnel, no doubt to sound the alarm. Missy ran after him. Tess wanted to yell out to her to wait, but the fact was, she would be safe with them.

The other three bigfoot crested the cliff in quick succession. They knelt down as Kong had, allowing the men to climb off, and then they, too, ran down the tunnel, leaving Tess and the men alone.

Tess looked everyone over. "You guys okay?"

Pax's complexion was gray. Dev held on to the cliff wall. Shawn, though, grinned. "We've got to do that again. You have the coolest friends."

Tess laughed. "Well, come meet the rest of them."

She led them down the tunnel to the valley. The sun shone brightly overhead, reflecting off the lake at the far side. As before, groups of bigfoot were scattered around the area, sitting, walking, and playing.

Just ahead, one bigfoot had Missy wrapped in a giant hug.

"That's Frank," Tess said to Dev and Pax. "He's the father."

A female bigfoot came sprinting across the valley. She took Missy from Frank with a squeal.

Tess smiled. "That's Mary, the mother."

She looked around for Sugar, but didn't see her. Then a tall female bigfoot loped down from one of the rocks and made her way over to them. *It can't be.*

The bigfoot ran her hand over Missy's hair. Then she let out a happy bark and sprinted over to Tess and the others. The men took an uneasy step back, but Tess took a step forward. Sugar pulled her off the ground and twirled her around.

Tess laughed. "Okay, okay. I'm getting dizzy."

Sugar put her down gently. Tess looked up at her. Sugar had grown nearly a foot since Tess had last seen her. She was now a few inches taller than Tess.

"You've grown," Tess said.

Sugar jabbered back at her. Then her eyes landed on the men behind her. Tess took Sugar's hand and led her over. "Sugar, these are my friends. Everybody—this is Sugar."

Sugar walked up to each man and tilted her head, inspecting them from head to toe. She inspected Shawn last. She reached up and tentatively rubbed her hand over his bald head. Then she laughed.

Tess laughed too. And for a moment, she forgot why they were here. She just enjoyed being here.

She felt Frank walk up behind her, and she turned. Missy was back in his arms.

"Did you tell him?" Tess asked Missy.

"He doesn't think they need to go. No one's ever found them before."

Tess had known this was going to be the hard part. They had no understanding of technology. They didn't realize how much easier it would be for humans to find them now.

Tess nodded toward her gun. "Tell them they have stronger guns and better eyes. They can see them from very far away. We have to go."

Missy relayed the message to Frank. Frank responded, and Missy shook her head at Tess. "He doesn't believe it."

Tess looked at Mary and saw the uneasiness on her face. Past her, she saw the tree that marked Charlie's grave. Tess had promised she would keep them safe. But how was she supposed to do that if they wouldn't let her?

CHAPTER ONE HUNDRED SEVENTEEN

Tess spent the next few minutes trying to convince Frank of the coming danger, but with no success. Eventually, he just turned and walked away.

Tess blew out a breath. Mary came and sat next to her. Tess took the female bigfoot's hand, wishing she could talk directly to her.

Mary nodded toward the men. And Tess saw the question in her eyes: *Which one is your mate?*

"Dev," Tess called, and he walked over. Tess looked at Mary and then placed her hand on Dev's arm with a smile. "This one."

Mary smiled. She whacked Dev on the arm, and he nearly fell over.

Tess laughed. "I think she approves."

Dev rubbed his arm with a grimace. "I'd hate to think of what she'd do if she didn't. Mind if I go back out of harm's way?"

"Sure."

The men were doing pretty well for their first interaction, but Tess could tell they were all pretty nervous. She supposed she couldn't blame them.

Tess and Mary sat together enjoying the quiet, but Tess couldn't help but worry about what was coming. They'd already been here for an hour. How much more time would they have? *I should try to talk to Frank again. Maybe—*

A yell went up from the entrance, and Tess looked over. Kong came charging through, letting out a bellow that shook the valley. Tess didn't need to know the words to understand the meaning. *They're coming.*

She leapt to her feet. Dev and Shawn were sprinting toward the tunnel, while Pax was running over to her. Frank came running over too, Missy clinging to his neck. A dozen bigfoot trailed them, all agitated.

"Missy, is there another way out of the valley besides the tunnel we came through?" Tess asked.

"There's a way under the ground over there." She pointed to the other side of the valley by the lake.

"Tell them they need to leave that way. Right now."

Missy spoke with Frank. Frank barked at the bigfoot behind them, and they turned and ran across the valley, sounding the alarm.

Dev sprinted back from the tunnel. "They're here," he said.

"How many?"

"Three dozen. Maybe more."

"Damn it." Then she looked around. "Where's Shawn?"

Dev grinned. "Leaving them a surprise."

CHAPTER ONE HUNDRED EIGHTEEN

Shawn sprinted out of the tunnel entrance, waving his arms. "Run! They're right behind me!"

Mary pulled Missy into her arms and took off running. Tess was about to race after her when she heard the sound she'd been dreading: chopper blades. She looked up just in time to see a black helicopter come over the high cliff wall and hover just above the valley.

Tess's heart clenched when she saw the guns mounted on the front of it.

Just then a cry echoed across the valley, and Tess turned to see Kong racing back toward the tunnel, his guard behind him.

"No!" Tess yelled. "We need to go the other way!"

But it was useless. They didn't understand, and even if they did, they wouldn't listen to her.

An explosion blasted through the entrance of the tunnel. The roof of the tunnel collapsed. *Shawn's surprise.* "Well, at least no one's getting in that way," Tess said.

"Yeah, but they'll find a way around. We've only slowed them down," Dev said.

Before Dev's words had even died away, the chopper opened fire. Dev launched himself at Tess and knocked her to the ground, covering her with her body.

One of Kong's men was hit and fell. Kong let out a yell and ripped a tree from the ground with his bare hands. Then, turning like a shot putter, he launched the tree at the chopper.

It slammed into the side of the chopper and busted the propeller. The chopper veered dangerously to one side, then overcorrected in the opposite direction. It began to spin. Even just watching it was dizzying. It was completely out of the pilot's control.

Tess held her breath as soldiers dove from the chopper, landing on the rocks above the clearing.

The chopper slammed into the cliff face at one side of the clearing. There was an explosion of fire and rock, and shrapnel flew across the valley. Shawn leapt out of the way as a piece of one of the rotors missed him by inches.

"Oh my God," Tess murmured, knowing the pilot couldn't have survived that crash.

Dev helped her to her feet. "Come on. We have to move."

"You okay?" she called to Pax, who also got to his feet.

Pax pointed a shaky finger at Shawn had nearly been killed. "Did you see—"

"He's okay," Tess said quickly.

Shawn ran full tilt across the clearing toward them. "Go, go!" Behind him, Kong's lieutenants descended with howls of outrage on the soldiers who'd escaped the chopper.

Dev grabbed Tess's arm. "Let's go."

"Pax!" Tess yelled.

Pax stood waiting for Shawn. Tess shook herself free from Dev and ran over to him. She yanked on his arm. "We need to move, Pax. Shawn will catch up."

"But—"

"There will be more coming. Come on!" Tess yelled, yanking him forward. Dev grabbed his other arm, and finally Pax began to run.

Tess looked ahead, but she couldn't see Mary and Missy anymore. She wasn't worried; she knew Mary would protect Missy with her very life. She just hoped she wouldn't have to.

Even through the terror of the approaching threat, Tess reeled at the scene around her: she was running in the midst of a tribe of bigfoot. A mother, her small child clutched to her, loped past Tess on the right, her longer stride eating up the ground. Smaller bigfoot, about Tess's size, outpaced her, their muscular legs propelling them. In fact, it didn't take long before all of the bigfoot had sprinted past the slower humans.

"Hope they wait for us," Shawn said as he caught up with them.

"Or at least leave the door open," Tess said.

But they hadn't been forgotten. Just then they saw Kong and three other guards running back to get them. They didn't kneel down and give piggyback rides this time, they just each grabbed a human, lifted them up into their arms, and ran. Tess swatted at Kong's hair as it blew around her face. Her lungs felt like they were going to burst. She pounded on Kong's arm, and he loosened up a little, allowing her to breathe. She sucked the air in greedily.

Ahead, at the rear of the valley, she saw the last of Kong's guards waiting for them beside the opening to a tunnel that looked like it might be too small for the bigfoot. But as soon as the guards saw them coming, they ducked inside. Without stopping, Kong and the other two guards followed. Tess held her breath as Kong's head barely passed under the cave ceiling.

This tunnel was much longer and winding than the entrance tunnel, and after the first turn Tess couldn't see a thing. But Kong slowed his run only slightly, and Tess said a small thank-you for his incredible vision. A few minutes later, they burst out once again into the sunlight, and Kong started running east.

Tess pounded on his arm. "No. We need to go north."

Kong ignored her.

Tess pounded again. "No. We're going the wrong way."

Kong grunted at her.

Soon they approached a gathering of waiting bigfoot. Kong came to a stop and unceremoniously dumped Tess on the ground. She landed hard on her butt. *That's going to leave a mark.*

The men were set down a little more kindly. Tess got to her feet and immediately scanned the group for Missy. Sugar came loping over to her, and Tess smiled with relief. If Sugar was here, then Mary, Frank and Missy couldn't be too far away.

Sugar started to chatter quickly. She was clearly agitated.

Tess reached up and rubbed the side of her face. "It's okay, Sugar. It's okay."

Sugar held Tess's hand to her face and closed her eyes. Tess felt the sadness from Sugar. Their home had been uncovered and destroyed. And even though they didn't have possessions, they did have a connection to the land. That mindless destruction was going to be tough on all of them.

Tess also felt uneasy, and that feeling was all her own. The bigfoot around her were giving her unhappy looks.

Shawn, Dev, and Pax came over to her. She glanced up at them and spoke in a low voice. "We need to find Missy fast."

"Yeah, I don't think your friends like us very much right now," Pax said.

"Come on." Shawn started forward.

Easing their way through the group, they finally spotted Missy in Frank's arms, Mary beside them.

"Tess!" Missy yelled. Frank turned, and Tess could have sworn she saw relief on his face. Missy scrambled down and ran for her.

Tess knelt down, and Missy nearly plowed her over when she leapt into her arms. "I didn't know what happened to you," Missy said, tears in her throat.

Tess hugged her tight. "I'm okay. Kong helped us get out."

Missy nodded into her shoulder and didn't seem inclined to let her go. Tess stood, and Missy wrapped her legs around Tess's waist. Tess patted the girl's back and carried her back over to Frank and Mary. The men followed.

Mary looked between Tess and Missy. Tess could sense her sadness—but also her relief that Missy had found a home with her own people.

"Missy?" Tess said quietly. "I need your help talking, okay?"

Missy nodded, wiping at the tears on her cheeks.

Tess turned to Frank. Kong muscled his way over to them, but Tess ignored him. "We have to head north," she said. "There will be more coming."

She waited while Missy translated. Kong grunted, which Tess took as disagreement. She ignored that too. "We have a plan to get everyone to safety, but it will only work if we head to the north. Please trust me."

Missy looked up at her. "There's no word for trust in their language."

"Well, come as close as you can."

Missy spoke with them again, and Tess waited anxiously. All of this hinged on the bigfoot trusting them right now. If they didn't... Tess shook her head. She didn't even want to think about that.

Kong grunted and gestured angrily. Frank chattered back at him. Mary also piped in. And a murmur rumbled around all them. Pax's hand found Tess's and she squeezed it tight.

Shawn leaned down and spoke quietly in Tess's ear. "We need to get moving soon. They'll have regrouped by now and focused their forces on our probable escape route."

Tess knew he was right, and she felt the seconds tick by. She wanted to yell at the bigfoot to hurry, but that wasn't how it was done. And she knew if she interrupted, she'd just slow things down. So she bit her tongue and prayed they would come to a decision soon.

Finally, they went quiet.

"Missy?" Tess asked.

Missy looked up at her. "They'll go."

CHAPTER ONE HUNDRED NINETEEN

Tess explained the plan to Missy, who translated it to the group. "Do they know where that is?" Tess asked.

"Yes," Missy said.

Tess knelt down in front of the girl. "Now I need you to go with Pax."

Missy looked confused. "What?"

"I need you safe. And this part is going to be dangerous."

Missy's eyes grew large and her bottom lip trembled. "You don't want me to come with you?"

Tess ran her hand over Missy's hair. "No, it's not like that. I need to know you're safe. It's my job to keep you safe. And if I bring us with you, I'm not doing my job. So you and Pax are going to head back home, out of harm's way."

Pax knelt down. "You're with me, kiddo."

Missy looked back and forth between them. Tess knew she wanted to argue, so Tess spoke before she could. "Please, Missy. I need to try to keep everyone safe. And you and Pax being out of the way will help with that."

"But you will come back? You're not sending me away?" Missy asked.

"Of course I'll come back. You're my family now. And you will always be my family. When we're done, I'll find you at the cabin."

Missy nodded even as tears filled her eyes. She threw her arms around Tess. Tess hugged her tight. *Please let me not be lying about returning to her. She's lost too much already.*

Tess pulled away and tried to keep her tone neutral. "Go hug everybody else, okay?"

Missy gave her a long look, then turned and ran for Mary.

"You sure this is for the best?" Pax said.

Tess kept her eyes on Missy, who was wrapped in Mary's and Sugar's arms. "I need her safe. I need *you* safe."

"I can fight if I need to."

Tess took his hand. "I know that. But I'm trusting you with something far more precious to me. If I don't make it back, I need you to take care of her, okay?"

Pax's jaw tightened. "Don't talk that way. And you don't even have to ask that. I love Missy. But you come back, you hear me?"

"That's the plan," Tess said lightly.

Pax gave a little laugh even as he wiped at a tear that escaped the corner of his eye. "Oh, good. Well, as long as you have a plan, nothing can go wrong."

"Look at how well everything's turned out so far," Tess joked, but it fell flat.

Pax pulled her into a hug. "Just come back. You're kind of important to me."

"I will," Tess said into his shoulder.

Pax pulled away and wiped at his eyes. "And bring back my husband. He's kind of important to me too."

"I will," Tess said.

Pax kissed her on the cheek and then walked over to Shawn.

Dev made his way to her side. "You okay?"

Tess sighed. "Not really. I can't let Missy come with us, but I hate for those two to go back alone."

"They'll be okay—safer than the rest of us."

"I'm counting on that."

Frank walked over with Missy in his arms and Kong at his heels. Tess looked between the unfriendly bigfoot and Missy. "What's going on?"

"Kong's going to take us home," Missy said.

Tess's eyes flew to Kong. He looked back at her with his usual flat expression. "Thank you," she said.

He gave her a nod.

Shawn and Pax joined them and Tess quickly relayed the new plan.

Pax paled a little. "Oh good. Another ride."

Shawn wrapped an arm around him. "Cheer up. Think of all the stories you'll have that you can never tell anyone."

"Oh, I'm telling people. Our son is going to hear every single one. Although I'll pretend they're all the result of my incredible imagination."

Tess smiled even though a large part of her felt like crying. "Okay then. Let's get this show on the road."

Missy hugged Frank and Mary one more time. Mary picked her up and placed her on Kong, then Kong knelt down and let Pax scramble up.

Pax gave a wobbly smile as Kong stood. "Well I guess it's time—"

Kong took off through the woods.

Tess smiled at Pax's yelp. Then she took a breath and turned to the rest of the group. "Okay. Now for the rest of us."

Tess held on to Mary's back as the female bigfoot ran through the trees. They were leading the tribe. Tess thought they were making good time, and she hadn't heard any forces behind her. But more than one chopper had flown above them. Each time she'd tensed, waiting for the gunfire. But so far, it hadn't yet come.

Tess pulled out her GPS. *Three miles to go.* She looked back at Dev, who was on one of Kong's men. He gave her a thumbs-up. Tess gave herself a moment of hope. *We're going to make it.*

Then she heard the undeniable sound of another helicopter. And this one sounded different, larger. She tapped Mary on the shoulder. Mary slowed down and then stopped. Frank stopped next to them, Shawn on his back, staring up at the sky.

"Shawn?" Tess asked.

Shawn tapped on Frank's shoulder. Frank knelt down so Shawn could disembark. Then Shawn pulled out his binoculars and scanned the sky, finally focusing on a spot to the north.

"Well?" Tess asked.

"It's not a gunship. It's a transport chopper. I think it's a Sikorsky. They can carry forty men." He lowered the binoculars. "They're landing. I'm guessing they've picked up on our heat signatures and know exactly where we are. They're trying to cut us off."

"We need to go around them then," Tess said.

"Let's head northwest," Shawn said.

"But—"

"I know. But we can't take them on. Not head on. They'll be armed to the teeth."

"We'll have to backtrack."

"There's no other choice." He paused. "Will you be able to use that gun on a human, if you have to?"

Tess looked over the tribe of bigfoot that stood behind them. There were over five dozen, ranging in age from elderly to newborn. They had stayed away from humans for centuries. And now humans were chasing them into a confrontation that they could never win. One that the bigfoot had never planned on engaging in. All they wanted was to be left alone, to live in peace. And humans wouldn't let them.

Tess felt only disgust at the reasons behind this life-and-death chase. Disgust at what her species would do to this other species. It was genocide. Could she shoot a human to save the tribe?

"If it comes to that…" She paused. "Yes."

They altered their course, heading more northwest than north. They were only a mile from their destination.

A gunshot rang out, and Tess's head popped up. *Damn it.*

"Take cover!" Shawn yelled.

The bigfoot didn't understand the words, but either Shawn's tone or the gunshot told them all they needed to know. Some of the bigfoot dropped to the ground, others slipped into the trees.

Mary crouched down, and Tess rolled off. Shawn crawled up next to her.

"Where's it coming from?" Tess asked.

"East," Shawn said, no doubt in his voice. "It's got to be the men from the chopper. Either they landed farther this way than I thought, or they've been tracking our direction this whole time."

A human scream echoed through the trees, and the hairs on the back of Tess's neck stood up. Dev made his way to Tess's other side. "I think your friends found one of the gunmen," he said.

The report of a weapon sounded behind them. Tess whirled around. "What the hell?"

"Damn it. They're flanking us, trying to box us in. Some of those choppers must have dropped more off and we didn't see it. We need to go, now." Shawn grabbed Tess's arm.

Together they made their way forward, the bigfoot doing the same.

Then all hell broke loose.

Dev pushed Tess to the ground, covering her as shots rang out. Shawn scurried behind a tree. He yelled over at them. "I'll cover you guys. Get ready to run."

Before Tess could argue, Shawn let off a barrage of gunfire. Dev and Tess crawled as quickly as they could to a rocky outcropping up ahead. Then using the rocks for cover, Dev provided cover for Shawn.

Shawn sprinted toward them and dove low. "How much farther?"

Tess checked the GPS. "Another mile."

"That's going to be a really long mile," Dev muttered.

Tess scanned the woods and saw the bigfoot making their way from tree to tree. So far, they looked all right.

"We can't stay here," Shawn said. "We're just giving them a chance to set up. We need to move faster."

As if on cue, Mary, Frank, and the bigfoot who had been carrying Dev grabbed the humans and began sprinting through the trees.

Tess held on for dear life, but she knew Mary would never drop her.

Then Sugar let out a yell, and Mary's head whipped to the side. Before Tess could even inhale, Sugar was sprinting through the trees away from them.

Mary didn't even hesitate—she ran after her daughter.

"Tess!" Dev yelled.

"I'll find you," Tess yelled back, not sure if he even heard her. She gripped her hands tighter in Mary's hair, trying to keep from losing her purchase. Tess tried to spy Sugar ahead, but the jostling from Mary made that impossible.

Then Mary let out a screech and dropped Tess to the ground, barely pausing. Tess rolled as she hit, but still felt the impact shimmy up her legs.

A scream—a human one—sounded up ahead. Tess got to her feet and stumbled forward.

Oh no.

Two of Sugar's friends were on the ground, blood seeping from their wounds. Sugar knelt next to them, immobilized. Behind them, two humans were also on the ground. One man's leg was bent at an unnatural angle. The other was trying to crawl away.

Mary stormed toward the second man.

Tess ran up to her. "No."

Mary glared down at her.

But Tess didn't move. The man was no threat. And in any other case, Mary wouldn't even consider harming him further. Tess nudged her chin toward the juveniles. "They need your help."

Mary stood in front of Tess, her hands curled into fists. Finally, she stepped back. Tess didn't spare the man another glance as she made her way toward the wounded bigfoot and dropped down beside one. The bullet had gone through her leg, but the wound was already clotting. The other had been shot in the side and in the foot. But neither wound looked overly serious. Which was good, because if they were serious, Tess wasn't sure what she could have done about it.

Mary picked up the one who'd been shot in the foot while Sugar wrapped her arm around the shoulders of the one who'd been hit in the leg.

Mary glanced back at Tess. And Tess knew Mary could not carry her as well. They both needed to get the injured bigfoot out of danger and quickly. Tess would only slow them down.

Tess nodded. "Go. I'll catch up."

Sugar glanced between Mary and Tess, her eyes growing wide. But Mary barked at her, and Sugar lowered her head. Tess touched Sugar's arm. "I'll be okay, Sugar. Get your friends to safety."

Mary nodded at Tess and took off at a run. Sugar gave Tess one last long look before following.

Tess let out a trembling breath. *Right, now it's just me.*

She took a step forward and then dove to the ground as gunfire sounded from only a hundred yards away.

CHAPTER ONE HUNDRED TWENTY-THREE

Tess crawled toward a tree, her heart pounding. More gunfire sounded, followed by screams. *No.*

Tess got to her feet but kept low, hoping it was only humans that were hurt. *And what kind of human does that make me?*

When she heard voices, she crept forward as quietly as she could, keeping herself low behind the scruff.

Taking shelter underneath the thick branches of a Douglas fir, she crawled toward the voices. A keening wail sounded from up ahead, and then was abruptly cut off. Tess's heart beat even faster. She moved forward on her belly, hidden by the fir's prickly leaves, and peeked through the branches.

Ahead of her a juvenile lay on the ground, a dart sticking out of his back. Beyond him, a larger bigfoot lay motionless, blood pooling next to him.

Tess put her hand to her mouth. Two men made their way into the clearing. One advanced on the larger bigfoot and kicked it. It didn't move. "This one's gone," he said.

The other man advanced on the small one. "This one's still

breathing. Not sure how long he'll be out. Let's get him caged before he wakes up."

"What about the big one?" the first man said, kicking the dead bigfoot again.

"We'll grab him later. He's not going anywhere."

"You sure he's out?" the first man asked, nodding at the smaller bigfoot.

"Yeah. These tranqs can take down an elephant. Grab an arm."

With a grunt, the two men started dragging the juvenile away. "He's heavier than he looks," the first man said.

"It's all that muscle. This thing is ripped."

Tess watched them leave, then let her gaze return to the dead bigfoot. *I'm so sorry*, she thought.

She crawled out from under the evergreen. She hesitated, glancing in the direction Dev, Shawn, and the rest of the bigfoot had gone. The direction she was supposed to go.

Then she turned and followed the men.

CHAPTER ONE HUNDRED TWENTY-FOUR

Tess was easily able to keep up with the two men—since they were dragging the bigfoot behind them—but she wasn't sure what to do. They were trained soldiers, and she was not. There was no way she could get the bigfoot away from them; even though he was only a juvenile, he was easily two hundred pounds, and she'd never be able to carry him or even drag him away.

And she knew she wouldn't be able to kill the men—she wasn't ready for that step.

So she followed them and watched from behind the trees as they joined up with two more men. The four of them picked up the juvenile and carried it to a camp of sorts. A row of six empty cages were lined up against one side of a clearing. To Tess's relief, they were all empty.

Until now. The juvenile was placed in one of the smaller cages.

Tess made her way slowly around the clearing, careful to stay well back behind the trees. When she got around to the cages, she moved closer so that she could get a better look. The back walls of the cages were solid metal. She couldn't even see into any of the cages from back here, much less open them.

Tess sank down on her heels, staying low out of sight. *What am I going to do?*

Just then there was a knocking sound from the trees on the other side of the clearing. The sound of wood on wood.

The four men turned and raised their weapons. One man nodded to the other three. "Check it out."

Tess watched as the three men slipped into the woods. *One to go.*

The last man checked the lock on the cage. He paused at the cage entrance and raised his gun, aiming it at the small bigfoot. Tess tensed, aiming her own weapon. *Please don't make me do this.*

The man laughed and lowered his weapon and then followed the other men into the woods.

Tess didn't waste a second. She burst into the vacated clearing and hurried to the front of the juvenile's cage. The bigfoot was beginning to come to. He rolled onto his back and sat up, his head hitting the top of the cage. *Oh, please know who I am.*

The juvenile reared back when it caught sight of her, rocking the cage.

"Shh, shh," Tess said.

The bigfoot's chest rose and fell quickly. The hair on the back of his neck stood up.

"I'm a friend. I'm a friend," Tess said.

The bigfoot watched her closely. It was a *Gigantopithecus* type, and it looked to be less than four feet tall. It probably wasn't even a teenager yet. It was still a child.

"Got that damn thing in a cage. I swear it nearly took my arm off," a voice said.

Tess dove around to the back of the cage again.

"We need to get this thing set up to transport."

"We're flying it out?"

"Yeah. Help me move it."

The two men who had originally grabbed the bigfoot reappeared from the woods and walked straight for the cage. But behind them, two shadows separated themselves from the trees. Two very tall shadows.

The bigfoot grabbed the men and threw them. They sailed through the air with a scream. Tess's heart rate picked up. The other men would hear that scream and be here soon.

Tess wasted no time. She sprinted back around the cage, pulled her rifle from her back, stepped back, and blasted the lock. She kicked the lock off and swung open the door just as more men appeared. Tess shot at the ground in front of them, forcing them to take cover. "Go, go!" she yelled at the juvenile, hoping he understood.

But the young bigfoot just cringed in the back of the cage. The men had taken cover and now that they realized it was only her, they opened fire.

Tess dove for the ground and rolled behind the cage, covering her head. She heard the men yell and she peeked out. Two bigfoot had appeared behind the men. They lifted them from the ground and flung them into the trees.

Tess ran back to the open cage door. She reached in, holding out her hand. "Please." She focused on her memories of Charlie, Mary, and Sugar, and did her best to pour out her feelings of trust.

The bigfoot finally reached out his hand. Tess grasped it and tugged him forward. The bigfoot needed no further urging. He ran forward and grabbed on to Tess. Tess nearly fell under his weight, but she managed to keep upright. "We need to go."

But before they could escape into the woods, a man stepped out right in front of them, his weapon aimed at the two of them.

Tess stepped in front of the bigfoot. She could feel the poor little one shaking, and her anger spiked, right along with her fear.

The man smirked. "What are you, one of those tree huggers? Get out of the way."

Tess looked at the rifle held confidently in the man's arms. It wasn't a tranquilizer gun.

"No," she said, although she would have preferred if the tremor in her voice hadn't been so noticeable.

"Your choice." He raised his weapon.

Tess tensed. But then a bigfoot swooped down from the trees above, both feet landing on the man and driving him into the ground. Tess cringed at the crunch of bones. She reached back for the child, grabbed his hand, and ran.

Together they sprinted through the trees, and Tess could hear the crashing of branches behind them. She knew bigfoot made no noise going through the trees—which meant it was humans giving chase. She willed herself to run faster.

The child stumbled and fell. Tess reached down and pulled him up, urging him on.

Their pursuers were getting closer. Tess knew she would have to confront them at some point, but she had no idea how to make the bigfoot continue on without her.

An arm suddenly wrapped around her waist, and Tess screamed as she struggled. The child's hand was yanked from hers. "No!"

Then she noticed the hair covering the arm. She glanced back —it was one of Kong's lieutenants. Another lieutenant had the young bigfoot wrapped in her arms.

Tess closed her eyes and took a deep breath. She was safe for the moment. But she knew that wasn't something she could count on for long.

Tess flew through the trees wrapped in the arms of one of Kong's lieutenants. She would love to check her GPS. She knew they were close. But in her present position, she couldn't reach it.

A gunshot sounded from behind them. The bigfoot carrying Tess stumbled and dropped Tess, who rolled to the side as the bigfoot crashed to his knees. Somewhere behind her a man screamed. The bigfoot next to her, who was carrying the child, sprinted away.

Tess crawled over to the downed bigfoot, but two of his friends reached him first and hoisted him up between them. They looked at her.

She waved them on. "Go, go!" she yelled. She scrambled behind a tree and pulled out her GPS. *Almost there.*

Movement in the woods caught her attention. She squinted. It was a man in camouflage. He leaned up against a rock, and raised his rifle. Tess's gaze flew to his target. He was aiming at a bigfoot about six foot tall, who was scanning the trees.

Sugar—she came back for me.

Heart pounding, Tess raised her own rifle and aimed. She pulled the trigger. Nothing. *Damn it.* She threw it down and pulled out Madge's rifle. *Oh, please God.*

She took aim and fired. Her bullet hit right a tree right beside the man, spitting bark. The man ducked and rolled. Sugar scampered away.

Tess let out a breath and sprinted forward.

In her mind, she counted the yards. Five more. She pushed harder and crossed the imaginary finish line. Gun blasts behind her celebrated her achievement, and she flung herself to the ground just as Sugar dashed toward her.

Behind Tess, six men stepped out of the trees, their weapons aimed at Sugar. Tess leaped to her feet and jumped in front of her. "No."

Tess's breaths came out in pants. Two more men moved in on her from the left. Tess pulled Sugar behind her so that none of the men had a clear shot. Tremors ran through her, and she was pretty sure her legs were going to give out at any moment. Nearby, bigfoot could be heard slamming branches into trees, voicing their displeasure.

Run, run, Tess yelled in her mind to Sugar as the armed men moved toward her. But Sugar stayed with her. Tess wanted to cry, knowing Sugar wouldn't leave her but wishing with all her might she would.

Then Shawn and Dev appeared out of nowhere. Their weapons were raised, and pointed right at the men. Even more threatening were the bigfoot who were lined up beside them.

The armed men swung their weapons between Sugar and these new bigfoot. Tess's heart stopped. This was precisely the nightmare that had kept her on edge since she'd first learned about the private army.

I'm going to lose them all.

A gray-haired man stepped forward from the group to her
left. "My name is Jeff Adams. I'm a retired colonel of the
US Army. We are under orders from the governor of California.
Stand aside."

Adams was a square-jawed man with sharp eyes. This was a
man who would follow through on his orders.

"And if we don't stand aside?" Tess asked.

Adams narrowed his eyes. "Casualties happen. Like I said,
I'm under orders."

"Well, that means next to nothing here," a familiar voice said.

Tess's head whipped to the side. Eric stepped out of the
woods. And he wasn't alone.

A dozen park rangers were with him, along with twice as
many men and women whom Tess recognized as members of the
Hoopa and Klamath tribes. There were more men, too, men she'd
never seen before, but she had no doubt who they were: Shawn's
fellow SEALs "on leave" from the Navy. They had made it.

The private military men seemed taken aback at this sudden

appearance. "You people need to clear out," Adams said. "We are under orders of—"

Eric stepped forward. "You're in Oregon. Your orders don't apply here." Tess felt a sense of hope as Eric stepped forward. "In fact, Governor Blackwell has ordered all of you arrested on sight if you set one foot into Oregon. So *I* am ordering *you* to drop your weapons. You are all under arrest."

The colonel slammed his mouth shut. He glared at Eric. But then he appeared to assess the situation. "Do as he says," he told his men. "Drop your weapons."

"Go," Tess whispered to Sugar. Sugar looked down at her, and Tess squeezed her hand. "It's okay. Go."

With one last look, Sugar disappeared into the trees, and the other bigfoot followed. Tess watched them go, then turned back to the stunned faces of everyone who'd watched them depart. That was not a sight they would soon forget.

The rangers made the military men kneel on the ground and placed zip ties around their wrists. The colonel looked up at Eric and Tess and narrowed his eyes. "I don't know what you think you've accomplished here. Everyone knows they exist now." He scoffed. "In fact, you just provided more than a dozen witnesses to their existence."

"I don't know what you're talking about," Tess said. "All I know is that my brother-in-law, boyfriend and I were walking through the woods when you started shooting at us."

The colonel laughed. "Right. And not the bigfoot standing next to you."

Tess reared back. "Bigfoot? What bigfoot?" She turned to Eric. "Did you see a bigfoot?"

Eric shook his head. "Can't say I did. But man, I would really like to." He turned back to the colonel. "You know, people often mistake bears for bigfoot. It's a common misidentification."

The colonel spluttered. "Who are you trying to kid? All these people saw them."

A few men and women had grabbed tree branches and were already busy swiping the ground in different spots, removing any traces of prints.

Tess called out to them. "This guy says he saw a bigfoot. Did you guys see one?"

They all shook their heads.

"Nope."

"No."

"Bigfoot's just a legend."

Tess turned back to the colonel. "You know, whenever people say they've seen bigfoot, they're viewed as being a little crazy. So you might want to keep that 'sighting' to yourself. Because none of the rest of us saw anything."

CHAPTER ONE HUNDRED TWENTY-EIGHT

Tess stepped away from Eric as he read Colonel Adams his Miranda rights. Dev was already doing to the same to the other captured men. Shawn and his friends had disappeared back into the woods. They were looking for any injured and any evidence left behind of the bigfoot.

Not that I think they left any. Tess stood still, staring at the woods to the north. Had she not just seen the bigfoot depart that way, she'd have no idea they had ever been here. She studied the ground. Nothing there either. Not a trace.

She walked north. She didn't expect to find any bigfoot still in the area. After all, they had plenty to take care of. She'd seen a few bigfoot carrying the bodies of other bigfoot, and her heart lurched at the memory.

But as soon as she rounded the curve of the path, Mary, Sugar, and Frank were there in front of her. Tess soaked in the sight of them. None of them seemed hurt. *Thank God.*

But Tess felt their sadness. Missy's family may have escaped injury, but they had lost their home, and other members of the tribe had been hurt or killed.

And she had the distinct impression they had been waiting for her. She looked at each of them. "Is everyone accounted for?"

She knew they couldn't answer her, or even understand her, but she needed to ask. Frank grunted, and Tess looked up at him. A vision of half a dozen bigfoot flew through her mind, vague and indistinct, except for the last one. Kong popped into her mind with perfect clarity.

Tess reared back. *Well, that's new.* But then she realized Frank was telling her that Kong and some others hadn't returned. She had no doubt that other bigfoot were out looking for them. But she also knew Frank was asking for her help.

Tess nodded. "I'll find them."

CHAPTER ONE HUNDRED TWENTY-NINE

Tess made her way back to Eric and the others, but everyone was busy dealing with the private army. Tess debated speaking with Dev before slipping away after the missing bigfoot, but she knew he would just try to talk her out of going. Kong might not be the friendliest bigfoot, but he had saved her life and Missy's. She owed him. She'd call in the cavalry if she found someone and needed help.

Without a word, she headed south. She knew there were probably still gunmen somewhere in these trees, but fear for Kong overrode all other considerations. At the same time, she thought she was crazy for even worrying. Kong was ridiculously capable. He could take care of himself. He was a ten-foot hominid, for goodness' sake—not exactly the stereotypical victim.

But she wasn't sure how familiar he was with the trickiness of humans.

Blowing out a breath, she checked that Madge's rifle was loaded—it wasn't. And she had no extra rounds with her. *Well, this was well thought out.*

Tess paused every few feet to listen. *What am I doing? Kong does not need my help.*

But maybe the others do.

She moved forward. Gunfire sounded through the forest followed by a scream of pain.

Tess ran forward, knowing that scream hadn't come from a human. She leapt over downed trees and moved faster than she ever let herself move in the woods.

She sprinted past a boulder and slammed to a stop. *How the hell—*

Abe Cascione stood ten feet away, a small bigfoot on the ground next to him. He reared back and kicked it in the side. It let out a whimper.

"Come on, you can scream louder than that." He kicked it again.

Tess's anger boiled. This bigfoot was barely a toddler. He didn't appear injured, but he did look absolutely terrified.

A bellow sounded from farther away, and Abe grinned. "Now that's more like it."

Abe pulled his gun into his shoulder and scanned for any movement. Tess quickly ducked behind a boulder.

A crashing sounded from the other side of Abe. Abe whirled around just as Kong stormed out of the woods, a body over his shoulders.

No. Tess knew Kong was fast, but he wouldn't outrun a bullet. She slid her rifle off her shoulder. It might not be loaded, but it would still work as a bat.

She adjusted her grip, not believing she was doing this. Was she actually about to take on an armed man with only an unloaded gun?

Abe pulled the trigger, and Kong reared back, the body he was carrying hitting the ground with a thump. The small bigfoot that Abe had been kicking darted into the trees, but Abe didn't seem to care. He was after the bigger trophy.

Tess raced forward, swinging the rifle for all she was worth.

Hearing her footsteps, Abe turned. "What the—?"

Tess swung, knocking his rifle aside. It clattered to the ground and out of his reach. Tess swung back and caught him in the shoulder. But he recovered quickly and tackled Tess around the waist, slamming her onto her back. Pain radiated through her skull, and her vision went blurry.

Abe held her arms down and stared at her. "You." He laughed. "Looks like I get to finish what I started." Abe reared back and aimed a punch at her face.

Tess shifted at the last second. He caught her ear instead of her cheek. But it still hurt like hell.

"Get off me!" Tess yelled. Squirming, she kneed him in the groin. He groaned. Tess managed to sit up, slamming her elbow into his chin. He fell back, and she scrambled out from underneath him.

Tess and Abe both dove for the rifle. But Abe got there first. Pointing the rifle at Tess, he rose to his feet. "Well, guess this didn't end the way you planned."

Still on her knees, Tess glared up at him. In her mind, though, she said her goodbyes. Her life flashed before her eyes, dominated by images of Dev, Missy, Shawn, and Pax. She pictured the four of them together. *I love you,* she thought, and then held her breath.

Abe smiled. And then his smile turned to an expression of horror as he was yanked into the air by an angry Kong. The rifle went off. The ground right next to Tess was torn up by the bullet.

Kong roared and slammed Abe into a tree. The tree cracked and bent. Tess cringed at the sickening thud Abe's body made. Then he flung Abe's broken body into the trees.

Kong stared down at her, breathing hard, rage coming off him in waves. Then he turned, scooped up the dead bigfoot, and disappeared into the trees.

Tess fell back, her stomach rolling. Her breaths came out in pants. She couldn't tear her gaze from the spot where Kong had disappeared. Then she turned on her side and threw up.

CHAPTER ONE HUNDRED THIRTY

After the incident with Kong, Tess had made her way slowly back to the group, feeling numb. She'd looked for the toddler on the way back, but she had no doubt Kong had found him and brought him back. And when she'd reappeared at the rendezvous point, it seemed that no one had even noticed she'd been gone. She'd grabbed a blanket and sat on the tailgate of Eric's pickup.

Now the sun was dipping below the horizon. All the private military individuals had been arrested and taken away, but the tribe and Eric's ranger friends stayed on. Someone had made a fire, and dinner soon followed. But Tess knew it wasn't the food that kept everyone here. It had been a once-in-a-lifetime event, and no one was ready to let it end.

The last few rays of sun hit her face. It was going to be a gorgeous sunset.

There had been no sign of the bigfoot since Tess had last spoken with Frank and Mary. *Or since I saw Kong.* Tess knew they wouldn't come back while all these people were here. But she hoped they'd come back one day. She wanted to see them again. She just hoped they wanted to see her again, too.

Dev came and sat next to her, pulling her into her arms. "You all right?"

"I think so." She lapsed into silence. "It all seems unreal, now, doesn't it? Like it was a dream."

"Yeah. But it was a shared dream."

Tess nodded to the group around the fire. "Do you think they'll all keep this a secret?"

"You have nothing to fear from the Hoopa and Klamath," he said. "My people have respected bigfoot long before you folks were around. They'll keep the secret. As for everyone else... I don't know. What do you think?"

Tess looked around. Eric had called in many of his ranger friends, and Shawn had brought in so many SEAL buddies, too. It was amazing. It was a tribe. The bigfoot had needed help, and Tess's friends, and friends of friends, had jumped in to pitch in. Humans might be violent, but they also could be amazing.

"Well, Shawn trusts his guys, so I do too. As for the rangers, I think they'll stay quiet. I mean, no one really believes bigfoot exists anyway. That hasn't changed. And there's still no proof. And these guys... they respect nature. They know what would happen to these parks if the bigfoot were exposed. So yeah, I think they're safe for now."

"Did Shawn make it back to the valley where the chopper crashed?" Dev asked.

"Yeah. He retrieved the camera that was on the chopper and he doesn't think it was linked. So that should be the only copy. He's going to oversee the cleanup, and then he'll head back to the cabin."

"How many soldiers were killed?"

"Believe it or not, none."

"Not even the pilot?" Tess asked remembering the crash.

Shawn shook his head. "Nope. Oh, he's in bad shape but he'll make it. As for the rest, there's a bunch of broken bones and some concussions, but everybody's breathing."

"Well, that's good news." Tess shuddered, though, as she remembered Abe's death. She should probably tell someone, but right now, she was a little too raw for that.

"Hey, you all right?" Dev said. "Do *you* want to head back?"

Tess looked over her shoulder at the trees. She did, but she needed to check and make sure the bigfoot were really gone. "In a little bit. I think I need to go for a walk, clear my head."

Dev kissed her on the forehead. "Just be careful."

Tess gave a rueful laugh. "I'm pretty sure the firefight scared off any predators in the area."

"True, but be careful anyway."

Tess hopped off the back of the truck. "I will."

Dev headed over to the group by the fire, where Eric poured him a cup of coffee. Tess watched the camaraderie for a little bit before slipping into the trees.

It felt good to stretch her legs. As she walked, the forest noises returned, and Tess breathed in deep. This is what she needed—a reminder of the peace of the forest, not the violence of today.

She made her way to a little brook and took a seat on a downed tree at its bank. She sat and just watched the water rippling over the rocks. Small fish surfaced and disappeared. The sun pierced through the trees. Tess sat there for a good long while, letting the peacefulness flow over her.

Goodbye, my friends. I hope to see you again.

Tess stood and dusted off her pants. With one last look at the peaceful scene, she turned for the camp.

And went still.

Standing twenty feet away from her was Kong. He had a few scratches but no major wounds. She squinted but couldn't make out where Abe's bullet had hit him. She was surprised at the relief she felt. She realized she viewed him like a grumpy uncle: he never had a good word for you, but he was still family.

Kong seemed to be inspecting her as well.

"Hi," Tess said.

Kong grunted at her, and Tess couldn't help but smile.

Kong covered the distance between them in three strides. He stared down at her, and a vision of the juvenile in the cage popped into her mind. Tess gasped. "He's your son."

Kong didn't say anything, but he held out his hand to her. An apple lay on his palm.

Tess looked at it in surprise. *They only feed you if they think you're worthy.* She reached out and took the fruit with a shaky hand. "Thank—"

Kong was already striding away. But then he stopped, paused, and walked back. Tess looked up at him. He patted her twice on the head. Then he turned again, and disappeared into the woods.

A laugh burst from Tess, and she hugged the apple to her, tears springing to her eyes. *I like you too, Kong.*

CHAPTER ONE HUNDRED THIRTY-ONE

Two Days Later

Queens, New York

Deloris Cameron sat in the small cramped office of Abe Cascione and Associates. There had never been any "associates," but Abe had liked the sound of it. The office contained only two rooms: a small reception area and Abe's office. There was a shared bathroom down the hall that Deloris tried to avoid using at all costs. The whole building reeked of cigarette smoke thanks to the pool hall on the first floor.

She'd been watching TV all morning. The governor of California was in lots of hot water over his decision to let a private army loose in a state park. The Feds were thinking about bringing charges against everyone involved, including the governor.

A few of the soldiers claimed they'd found and even killed bigfoot. They said there'd been a whole group of them. But they didn't have any proof. The bodies, if there had been any, had disappeared. The public seemed divided over whether or not they were telling the truth.

Carter Hayes had even jumped into the fray, releasing a statement claiming he had a hair sample that was conclusive proof that bigfoot did in fact exist.

Deloris hobbled over to the TV. Her arthritis had been acting up this last month, and she'd forgotten to take her meds this morning. She switched the TV off. The ensuing silence was startling. She realized she'd been playing the footage of "The Assault in Rogue River," as the media had dubbed it, nonstop for the last day and a half.

She looked at the clock. 10:59. The second hand seemed to echo through the room with each tick. 10:59 and 30 seconds. Then 45. Deloris's heart began to pound.

11:00.

She closed her eyes and pushed away from her desk with a sigh. She had known this day would come. You didn't work for a man like Abe Cascione for the job security.

She went to his office and took down the picture of dogs playing poker that hung behind his desk, revealing the office safe. She turned the dial with a shaky hand: 37-23-35. Marilyn Monroe's measurements. It popped open. Abe had made sure she knew the combination, although she'd never before been allowed to open it.

And she had hoped she would never have to.

Abe wasn't a nice man. He wasn't a decent man, or a good man. But he'd taken on an old woman as his receptionist when most people hadn't even allowed her to interview, and she was grateful for that.

Deloris pulled open the door. In the safe were a few file folders and several stacks of money. But what she was looking for was right on top: three manila envelopes. Deloris wasn't sure what was in them, but she had been told that if she didn't hear from Abe in forty-eight hours, she was required to mail them. That had been a running requirement whenever he went out in the field.

She closed up the safe, stopped back at her desk, and picked up the three flash drives she had updated this morning from Abe's drop box. She dropped one in each envelope, noticing there was already a hefty stack of papers in each.

The first envelope was addressed to the local FBI field office. The other envelopes were addressed to the *New York Times* and *CNN*.

Deloris sealed the packages, hefted them into her arms, and headed for the door. If she hurried, she'd make it in time for the noon mailing. Then she'd come back and clean out her desk. It would be her last day. And right before she locked the office for the last time, she'd be sure to grab all that money from the safe.

She didn't think Mr. Cascione would mind. In fact, he'd be disappointed if she didn't.

"Tess? Tess, wake up."

Tess pushed away the hand that shook her shoulder. "Go away."

Dev laughed. "You're not getting rid of me that easy."

Dev? Tess pushed her hair out of her eyes and looked up into his laughing face. "What's going on?"

He leaned down and kissed her. "Happy to see you too."

Tess smiled. "Sorry. It's always good to see you. But what's going on? Where's Missy?"

"She's fine. She's outside with Pax and Shelby."

"Okay. Good." Tess was still half asleep.

Dev stood up and offered her his hand. "There's something you need to see."

Tess took his hand. "What is it?"

"It's about Hayes."

Dread settled in a pit in her stomach. After the whole thing with the private army, Hayes had been quiet, but they all knew it was only a matter of time before he tried something new. "What happened?"

Dev didn't say anything; he just tugged her out into the living room, where Shawn sat with the TV remote in hand. The clock read 12:30. She'd slept through the morning. Of course, seeing as she'd slept only an hour or two a night for the whole last week, that was understandable. Her insomnia was all due to Carter Hayes. She kept worrying about what he was going to do next, and how they were going to keep him away from the bigfoot.

As soon as Tess and Dev settled on the couch, Shawn hit play.

"The business world is stunned today at the arrest of Carter Hayes," a newscaster's voiceover said. Tess's eyes grew large as she watched a group of FBI agents escorting Carter from his headquarters in cuffs. "Hayes is being charged with crimes ranging from racketeering, to unlawful restraint of trade, to half a dozen counts of murder. All Hayes's accounts have been frozen while the FBI discerns just how far Hayes's alleged illegal business practices extend. Sources inside the agency report that Hayes will be just one among many big names that will be arrested as part of this operation."

Shawn muted the TV. Tess stared between him and Dev. "What on earth happened?"

"It seems that Hayes had a man in his employ who kept very detailed notes," Shawn said.

Tess looked up at him, her eyes going large. "Abe?"

Shawn nodded. She had told them all about Abe's death, but seeing as his body had never been found and they had no proof besides Tess's testimony, they decided to keep it to themselves. Nothing good would come from that revelation.

"He kept all his emails and even recorded his phone conversations," Dev said.

"But why would he release that information?" Tess asked.

"Apparently to protect himself against any harm from his employers, he arranged that in the event of his disappearance, information would be released on all his illegal dealings with Hayes, among others," Shawn said.

"And what was that about murder charges?"

"It seems that Hayes used Abe Cascione as his hit man," Shawn said. "Those recordings went to the FBI as well."

"And one of the murders was Tyler Haven and his cameraman," Dev added.

Tess felt disbelief followed by joy. "Hayes is incapacitated. He can't go after them now."

Shawn smiled. "He's going to be battling legal attacks for years, if he can scrape together enough for a defense."

"And with Hayes out of the picture, the bigfoot are a lot safer now," Dev said.

Tess's good feelings began to fade as she thought of the hunters who had descended on Beauford ever since the governor's announcement. It seemed like more and more popped up each day. None of them had found anything, but with the number of them out there, Tess worried it was only a matter of time. "They're *safer* but not *safe*. We still have all those bigfoot hunters out there."

"Well, they know about Hayes's test results. They know there's a bigfoot in the woods."

"And I've been blogging about them for a year, further fanning the flames," Tess said. She had taken down her website, but nothing could ever be truly erased on the internet. Many of her blog entries had already reappeared on other sites.

"I don't know if there's any way to completely put that fire out," Shawn said.

Tess looked between the two of them. The reason she had finally been able to sleep last night was because she *had* thought of a way to throw some cold water on the blazing bigfoot fire raging across the country. She knew that if she took this route, though, her life would never be the same.

Her eyes drifted to the picture Missy had drawn of her bigfoot family. Tess remembered Charlie's kind brown eyes and all that he'd risked to protect Missy. Could she risk any less to protect them all?

She took a deep breath and released it. "Actually, I think I know how to get them all to go home."

CHAPTER ONE HUNDRED THIRTY-THREE

The next morning, Tess stood in the little room next to the city hall conference room. She had arranged for a press conference that would begin in about five minutes. She had fixed her hair, carefully applied her makeup, and even wore her conference suit. She ran her hands down the navy blue jacket, knowing this might be the last time she ever had occasion to wear it.

Pax linked his arm through hers. "You're sure you want to do this? We could still beat a hasty retreat."

Tess patted his hand as butterflies danced through her stomach. "If you have an idea that would achieve the same result, I'm all ears."

Pax frowned and shook his head. "I hate this. You've worked so hard."

She kissed his cheek. "It'll be okay. I have you guys, Missy, Dev. The rest doesn't matter."

"You sure you'll be able to live with this decision?"

Tess thought about everything she had been through. The thrill at every discovery, her absolute shock, joy, and fear at meeting Charlie—and everything that had resulted from his trust in her.

He had taken a leap of faith. He had trusted her with the people most important to him—and all to save the life of a child from a different species. A child Tess now loved with all her heart.

"I can live with it," she said.

The door opened, sending Tess's heart racing. Dev and Shawn stepped in.

Dev's hazel eyes searched hers before he nodded. "They're ready."

"You're sure you don't want us up there with you?" Shawn asked.

Tess shook her head. "No. This is on me."

Shawn leaned over and kissed her cheek. "We'll be in the front row. Madge saved us seats."

Tess nearly cried at those words. Even Madge had left the farm to come support her. "Okay."

Pax wrapped her in a hug. "I am so proud of you."

Tess clung to him, then pushed him away. "Go. I need to not be an emotional mess when I do this."

Shawn took Pax by the shoulders and steered him out of the room. Now it was only her and Dev.

"So... you want to grab some lunch after this?" Dev asked.

Tess laughed. "Sure, but you'll have to buy. I'm kind of out of a job."

"I suppose I can manage that." He paused. "You ready?"

Tess straightened her shoulders. "Yeah. Let's go."

Dev led her to the door to the conference room and opened it. Immediately the noise level ratcheted up tremendously. Flashbulbs exploded. Tess ignored all of it, her focus only on the podium with the microphone attached to it. Dev escorted her there. With his back to the room, he smiled. *You've got this*, he mouthed.

Tess nodded. Reporters were already shouting questions at her, but she stood silently until everyone quieted down. Feeling shaky, she looked at her support group in the front row: Shawn, Pax, Madge, and Abby. And she knew Sasha was supporting her at home while she kept an eye on Missy.

She took a deep breath and expelled it. *Showtime.* "I am here today to rectify a grievous hoax perpetuated on my part. Due to the injuries sustained in the last few weeks, and..." She swallowed, her mouth felt dry. "I can no longer in good conscience stay silent."

She paused. "All of the evidence I have gathered on the bigfoot has been falsified. None of it was real."

The reporters stirred. Tess continued on. "I did it because while I have been searching for bigfoot, there have been absolutely no signs of the creature. Therefore, in order to continue my search, I manufactured evidence to support myself. And while I continue to believe and hope that the creature exists, I have not personally seen any verifiable proof of the existence of a bipedal hominid living in North America."

A reporter in the second row called out, "Dr. Brannick, what about the report on the hair sample you provided to Carter Hayes?"

Tess knew she was on tricky ground here. So far all she'd done was implicate herself. "I can't speak to that directly. But I will tell you that the hair I provided came from a black bear. I don't know how the results turned up the way they did. You'll have to speak with Mr. Hayes about that."

Questions flew at Tess fast and furious after that. Tess answered them for twenty minutes, wanting the assembled reporters to have no doubt that her life's work was entirely fraudulent. Finally, though, she could take no more. She put up her hand. "Thank you for your time. I will not answer any more questions on this subject at any point again." She stepped from the podium as flashbulbs exploded.

Dev quickly escorted her out of the room and closed the door behind them, shutting out the questions still being hurled at her by reporters.

Tess began to shake. "I did it. I just ruined my career. No one will ever believe me again."

Dev pulled her into his arms. "And you just saved a population—an entire species. That was one of the bravest things I've ever seen anyone do."

Tess wrapped her arms around him and held him tight. "Thank you for standing by me."

He looked down into her face. "I have been waiting forever to have the chance to stand with you. Bigfoot, journalists, hit men, heck, you can throw in UFOs, and I'll still be standing here. By your side is where I always want to be."

"Same goes." Tess leaned up and kissed him, feeling a peace that only comes from doing the right thing.

EPILOGUE

Two Years Later

Rogue River National Park, Oregon

Tess walked along the path in Rogue River Park. Her park ranger uniform was getting a little tight. She'd have to get a new one soon.

Sunlight glinted off her wedding ring, and she ran her thumb over it. Even though she had worn it for over a year, she still loved looking at it. It wasn't fancy, it wasn't expensive, but it was a part of Dev. And that's all she wanted.

She approached a campsite where a group had been camped out for the last week. She noted with approval that they had policed their own garbage. She loved when people respected the park. She wanted people to enjoy the outdoors, but in a way that allowed others to do the same after them.

Tess pulled her radio off her belt. "Brannick to base."

Eric's voice came over the line. "How's it looking out there, Tess?"

"It's good. They cleaned up great. I'll be heading back in."

"Good. Dev said he'll be here at three to pick you up."

"Okay, great."

"Oh, and Jeanne wanted to ask if it's okay if she brings flowers tonight."

Tess smiled. Missy had her first dance recital tonight, and everyone was coming to see her: Pax, Shawn, their son Dylan, Sasha and her latest boyfriend, Abby and her husband, Madge, Eric and his wife Jeanne. It was going to be a packed house.

"Tell Jeanne that would be great."

"Will do. See you in a little bit."

Tess keyed off the radio. Missy now had a full-fledged extended family—her own little tribe.

Tess felt eyes on her, and the hairs on the back of her neck stood up. Very carefully, she unsnapped her holster and placed her hand on the Browning there. But the fear she felt disappeared as quickly as it had appeared. It was replaced by an over-whelming feeling of trust.

Tess looked around, trying to find the source. And then a seven-foot bigfoot stepped out from the woods. Tess recognized her immediately, even though she was now fully grown. As Sugar approached, Tess's initial happiness turned to surprise and then joy. She gently placed her hand on Sugar's protruding belly. "Congratulations."

Since she'd become a ranger at Rogue River almost two years ago, she'd seen her friends every few months, sometimes more often. She and Dev had brought Missy out camping a few times, and inevitably their friends found them. The last time she'd seen Sugar had been two months ago, and there'd been no sign of the pregnancy. She wasn't sure how long bigfoot pregnancies lasted, but she really hoped she got to see this little one.

Tess never would have believed after everything they had all been through that this would be the end result. After the press conference, Tess had been raked over the coals in the media. It hadn't been easy, but the fact that everyone thought she was an unscrupulous liar at least meant that people had lost interest in investigating the areas where she'd said bigfoot were—and that in turn meant the bigfoot were at least as safe as they were back before any of this happened.

Sugar tilted her head and then sniffed. Her eyes grew large. Gently, Sugar placed her hand on Tess's stomach. Tess laughed. "Yup, me too."

Tess took a seat on a downed tree. Sugar sat next to her and looked at her expectantly. Tess pulled the Twinkies from her bag. Carefully unwrapping them, she handed one to Sugar.

Then she took a bite of the other one, listening to the sounds of life in the forest scurry by. She knew she should probably head back to the station.

Sugar sat next to her, already having finished her Twinkie, her head tilted back, her eyes closed as she enjoyed the feel of the sun on her face.

Tess smiled and did the same. *But there's no rush. I've got time.*

FACT OR FICTION?

A lot of different factors led to the creation of *Hominid*. Since I was a kid, I have always been fascinated by the idea of bigfoot. I asked my kids—my oldest is eight—if they knew about bigfoot, and they did as well. Bigfoot is pervasive in American culture.

The idea for this story came about when I was conducting research for a different book, *The Belial Children*. I was looking for information about giants interacting with humans. Everywhere I looked, I found mention of bigfoot. And a seed took root.

When I first came up with the idea for *Hominid*, though, it was going to go in a completely different direction. I had just seen a documentary on the 1959 deaths of a group of nine college students in the Ural Mountains of Russia. Their broken bodies were found, but the autopsies were withheld from the public for years. The documentary made the case that the menk—the Russian name for bigfoot—was responsible for the gruesome deaths. So when I first started thinking about a bigfoot book, that event stuck in my head.

But then I started doing more research. First off, if you're looking to do research on bigfoot, go for the books and not the

websites. The websites tend to provide good examples of incidents, but I was looking for something that drew conclusions
from those incidents.

So with the Russian Yeti documentary fresh on my mind, I
started looking for reports of violent attacks by bigfoot, sasquatch
or yeti—and I was coming up empty. Oh, they threw trees, chased
some people, and seemed to really dislike dogs, but there just
wasn't a lot about them attacking humans, which seemed odd.

Almost all the research agreed that the beings were between
six and eight feet tall, although some suggested that ten to twelve
feet might be possible. And reports consistently said they were
seriously fast. And I thought, if that's the case, if they wanted to
catch humans, or to hurt humans, they should have no problem
doing so. So why weren't there more reports of injuries from
bigfoot encounters?

I realized that if I wanted to write a book on bigfoot, even
though it's fiction, bigfoot needed to peaceful toward humans—
because that fit with the actual encounters.

And even though *Hominid* is indeed a work of fiction, there
was a lot of research that went into making it *believable* fiction.
So here are some of the facts incorporated, in no particular order.

Bigfoot Scenic Byway. Yes, it exists. It's an eighty-six mile stretch
of roadway in Northern California. And the land along the
highway is known for bigfoot sightings.

Names. All the names for bigfoot mentioned in *Hominid* are real:
Yeren, yowie, skunk ape, etc. There are dozens of names for a tall,
hairy hominid across the country and the globe.

Bigfoot and Early Humans. There really is a pictograph in Sonora California called the Hairy Man, which depicts a bigfoot family where the bigfoot is crying as man runs away. And the Hoopa story of how humans came to be through animals deciding their fate is a real story. And there are other stories, hundreds of years old, about man's interaction with a hairy bipedal wild man.

Jane Goodall Quote. The Goodall quote at the beginning of the book is real. Jane Goodall, according to interviews, *does* believe that bigfoot exists. A large reason why, according to Goodall, is the tales she has heard from indigenous people in areas said to be inhabited by bigfoot.

Bigfoot Erotica. Yup, it's real. No, it's not something I read... regularly. Seriously though, when I was doing research on bigfoot, I put in all sorts of keyword searches. One of them revealed the tale of a woman who fell in love with bigfoot. Or at least, part of bigfoot. Needless, to say, I was a little surprised.

Gigantopithecus. A ten-foot-tall ape did once roam the earth. *Gigantopithecus* is believed to have come into existence about a million years ago and survived until almost one hundred thousand years ago. It was believed to have gone extinct due to the lack of availability of bamboo. But as mentioned in *Hominid*, *Gigantopithecus* has actually been found to have been an omnivore—eating both meat and plants. So people don't know why exactly the giant ape went extinct—or if it really did. And the realization that *Gigantopithecus* existed came about just as described in *Hominid*: a doctor found a giant tooth in a bazaar in China.

Annual Cryptozoology Conference. There is no single annual cryptozoology conference. There are, however, different cryptozoology conferences held across the country to discuss cryptids.

Land Bridge. The land bridge between North America and Asia was around when *Gigantopithecus* existed. Bigfoot believers have made the argument that *Gigantopithecus* could have crossed the bridge from Asia and ended up in North America. It is known that other Asian animals did so, such as the red panda, whose remains have been found in Tennessee. And as indicated by the fossil record, the land bridge had lots of vegetation to support animal life.

Fossil Record. Speaking of the fossil record, it is indeed spotty. Environment plays a role here: damp, heavily forested areas are notoriously unreliable in the creation of fossils. But the larger issue is that a fossil or lack thereof is not indicative of when an animal ceased to be, but only when it actually was. Take for example the coelacanth, which disappeared from the fossil record for sixty-five million years before it was spotted in the Indian Ocean.

Ancient Hominids. As anyone who's read the *Belial* series knows, there have been many different types of hominids on planet Earth at one time or another. Science has now demonstrated that those hominids' existences have overlapped. *Homo sapiens* existed alongside both Neanderthals and *Homo denisova*. In fact, as mentioned in the book, research has indicated that the *Homo sapiens* gene pool is not pure *homo sapiens*. It includes indications of other hominids, although these percentages are very low. But the existence of different hominids in our gene pool at all suggests there was interbreeding between these different hominid groups.

Homo Denisova. All of the information provided in *Hominid* on *Homo denisova* is accurate to the best of my ability. And yes, new hominids are being discovered at a quick rate—such as the previously unknown hominid whose jawbone was found in Taiwan in 2014. Our family tree seems to be continually growing branches.

Bili Ape. The Bili ape is a real animal. For generations, there were reports in Congo of giant chimpanzees that walked on two legs, hunted lions, howled at the moon, and made nests on the ground. These tales weren't taken seriously—chimps couldn't possibly behave that way and they were not that large. Then in 2005, primatologist Shelly Williams discovered them.

Troglodytes. In 1735, Carl Linnaeus did indeed write the first codex on all the animals in the world. It was called *Systema Naturea* and included nine thousand species. In it, he said there were two types of humans: man and the troglodytes. The troglodytes, whom Merlin was said to reside with, were described as wild hairy men.

Invisible Gorilla. The invisible gorilla experiment was an actual experiment conducted at Harvard University, and the results were just as depicted in *Hominid*: half the subjects did not even notice the gorilla walking through the middle of the basketball game. The video used for the study can still be found online.

Leif Ericson. The tale of Leif Ericson's interaction with bigfoot comes from Leif Ericson's own journal. According to the tale, around 1000 AD Leif and his crew landed in Newfoundland, where they found towering hairy men of incredible strength and odor.

Cross-Species Breeding. Dr. Ivanov was a real individual who attempted, on behalf of the USSR, to create soldiers who were half human and half ape. As mentioned in *Hominid*, he attempted to inseminate chimps with human sperm, but no fertilization took place. He was in the process of soliciting human volunteers when the project was scrapped.

New Jersey Red Eye. In the late 1970s there were reports of a bigfoot-like creature with bright red eyes in the northwestern section of New Jersey. During the time when the sightings occurred, bloodcurdling screams were also heard late in the night.

EPAS1. EPAS1 is a real genetic marker found in the people of Nepal. And as mentioned in *Hominid*, it allows the Nepalese people to thrive at high altitudes. Individuals without the genetic marker are unable to sustain the high altitude for long without getting sick, and in many cases, dying. It has also been theorized that EPAS1 is allows people to resist cold weather.

*DUF*1220. Researchers have identified DUF1220 as being responsible for increases in human brain capacity. It is believed to have allowed us to evolve beyond animals. It has also been linked to autism. Autistic individuals with a higher number of copies of DUF1220 have more severe symptoms of the disorder: repetitive behaviors, communications difficulties, and social deficits. It's a new direction for autism research.

Legal Rights of Bigfoot. There is only one county in the United States where it is illegal to shoot a bigfoot: Skamania County, Washington. In 1969, Skamania passed the Undiscovered Species Act, which contends that any individual who kills a bigfoot is subject to a substantial fine and/or imprisonment.

Tree Structures. Structures built from tree limbs have been found in areas where bigfoot have been sighted. The limbs are not rotted at the end and show no evidence of having been cut with a tool, even though they are between four and eight inches thick. The limbs are often interwoven, but not in a way that would provide shelter.

Twinkies. I have no idea if bigfoot likes Twinkies.

Yeti and ancient polar bears. In 2013, Oxford University emeritus professor and geneticist Bryan Sykes conducted an analysis on twenty-seven samples of alleged bigfoot hair. Some samples came back with matches to known animals such as bears, but two of the samples came back matching an ancient form of polar bear believed to have gone extinct forty thousand years prior. Then, in

2014, new analyses of the same sample indicated that the sample was actually that of a subspecies of a type of Himalayan bear.

Infrasound. Infrasound refers to low frequency sounds that occur below the hearing range of humans, and it has been found to be used by lions, giraffes, hippos, and even elephants. In humans, these low frequency sounds can result in nausea and dizziness.

Bigfoot Must Die. There is not a TV show called *Bigfoot Must Die.* There is, however, one called *Killing Bigfoot* and another called *10 Million Dollar Bigfoot Bounty.* I have never watched the shows, although I did read about them. They involve groups of individuals going out to track down and—yup—kill bigfoot. There are also *Finding Bigfoot, Bigfootville,* a few radio shows dedicated to the topic, and dozens of websites. Not to mention the individual episodes on shows like *MonsterQuest* and *Survivorman,* Les Stroud just did a season on bigfoot as well. Bigfoot is actually big entertainment. In fact, once you start looking for bigfoot, you find it everywhere.

So do I believe in Bigfoot? I don't know. But there is someone much better qualified to comment on them than me: Jane Goodall. In a 2003 interview, when asked why no one had found a body of a bigfoot, she said: "You know why isn't there a body? I can't answer that, and maybe they don't exist, but I want them to."

So thank you for reading. I hope you enjoyed yourself. If you have the time, I would appreciate if you left a review. It makes it easier for other people to find the book and decide if it might be right for them.

Take care,
    R.D.

P.S. If you are looking for some books on the topic, here are some of the books I found very helpful:

Meldrum, Jeff. *Sasquatch: Legend Meets Science.* Forge Books, 2007.

Williams, Autumn. *Enoch.* Amazon, 2010.

Coleman, Loren. *Bigfoot! The True Story of Apes in America.* Paraview Pocket Books, 2003.

Burnette, Tom and Rob Riggs. *Bigfoot: Exploring the Myth and Discovering the Truth.* Llewellyn Publications, 2014.

BOOKS BY R.D. BRADY

The Belial Series (in order)

The Belial Stone

The Belial Library

The Belial Ring

Recruit: A Belial Series Novella

The Belial Children

The Belial Origins

The Belial Search

The Belial Guard

The Belial Warrior

The Belial Plan

The Belial Witches

Stand-Alone Books

Runs Deep

Hominid

The A.L.I.V.E. Series

B.E.G.I.N.

A.L.I.V.E.

D.E.A.D.

Be sure to sign up for R.D.'s mailing list to be the first to hear when she has a new release and receive a free short story!

ACKNOWLEDGMENTS

Thanks to all those who helped make this book happen. First and foremost, thank you Tae. Thank you for all your support, time, and love. Thank you for letting me take the time I needed to complete this book. Thank you for always being in my corner and being unfailingly there when I needed you. You are my rock.

Thank you to my little gang of three who is always asking how Mommy's books are coming along. Your innocent inquisitiveness keeps me pushing forward and your love keeps me happy.

Thanks to Syracuse Martial Arts Academy and the larger martial arts community for their indispensible help not just with this book but with life lessons. I am blessed to have found you.

Thanks to my editorial team. Thank you to Damonza for their incredible cover design. You guys are incredible.

Thank you to David Gatewood for the incredible editing. My writing had improved greatly since meeting you. Thank you, thank you!

And thank you to all you readers who have gotten in touch. Your notes and comments are make my day! Thank you so much for taking the time to drop me a note and of course, for reading.

ABOUT THE AUTHOR

R.D. Brady is an American writer who grew up on Long Island, NY but has made her home in both the South and Midwest before settling in upstate New York. On her way to becoming a full-time writer, R.D. received a Ph.D. in Criminology and taught for ten years at a small liberal arts college.

R.D. left the glamorous life of grading papers behind in 2013 with the publication of her first novel, the supernatural action adventure, *The Belial Stone*. Over a dozen novels later and hundreds of thousands of books sold, and she hasn't looked back. Her novels tap into her criminological background, her years spent studying martial arts, and the unexplained aspects of our history.

If you would like to be notified about her upcoming publications, you can sign up for her mailing list. Those who sign up will receive a free e-book copy of *B.E.G.I.N.* and other freebies over time. Email addresses are never provided to any other sources.

For more information,
rdbradybooks.com
rdbradywriter@gmail.com

Scottish Seoul Publishing.

Syracuse, NY

Copyright © 2015 by R.D. Brady

Hominid

Printed in the United States of America.

This book is a work of fiction. All characters, places, and events herein are a product of the author's imagination. Any resemblance to real individuals, situations or events are purely coincidental.

Made in the USA
Coppell, TX
17 November 2019

11475154R00275